MW00488241

Worst Enemies

"You're going to be surprised and delighted. It's a great book, and I recommend it unreservedly."

—Leighton Gage, author of
the Inspector Mario Silva series

"By the end, *Worst Enemies* was miles from *Strangers On a Train...* When a crime novel goes above and beyond a mere interpretation of a classic, the reader is left as satisfied as the author."

—Benjamin Sobieck, author of *Cleansing Eden*
and *The Writer's Guide to Weapons*

"I finished reading this book on a gurney in an Emergency Room with crying kids, a car accident victim and a loud drunk keeping me company, and barely noticed them. If that's not a recommendation, I don't know what is!"

—New Mystery Reader

Praise for
Grind Joint

"King has created vividly drawn characters, a plot the late Elmore Leonard would appreciate, and dialogue that hits all the right notes. Let's hope *Grind Joint* is the first in a new series chronicling life and crime in the Alleghenies."

—Booklist

"One of the best novels I've read this year. Period."

—Les Edgerton, author of *Bomb*,
The Bitch and *The Rapist*

"I cannot remember a book I've read—including anything by Elmore —where the cops sounded more like cops, tricking suspects, stumbling with women, smart-talking the tough guys, and finally getting out of a big shootout with brains, brawn, and guts."

—Jack Getze, author of the
award-winning Austin Carr series

WORST ENEMIES

A PENNS RIVER NOVEL

ALSO BY DANA KING

The Penns River Novels
Worst Enemies
Grind Joint
Resurrection Mall (*)

The Nick Forte Mysteries
A Small Sacrifice
The Stuff That Dreams Are Made Of
The Man in the Window
A Dangerous Lesson

Stand Alone Novels
Wild Bill

(*) Coming Soon

DANA KiNG

WORST ENEMiES

A PENNS RiVER NOVEL

Copyright © 2012 by Dana King
Down & Out Books edition: October, 2016

All rights reserved. No part of the book may be reproduced in any form or by
any electronic or mechanical means, including information storage and
retrieval systems, without permission in writing from the publisher, except by a
reviewer who may quote brief passages in a review.

Down & Out Books
3959 Van Dyke Rd, Ste. 265
Lutz, FL 33558
www.DownAndOutBooks.com

The characters and events in this book are fictitious. Any similarity to real
persons, living or dead, is coincidental and not intended by the author.

Cover design by Eric Beetner

ISBN: 1-943402-42-6
ISBN-13: 978-1-943402-42-7

To the Tri-Cities,
the Hotel California
of the Rust Belt

PRONUNCIATION KEY

Western Pennsylvania has a rich ethnic heritage that is obvious from even a quick glance at the phone listings or any high school yearbook. Many of the names are hard to pronounce to outsiders who don't come across them often. Even for those who do, Western Pennsylvania natives have developed unique accents and pronunciations that bear little resemblance to how relatives in the old country would speak.

Charlie Stella, in addition to being the Godfather of mob fiction, has been a priceless source of inspiration and encouragement to me. I had no thought of having any of the Penns River books published until Charlie told me I really needed to do something with them. He had but one negative comment: "I can't pronounce any of the names in this frigging book. Ain't no one in this town named Smith?"

This is for you, Charlie.

Allegheny — al-i-GAY-nee
Dougherty — DOCK-ur-dee
Dolewicz — DOLE-uh-wits
Faison — FAY-zon
Grabek — GRAY-beck
Gwynn — Gwin
Mannarino — Man-uh-REE-no
Napierkowski — Napper-KOW-ski
Neshannock — Ne-SHAN-ik
Neuschwander — NOO-shwan-der
Obbink — OH-bink
Orszulak — OR-suh-lack
Schoepf — Shef
Smith — Smith
Wierzbicki — Weerz-BICK-ee
Zywiciel — Suh-WISS-ee-ul

Until I got married, I was my own worst enemy.
—Unknown

CHAPTER 1

Tom Widmer needed to pay attention. It's not every night someone tells you how to kill his wife.

Hard enough to hear in Tease as it was, the tekno/disco/hip-hop cranked to Volume Eleven, so loud the pulsing in his eardrums ruined the floor's foot massage. Chastity's nipple in his ear didn't help. She had the rest of her tit wrapped against his cheek like she was about to go off shift in fifteen minutes and needed to get him into the VIP Room *now*, which she was and did. This was her go-to move when time got short: sit on the arm of his chair, slip the teddy or camisole or whatever they call that thing she wore off-stage out of the way, then ease it in. Usually he didn't mind. Usually it cost him an extra fifty for a trip to the VIP Room. Not tonight.

Tom turned his head and Chastity gave him a mouthful. He couldn't resist a quick lick before he pulled away. "I'm sorry, baby. Marty and I gotta talk. Maybe later."

Chastity pulled a pout. "I go off shift in fifteen minutes, Tommy. Can't it wait?"

Tom looked at Marty and saw no, it couldn't wait. "Sorry, babe. Next time."

"You're just a tease." The smile that never reached her eyes didn't hide the irritation in her voice. Fifteen minutes wasted. She made a show of tucking the nipple away and ran her tongue around his ear. Bit the lobe for good measure.

1

"Next time. You'll be sorry you passed."

Marty waited for her to get out of hearing range, about three feet. "Can I have your attention now, or do I have to wait for your dick to get soft again?"

"You're sure it has to be tomorrow?" Tom swallowed the bottom half of his gin and tonic, looked for the waitress.

Marty put his hand over Tom's and forced the empty glass onto the table. "Pay attention. This has to be done before Monday. She hired a lawyer. You understand me? She already hired a fucking lawyer. Once they serve me with papers, there's no way anyone will believe a burglar killed her. Thursday's my regular night out and we have this thing with her family over the weekend. It has to be tomorrow."

"That's not a lot of time to plan."

"Fucking A, and I got tired of waiting for you to do it. Everything you need's in the car."

"My car?"

"No, dumbass, in *my* car. How the fuck would I get it into your car?"

Tom really wanted that gin; the tonic had become optional. He'd had fun the past few months, basking in young pussy while he and Marty talked about killing each other's wives, a couple of lap dances for the road. He figured his divorce was almost as close as Marty's, and Marian would get half of what was already only half as much as it had been, the market's death by a thousand cuts bleeding him every day. The sun would shine brighter in a world without Marian.

Now Marty was good to go. Carol had a lawyer and Tom didn't know for a fact that Marian didn't. Marty was right: once papers were filed, neither wife could catch cold without her husband falling under suspicion. Of course, wife killing was much more entertaining as an abstraction, and Tom had never killed anything more evolved than an insect in his life. Buried the whole cage when the kids' pet hamster died so he wouldn't have to touch Fluffy. Still, it was now or never. Kill her or face the idea of living like an intern again, running the copier for guys whose cufflinks cost more than his car.

Marty was talking. Probably had been, now that Tom thought about it. "You gotta be there at ten o'clock. Earlier and she'll still be up. Later and it's too close to when I come home."

"Huh? Wait. Run that first part by me again."

Marty squeezed Tom's wrist until he grimaced. "Pay attention, dickhead. You fuck this up and I'll come after you myself. There's no way you're doing this half-assed and taking me down with you. You listening to me?"

Tom nodded, tried to make eye contact with the waitress without moving his head. She wanted fifty bucks, he'd give her fifty bucks. A hundred. Just someone bring him a *drink*, for Christ's sake.

Marty didn't need a drink. "One more time. The stuff's in the car. Black pullover, black jeans, black shoes and socks. One of those head things like Hines Ward wears when it's cold."

"What? You mean like a helmet?"

"No, not a helmet. Jesus Christ. Are all stockbrokers this dumb? No wonder the economy's in the shitter. It's like a skull cap, tight, pulls over your head, covers everything except your face. Race car drivers wear them."

"Balaclavas?"

"If you say so. At least you're listening. Put everything on, darken your face up some—"

"How should I do that?"

"Do what?"

"Darken my face."

"I don't know. Use some charcoal from the grill."

"We have a gas grill."

"Then *buy* some charcoal. Jesus Christ. We're talking hundreds of thousands of dollars here. Spend three bucks on a lousy bag of Kingsford."

"It's not the money. How am I going to explain the charcoal when I have a gas grill? It won't look right."

Marty rubbed his forehead with a thumb and index finger, closed his eyes for a couple of seconds. "What are you, autistic? Throw the rest of the bag away. It's just charcoal. It ain't like they got serial numbers on them. Use dirt if you want to. Just darken up your face."

Tom had a thing about being dirty, showered before and after work every day. Sanitized his hands after he blew his nose, snot on them or not. Right now he'd swim naked through a pig trough if someone would just bring him a beer. Lite beer, even.

"Look at me, you son of a bitch." Marty grabbed Tom's cheeks between a thumb and forefinger. "I'm desperate here. This has to happen, and it has to happen *tomorrow*. You don't do this and I'll ruin you. I'll tell your wife what I know and she'll get half of what you got left *plus* child support. And you'll probably lose your license. Then what are you gonna do?"

"How you figure to get my license?" Marty could tell stories about Tom lawyers would line up for like politicians at a microphone. Being a randy drunk couldn't cost him his stockbroker's license.

"Remember that time you told me about that old broad—what's her name?—Finnegan? How you used money in her account for what you called 'leverage' to float that hedge fund thing a few years ago? You made a bundle off that, didn't you?"

"She didn't lose a dime."

"She didn't make any, either. You told me how you got her to sign shit she wasn't sure what it was? Got to be records of that, right? You move money around, something she has to sign for, I can't believe they just throw the paperwork away when the money gets moved back. I'm no stockbroker, but they must be pretty fussy about their bookkeeping. I mean, it's money, right? No other reason for a stockbroker to be in business."

Fuck. *Fuck.* Marty told anyone about that and it was over for Tom. He'd be lucky if his old man could get him a job delivering uniforms. *If* he didn't go to jail. He opened his mouth to talk. Marty beat him to it.

"Wait. Don't say it. How do you know I won't tell anyway? Right? That's what you're thinking. Well, think again. You already have me dead to rights for solicitation of murder. That's a capital offense. If we quit dicking around and go through with it, both of us have enough on the other guy that neither one can afford to talk." Marty cocked his head, raised his eyebrows. Showed the palms of his hands like he'd just said something so self-explanatory a retard would understand.

Tom was drunk, not retarded. He understood perfectly that he was well and truly fucked. Didn't matter anymore whether he killed her or not. Don't kill her and Marty would ruin him, maybe even send him to jail. Much as Tom disliked getting dirty, he liked the idea of taking one up the ass even less. Kill this woman he'd never met, never ever seen, who'd never done him any harm, and he knew Marty would hold up his end of the deal. Just watching him, the way he acted when he talked about it, Tom knew Marty wanted to do Marian. Hell, he was looking forward to it. Then Tom would be out from under forever.

Maybe he should pretend she was Marian.

CHAPTER 2

Tom took twenty minutes to decide where to park the car. Right in front of the Cropcho house was too obvious. Up the street either direction meant leaving it where someone might notice it in front of his house. Nothing but trees around the corner where Argonne made the bend to go down the hill, but then he'd have to walk. No telling who'd see him, and the car could get clipped by someone taking the blind turn too fast. He settled for across the street, more or less between two houses so each could think the car was visiting the other. Made him feel good, thinking of that. Like he knew what he was doing.

Last week of September, steam from his breath reflected the streetlights. Made him feel practically luminescent, like people watching television in their homes would run to the window to see what the hell was *glowing* out there? His footfalls loud as someone striking an oil drum with a ball peen hammer. How could anyone not see or hear him?

Relax. Take a breath. He had the key and knew the security code. Might not even need the code; Marty said Carol hardly ever turned on the alarm. She'd be in bed watching *20/20* or a doctor show or some queers designing clothes or cooking. Even if the alarm did go off, she'd assume Marty came home early and wouldn't get up. Bedroom to the right at the top of the stairs. Walk up, surprise her—she might even be asleep, that would be nice—put a pillow over

7

her face and press. Take a few things to make it look good, break a window on the way out. Easy.

He paused on the front porch to steady his breathing, try to get a handle on his heart rate. Looked for signs of trouble, not that he'd recognize any. Most houses had a tree or two in the front yard; at least some shrubs. Leaves already falling, more every time the breeze picked up. Made rustling sounds so he couldn't hear if anyone was coming. Moving shadows in odd patterns, someone could be in any of them. A kid sneaking in late. Sneaking out. Someone walking a dog. Too exposed out here. Time to get inside.

He probably should have skipped that third drink, the double, but he couldn't bring himself to think of what he had to do with just two in him. The last one got him feeling sorry for himself, how that bitch Marian was ruining his life and what he had to do tonight would be the first step toward setting things right. Not equating it to killing Carol Cropcho, he kept it an abstract concept, like all those discussions at Tease. As much booze as he had in him, it *was* more or less an abstract concept, though he felt dead sober now. He adjusted the balaclava, tucked the long sleeve tee into his gloves. The breeze died and took all sound with it except the porch creaking as he walked to the door. Put the key in the lock, rested his hand there and closed his eyes. Leave now and no one would ever know. No going back once the door was open. He thought of what he'd tell Marty, what it would be like to face him, try to explain why Carol was alive. Then he turned the key and pushed.

The beeping of the alarm sounded like an air raid siren. He reached for the panel on the wall to his left. Fat fingered the code twice, got it right the third time. Stared at the wall until his heart worked its way out of his throat. Stepped across the vestibule to the stairs. Looked up and saw Carol Cropcho standing at the top looking down at him.

A powder blue nightshirt hung below her knees. Auburn hair to her shoulders in the twenty-first century version of a shag, rumpled from the bed. Her breasts filled the nightshirt as she breathed, nipples visible though the material in the cool house. Neither moved for three seconds that lasted a week. Gawked at each other like two cartoon characters who'd walked off a cliff, waiting to fall. For a nanosecond Tom's mind considered stepping back out the door and pretending it never happened.

Carol turned and ran into the bedroom. Three words ran through Tom's mind: Nine. One. One.

He took the stairs two at a time, saw her in the bedroom to the right crawling across the bed to get at the phone. Dove onto the bed, wrapped his arms around her as his momentum pushed them off the other side. The phone glanced off his head. She screamed and rolled away when they landed unevenly on the floor. Reached for the phone and he swatted it under the bed. Carol screamed again.

Carol got to her feet and backed to the wall nearest the bathroom. Hands hooked near her face, eyes locked on Tom. Screaming, not hysterical. Screaming with a purpose. For someone to hear. To get help. Tom thought of how quiet the neighborhood was. How close the other houses were.

Someone would hear.

He stepped up, put his hands on her throat to stop her. Carol scratched for his face and missed, snagged his collar. Twisted her head away. He got one hand on her neck, felt the cartilage under his thumb as he pulled her back toward

9

the bedroom. Her nails raked across his eyes and he let go to swat them away.

She stepped aside and ran for the bathroom. He grabbed for her, snared an ankle to trip her onto the tile floor. Carol rolled onto her back as he crawled on top of her. Used her heels to kick his shoulders, then his stomach. Not a small woman, in good shape. The kicks hurt. He fell off her and backed away on his knees to catch his breath.

She made too much noise and he moved his head aside in time for her to miss with the scissors. She tried to bounce off the bed and face him, but he lowered a shoulder into her and drove her back. Took the scissors and threw them away without thinking they'd work as a weapon for him, too. Carol slapped his face hard when he shifted position to take her arms. He caught her wrist before the second slap and realized how strong she was. A knee missed his groin, connected higher, knocked some wind out of him. He raised up to catch his breath and she scratched his face hard enough to draw blood. He tried to pin her arms and she drew up her knees to beat him to the leverage, kicked out hard. He lost the grip and she went after his face again. Tears blinded him when a nail caught a corner of his left eye and it occurred to him he could lose this fight he never expected to have. Nervousness passed through fear into terror.

Adrenaline cleared his mind. He forced his hands inside her thighs to spread them. Leaned in to press her onto the bed. Positioned himself between her legs, letting his weight hold her down, and drove her arms into the mattress. Desperation gave him the speed to get one hand around her throat, then the other. Rose up so he could press straight down and use his size to keep her hands off his face. Pressed his thighs into the backs of her knees to stifle her movements. Carol writhed against him, her mound pressing against his groin made him hard. She got her knees loose and kicked at his back with her heels like spurring a horse. He ignored the pain in his kidneys, watched her face start to change color. The kicks and thrusts got weaker. Slower. He pressed down harder. Her eyes rolled up. The kicks stopped. Then the punches. Carol's arms and legs fell away. Then she was still and he relaxed.

Tom stood and tasted the salt of his tears and blood on his lips. Carol's nightshirt had ridden up to expose her trimmed pubic hair. He became aware of his arousal and fought back a throat full of bile. He had to get out, he'd been there too long already, but he needed some jewelry and cash first. To make it look good.

He trashed the jewel boxes and knick-knacks on the dressers and nightstands. Pieces of colored, shaped glass that bounced when they hit the floor, too heavy to break. Dumped the contents of the drawers. He knew there was nothing here but paste, the real jewels in the walk-in closet. Marty told him what to take, made him write it down so he'd get the right stuff, look like a knowledgeable thief. Threw around shoes, clothes, hat boxes, anything to make a mess. Stuffed jewelry into a Crown Royal bag, then stood with a handful of cash to catch his breath and be sure he hadn't forgotten anything.

The television seemed louder than before in the unnatural quiet. Some movie on HBO from the language. He listened to it for a minute, hearing only the voices, not what they said, the sound muffled by the weight of the house's sudden stillness. Tom felt his heart beating in his chest and ears,

11

wondered if he could hear it if he tried. Stood perfectly still to listen and what he heard was a sound like a person coming up from a long time under water, and movement.

From inside the house.

His watch read 10:23. Marty wasn't due until midnight and he wouldn't come back early tonight of all nights. Someone must have heard. Did they come over, or call the police? The police would have knocked, rung the doorbell, something. They wouldn't just come in. And they wouldn't come sneaking around. They'd announce themselves. He'd watched ten thousand cop shows. "Police! Is anyone home?" They'd do that, right?

Time to go. He pulled shut the bag full of jewels. Left the cash. Too bulky. All he wanted now was out. He stepped back into the bedroom and heard what sounded like sobs and saw Carol Cropcho wasn't on the bed.

Oh. Fuck. Me.

He heard her crying on the floor the other side of the mattress. He dropped the bag and fell to his knees to look under the bed. Her hand swept back and forth reaching for the phone. He got to it first. Carol screamed, *"No!"* loud and long and broke into sobbing as he threw it against the wall.

Tom rose and came around the foot of the bed. Carol screamed, hysterical now, gibberish coming out, too frantic to form words. She threw whatever she could reach. A baseball-sized glass sculpture he'd dumped onto the floor hit his shoulder like a rock. The next one would have dented his temple if he hadn't got his hands up. He turned the corner of the bed. Saw the bruises on her throat and the panic in her eyes as she scrabbled around the floor for something else to throw. He picked up an oblong piece of the same type she'd been throwing by the narrow end and drove it into the side of Carol's head. The first one put her down. The second probably finished the job, but he didn't stop until bits of blood and brain spattered onto his gloves and cheeks. He stopped and his eyes eased into focus. The left side of Carol's face and head were completely stove in, hard to tell where hair stopped and gore started.

Tom almost made it to the toilet before he vomited.

CHAPTER 3

Ben Dougherty leaned against the doorframe of the Cropcho bedroom and watched Rick Neuschwander work. He didn't touch anything. He didn't say anything. Neuschwander even more methodical than usual, homicides not everyday occurrences in Penns River. He picked up anything on or around Carol Cropcho's body that might be evidence; never touched the body itself. Strict letter of the law, Neuschwander should have waited for the Medical Examiner, but the ME had to come from Allegheny County and time was wasting. It didn't take House to know Carol was dead, half her brain on her face.

"How much longer, Noosh? My hands are starting to sweat in these gloves."

"Take them off." Neuschwander didn't look up. "Just don't come in here. Go talk to the husband or something."

"Willie's doing that. I'm waiting for you."

"Go help Willie. Try some of that 'good cop-bad cop' shit. Get a confession."

"You see anything makes the husband look guilty?"

Neuschwander eased a glass sculpture eight inches long into an evidence bag. The glass was caked with blood and hair and something Doc guessed was brain. "All I see is stuff. I don't know what anything means until the tests come back from the lab. The husband called it in, though, right?"

"Yeah. So?"

"Isn't the guy who called it in guilty about half the time?"

"Yeah, but—"

"And isn't the husband usually who kills a wife?" Neuschwander sealed the bag, wrote something on the evidence tag.

"Right."

"So you have at least a seventy-five percent chance he's the guy and you want physical evidence, too? I thought you were supposed to be good."

Doc peeled off the gloves, put them in his jacket pocket. "When should I come back?"

"I got most of what I need. Half an hour, assuming the ME drags his ass in here by then."

Doc went downstairs to find the kitchen and get a drink of water. Willie Grabek leaned over the island, jotting notes. Doc took a glass from the drain board and filled it from the tap.

"How's the husband?"

"About what you'd expect." Grabek wrote a few lines in his pocket notebook, flipped back a few pages. "Thursday's his night out. He works downtown, meets a couple of guys at Veltri's for prime rib and a few beers after. They hook up with a couple other guys for a rotating Hold-Em game and he gets home around midnight. Done it almost every Thursday for three years.

"Tonight's game was in Holiday Park, before you get to 380. The husband dropped twenty bucks. Got home about quarter to twelve. Thought it was funny the alarm was off and the lights were on upstairs. Said the wife was always asleep when he got home, he'd just slide into bed beside her. Went up the stairs, saw the mess, found her when he came around the side of the bed."

"He mentioned he lost twenty dollars?"

"I asked."

"How come?"

"Because I'm gonna ask his friends, too."

A murmur of voices from the living room. Doc nodded in that direction. "Who's with him?"

"Paramedics are giving him something. He's pretty shook up."

"Where's he going to stay?"

"Brother's coming for him." Grabek checked his watch. "Should be here any minute."

Doc finished his water, put the glass on the drain board. "You like him for it?"

"Not really. He called it in and he's the husband. That's two strikes, but his alibi's too easy to check. You get a time of death from—what's his name? Upstairs."

"Neuschwander. No, but he says it's been at least a few hours from the drying of the blood and what he can see of lividity."

"So make it around ten-thirty. The nine-one-one call came at eleven-fifty-two. His boys say he was with them past eleven o'clock, quarter after, and he's home free."

"Yeah, but what do you think of him? You worked a lot of these, thirty years in the Burgh. How's he strike you?"

"I don't put too much faith in first impressions. Only cops I know solve cases off hunches are on television. Still, he seems legit. People act all kinds of different ways when something like this happens. He was rattled, not hysterical. Didn't take it personal when I asked about his alibi, did they have family trouble, stuff like that. Distracted enough to seem for real."

Doc leaned back against the sink. Grabek read over his notes. Together barely three weeks, their first serious case. Paramedics had the husband, Neuschwander had the crime scene, and neither knew enough about the crime or each other to have much to say.

Doc broke first. "It'll be another half hour before he's done upstairs. How about we talk to some of the ghouls?" The emergency vehicle lights had attracted half a dozen neighbors to the sidewalk in front of the house.

"You go. I wanted to work in the middle of the night, I could've stayed in Pittsburgh." Grabek's eyes showed he'd had a few, maybe more, before the call came in. His breath was fine, but anyone standing close would smell the alcohol in his sweat. "Thought this was a nice quiet town, maybe I'd scare a kid smoking reefer once in a while. Live off the salary and send my daughter to Penn State with the pension. I'm here three lousy weeks and I'm out of bed working a genuine whodunit." He took a seat at one of the elevated island stools. "It's cold out there. I'll call you when Neusch-whatever's ready."

Doc walked to the front door. He'd heard Grabek's story before. Guy was smart, experienced, and the laziest prick Doc had ever worked with. Lived in the gray area between drinking too much and being a drunk. Still, it was only three weeks. Some people's virtues took a while to surface.

Outside, police and emergency lights reflected off the clouds; it would look like half the town was on fire to someone on Coxcomb Hill. Two hours ago Argonne Drive would have been as quiet as a nursery at nap time. Dark enough to be peaceful, sufficient light for everyone to feel safe. No one around but the stray kid sneaking in or out.

Maybe someone taking a dog for an evening stroll in the still. Safest place in the world.

Mike Zywiciel kept a knot of the curious away from the house. He had his hands full with a neighbor who looked like he'd been over-served and wanted to make up for it by going out of his way to act responsible now.

"Listen, Officer, uh, Zy-wuh-keel, how are my kids supposed to sleep with those goddamn lights flashing in their bedroom window?"

"It's Zuh-*wiss*-ee-ul, sir, and I'm sorry. We have to keep them on while the street's partially blocked. It shouldn't be too much longer."

The man leaned over, traced the letters on Zywiciel's nametag. "Yeah, right. Zy-wuh-keel. What did I say?"

"You said Zy-wuh-keel, sir. It's Zuh-*wiss*-ee-ul." Pronouncing every syllable.

"That's what I've been saying, *Zy*-wuh-keel. Says right here: Officer Zy-wuh-keel."

"Actually, sir, it's Sergeant Zy-wuh-keel, and I'm going to have to ask you to step back a little. We'll get these lights out as soon as the medical examiner's done."

The neighbor looked like he wasn't finished debating the lights or Zywiciel's name when Doc interrupted them.

"Hey, Eye Chart. What are you doing out in the field? I thought you requested per diem for anything farther away than Clementine's."

"I just come to see how detectives justify drawing a check. Patrol cops actually go to crimes in progress. Nothing much to do by the time you guys get here."

"Don't forget I rode patrol with you. You taught me everything you know. Took you almost twenty minutes."

"Shouldn't have taken me that long if you had any talent. What do you need?"

"I know your guys did a quick canvass of this crew, names and addresses, basic statements."

"Yeah. They're searching the area now. We'll get the other shifts out tomorrow to catch people when they're awake."

"I want to cut a few from this herd while I wait for Noosh to finish up with the scene. Anyone worth starting with?"

Zywiciel lit a cigarette, shook his head. "Uh-uh. Take your pick. No one here knows dick." He switched to his generic "female citizen" voice, an octave higher, hinting at a room temperature IQ. "Oh my God, Carol's such a sweetheart, Marty's such a nice guy, what's the world coming to?" Returned to his normal voice. "You know. The usual bullshit."

"Yeah, I know. I'll start with her." Doc pointed to a fortyish woman whose idea of bundling up didn't include hiding her cleavage. "Looks like she might have a couple of guns in that housecoat."

"I talked to her already. She has issues with authority."

"She doesn't like cops?"

"I don't think she likes anybody. I get the feeling she's only flashing her knockers to show us what we're missing. You get up close and they're not all that impressive"

Zywiciel was right: Michelle Prince didn't appear to like anybody, and her breasts didn't justify her high opinion of them. She didn't have much to say about the Cropchos, not wanting to speak ill of the dead and Marty suffering like he must be. She didn't spare anyone else. Doc could have kissed Grabek on the mouth for calling him back to the house.

They found Neuschwander in the bedroom packing up. "It's all yours, soon as the ME's done. I'll get what I have here out to the lab soon as I get it logged and separated. When it comes back is anyone's guess." He held up a hand before Grabek could speak. "This ain't the big city. We suck hind tit on this kind of stuff. I'll give them the usual 'violent offender at large' spiel, so maybe you'll get it in six weeks instead of eight. Except for the DNA. Jesus Christ couldn't come down from heaven and get you DNA results in less than four months."

"You have DNA?" Doc said.

"We should. She put up a hell of a fight. There's skin, blood, and fiber under her nails. The ME will bag her hands and send what we find to the lab. If you luck into a suspect in the next few days, he'll have scratches on him. Willie, you talked to the husband. Did he say anything about puking when he found her?"

"No."

Neuschwander smiled. "Someone did. I'd guess he lost it when he got a good look at her. I see some swirls and a wipe pattern, so he tried a half-assed clean-up job, but I got a good enough sample to use."

"What do you think happened?" Grabek said.

"I don't know how it started, just how it ended. Television's on and she's dressed for bed, so let's say she's watching whatever HBO had on at ten."

"I thought you didn't have time of death."

"That's just a guess. The ME will take her temperature here and check her stomach contents at the autopsy."

"Speaking of which, where the hell is the ME?" Grabek said. "This call went out a couple of hours ago."

"Didn't you hear? There was gang trouble down Wilkensburg tonight. Two dead for sure and a couple wandered off they're not sure about. He's been busy, but I just talked to him. He's on the way."

"What's our guy doing in Allegheny County?"

"Allegheny County *is* our guy. We don't do enough business here in Neshannock to rate a full-time ME, so we borrow whoever's on call in Allegheny. Sometimes they get backed up."

Grabek stared like he held Neuschwander personally responsible and had more to say, as usual. Doc kept the conversation on track.

"Let me get this straight. What the hell kind of burglar walks into the bedroom not too late at night with the TV on?"

"Home invasion," Grabek said. "He might like the idea of someone home. Might even have looked for a place with the lights on."

Neuschwander shrugged and opened his hands. "Could be. No rational burglar would do it that way. Even a cat, some guy gets off creeping rooms with people in them, even he'd do it in the dark. No burglar likes to be seen."

"You really think it's a home invasion, Willie?" Doc said.

"I can't say for sure, but I'll see if there've been any others in the area."

Neuschwander closed his equipment case, said, "I don't have anything argues against it. Anyway, he comes in, she sees him, they fight. Hell of a fight, from the mess and the scratches she must have given him. Bruises on her neck say he choked her. After that I'm not sure. She either gets away and he beats her with this piece of glass," he held up the

21

evidence bag, "or he got tired of choking her, or pissed, or whatever, and bashed her head in. Autopsy should tell us more."

"Sexual assault?" Grabek said.

"Not that I can see."

"Anything else?" Doc said.

"He's done this before." Neuschwander paused while both detectives looked away from the body to his face. "Not the murder, I don't know about that, but the theft. He knows his jewelry. See this mess spread around the room? All paste and cheap shit. The good stuff was in the closet."

Grabek leaned in for a view of the closet. "He still left a lot of cash and stones behind for a pro."

"Maybe something startled him. Maybe he figured he'd been here too long. All this damage took time and made noise. Could've thought he'd been heard."

Zywiciel stood in the doorway. "Examiner's here with the wagon."

The Allegheny County Medical Examiner talked with Neuschwander for a few minutes before bothering with Carol Cropcho. Bagged her hands, took some notes, told them what he thought. Coming from the big city didn't make him any smarter than Neuschwander; he taught them nothing they didn't already know.

Patrol officers canvassed awakening homes as first light crawled over the tops of the eastern hills. Doc and Grabek walked to their separate cars.

"You want to hit the Clarion for the two-twenty-nine breakfast before we go see Stush?" Grabek said.

"It's two-sixty-nine now," Doc said.

"Since when?"

"At least a week."

"Bastards. I knew I made a mistake coming here."

CHAPTER 4

Grabek sat in the lone interrogation room, feet on the table, second cup of coffee in his right hand, rubbing sleep from his eyes with the left. Doc looked over their notes from the Cropcho house. Rick Neuschwander had just finished catching everyone up on what he'd found and done since returning.

Stush Napier turned the leather desk chair he'd rolled in from his office toward Grabek. "Anything else?"

"I called the alarm company." Still rubbing his eyes. "She set the alarm at nine-thirty-two. There were two unsuccessful attempts to disarm it at ten-oh-four. Third try worked at ten-oh-five. It was the wife's code that got used."

"So he figured it out in three tries?" Stush said. "What are there, ten thousand possible combinations?"

"He knew it coming in. He might not have expected it to go off and hurried too much."

"That's all?"

"What Neuschwander told you. Uniforms are canvassing now."

Stush turned the chair again. "Doc?"

"Ulizio found something interesting after the sun came up. There's a broken window in the basement big enough for someone to come in, but the pane isn't broken completely out and there's no dirt or crushed glass on the floor."

Stush stared at him like he expected more, said, "This is my first cup of coffee. Spell it out."

Grabek spoke up. "It means that's not how he got in. He broke the window so we'd think he used it, but he would have brought in some dirt or mulch from the flower bed if he crawled in that way, or crushed some of the broken glass under his feet."

"So he came in the front door?"

"Had to," Doc said. "No other door is close enough to the alarm panel for him to get there in time. No signs of forced entry or jimmy marks, either."

"So he had a key," Stush said.

"Looks that way," Grabek said.

"The husband?"

"No," Doc said. "His alibi checks out. He was in Holiday Park playing cards until quarter after eleven."

"So someone else had a key."

"And the wife's code."

"Be nice to know where he got them," Stush said.

"It might be, depending on how he got them, but we're not likely to figure it out and it won't matter anyway." Grabek stopped like he might not explain himself until Stush leaned in his direction like he might as well. "Take the key. He could've stolen one. He could've made an impression of the lock. He might be a parking lot attendant and made a copy while she was shopping. Same thing with the code. Women forget shit like that all the time. Leave notes in their wallets, or use some dumbass thing like their birthday or address. If we luck into something, great. It's not worth spending a lot of time."

Stush already getting sick of listening to Grabek tell him

25

how to be a cop. Not that he had any illusions about being Dick Tracy. Stush got his job the old-fashioned way: some seniority, a willingness to do dirty jobs, and his sister's husband was mayor. Smaller town then, different demographic. Not much to do but break up the occasional millhunk fight born of too many boilermakers and not enough work. No serious poverty then, no one dramatically more affluent than anyone else, except for the handful of doctors and lawyers on Pill Hill, by the country club.

That all changed when the steel and aluminum mills started closing. After a while even the diehards gave up on an industrial renaissance. Small subsistence businesses popped up, locals selling things to their neighbors and buying in return. Money moved back and forth, no one getting rich so much as they were helping each other go under slower.

Pittsburgh rode medicine, finance, and education into the twenty-first century and parts of Penns River became a bedroom community for young professionals with more income than patience. The old Meadow Gold dairy farm was broken up into multi-acre lots for McMansions. The yuppies treated Stush's cops like their personal security detail and spent their disposable income at Pittsburgh Mills, the Strip District, and Walnut Street, not in Penns River.

Only a matter of time before someone figured out it was easier to drop drug shipments off in a little town with forty cops and a lot of abandoned real estate by the river than run the risk of dealing with serious police downtown. Stush Napier found himself the chief of a town with its demographics stretched both ways, and law enforcement problems he never signed on for. Knowing he was in over his head didn't make it any easier to listen to endless rations of Willie

Grabek telling him how to be a cop. Right now he needed Grabek more than Willie needed this job.

Stush pivoted his chair to more or less face everyone. "I don't need to tell you guys this is a big deal. I already had a dozen calls from reporters and Eye Chart says there were three Pittsburgh TV trucks parked when he left this morning. So, you know, anything you can do to speed this along..."

Doc spoke before Grabek had a chance. "Day shift has all but one man canvassing the neighborhood and doing perimeter searches. Called in a couple on their days off to help. Noosh has some good physical evidence. We'll push hard. Someone must've seen something. It wasn't *that* late at night."

He almost convinced himself. With a key, the killer didn't have to waste time on the porch where he might draw attention. He could park in the street right in front of the house and walk in. No one would have thought twice about it, backs turned against the first chill of autumn. Even if someone had looked out the window, what would they see? A car? Someone walking down the street? Cars park. People walk down streets.

"State police called, too," Stush said. "Asked if we needed any help. I told them not right now, but I'm not too proud to ask for it. This guy needs caught. How we do it don't matter much to me."

"We're on it, Chief," Doc said. "I want this guy myself, but like you said, so long as he goes down."

Someone knocked twice on the door and Janine Schoepf from the dispatcher's desk stuck her head in. "I have a call here for the detective who's working on the Cropcho murder."

Doc had more time in Penns River, looked to Grabek, the more experienced homicide cop. Willie waved his fingers in a dismissive gesture. Doc followed Janine to her desk, picked up the phone and identified himself.

A man's voice. "You the one looking into that woman got killed on Argonne Drive last night?"

"Yes, sir. Do you know anything about that?"

"About what time was she killed? You know, approximately."

"I'm sorry, sir, we can't give out details of an ongoing investigation. The paper and TV news will have everything we can share."

"Okay, I probably should've known better. Here's what I got. About ten-thirty last night I was sitting in Arby's eating a sandwich. You know, the one on Greensburg Road, right at the bottom of the hill?"

"Yes, sir. I know where it is."

"Anyhow, this guy come in like he was in a hurry. Dressed all in black, carrying clothes and one of them big trash bags, like contractors use."

Doc picked up a pen from Janine's desk, gestured for something to write on. "Go ahead."

"This guy, he goes back to the men's room, comes out a couple minutes later. He washed his face—oh, yeah, his face was all dirty when he come in—changed his clothes and that bag was full of something."

"Sir, what did this man look like?"

"What did he look like? Hard to say, you know, me not expecting anything like that, just eating my sandwich, minding my own business. Average size, white guy, dark hair, looked like he was in decent shape, you know, not fat but not all bulked up, either."

"You said his face was dirty when he came in. Could it have been blood?"

"Coulda been, maybe. Sure, I guess. Anyway, he goes back outside and I seen him throw the trash bag into the Dumpster behind the joint, the one closest. They got two there, you know, and he threw it in the closer one."

"Sir, did you notice anything else? The car he drove, for example?"

"No, I didn't see his car. Guess he must've had one, though. No one walks to Arby's that time of night."

"Sir, can I have your name, please? It's very important to be able to talk to you some more, maybe look at some pictures for us."

"No, I ain't coming in. I did my thing. If this is the killer, he's a psycho, and I don't want him making bail and come looking for me. No, you got what I have to give. If you can't use it, that's on you. I gotta go."

"Wait, don't hang up." Too late.

"Janine, you got anything on Caller ID?" Not a 911 call, so no recording.

"Looking it up now." Janine typed, clicked, typed some more. "It's a pay phone in Pittsburgh."

"Shit. What part?"

"Says here it's a lounge on Crawford Street. You want me to call Pittsburgh?"

"What are we gonna ask them? 'A guy made a phone call. Pick him up?' Maybe he'll call back."

Doc trotted back to the interrogation room, almost ran over John Harriger coming out of his office. "Jesus Christ,

Dougherty. This isn't high school. Do I have to send you back down the hall and make you walk?"

Anyone else and it would have been a joke. In a department where the chief was universally known as "Stush," everyone other than Stush had to call Harriger "Deputy," as in "Deputy Chief." At least to his face.

"Sorry, Jack." Haste would do for an excuse to cover Doc's breach of etiquette. "I need Willie right away. Might be a break in the Cropcho murder."

He ducked his head into the interrogation room. "Saddle up, Willie. We got us an honest to shit clue."

CHAPTER 5

Ten in the morning, day warming up like Indian summer. Traces of frost in the shade, damp grass in the light. Warm enough in the sun for flies. Arby's Dumpsters were in the sun.

Doc was tall enough to see over the side and spot a likely-looking black bag near the back. The trash hauler left the Dumpster too close to some trees and the lid didn't have room to fall open all the way. No way to reach around it, grab the bag from the close side. He had to go overland. The manager loaned him a step ladder.

He looked at his slacks, the second time he'd worn them. Only put them on last night because they were handy. Grabbed them off the door hook where he'd left them, coming out of the dryer damp. Forty bucks about to go in the trash. Literally.

He looked at Grabek in jeans and a sweatshirt. "You want me to boost you up?"

Grabek smiled like he was watching someone fall down stairs. "Nice try. I'm fifty-seven years old, thirty pounds overweight, and five inches shorter than you. Even if you got me in, you'd never get me out. I didn't take this job to die in no Dumpster. Up you go."

Doc stepped onto the ladder. The Dumpster was half full. Or half empty, the way he looked at it. He'd have to climb up to climb down into whatever crud a fast food Dumpster accumulates over however long this one had been there. Old grease was the best he could hope for.

He grabbed the edge and lifted himself up. Turned as he crossed the lip and tried to ease himself down. His feet slipped on the greasy angle and he half fell, half slid into the can. Broke a bag of paper cups and half-eaten food when he landed on it. The residue of unfinished drinks seeped through his pants and he made an appropriate comment.

"Hey, Doc." Grabek started chuckling as soon as Doc disappeared over the side. "It ain't a sand box. Quit playing around and get the bag."

What Doc wanted to do was throw the goddamn bag out and hit that Polack prick in the head with it and whatever was stuck to it. Breaking the bag would contaminate the evidence, if it wasn't already. His slacks were ruined. No point wasting the trip. Grabek's time would come.

He stumbled over piles of trash to get to the bag he wanted. Flies buzzed, bounced off his hands and face. A foot slipped on what he thought was a patch of grease. Closer inspection showed fresh maggots. Picked up the bag he wanted. A half-assed effort had been made to tie off the top. The knot came open with a gentle pull. Doc held the top shut to hand it out to Grabek. "See what this is so I don't have to crawl back in."

Grabek handled the bag like it was radioactive. Set it on the pavement and peeled back a corner. "Looks good. I see a long sleeve shirt. There's a glove. Two gloves. Shoes. I'm not going to touch anything until Neuschwander gets it, but I think we're all set."

Doc waded to the front of the can. Gripped the lip but couldn't get enough purchase with his shoes to climb out.

Gave up after the third try. "A little help here, Willie?"

Grabek tied off the bag, looked at him like he was a rotting corpse. "You mean like, give you my hand? For real?" Reached out before Doc had time to wonder if he was serious. "Jesus, did you have to touch everything in there?"

Doc picked the most obvious pieces off his clothes. Almost ran a hand through his hair. Caught himself in time and used it to gesture toward Arby's roof. "You see what I see up there?"

"Yeah. Security camera. Noticed it while you were Dumpster diving."

"See if you can get us a tape while I get cleaned up a little."

"You're still sitting in back on the way to the station."

CHAPTER 6

Tom Widmer called in sick on Friday. He was sick, too. The nausea that hit him in Carol Cropcho's bedroom didn't leave overnight. He tossed in Arby's men's room and once on the way home. The only thing kept him from heaving now was he was empty. He tried water, Pepsi, orange juice, vodka, and bourbon to get the taste out of his mouth. Nothing worked and now he was half buzzed to boot, eleven o'clock in the morning.

He showered until the hot water was gone last night, and again this morning. Tried to sleep in bed with Marian, like nothing was wrong, gave up after forty-five minutes. Laid on the couch and watched *Baseball Tonight* and *SportsCenter* reruns until after four. Decided he should at least try to get some sleep. Turned off the television and rolled over on his side on the big sectional.

Lay in the dark until he heard the newspaper delivery. Ran out to the box at the end of the driveway in his underwear and robe. Afraid to open it, afraid not to. Marty must have called it in around midnight. Was that time to get it in the morning paper? Was this more important than West Coast box scores?

The *Post-Gazette* had nothing. Tom couldn't decide if that was good or not. Bad as it would be to read about it, not knowing anything was worse. Nothing on the early morning TV news, sneaking looks around telling the kids why he was still home. Marian didn't have much to say; nothing unusual there.

He spent most of the morning in the extra bedroom he used as an office. The *Post-Gazette* web site had the story now. No details, just that a Penns River woman had been brutally murdered in her home last night between ten and midnight. Local police said it looked like a burglary gone wrong. Signs of forced entry, valuables stolen, costume pieces left behind. A professional job. Just like Marty drew it up.

"Aren't you at least going to get dressed? I mean, before the kids come home from school, anyway?"

He hadn't heard Marian come in. Nursing a little gin in a water glass, keeping the edge off, focused on the computer screen. "In a while. I'm still deciding if I want to lie down. I feel like shit."

Marian came around the side of his desk. Arched her eyebrows when she got a good look at him. "What happened to your face? Did one of your chippies get rough with you?"

Tom's hand went to his cheek, felt the scratches. He tried not to stammer too quick an answer. His blush was faster than his brain and he had to settle for, "It's stupid. I walked into a tree last night. Like a big shrub. Scratched hell out of me."

Marian gave that the credence it deserved. "Where did you come across a tree or—never mind. I don't think I want to know." She put a hand on his forehead. "You're not warm. Are you sure you're not just hung over? You were out with your little friends pretty late last night. And you were drunk enough to walk into a tree."

"No, it's not that. I only had a couple. This is something I ate. Food poisoning, maybe."

She sat on the corner of the desk. Leaned in until he could see the swell of one breast disappear into her bra under the blouse. "Smells like you're had a few already today. I know you swear you don't have a problem, but it's not even noon yet."

"I told you I threw up last night. I used some Listerine to kill the taste in my mouth."

"Smells like you used enough to kill some brain cells."

"What do you want, Marian? I feel shitty enough without getting my balls busted."

She looked at him long enough to give the impression there was a wide and varied range of things she wanted before she said, "Nothing right now. Someday, though."

Marian leaned further and gave him the kiss on his ear lobe that could get him hard at his mother's funeral. Only she had found the right spot and pressure to do it. He didn't even know it was possible until she did it one night in his car on a date. That little kiss, a touch of her lips on his ear, was responsible for much of what had happened since. In its way, that kiss had killed Carol Cropcho. No exaggeration. That kiss, Marian's ability to turn any situation sexual whenever she wanted, pushed him past his doubts into a proposal. That kiss, on that one night, led to this marriage and the current situation. Carol Cropcho would be alive today but for the kiss of a woman she'd never heard of.

Marian left with no more preamble than when she'd come. Tom had no idea what got into the goofy bitch sometimes. Came in, jerked him around, but didn't want anything. *Someday, though.* He wanted to tell her "someday" is a vague concept. Not good to look too far into the future. No one ever knew for sure how much future they had. If anyone should live her life like each day might be her last, it was Marian.

He snuck a little more gin into his glass. It would be a while before he could talk with Marty again. Not good to be associated with the grieving husband, not when the bereaved still had work to do. They could be fast friends after Marian was gone. Two sudden widowers sharing their grief. People could think what they wanted then.

Tom finished his drink and refreshed the web page. This bitch couldn't be dead soon enough.

CHAPTER 7

"There. Back it up a little. Stop. Are those scratches on his face?"

Doc and Grabek were into their second hour reviewing the same thirty-eight seconds of tape. A dark sedan pulls into the lot, parks out of sight. Eight minutes twenty-three seconds of nothing. Then a man walks to the Dumpster holding a large dark plastic bag, half full. Throws it in. His face is visible for no more than six seconds trotting back to the car. Another forty-seven seconds of nothing. The car leaves the way it came. The rear license plate is visible, but indistinguishable.

Doc leaned closer to the monitor. "Could be. Hard to tell, shitty as this tape is. Guess it was too much to ask for a small town Arby's to have a disc recorder."

"We're lucky we got there when we did. This tape's probably been overwritten a thousand times. I'm half surprised we can see anything at all."

"Noosh, can you do anything with this?"

Neuschwander shook his head. "Not me. I know a guy at Pissper might be able to." Pissper meaning Penn State, Penns River. "He teaches AV up there, does a nice job for someone stuck in a branch campus. We send him contract work when we have to."

"We don't need all the dead air. Just where the guy is visible, or the car is moving. Should save him some time."

"I'll make a copy and call him." Neuschwander held up a hand to stop Grabek from saying it. "I know, we'll lose even more resolution if I make a copy. We can't let a civilian handle the original without breaking the chain of evidence. It's not like it'll make a big difference, as many times as this tape's been overwritten. If he can't work with my copy, the original won't help him."

Doc rubbed his eyes. He'd been home long enough to shower and change. Got his pants into the washer with an old towel, worth a try. Split a pizza from Elena's with Grabek while they watched the video. Now he was full and warm, coming down from the morning's caffeine overdose, running on two hours' sleep. Exhausted and jitty at the same time. "What else you got?"

Grabek's eyes had drifted shut. Neuschwander nudged his foot. "You're going to want to hear this, Willie. Everything that had to go to the lab is gone. They promised to bump us up the list, but they say that to all the girls. I did a little work myself while you two were in here playing video games."

He waited. Doc refused to beg. Grabek's lids were reuniting when Neuschwander realized he was losing his audience.

"I typed the blood from some of the evidence samples we got. There's quite a bit on the gloves you pulled out of the trash, especially the right, and on that glass thing we figure was the murder weapon. The blood type on the gloves and on the weapon matches Carol Cropcho's. These aren't positive matches, but what are the odds someone unrelated to this case decided to ditch clothes covered with A-positive blood at what's probably the closest Dumpster to where she was killed, right after she was killed? I mean, A-plus is fairly

39

common, but we're still talking only about a third of the population."

Neuschwander sat back like he expected more acclaim than he got. Grabek looked even more asleep than before. Doc let it lay for almost a minute before he picked it up. "There's more, isn't there? You're not that smug because of what you just told us."

"No one seems too excited. I'll just type up the report and you two can read it when you have more energy."

Doc rested his left elbow on the table, forearm vertical. Made a loose fist with his left hand. Reached over with his right and took hold of the middle finger, extended it from the others like it weighed thirty pounds. "You see that, Noosh? That's how tired I am. I can't even tell you to fuck off without help. What else do you have?"

Neuschwander kicked the table, startled Grabek awake. "You pussies forget I didn't get any more sleep than you did. Since I plan on leaving here in the next fifteen minutes and I don't want you calling me at home asking what's going to be in my report, I'll tell you now. There are minute traces of blood on the sleeve of the shirt, and near the collar. Both are Type O."

Doc sat up straighter, not as sleepy as five seconds ago. "His blood."

"I don't see who the hell else it could belong to. Now, O-plus doesn't help you a lot. It's the only type more common than A."

"Still, if we get a suspect and he's not O-plus..."

"He's probably clean."

Doc rubbed sleep from his eyes. Still exhausted, but fully awake. "That's good, Noosh. Very good. That won't tell us who did her, but it will sure tell us a lot about who didn't. Save an assload of time."

Neuschwander basked in Doc's appreciation for a few seconds. Grabek's eyes were one-third open, no other sign of life. "There's more."

"More? More?" Doc leaned on the table toward Neuschwander. "Did you ever think of making late night TV ads? 'Already a great bargain for nineteen-ninety-five! But wait! There's more!' Billy Mays is dead, Noosh. Cut to the chase."

Neuschwander looked like he might let Doc suffer, then stifled a yawn. Rubbed his eyes, said, "While I was looking for blood on his clothing, I came across some possible clear fluids that had dried on the shirt and gloves. Could be saliva, could be tears. We're talking really minute traces here, I don't know if it will be enough to get a sample, but if we get anything from them, or from the barf by the toilet, we can lock your boy in tighter than a frog's asshole. Assuming you can bring him in."

There it was, the catch with DNA and most forms of trace evidence: they never helped find the guy. Neuschwander's work could convict the right suspect, but the detectives had to catch him first. It pained Doc to watch *CSI*; he'd never seen either the New York or Miami versions. Not even the lust he felt for Marg Helgenberger got him past the idea the show planted in people's minds, that suspects walked around with DNA bar codes stamped on their foreheads, just waiting to be picked up as soon as Grissom got results in fifteen minutes from a sample that couldn't help but be contaminated because of how it was handled while it was carried to the testers, who had nothing better to do than wait for this specific piece of evidence, crime in Las Vegas so low the techs only worked one case at a time.

So, yeah, they still had to catch the guy. Doc thanked Neuschwander, then slapped the flat of his hand against the table to wake Grabek. Turned out the lights and staggered down the hall to his cube for his coat, already thinking of what his bed would feel like. He could be asleep fifteen minutes from now, and he was prepared to use siren and lights to do it.

He had one arm through his coat when Stush Napier leaned through the doorway. "Got a minute before you go?"

"Sure, Stush. Let me run to the head first."

Doc splashed water on his face, left his coat in his cube. He didn't want to look like he was hurrying Stush.

CHAPTER 8

"You want some coffee?"

Doc tried not to slump in the chair. He knew Stush didn't like keeping him here any more than he liked staying. "I'm good. What's up?"

Stush poured himself half a cup from the coffee maker on the lateral filing cabinet. Stirred in sugar and milk. Brought it back to his chair. "So, are things working out okay with you and Grabek?"

"I got no problems working with Willie."

Stush sipped coffee, gave Doc time to say more. "How long we known each other, Benny?"

Only a handful of people called Doc Benny. "How old am I? Thirty-seven years."

"I've known your old man almost fifty. This is your Uncle Stush asking you: How is he to work with?"

"Lazy. When he retired from Pittsburgh, he meant it."

"He stiffing you on the Cropcho thing?"

Doc thought for a second about the Dumpster at Arby's. "No, he's there. He just does the absolute minimum to get by, is all."

"You're the lead, right?"

"Yeah, but still. I mean, show some interest."

Stush drank more coffee. Swirled it around his mouth like he wasn't sure he liked it. "I knew him from before, you know. When he was in Pittsburgh."

"You worked downtown?"

"Exchange program, twenty years ago. I just made lieutenant, so the old chief sent me down to see how real cops work. Willie was still the new guy, working Night Felonies. Never saw him do anything he didn't have to do, even then, but man, he was smart. Smart mouth, too, but he's natural police. You can learn a lot from him. That's why I wanted him here when I heard he was looking for a soft landing."

"Stush, you're the chief. I work with whoever you say. I've never had a problem with that, and I don't now. I know you'll take care of me."

"Benny." Stush waited for Doc to remember they were having a personal conversation. "You know how much I appreciate how you insisted on working your way up through patrol when you came back here. All that time in the army, the shit you'd done? Hell, boy, you were more qualified for my job than I was when you walked through the door. You think I want that pompous prick Harriger running things when I retire? That's your job." He went on before Doc could speak. "If you want it."

Doc sat back. He was too tired to argue and this wasn't the time. They'd been here before and would be again.

"It's okay," Stush said. "That'll be up to you. I'd just like you to have the option when the time comes. That's why I wanted to talk to you today. I never ask you for anything special because of how we go back and you've earned everything you got here. But I need something from you now."

"Anything, Stush. You know that."

"I need you and Willie to break this case quick. Without help. I'll call for the states if I have to because I want it to go down. But I would consider it a personal favor if we could keep it in house. I'll give you all the help I can."

"Can I ask a question?"

"You can always ask me a question, Benny. You know that."

"I've known you almost as long as you've known me. You want to close every case we get. I know this is a bad one, but what makes it special?"

"You know how I got this job, right?"

"The old chief retired and you stepped up."

Stush locked his hands on his belly. Stared at them while he spoke. "It's not completely fair to say I stepped up, not like it was my turn. I got jumped ahead of a couple of guys who outranked me and had more time in. You know why?"

Doc knew, didn't say. He waited to hear how Stush told it.

"My sister Helen's husband used to be mayor. We drank together a couple a nights a week at the Warszawa Hotel since before they were married, back when it was a decent place. He give me the job over the deputy chief and another lieutenant with five years on me. I didn't ask for it and he never asked me. He knew I wanted to be chief one day, and he had the juice to do it. So he did."

Doc waited before he asked. "How'd it go over?"

"How do you think?" Stush picked at a loose thread on his shirt. "Council pissed and moaned, but Dave could handle them. It didn't take Elliott Ness to run things in those days, and I think he told them I'd be grateful enough not to fuss about whatever I was told not to fuss about."

"Small town politics."

"Nothing new there, right? Anyhow, Mike Sepelyak—the

45

other lieutenant, the one with more time in than me—him and me went way back, too, and he didn't really want the job. He wound up being deputy when Eddie Farina quit. Eddie was deputy chief and thought he should've at least been offered the job. He was right. He should have. But that wasn't how it came down. Eddie didn't like it and went to work in the front office of some uniformed security company in Pittsburgh. Made nice money there, I hear. So I guess it worked out."

Doc knew most of this. Not about Eddie Farina, or Sepelyak's history, but the basic facts weren't news. Stush knew it, too, so a punch line was coming.

"Mike had a heart attack before you came back. He retired with disability, but he died a few years later."

"I remember his funeral. It was right after I started here, maybe three months in."

"That's about right. Mike retiring meant we had an opening for deputy, and no one qualified for the job. Things were getting rougher, especially down the Allegheny Estates and the Flats. By this time Dave's not mayor anymore and the council isn't too sure I'm up to handling what the town's turning into. They go looking outside and find Jack Harriger working for the State Police way the hell up Emporium. He was nothing special, putting in time, but he was from Tarentum originally, so he was a local boy with some training and experience and they hired him.

"I didn't like the idea. I thought he was too rigid, wanted to run a small town police department like an Airborne outfit. Everyone thought I was too easy, and a couple on the council wanted to show me who was boss, so they hired

Jack, who just happens to be Eddie's nephew. His sister's boy."

"Him and Uncle Eddie close?"

"Like two fingers in an asshole."

Doc stayed as far from politics as a cop could in a town the size of Penns River. He couldn't help knowing how Jack Harriger worked the council. There were five members, plus the mayor. One Jack grilled steaks for two or three times a summer. Went to a couple of Steelers games every fall with another. One more and Stush had a problem.

Stush connected the dots for him. "Last week I seen that little cocksucker come out of the Vets with Jimmy Briscoe. I don't like wondering what they talk about with this heater case dumped in our laps."

"I don't guess you would." Part of Doc wished Stush hadn't said anything. Neuschwander had some good evidence; finding who it belonged to was no cinch. The phantom phone call probably burned up their luck allotment for this case. Doc thought their chances of an arrest were no better than fifty-fifty.

Another part of him was glad Stush told him. He couldn't love the old man more if he really was his uncle. Took him to watch softball tournaments down at Sokol Camp when his dad couldn't go. Showed him where Forbes Field used to be, home plate in one of Pitt's libraries now, and the spot where Mazeroski's home run cleared the wall to beat the Yankees in 1960. Told Doc exactly where he was, what he was doing, when Jim Woods made the call on KDKA. There wasn't much Doc wouldn't do for Stush Napier.

"We'll get him, Stush. I ain't working for Jack Harriger."

CHAPTER 9

Eve Stepler flopped on the chair next to Doc during rehearsal break. "What are you this time?"

The Penns River Players did two productions a year. This year's fall show was *Inherit the Wind*.

"A cop. Do you believe that?" Doc less than fully conscious, the three hours of sleep he grabbed between work and rehearsal not doing much more than remind him how tired he was. "I volunteer my valuable free time to the local theater company, hoping to broaden my horizons, and they cast me as a cop."

"Don't exaggerate. You're just the bailiff."

"Still, I have to wear a uniform and stand for the whole show. My feet will hurt like bastards."

"Didn't you tell me once there are no small parts, only small actors?"

"I don't care how small the part is. I'd just like to do something besides be a cop, which is what I do all day. I could be a juror. Then I'd just have to sit there. I could do that. Hell, I'm *good* at that."

"Jurors can't have doughnuts." Doc flashed her the finger. "You want a different part, talk to Fred." The director.

"I did."

"What did he say?"

Doc elevated his voice a fifth and used enough British accent to sound haughty. Or artsy. "Your authoritarian presence commands the stage." Back to his regular voice. "Said I was too dominant to sit in the jury box. Everyone would wonder what I was going to do instead of listening to the actors."

"Maybe he just needs a little doctoring, Doc."

Doc pursed his lips like he was suppressing a suitable reply. Or a burp. "As no one knows better than you, Eve, when choosing my friends I do not discriminate on the grounds of whether a person desires complementary plumbing to have a satisfying relationship. Fred's just a little too precious for my taste, no matter how he spends his free time. When's Gene coming back?"

"Might be a while. I heard his wife might not make it."

"I didn't know. What's wrong?"

"Breast cancer. You know, it pisses me off when someone dies of breast cancer at her age. What is she? Fifty? Fifty-five? I know she's younger than Gene, and he can't be sixty. She just didn't get her mammograms."

"Do you know that?"

Eve pulled back her first answer. "No. No, I don't. It's just that my mother had breast cancer. Both her sisters and their mother died from it. It's like a fucking heirloom, and I get it next. The only way I keep from lying awake nights worrying about it is if I tell myself to stay on top of it. Take the mammogram every time they'll pay for it, then it won't get me. So I tell myself every woman who dies of breast cancer didn't keep up with her mammograms until I hear different. And I don't want to hear different."

Doc waited to be sure there wasn't more, and for Eve to get her wind back. She beat him to it. "I'm a little surprised to see you here tonight, what with that big murder all over the television."

Doc didn't want to talk about the Cropcho murder, but not as much as he didn't want to talk about breast cancer. "We're working it, just not twenty-four hours a day. Cops have lives, too, you know."

"You're the only cop I know, so, no, I didn't. You see the new girl?"

"Which one?"

Eve exhaled hard through her nose. "The juror? Copper blond hair and green eyes."

"Oh, her. I saw you chatting her up when she came in. I didn't know she was in the cast. What's her name?"

Eve took a swig of bottled water. Tiny curls of sawdust nestled in her hair. "Jillian something. Starts with an O, I think."

"Evie, that's disgusting. You were too busy checking out her rack to even get her full name. Shame on you."

"I saw her first, Doc. There's someone new playing Mrs. Krebs. Why don't you try her?"

"We already met. Remember Greg Gilligan, played clarinet? She's his aunt. Can't be more than sixty years old."

"She looks like a cougar to me. Just the kind of experienced woman who'd go for a somewhat younger man who's been around a little."

Doc waited until it was obvious they weren't having that conversation. "So what's the deal with Jillian Whatshername?"

"Let me at least take one shot. Please?"

"Are you sure you're even playing on the same team? You're usually running to me. 'Ask this one out. Ask that one out.' What's different here?"

Eve pretended to drink from the empty bottle. "The ones I send your way aren't usually this good looking."

"So you're saying I only get your rejects."

"They're not really rejects. I mean, well, I usually at least ask about them, you know, kind of feel them out, and if they're not interested in a girl like me, I, like, tell you about them."

"And you haven't written this one off yet. Don't you feel like you owe me one?"

"You know, Doc, if I was a guy you wouldn't be poaching like this. I know you. You're a good wing man."

"The reason you know is because I've done it for you. Remember the cast party for *Rosencrantz and Guildenstern Are Dead* two years ago? How'd that work out for you?"

"That was three years ago."

"And? How'd it go?"

"For the whole weekend. Too bad she was from out of town just visiting family. Okay, you took care of me that time. Steered the ugly friend away. Fine. You can have Jillian. I think she's a breeder, anyway."

"Jesus Christ, Eve. You make it sound like we're dividing up Poland here. I just asked a question to see if you thought she'd like me."

Eve stood. "You're not going to pull that old high school crap again, are you? 'Gee, who's that pretty girl? Maybe she'll like me. Ooh, but what if she doesn't?' Damn, Doc. You're like Charlie Brown and the little red-haired girl. We graduated together. You're thirty-seven years old. Get over it and make move on her, or I will. Even worse, I'll tell her you're hot for her."

51

Doc shot her a look. "All right. I won't do that. But if you don't at least make an effort, I'll find ways for you to bump into each other. You know I'm sneaky like that."

What Doc knew for sure was he'd given Penns River's leading lesbian *yenta* an excuse to practice her trade. He'd need something legitimate to account for his free time or Eve would have him married by Christmas.

CHAPTER 10

Tom Widmer skipped his usual Thursday night out. A week now since he'd killed Carol Cropcho. He'd been careful to be home every night by six to see the news. Flipped through the channels so he wouldn't miss it because they were showing some asshole's house burn down in McKeesport. Working almost regular days now, hard to believe how much better he felt compared to last Friday. He still started awake a couple of times a night. Looked hard at any car he didn't recognize going past the house.

Marian yelled to watch the kids, she was going down the hill for milk or something. She used to call him to get milk on his way home. Now she took any excuse to drive that new Beemer. Their portfolio dropped five percent some days, his commissions not enough to rent a video, and she bought a new car. There wouldn't be anything left if this Cropcho business didn't blow over soon so Marty could hold up his end of the deal.

Kids were wrecking the joint, as usual. Toys and video game sleeves on every flat surface. Potato chips in and around a bowl on the coffee table, a few strays ground into the carpet. Three—no, four—half-drunk sodas. They only had two kids. Either she was importing the little bastards to irritate him, or his pair were working overtime. Fucking cow home all day and couldn't keep them in line. Looked like this every time he came home. He popped open a beer and turned on KDKA.

The big story was a school bus crash in Monessen. No one hurt, bunch of parents yakking about how they've been asking for a stop sign for years, that's always been a bad intersection. Try WPXI. Weather teaser. Switched to WTAE. Transformer blew in Braddock. Never any news from up this way. Back to KDKA. Commercial. WPXI just got to the bus crash. Different parents, same bullshit. Clicked the remote for WTAE and the doorbell rang.

"Dad! Door!"

"See who it is, Mark! I'm busy!"

"Why do I have to do it? Peter's closer!"

Bingo! Jennifer Marhefka on Channel 4. "I don't care who's closer! One of you answer the goddamned door! Now!"

They must have just thrown it over to her. "Police still have not made an arrest and have not released the names of any suspects in the brutal killing of a Penns River woman last week." The picture cut away from Jennifer to show footage of the body's removal. "Carol Cropcho is believed to have been beaten to death after surprising a burglar last Thursday night. The brutal slaying has shocked this Neshannock County community, and left Martin Cropcho with many questions."

"Hey, Dad! It's some guys for you!"

No way Tom was leaving before he saw how Marty would pull this off. "All right! I'll be there in a second!"

Stood in front of the couch so he could go to the door right away, shut up whichever kid was busting his balls. Took a swig of beer. Spilled half of what was left when he saw the graphic on the screen. *Martin Cropcho. Husband of Victim.* Talking to Jennifer about how ironic it was, all the time and money they spent trying to have kids and now he was glad there weren't any, or they might be dead, too. Helluva performance.

Tom had never seen him before in his life.

"DAD!!"

He bumped into the side of the couch as he backed around it. Almost fell. His eyes kept the television in the center of his vision wherever he moved. Not thinking anything, his brain not processing. All he knew was he didn't recognize the guy passing himself off as Marty Cropcho.

Two men at the door. One about Tom's age. A little over six feet, good shape. Other guy was older, fifties maybe, shorter and fatter. "Yeah? What can I do for you?"

The younger one said, "Hello, sir. Are you Thomas Harold Widmer?"

"Yeah?"

He held up a badge. "I'm Detective Dougherty of the Penns River police. This is Detective Grabek. We have a warrant for your arrest for the murder of Carol Cropcho in her home on or about September twenty-fifth of this year."

"Huh? What the fuck?"

The older one—Grabek, did he say?—stepped forward and cuffed Tom's hands behind his back before he had a chance to move. The can of beer fell to the porch. Not much left to spill.

Dougherty said, "We also have a warrant to search your house, garage, and grounds. Please go with Officer Ulizio to his squad car and wait for us there."

Tom tried to gesture with his hands. Looked at Dougherty

like he'd just beamed down from a *Star Trek* movie. "Wh-what about the kids? I mean, I'm the only adult home."

"Officer Pazul will keep an eye on them for the time being if you'll help us get them all on the porch." Dougherty gestured for a big woman in uniform, curly hair frizzing in the light rain. "We'll call your wife or someone else to come over if you'll give us the number."

Tom said, "I don't understand," his mind screaming *ShutupShutupShutup!*

Dougherty slid a folded piece of paper into Tom's shirt pocket. "U, put him in the squad. No one talks to him, not even you." Then he and Grabek walked into Tom's house like they owned it.

CHAPTER 11

Stush, Doc, Grabek, and Jack Harriger were jammed into Stush's office like tissues in a box. Stush had his own chair; Harriger and Grabek took the visitors'. Doc sat on the HVAC unit.

"You're getting too cute," Harriger said. "Mirandize him and be done with it. No screwing around."

Grabek didn't play favorites. He spoke to Harriger in the same patronizing tone he'd used with Stush.

"He doesn't need Miranda until we ask him a question. No one's said dick to him yet, so we're okay there." He sipped his coffee. "This isn't just another asshole criminal. He's a white collar guy with some smarts. As soon as we read him his rights, he'll ask for a lawyer. We don't have a good motive. It would be nice if he gives us one and I doubt we can browbeat it out of him, especially not after the kind of lawyer he can afford shows up. We might be able to scare it out of him if we're careful."

"Statements are only admissible without Miranda if the perp blurts something out at the time of arrest," Harriger said. Doc shook his head. He couldn't decide who irritated him more. Even in private conversation Harriger spoke like he was being interviewed for the TV news. Only he said "perps" in Penns River. Suspects, criminals, crooks, or bad guys was good enough for everyone else.

Grabek was no better. He might have a good idea. Even if he did break Widmer down this way, it left too much to a judge's discretion, or the uncertainties of endless appeals. Get the guy a lawyer and move on. Let the motive come out later. Or not. It wouldn't matter if Neuschwander's DNA came through.

Harriger hadn't finished talking. "The lawyer's going to see how much time elapsed and get everything he says thrown out. You'll be left with an empty bag."

"Maybe." Grabek's tone got more condescending every time he opened his mouth. "I'll get over it. We can probably convict with what we have, especially if the DNA comes back worth a shit. At least this way we'll know, instead of having to wait for the lab to squeeze us into their busy schedule. If they don't lose the samples. Or miscode them. Or any of the thousand other things they can do to hose a good case."

"You're in the process of hosing a good case all on your own, De-*tec*-tive Grabek." Doc might have enjoyed watching these two assholes piss on each other if this wasn't a murder case. Harringer looked to Stush while he spoke at Grabek. "There's a reason procedures are written the way they are."

Stush spoke for the first time since he offered everyone coffee and seats. "We got the general outline, Willie. Tell me how it'll go down. Be specific."

Grabek threw a dismissive glance at Harriger and spoke to Stush. "Me and Doc go in. Lay out all the evidence we have, show him how deep he's in. No loss to us, we'll have to give it to his lawyer in discovery, anyway. Tick it off piece by piece. We know the burglary is bullshit. The jewelry we found in his house proves he knew her." The search warrant had paid off big. "Nice of the cheap bastard to keep the receipt. Then there's the tape from Arby's. Eyeball witness. We can tie the clothes in the bag to him and the dead woman."

"Eyeball witness, my ass," Harriger said. "You got an anonymous phone call. No one to testify."

"We don't need him to testify, Jack." Grabek of the "in for a penny, in for a pound" school of insubordination. "Doesn't matter if an angel came down from heaven and give us the tip. The tape shows a man fitting Widmer's general description get out of a car that matches four digits of the license plate with his make and model. This mystery man throws a bag into the trash, which makes it public property, no warrants necessary. The clothes in that bag have stains that match Carol Cropcho's blood type, and probably his. DNA's not back yet, but when we mention it's coming I say he's even money to piss himself and cry for a deal."

"Until his lawyer backs him out."

"The hell with his lawyer. We'll have his statements. Make the judge earn his money for a change. What's her name—Sally? The prosecutor?—she should be able to convince the judge the original statement's true. It's practically a deathbed confession."

"Never let a judge have that kind of control over a case," Harriger said. "I want T's crossed and I's dotted. By the numbers, Detective. This is a murder investigation."

"And how many homicide cases have you worked, Jack? I've closed over a hundred. What did you investigate up Emporium? Poaching? Take the antlers home, tell your friends you shot the bastard yourself?"

"Detective Grabek, that's insubordination!" Harriger half out of his chair, cords showing in his neck.

Stush looked past him to Doc, who'd lost interest. Stush said, "All right, that's enough."

"Chief Napier, I'm the deputy here. I don't have to take that kind of insolence from a subordinate. I don't care how many cases he closed in Pittsburgh. I want his ass put down, and I want it down now."

"Take it easy, Deputy." A hardness came into Stush's eyes Doc had seen before, not often. "I'm entitled to a little respect myself. Willie's been working long days. I'll speak to him about his tone of voice later. Here's what we're going to do now. Neuschwander will get the video running, and Willie and Doc'll tell Widmer how it lays. I'll watch through the mirror. First time Widmer even hints he wants a lawyer, he gets one."

"Chief, you're making a mistake here."

"I've made them before, Jack. As you well know." Stush's eyes lingered on Harriger's. "Anything rolls back will roll back on me. That's why I'm sending you home, so your hands will be clean. You good with that?"

Everything about Harriger said he wasn't except his mouth. "Yes, sir."

"Willie, Doc, give me a couple minutes so I can take a leak. I'll wave when I'm ready."

Stush moved for the men's room. Doc and Grabek waited in the hallway outside the interview room.

Grabek was too short to look through the window without standing close enough to be visible from inside. "Can you see him in there, Doc?"

"Yeah, I see him."

"How's he look?"

Doc took his time letting the smile grow. "He fell asleep."

Grabek smiled right away. "Bingo."

CHAPTER 12

Grabek snuck the door open, slammed it shut when he and Doc were inside. Widmer's head slipped off the hand that cradled it.

"Sorry to make you wait," Grabek said. He turned a chair to straddle it, draped his arms over the back. Casual. Routine business. "We had things to do."

The two cops sat at opposite ends of the rectangular table, so Widmer had to turn his head to see either. Both never in his field of vision at the same time. Doc pushed his front chair legs off the floor, hung a knee over a corner of the table. His job was to look uninterested and write key points on a legal pad as Grabek made them. Don't show the pad to Widmer, but make sure he could see it.

"Can I get something to drink?" Widmer ran a thumb and forefinger through his eyes to join at his nose, waking himself. "I'm dying of thirst here."

Grabek handed him the bottle of water in his hand. "Here. Seal's still on it."

Widmer took the bottle. "It's not very cold."

"Friend, cold water is the least of your troubles right now. Do you want the water or not?"

He did. Unscrewed the cap and took a long pull. Everyone sat. No one spoke. Widmer tried more water. A small red LED went on in the light switch panel. Doc rapped twice on the table and Grabek said, "Here's how this works. We're going to lay out what we have on you, and—"

"Don't you have to read me my rights?"

"Your rights aren't in jeopardy until someone asks you a question. I know everything I need already. I'm just going to tell you what's what, so you can appreciate the situation."

"What about my right to remain silent?"

"Exercise it. When I want to hear from you, I'll say so. For now, just sit there and listen."

Widmer's confusion couldn't be more obvious if a question mark was tattooed on his forehead. He glanced at Doc, then looked back to Grabek like he wanted to ask something but didn't know what. Doc scratched a series of squares on his pad.

Grabek spoke only loud enough to be sure the tape picked everything up. "About ten-thirty last Thursday night a man drove to the Arby's at the intersection of Fourth and Stevenson. Parked around the side. He was dressed all in black. Black tee shirt, black jeans, black shoes, black hood. Dark smudges on his face. Looked like someone straight out of ninja camp. He was nervous, kept looking around all the way to the crapper in back. These facts are not in dispute. A witness saw him come in and thought he looked a little squirrelly, so he paid attention."

Color ran from Widmer's face like snow melting off a roof. His body seemed to shrink in on itself as Grabek spoke.

"The witness also took notice when the man came out of the john five minutes later with a clean face, clean clothes, and a big trash bag under his arm. He looked out the window and watched the man throw the bag into the Dumpster on the right. The one closest to the building. Then he got back in his car and drove out the way you came in."

"That's bullshit," Widmer said. "It wasn't me. I wasn't there." He didn't sound too sure.

"It's not bullshit. We know it's not because Arby's has a video surveillance camera. We got a good look at you walking to the Dumpster, jogging back, and driving away." Not really. Neuschwander's friend at PSPR couldn't make Widmer's face recognizable. Grabek wasn't under oath. "The videotape also got four of the six digits from your license plate on the way out. There's only one dark—blue, black, maroon, whatever—Mercedes with those four digits in those exact places registered in the entire Commonwealth of Pennsylvania.

"Next morning, bright and early, Detective Dougherty went Dumpster diving and recovered the trash bag you threw away. We know it's the same bag because the clothes in it match what the witness says he saw you wear into the men's room. There's blood on the gloves, and on the tee shirt. A lot of blood. It's the same type as Carol Cropcho's. We can't prove it's her blood yet, but you know we will when the DNA tests come back.

"Now here's the hell of it. There's someone else's blood on the shirt. One of the gloves, too. And you here with almost healed scratches on your face. Damnedest thing, isn't it?"

Doc wrote each point on his pad as Grabek laid them out. Widmer stole glances at the list. Watched it grow. The color in his face changed to the human flesh version of green. Doc looked for a trash can without moving his head in case Widmer ralphed again.

Grabek wasn't finished. "So I'm looking at all this before I come in here. Playing jury, giving you every reasonable doubt. Hell, I'm even giving you unreasonable doubts. Thinking of all the ways you and your attorney are going to explain away the evidence. Someone good, right? You're not thinking you can get off using some overworked public defender that passed the bar by two points on his eighth try, are you?

"Here's the lawyer's closing argument. 'Someone stole the car, brought it right back where you left it before you even knew it was gone.' Not too likely, but I'll give you that one. 'The witness in Arby's didn't get a good enough look at who threw the bag in the Dumpster. Could've been anyone.' That one's better, but the two of them together are a little more of a reach. Listen to me now. I'm just getting to the good part. 'The police don't know who might have been in and out of that Dumpster between ten-thirty Thursday night and Friday morning It might not be the same bag.' You know, I thought of that myself. I almost talked myself out of it. I was just starting to think you could beat this."

Widmer looked into a high corner like there might be a window there he could crawl through. They all look for it, like there's something they can say or do to make it magically appear. They'd crawl up the wall like centipedes if it opened, hoping once they were out, they'd stay out. No one had found it yet.

Grabek waited for Widmer to look at him. "You could, too. Beat this. Except that's your blood on the clothes with hers. I'd pay money to watch any lawyer convince a jury how her blood *and* your blood get on those clothes if you didn't kill her.

"Your lawyer's good, though. He's not giving up. He better not, for what you're paying him. He says, 'The

Commonwealth can't even prove my client was ever in the house.' That's a good point. I left one thing out. I shouldn't have—it's cheating—and the DA won't be so sloppy. You don't help the wife around the house much, do you? Use a maid service, maybe? I've seen your house and car, so I know you don't do it, because you did a half-assed job on the single most important clean-up of your life. You didn't know there's DNA in vomit, did you?"

Widmer dropped his head and started to cry. Soft, like someone behind a curtain. Tears dripped onto the table.

"That DNA puts you in the house, in the master bathroom not ten feet from where we found the body. Had to be that night, too. Who the hell lets someone else's puke sit around their house?

"All that's good, but my favorite part is the confession."

That retrieved Widmer's attention. "Confession? I didn't confess to anything. You won't even let me talk."

"The written confession's a formality. An innocent man, he's under arrest for murder, looking at a death sentence, he's shitting his pants. 'How did this happen? Oh, my God. Sweet Jesus, when are they going to realize they got the wrong man?' Not you, Tommy. Uh-uh. You were sawing logs when we came in here. Probably the first good sleep you've had in a week. No more wondering when we'll kick down your door. The suspense is gone, the waiting's over. Your body finally runs out of adrenaline and you conk out. Cops have a saying: Only the guilty sleep. You just slept yourself into the death house, motherfucker."

Widmer sniffed snot back into his nose. Spoke to the table. "No. I didn't kill her. Why would I kill her? I didn't even know her. You're making a mistake. I swear to God. I didn't know her. I'm not a criminal."

Grabek let him cry. Looked over at Doc, nodded with his eyes at the pathetic spectacle. His voice so low Widmer had to quit sniffing and sobbing to hear.

"We wondered about that. There was no obvious connection between you. No mention in her address book or calendar. You're not in her cell phone call log. No one had ever seen you together. Her husband didn't suspect anything. Your wife had no hint."

He slid an evidence bag across the table. It held a small diamond bracelet and a standard sheet of printer paper folded in half. "This was in that two-drawer lateral file you have in your home office or den or study, whatever you call it. Engraved on the inside. I'm guessing CLC means Carol Lynne Cropcho. Her husband listed a similar piece as missing."

Grabek leaned forward over the back of the chair until it leaned with him. "Only the guilty sleep, Tom. Tell me what happened and I'll get you a pillow."

Tom Widmer heard about half of what Grabek said after, "A witness saw you come in." Words and phrases here and there. Video surveillance camera. Only one dark Mercedes. Her blood *and* his blood on the clothes. DNA in vomit. Each one drove him deeper into himself until he felt so small he might blow away if Grabek breathed on him. His resolve crumbled like a ball of sand the first time he heard, "only the guilty sleep." Take me where I have to go. Show me what to sign. Just please don't kill me. An even bigger coward than he always thought he might be.

The bracelet brought him around. They found it in his house? In his *den?* He thought back to the TV news, Jennifer Marhefka interviewing a man they claimed was Marty Cropcho, it had almost slipped his mind once the police got hold of him. Tom was so stunned at first he thought he saw it wrong, or that Marty had on a disguise, or the police slipped a ringer in there as some kind of investigative trick. The bracelet shocked his brain into working like it should for a man with a triple-digit IQ. The poor bastard on TV *was* Marty Cropcho. Tom had been drinking and wenching around with someone else.

He ground his fists into his eyes. Looked at Dougherty, then straight at Grabek. "Fuck you and your evidence. I want a lawyer."

CHAPTER 13

Fat Jimmy's smelled of sweat, beer, and cigarette smoke tempered by piss and urinal cakes near the rest rooms. Jimmy spent an average of fourteen hours a day there. He didn't smell much better.

Doc spotted Eve with three other Penns River Players in the corner farthest from the toilets. He'd tried to beg off. Told Eve the Widmer arrest would keep him from rehearsal. "Screw the rehearsal," she said. "We got a group going to Fat Jimmy's after to make the rednecks queasy. Everyone will be there."

"Everyone" was an exaggeration. Three-quarters of the Penns River Players wouldn't go within a mile of Fat Jimmy's if Patty LuPone promised to sing *Don't Cry for Me, Argentina* sitting on their laps. Eve liked scandalizing the locals and could usually round up two or three thrill seekers who thought an hour in Fat Jimmy's was like touring a West Baltimore shooting gallery. And, tonight, Jillian Obbink. Eve made a point of mentioning her last name.

Fat Jimmy sat on the last stool where the short side of the L-shaped bar met the wall. In most places this would be the service area. Fat Jimmy's had no table service. You want a drink, get your ass up and get it. Strictly a BYOF joint: Bring Your Own Food. Anyone got desperate, a chalkboard leaning where most places kept the better liquor listed chipped ham barbecues, kolbassi—not kielbasa—with sauerkraut, and potato salad Jimmy picked up at Shop 'N' Save on his way to work if he thought he'd need some.

"I stayed late just for you, Dougherty," Jimmy said when Doc ordered another round for his table and a MGD for himself. Nothing ironic about Fat Jimmy. Not some hundred thirty pound hockey stick who called himself fat for laughs. Jimmy weighed close to four bills and stood five-ten on the rare occasions he stood at all.

"I'm touched, Jimmy. I thought you were always out of here by nine."

"Usually. I had my coat on when your dyke friend and her little pals walked in. They never come slumming unless you're around, so I stayed. You catch that asshole killed the woman on top of the hill last week?"

"That's where I just came from. We picked him up this afternoon."

Doris the barmaid put Doc's bottle and a draft in front of him. "I owe you three white wines, but I gotta open another box. I'll be right back."

Doc touched his bottle to Jimmy's glass. Took a swallow, felt the beer move through his throat, extended it until half the bottle was gone. "That went down nice. Been a long week. How've you been, Jimmy?"

"Fat." Jimmy finished what was in his glass and left it where Doris could see. "I open at seven, work till five, and drink beer until nine. I get home a quarter after, jack off, watch the news, and go to bed." He bounced his paunch with both hands. "I gotta lose some weight. Getting so I need a mirror to find Little Jimmy."

Doris brought Jimmy a fresh beer and three glasses of wine for Doc. He handed her a ten, told her to keep the change. Said to Jimmy, "Don't be so cheap all the time. Spice things up a little. Buy yourself some flowers, maybe a new magazine. Get Little Jimmy to come to you for a change."

"This is why you don't have any friends."

Doc picked up his drinks. "I don't need any other friends with you around, Jimbo. Lotta guys would just bend me over the bar and have their way. At least you'll give me a reach around."

Doc weaved through the tables to the theater party. The open chair was between Eve and Jillian. "Any room for me? Or should I go back and discuss Jimmy's monosexual love life with him?"

Eve pulled the chair away from the table. "Sit your ass down and tell us about the high speed chase and gunfight you had tonight."

Doc smiled for Jillian's benefit and sat. "Sorry to disappoint you, but all we did was ring his doorbell and ask him to come with us. His kids were playing on the porch."

"No high speed chase?"

"No."

"No gunfight?"

"Uh-uh."

Jillian said, "Were his kids really playing on the porch when you arrested him?"

Doc sipped his beer. Wiped foam from his lip. "And a neighbor's, too, I think."

"Was that safe?" Jillian had green eyes and copper blond hair and a voice like Sigourney Weaver on the make.

"It was fine." Another sip and Doc's beer was done. "I'm not making light of it. We looked around first and took plenty of backup. It's not like in the movies. We went in when he wasn't expecting us and had him handcuffed before he was sure what was going on."

"Was anyone there to watch the kids? His wife? Another adult?"

"We took a female patrol officer with us just in case." He went on before Jillian could continue. "Cheryl Pazul has a gift with kids. We had Dad in handcuffs and she had the kids collected on the porch before we got him to the car. No crying or yelling. Couple a long faces, but she didn't have any trouble with them while they waited for Mom."

Eve stood, picked up Doc's empty. "Must have been thirsty work. Don't get up. Tell Jillian all about it. This one's on me."

Doc turned to include the rest of the group. The others were watching four guys with goatees and unbuttoned flannel shirts shoot pool at the seven-foot table in the back like it was the National Geographic Channel.

Jillian was already looking at him when he turned to her. "It's not like on *Cops*. Good police work is boring to watch. Do you have any idea how much footage they shoot to get that half hour of dimwits?"

"I've never seen *Cops*."

"You haven't missed much." Nothing to drink, nothing to eat. Nothing to fill the conversational void made it obvious he had nothing to say.

Jillian did. "I don't think I've ever met a police officer in a theater company before. The two don't seem to go together."

"I was an MP in the Army. They were training me for some undercover work and the guy running the class suggested acting classes. You know, learn how to get into character. Observe people like who I was supposed to be. So

I'd fit in. I liked it and stayed with it. Kept me off the streets at night." He nodded toward the bar, where Jimmy pretended not to listen to Eve tell him something probably calculated to ick him out. "I knew Eve from high school and she told me about the group. This is my fifth season."

"She said you don't like your part."

"It's fine. I complain for her, mostly. Give her something to do besides worry about me."

Jillian tasted some wine. Let it stay in her mouth a few seconds. Her lip gloss shone when she spoke. "She does worry about you. She thinks you don't get out enough."

"She told you that."

"Not in those exact words, but yes." Speaking softer. Doc leaned in to hear above the bar noise. "I'm glad she got you out tonight."

"I guess I earned it. It's been a long week. What brings you to our off-off-off-Broadway company?"

"I acted in high school and college. I thought of making it a career for a while. Now I have a 'real' job, but I still like to stay close to it. The roar of the greasepaint and all that." She smiled at her own joke. "This little organization is pretty well thought of as local theater companies go and I live in Fox Chapel, so it's not far."

"You only thought of making a career of it?"

Jillian lowered her eyes only a second. "I did more than think about it. I tried for a while. Not enough work. To be honest, *no* work." She set down her glass. "I guess I wasn't pretty enough."

He knew he was supposed to say something here. "I guess they set the bar pretty high."

"Do you?" Even softer.

Doc's glance flitted around the room. Their companions might as well be in Ohio, engrossed by the pool game. Jillian's hands were one over the other on the table. The IC Lite clock read 11:04. Jillian's eyes didn't get any less green. "Yeah. They set the bar awfully high." The corners of her mouth turned up. "Fox Chapel's a nice area. What do you do?"

"I'm a surgical nurse." Doc cocked an eyebrow. "My ex is a surgeon. I got the house."

"Good for you."

"I suppose. It'll be too big when the kids move out. It's already too big sometimes."

"How many do you have?"

"Two boys. One's a sophomore at Rensselaer, in New York. He wants to be an engineer. The other's a senior in high school."

Doc did the math in his head. College sophomore had to be twenty, right? So Jillian was, what? Forty-five? Older? The bar must be higher than he thought if she hadn't been pretty enough, the way she looked now.

"This murder case has kept me pretty busy, but it'll wind down once the DA takes over. After I take a little time to decompress, you think you might like to go out for dinner? I mean, I can't promise a place as nice as this, but—"

"Do you have your phone with you?"

"Right here." He took it from his front jacket pocket.

"Let me see." She reached across for the phone, flipped it open, pushed buttons, gave it back. "There. It's too easy to misplace a piece of paper, and that would cause an awkward situation. I'd wonder why you didn't call, and you'd be embarrassed to say you lost the number. Now we're all set."

Eve rubbed Doc's fresh bottle of beer against the back of his neck. It was room temperature. "That Jimmy. He just never shuts up. Yak yak yak yak. Did I miss anything?"

CHAPTER 14

Willie Grabek raised his right hand and swore the truth and nothing but. Smoothed his pants before he sat in the witness chair. He wore a suit, not the short-sleeve shirt and loose tie he usually had on under a sport coat that hadn't been cleaned since the invention of perchloroethylene. Combed what hair he had. Doc sat in the gallery and guessed he even had clean underwear on.

Grabek's manner bore no more resemblance to everyday than his attire. Clear diction, grammatical sentences. Sounded like a TV cop. Blasé, polite, direct, gave the impression catching murderers was routine for him. Wore that old-time good cop aura like he put it on with his suit. No one could listen to him and not believe he caught the right guy.

Sally Gwynn finished with him in nineteen minutes, including swearing in and introduction. Widmer's lawyer was even more perfunctory. How unusual is it to get anonymous tips? Isn't it true a lot of people have Tom's blood type? How could he be sure it was Tom in the Cropcho house with no DNA result to back him up? Disappointing for a big shot in from Pittsburgh. Willie left the room like he was on his way to catch some other ne'er-do-well before lunch. No hurry. He'd get this guy, too.

Neshannock County bail hearings are predictable affairs. First the prosecutor gets up and describes the horrible nature of the crime, what a conscienceless and remorseless bastard the accused is, how old women will be raped and innocent children killed all over the country if this Genghis Khan of the Rust Belt is allowed to walk free. Doing this with a straight face is how the Assistant District Attorney earn much of her money.

The defense lawyer then tells the judge how his client is a bulwark of the community, the word "bulwark" invented for just such an oration. His client has never been in trouble before, unless the Commonwealth provides a rap sheet the size of a dictionary, which esteemed counsel will blame on youthful indiscretion and overzealous law enforcement. His clients always have strong ties to the community and would never dream of failing to make a scheduled court appearance. He's appalled that anyone, especially an attorney as respected as counsel for the Commonwealth, could think this upstanding gentleman might seek vengeance or want to coerce a witness. Saying this with a straight face is why defense attorneys make much more money than the Assistant District Attorney.

Sally added a nice wrinkle for Tom Widmer's hearing. The defendant's wife and next of kin are predictable character witnesses. Not much point contesting bail if your family won't vouch for you. Not only did Marian Widmer not appear on Tom's behalf, she testified for the Commonwealth, which meant Tom was well and truly hosed.

Doc had never seen Marian before; she wasn't home when the arrest went down. She made quite a impression when her name was called and the door at the back of the double-wide—in use while water damage was repaired in the real courthouse—opened. Eleven of the twelve people in the room turned their heads when she made her entrance. Tom stared at the table in front of him like the loophole that would spring him was seeping through the wood veneer for him to read.

She was an attractive woman by any standard. Five-eight, good posture, her business suit cut to inspire the imagination and provide plausible deniability. Heels arched her calves without seeming obvious. Ash-blonde hair and slate-gray eyes, make-up applied to make her skin appear flawless to anyone more than ten feet away. She passed within three feet of Doc and even then the flaws weren't deal breakers. She stepped up into the witness box and the slit on her skirt allowed a glimpse of pale thigh not hinted at before. Late thirties, no more than forty. Still getting it done, though she had to work at it.

Sally Gwynn was thirty-two and inspired courthouse fantasies herself. She didn't often question a woman more attractive than she; it didn't faze her a bit. Marian was sworn in and Sally got right to business. "Mrs. Widmer, do you think it would be safe for your husband to be released on bail?"

Marian looked at Sally like no one else was in the room. "I would have before. I mean, before he killed someone. But now—"

"Objection, Your Honor." Tom's lawyer, a big timer from Pittsburgh named Aiden Flaherty. Didn't exactly leap to his feet when he said it, not at his age and size. Judge Molchan shot him down before he was all the way up.

"Take it easy, Counselor. There's no jury here. I think I can tell what's prejudicial and what isn't. Proceed, Miss Gwynn."

Sally had corrected judges before. *May it please the Court, I prefer Ms. Gwynn, Your Honor.* Not today. Molchan didn't mean anything by it. Pushing seventy, he'd learned "Mrs." and "Miss," and that's what he knew. She'd tease him about it if they bumped into each other later and he'd laugh with her.

"Mrs. Widmer, leaving aside whether your husband may, or may not," a quick look at Flaherty, "have killed anyone, do you have reason to believe he might be dangerous to himself or others?"

Marian had deflected her glance into her lap during Flaherty's objection. Now it was just her and Sally again. "He beats me sometimes. When he's drunk." Tom Widmer sat up like someone had shoved a cattle prod under him. "For about a year now. It wasn't bad at first, but lately..."

"But lately..." Sally said, her tone inviting Marian to finish the sentence.

"Lately it's been worse, since the market started to drop. He drinks more, comes home later. He used to just slap me. Now he pushes me, and-and the last couple of times...he hit me. Hit me with, you know, different things."

Sally moved to within a foot of the box. "What kinds of things?"

"A hair brush at first. Across my backside. Then, well, I mean I don't know what was special about last time, but he came into the bedroom with...with..."

"With what, Mrs. Widmer?"

"A phone book. The Yellow Pages."

Widmer launched a one-sided discussion with Flaherty. Molchan banged his gavel.

"Mr. Flaherty, is there a problem? Does your client need assistance?"

Flaherty spoke as he rose. Taking the time to stand first risked a contempt citation for non-responsiveness. "No, Your Honor, no problem. This testimony is a bit of a surprise, is all."

"You'll have ample opportunity to register your surprise and, I assume, dismay. Please direct him to be quiet so we may proceed."

"Yes, Your Honor. Thank you." Flaherty took almost as much time to sit as to stand. Whispered to Widmer and glared. Widmer wrote something on the pad in front of him.

Molchan nodded to Sally. "Miss Gwynn."

"Thank you, Your Honor. Did he beat you with the phone book, Mrs. Widmer?"

"Yes."

"Why did he do that?"

"He said it was because it wouldn't leave marks."

Sally left the answer out there for a while, then, "I mean, why did he beat you at all?"

"He said he knew I was planning to divorce him, and he knew I'd do it soon, while there was still something worth taking. You know, before it was all lost in the stock market."

"Were you planning to divorce him?"

"No."

"Not even after he started beating you?"

"He's a good father. I knew he'd never hurt the kids. This is a tough time for him, for everyone at his work. I hoped it would pass."

"Do you think your husband should be free on bail, Mrs. Widmer?"

A quick peek at Tom, like she was afraid he'd see her looking. "I would say yes. Would have, I mean, but he's getting more violent all the time. I don't know what he'd do anymore. I know I don't want him around me or the kids now, not after this."

Flaherty opened his mouth, closed it when Molchan shot him a look.

"I have nothing more, Your Honor." Sally walked back to her seat in a manner that said Marian was hot, but she had a few things going on herself.

"Your witness, Mr. Flaherty."

Flaherty stayed seated. "Mrs. Widmer, did you ever call the police after one of these alleged beatings?"

Marian snugged her knees together. Her eyes flickered in Sally's direction before looking toward Flaherty, not at him. "No."

"Why not?"

Marian mumbled something. Flaherty said, "Speak up, please" before the stenographer had a chance to ask her to repeat it.

"He said he'd kill me if I told anyone. He said he knew how to make it look like someone broke in and did it, and that way he'd get everything."

Tom Widmer shouted something unintelligible. Judge Molchan pounded his gavel and shouted just as loud for silence. Doc stood and walked out of the courtroom thinking *Nice work, Counselor.*

CHAPTER 15

Doc had his hand on the panic bar of the courthouse door when someone called his name. He turned and saw a man he couldn't place right away. Familiar, he'd been in the courtroom, what the hell's his name?

The man extended his hand and said, "I'm Marty Cropcho."

Yeah. That's his name.

"I was wondering if I could have a minute. If it's okay, I mean. Detective Grabek spent a lot of time with me and I have his card and all. Should I only talk to him?"

Doc steered him away from the flow of courthouse traffic. "No, it's fine, Mr. Cropcho. I'm sorry I didn't recognize you right away. Would you like some coffee? A cold drink, maybe?"

"This will sound stupid, but I'm dying for a milkshake. Do they sell them in the cafeteria here?"

"They sell something they call a milkshake. You want to take a little ride, we can go to Bruster's. It's right up the street here."

"You're busy. I don't want to make a special trip or anything."

"It's fine. Let's get you away from the court people and talk. It'll be easier."

Safe conversation in the car. The weather. Construction on the bypass. Doc ordered chocolate. Cropcho got strawberry. He wanted to pay but Doc insisted. They sat at the picnic bench next to the building. Not quite Indian summer, warm enough for a milkshake if your jacket was closed.

Cropcho sucked on his straw, let his shake melt in his mouth before he swallowed. "I can't remember the last time I had a milkshake. High school, maybe. I had an aunt and uncle lived in Cheswick, by the power plant. We used to walk up to Glen's and get shakes in the summer. I don't even know if it's still there."

"It's there. I go every so often when the weather's good. They have a little miniature golf course behind it now. I guess business is okay."

The men sipped their milkshakes. Traffic went past on Leechburg Road. They drank some more. A breeze picked up and blew wisps of hair away from Cropcho's forehead. No one spoke until Doc sucked air through his straw.

"Are you sure it's him?" Cropcho said into his cup.

"Yes, sir. There are a few tests to come back from the lab that might make a jury more comfortable if it goes that far, but there's no question he did it."

"Do you know why?"

Doc wanted to take another sip. Buy some time. He didn't want to take the chance of sucking up a straw full of air again. It seemed somehow disrespectful. Inappropriate to the question.

"Just theories. We don't usually go forward without knowing more, but the physical evidence is so over-whelming—well, we didn't want him to leave town on us, so we picked him up. The DA's office will continue investi-gating."

"You think they were having an affair."

"It's one of the things they'll look into."

"Will you tell me when they find out?"

"Do you think they were having an affair?"

"No."

"Then why assume the worst? Don't think 'when' they find out. Think 'if.' If that, even."

"I didn't think someone was going to beat her to death, either. I thought everything was fine. Who knows what else I didn't know?"

"Does it matter? Now?"

Cropcho shot him a look, then let his eyes drift off to the traffic. "Yeah. It does. Not the way you think, though. Everything about her matters now. I don't mean it matters like it was good or bad, or she was good or bad. It matters because I took it for granted, little things about her. Never her. I love her—loved her. I wish every day since it happened I could trade with her. It was little things I took for granted. Like her favorite sweater. I knew which one it was, and I knew what it meant to her when she wore it. But I didn't think about it, you know? It was just there, her favorite, so what? But it was something unique to her. No one else." Cropcho didn't seem to notice the tears running off his cheeks in sheets, like summer rain. "I don't know how many women own that sweater. You know, one just like it. Thousands. Is it anyone else's favorite? I don't know. Maybe. Maybe it really was something unique to her. Maybe out of all the thousands of women who own a sweater just like that, maybe Carol was the only one who thought it was her favorite. And now she's gone. I mean, that was something special about her, right?"

Doc didn't answer.

"I don't care if she was having an affair. Not now. I might if she was alive. Just because I don't care doesn't mean it doesn't matter to me. It matters that she fought him. That she wanted to live. It matters—to me it matters—what she was watching on television. What book was on the nightstand." Cropcho dried his eyes with the back of his hand. "Have you ever lost someone suddenly? Someone who it shouldn't have been time for yet?"

Doc spoke just loud enough to be heard over the traffic. "No. Not like you mean."

"I came home, I'd had a good time. Thursday was my night out. You know that, I guess. We each had one. I'd go out for steaks and poker on Thursday and Tuesday was her night. She and some friends would go to a movie and have coffee after while they talked about it. 'Soul-wrenching dramas,' she used to call them." Cropcho chuckled under his breath. "She used to kid about it. I'd ask what they saw when she got home and she'd name something I never heard of and say it was an 'important film' in this voice she used just for that, or when she was making fun of someone who had a high opinion of himself. Then we'd talk about whether it measured up as a 'soul-wrenching drama,' or if it was just 'weighty.' We had a lot a lot of fun, talking about those movies."

"Did you ever check out any of the movies yourself?" Doc on the clock, even with a milkshake.

Cropcho gave him another look. His lips wrinkled into almost a smile. "Sometimes. She'd mention when she thought I might like one. We rented a few when they came out on DVD. If she was using her nights out to cheat on me, she was very good."

"I had to ask."

"I understand." Cropcho stirred what was left of his shake with the straw. "She'd like you. You're a good listener. Patient. No offense to Detective Grabek, but you're a better listener. You seem to like it."

"He was working."

"You're working."

"I'm on duty. He was working a homicide. The first twenty-four, forty-eight hours are critical. Ninety percent of the time, you find out everything you need in the first day or two. The rest of the time is spent figuring out what it all means."

"Is that what happened here?"

"Pretty much. Everything we've learned since the first twenty-four hours or so is just clarification of evidence we found that first day. Enhancement of a video. Lab results. Sitting around bouncing ideas back and forth. Not too much new."

Cropcho slurped the last of his milkshake, pushed the straw down under the lid. "Do you like your job?"

"Usually,"

"Not right now, though."

Doc finished his shake. "I enjoy the problem solving. Putting things right. That's why I don't like homicides much. Things are never really put right after a homicide. Then I go for the satisfaction of putting the killer away. I wouldn't say I liked it."

"So in this case you'll settle for justice?"

"Justice never enters into it. That part's not up to me. I'll settle for vengeance." Doc had more to say, but not to Cropcho.

"So you think they should execute this man. The one who killed Carol."

"They won't."

"But do you think they should?"

Doc wished he had more milkshake. Funny how he never had a prop when he needed to buy time.

"No. Not this one. This one should spend the rest of his life locked up, thinking about what he did. We should take small-timers in to see him like it was a zoo. 'This is what happens if you mess up bad enough.' Leave him in gen pop and let him take his chances. He's soft. His time might not go too well for him. I'm okay with that. Now, if he was a hard case who'd been in before and knew how to deal with prison, then, yeah. Take him out."

Neither spoke on the ride back. Doc asked before Cropcho got out of the car at the City-County Building, "Did this help you at all, Mr. Cropcho? The talk and the milk-shake?"

Cropcho took time to think. "Yes, it did. People have been coming up to me asking what they could do for a week, and there's nothing they can do, but how do you tell them that? They just want to help. You were about the only person in a position to *do* anything about this, and you did. You and Detective Grabek. So I wanted to hear what you had to say. Thank you for not telling me how sorry you are, or asking what else you could do. It's done, and I'll go on. I'm not sure exactly what you did that helped, but I feel better now, so it must have been something. Thank you."

They shook hands. Doc gave him a card, told him to call any time. He hoped he never heard from him again.

CHAPTER 16

"I told you to wait. We needed time for research and we needed time to find you a real criminal attorney. I told you all of this, but you couldn't stand to spend another night in jail. Where was the hurry? It's not like your loving wife needed time to take out a second mortgage for your bail."

Aiden Flaherty had never been in the Neshannock County lockup before. Not too impressive, even after his expectations were lowered by having the bail hearing in a double-wide trailer. The room he met Tom Widmer in looked like every other interview room in ninety percent of the jails in the country, not that Aiden had seen many of them. He did financial law now. Made a nice buck at it. Dickman, Ibrahimi, Flaherty, and Wertkin handled all the legal issues for the brokerage where Tom Widmer worked. Flaherty was called away from home to handle this crisis because he spent two years as a prosecutor in Allegheny County back when no one thought twice about cops eating free and Miranda was some broad with bananas on her head. That made him Dickman, Ibrahimi, Flaherty, and Wertkin's most experienced criminal lawyer.

To Aiden Flaherty, "criminal law" meant drunk driving and SEC hearings. Never handled a murder case in his life, not even as a prosecutor, when he drew two checks a month for DUI, shoplifting, and disorderly conduct beefs. Had to ask the guards where the courtrooms were on the rare occasions he actually went to the courthouse. Pled everything out. A master negotiator, even then. A natural for financial law. Now he sat in a block room in the Bumfuck County jail with a broker he'd met and didn't like at a Christmas party, whose crime—alleged crime—disgusted even Flaherty.

"I can't believe the firm wouldn't post the ten percent. They know I'm good for it."

Flaherty shook his head. He knew brokers could be delusional. This one was climbing Everest without oxygen or Sherpas. Didn't just need medication, he needed restraints, if he thought a brokerage that dodged Lehman-ville thanks to government intervention would stick its neck out for a murder charge. The only thing standing between Tom Widmer and official unemployment was the paperwork.

"There's something you need to understand. The firm only authorized me to represent you long enough to find suitable counsel. I'm not a criminal lawyer. That's why I asked—why I *begged* you to wait on this bail hearing. I didn't have everything I needed, and I freely admit I was in over my head. Today was my first time in a criminal courtroom in over twenty years. Why wouldn't you wait?"

"The whole point was so I wouldn't have to spend the weekend here. Jesus Christ, I'm being set up. I didn't think it would take Perry Mason to see that."

"Perry Mason is fiction." Flaherty tried to remember the last time he lost his temper. Not just showed it to provoke a response, actually lost it. Widmer's insistence on almost willful ignorance pushed the right button. "Haven't you ever read a book? Watched a movie? It doesn't matter what I think. It doesn't even matter what I know. All that matters is what I can prove. Given the amount of time you allowed me,

I didn't get a chance to form an opinion, let alone come up with any good reasons why you shouldn't be in jail. The police had solid evidence. All I could offer was my gratitude if he let you go. You're lucky he set bail at all."

"Lucky? You call a million dollars lucky? Where the fuck am I supposed to come up with a hundred thousand dollars to pay for that?"

"Given the weekend, I might've been able to find something in your favor to lower it. Character witnesses. A flaw in their case. That's your fault, plain and simple. Start accepting responsibility or you'll never get out of here."

Widmer pounded the table between them. He stood and stepped on the legs of the three size too large county-issue jump suit. Stumbled before he grabbed the crotch like a gangbanger to hold them up. "You could've at least showed what a lying bitch my whore of a wife is! I never laid a hand on her! Never! She sat up there this morning and lied through her teeth and you let her get away with it."

"Sit down." Flaherty had little patience with unreasonable clients, none with those who questioned his skill. "We had no way to disprove anything she said. Not today. There will be time to work on that angle before you go to trial, to find people you both know who never saw any signs. Ask her for particulars that can be disproved. A lot can be done with six months to a year to build a case. Things only happen overnight on television."

"You gave up. You stepped in it with your first fucking question and you quit."

"You're right, I did. If it makes you feel any better, I think she's lying, too. I doubt someone telling the truth would've had that answer ready as quickly as she did. Still, what's the best we could hope for? It's he said, she said. The police showed good reason to think you smashed a woman's head in. Who's the judge going to believe? You? Or her, the victim who put up with your abuse for the sake of her children? Now sit down so we can talk. I'm not going to argue with you."

Flaherty sat with a practiced look of indifferent invitation, like he'd asked an unexpected and only somewhat welcome guest to stay for a beer. Widmer shuffled back to his chair and sat. "All right. What do we do?"

Flaherty relaxed, on familiar ground now, someone paying him to tell them what to do. "First, make peace with the situation. You're not going anywhere for a while. This isn't an overcrowded jail, so I got them to leave you out of the general population, at least for a while. Get some sleep. Think of who might want to frame you for this. Most of all, relax. No one can think straight as wound up as you are.

"I'll look for another lawyer with the kind of experience and resources you need. It's going to be expensive. Even if you win, it'll probably break you. Make peace with that, too. You can't count nickels once you start the process."

"Don't they have to pay my bills if I win? I mean, once I'm proven innocent. It's false arrest, right? Arresting an innocent man?"

Flaherty sighed so Widmer could see it. "No. They won't pay your bills, and it's not false arrest unless you can prove they falsified evidence."

"It's all false. I just told you that."

"You told me you were framed. It's not the same thing. If the police find evidence assumed in good faith to be true, and it's sufficient for a magistrate to sign an arrest warrant, then it's not false arrest. Now let's move on."

Widmer pulled a pout. Flaherty didn't know if he was guilty or not. Didn't care. Wanted Tom Widmer out of his life as soon as possible. "Let's assume you are being framed. There are lawyers in Pittsburgh who are good at that sort of thing, but you want one who will work with Daniel Rollison."

"Who's this Rollison guy?"

"Private investigator. Retired spy, I think. Doesn't work regularly for anyone, likes to cherry pick his cases. I'm telling you now, he's expensive, too. He also gets results. If you think it's a frame, he's your best bet to find out who, and how."

"Will he work with me?"

"He might. He's a publicity hound and might like the idea of breaking a frame. I don't know him personally, but he has quite a reputation." Flaherty squeezed the bridge of his nose between a thumb and finger. "You should also be aware there are questions about his methods. He, ah, keeps a lot of things to himself."

"They're talking about the death penalty. I don't care how he does it. How do I get a hold of him?"

"The new attorney will have to do it. You see, there's no privilege between you and an investigator like there is between you and a lawyer. If your attorney hires him, then he's covered as if you were talking to the lawyer. Do you understand?"

"So you call him. Let's get a move on. I don't have time to waste."

Stockbrokers were all alike. Flaherty once decided he made twenty bucks an hour for his legal expertise. The rest was for putting up with these guys. Now. Fast. Me first. Flaherty thought of himself as a gentleman. Said "fuck" about once a month, always when discussing a broker. Worse than lawyers, if people knew them like he did.

"It's twelve-thirty now. I'll make some calls to see if I can get someone to take you on. A couple who come to mind might be hard to get a hold of on a Friday afternoon, and no one will be looking forward to my call. If I don't get an answer right away, I'll call Rollison and hire him on myself so he can get started. You can transfer him over to the other attorney when the time comes. *If* he takes the job."

Widmer showed the first sign of energy all day. "Set it up. I talked people into going long on GM during the bailout. He'll take the job."

CHAPTER 17

"Hit it right here, not too hard." Tom Dougherty put his index finger halfway between the center and right edge of the seven ball. "Give it a little left English and it'll throw the cue ball off the rail and set you up for the three."

"Hey, Doc." Skip Jacobs stopped chalking his cue. "I know we're playing teams, but wait your turn. Let Little Doc beat us like a man."

He'd always be "Little Doc" at the American Legion. Still in high school when he started coming in to swap cars with his dad. Leave one in the lot of his aunt's restaurant for his mother working the night shift, walk two blocks to the Legion for a ride home. Minors not supposed to sit at the bar, but he was Doc's kid. Give him a Coke and let him watch the ball game. Listen to Doc's friends tease him about how much they looked and acted alike. How it should worry him, seeing what he'd be in thirty years. Thirty-seven years old now, four inches and forty pounds bigger than his old man, still Little Doc in the Legion.

"You're free to help Augie if you want, Skip," Big Doc said.

Doc used too much English, spun the seven off the rail and left Dewey Augustine a bunny on the eleven.

Augie rested his gut on the edge of the table to reach his shot. A bandy-legged guy, skinny everywhere except his middle. "The only help I want from Skippy is a step outside

94

his bedroom window so's I don't break my neck getting out when he comes home early." He made the eleven.

"I'd give you a goddamn key if I thought you'd keep Lorraine off my back," Skip said.

"Maybe that's your problem, Skip. She's not supposed to be on *your* back." Down went the fifteen. "One more thing you do ass backward."

The Doughertys stood silent and watched the show. Three nights a week Skip and Augie fought like an old married couple.

Augie drained the twelve. "If you're not going to miss, just say so," Big Doc said. "We can get our seats back and have a couple of beers."

"You should take your old man on a stakeout sometime," Augie said as the nine fell. "Teach him some patience."

"We don't do stakeouts anymore, Mr. Augustine," Doc said. "Don't you read the news? We walk right up to the front door and arrest them."

"That how you got that peckerhead killed the Cropcho woman? Walked up to his door?" The thirteen rattled in the pocket, stayed out.

Skip groaned. "Goddamn it, why do you distract my partner like that? We don't beat you assholes more than once or twice a month and you still try to cheat us."

"Cheat you?" Big Doc stepped back with his arms outstretched. "How the hell did he cheat you? They were just discussing the events of the day. You want us to talk about your sexual deficiencies again?"

"Yeah, if we're shooting pool. You know he's like a dog with a fire truck if you talk cop stuff." Skip looked at the remaining balls. "At least he didn't leave nothing."

Big Doc circled the table. Five balls left. Skip and Augie had only the thirteen, hanging on the lip where Augie left it. He stopped halfway between a corner and a side to lean over the table. No one spoke. Big Doc had a reputation for inventing shots no one else could see, his imagination working overtime to cover for hands stiff and bent with arthritis.

A minute smile touched the corners of his lips. Turned his head just enough for Doc to see him wink. "Safe." Bent over the cue ball, hands in a more or less permanent bridge. Slid the cue over his index finger, twice, three times, four, stroked the cue ball on the fifth. Kissed the six and caromed off three cushions, coming to rest behind a picket line of solid balls blocking access to the thirteen. A legal safety.

"Son of a bitch." Skip leaned on his cue, didn't approach the table. "Goddamn it, Doc, that's faggot pool. You're not even trying to win. I don't have a legal shot."

"Ooh, Mr. Jacobs" Doc said. "It's a good thing I'm just regular police, and not PC police. I think the preferred term is gay pool. And besides, he did leave you a shot. It's hard, though."

"You should thank him, Skip," Augie said. "That's the first hard thing you've had in a month. No wonder Lorraine leaves that window open for me."

Skip flipped him the finger and circled the table. Muttered under his breath. "Goddamn rule book...didn't even try to make a ball...poor loser..."

Big Doc walked to the corner pocket farthest from the thirteen ball. "Here, Skip." Placed a finger a few inches to one side of the pocket. "Hit it here just hard enough to make it around the table. Three cushions and you'll clip the thirteen on your way to the fourth rail."

Skip stopped to look at the line Big Doc gave him. "Yeah, I guess. You know if I'm off even a cunt hair we lose."

"So it's not enough I leave you a shot *and* show you what it is. It has to be easy, too?"

Skip missed. Bitched about Big Doc giving him a bad line. Big Doc reset the balls, showed Doc the mark, and Doc put it down. Skip jammed his cue in the locker and went home. He'd be back tomorrow.

The two Docs reclaimed their chairs and ordered fresh drafts. Each swallowed a mouthful. Big Doc said, "Did you really just walk up to that guy's house last night and arrest him?"

"He was home. Best place to take him."

"You weren't worried about any kids getting hurt?"

Doc swirled beer around his mouth before he swallowed. "Nah. This isn't a hardened criminal. You should've seen the look on his face when Willie cuffed him. Practically relieved."

"Why'd he do it?"

"Near as we can figure, they were having an affair and it went bad. Neither spouse suspected anything, but we found a bracelet that belonged to her in his house, with a receipt. I think he ditched the other stuff, but wanted to get his money back on this one."

"Christ, Benny. How dumb is this guy?"

"He's not dumb like you think. Even smart people are dumb criminals. Doing something that can get you locked up is hardly ever a smart move."

They drank in peace for a couple of minutes. Doc watched the Pirates work on losing their ninety-first game of the year. If they split their last two over the weekend they'd win seventy for the season. Not bad by Pirate standards. Big Doc watched college football on the screen over the other corner of the bar. Their lines of sight intersected.

"You coming to the house on Sunday?"

Doc nodded. "Steelers play at one, right?"

"Yeah. They're home against Cleveland. Your mother said she'll make chicken wings and onion rings for halftime."

"Can I ask a question?" Both of them still watching their respective ball games. "When's the last time I didn't come over on Sunday, except for when you guys are in Colorado?"

"I don't know. Probably when you were sick last Christmas, first of the year. We didn't want you then."

"That's my point. Why does she ask every week if I'm coming over?"

"She worries about you." Big Doc finished his beer, raised his eyebrows. Doc looked in his glass, drained it, set it back on the bar. Big Doc gestured for two more, waved to include Augie and Dick Palumbo a few seats away. "If you didn't like the last question, you'll love the next one."

"No, I didn't have a date last week, and I'm not going out this weekend. Tell her I was a little busy, what with this murder investigation and all. Pitt plays South Florida on TV tomorrow night. I plan on falling asleep watching the game. It's not like Pitt's offense will keep me awake."

"She worries about you, is all." Big Doc gathered his fresh beer. Waved an acknowledgement to Augie and Dick. Took a sip. "We both do."

Doc wiped foam from his lip with the back of his hand. "You know, Dad, I'm not gay."

"That's not what we're worried about."

"What is?"

"You're thirty-seven years old, Benny."

"You think it's time I settled down?"

"Not like it sounds when you say it like that." A receiver let a sure touchdown slide through his hands. "Ah. Dumbass. No, we don't mean it like that. Well, maybe your mother does. We just don't want you to wind up all by yourself. That's all I'm going to say. I'm not here to nag."

Doc watched Andrew McCutchen send the left fielder to the wall to pull in a drive that could have made the game close. Down 4-0 after three innings. Again. Kept looking at the television even when the commercial came on.

"You remember what Groucho Marx said? About how he would never join a club that would have him as a member? It's not that I don't like girls, but the ones I like can get along without me, and the ones that like me, well, they pretty much fall into two categories. One's women I'm not crazy about. They're okay, you know, but not someone I'd want to spend too much time with."

"What's the other?"

"The other what?"

"The other category."

"Cop fuckers. I mean, God love 'em and all, it's nice once in a while for one to come on to you, but half of them just want to see my gun."

"You show it to them?"

"Sometimes. If she doesn't look too much like someone who has a brother I'm likely to have to arrest, or just wants a ticket fixed."

"You're telling me a woman would sleep with you just to get out of a ticket?"

"I didn't say *just* to get out of the ticket. Give me some

credit. Some of them figure they've shown their appreciation for my contribution to community safety, maybe I should show a little appreciation in return."

"Do you?"

"Appreciate them? Hell, yeah. I always say nice things, treat them great. Fix the ticket? Never. I look at it this way. Tickets cost money. Any woman sleeps with me to avoid paying a ticket is really doing it for the money. There's a name for women who fuck for money."

"Trophy wives?"

Doc snorted in his beer. Swallowed and wiped foam off his nose. "You want me to tell Mom a story on Sunday? Not lie, exactly, but maybe embellish my social life a little?"

"Now that you bring it up. Not like I asked you to do it, right? You volunteered."

"You're covered. I feel a big night coming on. Maybe a celebration for closing this case. I better get home so I can rest up. See you about twelve-thirty Sunday."

CHAPTER 18

Tom Widmer made a sorry spectacle shuffling into the interrogation room Saturday morning. Two nights in jail, he'd figured out how to cinch up the jumpsuit so it only seemed one size too big. Hands manacled to a waist chain didn't ease his movements any.

"You can take the chains off." Daniel Rollison looked at the guard like an eagle eyes a sparrow. He chewed his gum with only his front teeth, jaw barely moving.

"Sorry. County policy. Capital case, no bail. He can't leave the common areas of the jail without restraints." The guard about Rollison's size. Six feet, pushing two hundred pounds. Middle forties. Looked like someone who'd been around long enough to know what to do and still young enough to be able to do it. Not that a lot of "it" came up in the Neshannock County lockup. "He don't look like much trouble to me, but my boss is. I'd rather deal with you bitching than have to answer for letting this one loose."

Rollison turned to Widmer. "You all right like that?" He'd bitch if he was the lawyer. Bring in the warden or whatever they called the head man in a dump like this. Talk about rights and *habeas corpus* and half a dozen amendments. Rollison wasn't a lawyer; he was a professional investigator, and he didn't really give a shit, so he let it go.

"I'm fine," Widmer said. "Let's get busy."

The guard left. Widmer waited twenty seconds after the

door closed. "Everything we say is privileged, right? Just like I'm talking to a lawyer."

"Here." Rollison took a few stapled papers from a briefcase. Slid them over to Widmer. "That's the agreement. I officially work for Dickman Ibrahimi. Talking to me is like talking to Flaherty."

"Do you have to tell them everything I tell you?"

"I'm not sure I follow." Rollison's lips didn't move much more when he talked.

"Can I tell you things you won't tell Flaherty? Or whoever else takes over, for that matter. I know he's trying to ditch this case."

"First off, Flaherty's your man. He called every decent criminal lawyer in Pittsburgh. No one will touch you. They think the case is a loser, and you won't be able to pay. To be fair about it, so does he. Now you're my problem."

"Sons of bitches. I thought they were supposed to be about justice."

"No one wants justice. Ever. They want it to come out the best way for them. Then they'll call it justice. A big time criminal lawyer takes a case for two reasons: make money, or build a reputation. This is likely to be a six figure case and if you had that kind of money you'd have made bail. No one believes that frame story enough to risk their reputation on it. So it's Flaherty. And me."

"Why are you here? If you figure I can't pay a lawyer, how can I pay you?"

Rollison took back the papers. "Reputations get built in different ways. Lawyers need to win. I just have to break the frame. It's not my problem if they can't win it."

Widmer jangled chains trying to sit up straighter. "So you think I've been framed?"

"That's not what I said. I said my reputation would be enhanced if I break the frame. I don't really care whether you were framed or not. My job is to tear that story down. Did Flaherty give you the old 'it's not what happened that matters, just what I can prove' speech?"

"Yeah."

"Okay, then. Same deal with me. I don't care if you were framed. All that matters is what I can prove. Which means you better tell me everything. I go out there asking questions thinking you're innocent and find out you lied to me, well, that's going to go badly for you. You want this to go well, I have to know everything, and I have to know it for real. You with me?"

Widmer nodded. Got his hands folded on the table after some contortions.

"Okay, then. Did you kill her?"

Widmer almost ruptured himself sitting up too straight too fast. "Just like that? I thought Flaherty didn't want to know about that."

"That's Flaherty. I *do* want to know."

"Yeah, okay, but, you know, that's what I was asking about. Do you *have* to tell Flaherty everything I tell you?"

"Listen. I know you killed her. I haven't been in a room with anyone that acted guiltier than you since I caught my wife in the act with my partner. Both of them were worried about who else I'd tell, too, though I still can't think of anyone they'd rather not find out about it than me. I don't need to hear you say it to know you're guilty. I just want to hear it so there are no illusions between us."

The shock on Widmer's face gave way in stages. First the forehead. Next the eyes and on down until his expression changed from stupefaction to confusion, then slower into connivance. Rollison watched the metamorphosis like the changing of the seasons. He knew how long each stage would last, and what came next. Widmer would tell him—he was dying to tell someone—when the process finished playing itself out. Not before, so there was no point rushing him. Not too long after, either, or Widmer would explode.

It took about a minute and a half. Rollison had waited longer. "How do I know you're any good? I'm not telling everything to someone who just finished some online training school."

"Okay, then. Fair enough." Rollison knew Flaherty must have told Widmer something about him, but he never minded talking about himself. "I used to work for a government agency. You don't need to know which one. Let's just say we did a lot of stuff you're not going to read in the papers or see on *60 Minutes*. I was good at my job, and learned a lot of things that might be helpful to you, considering your present situation." He gestured to include the block-walled room with its smooth coat of not yellow, not white paint.

"Why did you leave?"

"I spent thirty years developing and using skills for a quarter of what they were worth. Now I draw a pension and make what someone with my abilities deserves to make."

"And the government lets you do that, with all the shit you must know?"

"It's a free country. I was trustworthy enough to keep my mouth shut all those years, why would it change now?

Besides, I didn't just quit or get fired. I retired. They want me for, they know where to find me."

"The ways you find things out. What kind of stuff—do you—I mean, is it legal?"

"All you need to know is that I get results. And I won't go to jail for you. I'm fifty-six years old and never spent a night in jail. Anywhere, and I've been some places. I'm not going to start for you."

Widmer didn't like him. His body language—even allowing for the chains—tone of voice, the way he looked at Rollison all said so. Rollison had seen it all before. Not kidding when he told Widmer he didn't give a shit if he'd been framed or not. He didn't care if Widmer liked him. Or trusted him. He'd just better not lie. Not if he knew what was good for him.

They waited again. Rollison watched thoughts play across Widmer's face, below the skin. The decision made. Just a question of how to tell him. Widmer opened his mouth a couple of times. Pulled back. What he said wasn't what Rollison was waiting for, but not unexpected.

"It's dry in here. You think you can get me some water?"

Rollison walked to the door. Knocked. Asked the guard for some water for each of them. Waited at the door, not looking at Widmer. Giving him whatever time he needed to get himself right.

The water came in two plastic bottles. Rollison opened one, handed it to Widmer. Sat and opened one for himself. Waited.

Widmer took a quick drink, then a longer one as he figured out how to position himself to get the bottle to his mouth. Stayed in that posture like he didn't want to forget how he got there in case he got thirsty again.

"I met this guy at a joint in Pittsburgh. Tease. You know it?" Rollison did. "Said his name was Marty Cropcho. We hit it off, couple of guys looking at tits, you know? Few drinks, lap dance or two, discussing events of the day. Bitching about our wives. Like guys do, right?"

"How long ago was this?"

"About a year? Less, maybe. Baseball was over, I think, or I was going home to watch the World Series that first time. Around there." More water. "Anyway, both of us are married to real bitches. I mean, that's what makes us friends, we hate our wives. It's just a matter of who gets fed up first, us or them. Only difference is, we have a lot more to lose than they do. I mean, they'll get half of what we busted our humps for and all they do is exercise enough to keep their asses from getting out of control. If they feel like it. And they're going to get half."

"You're a stockbroker, right?" Widmer nodded. "The half that's left for you won't be nearly what it was a year ago if she pulls the pin, will it?"

"Fucking-A. Every time the market takes a hit, I figure she's one step closer to calling a lawyer. Before it's not worth fighting over." A quick sip. "So that's what got us thinking about it. Not even thinking about it, not like thinking about it thinking about it. Just like talking about it. You know, two guys talking, like what would you do if you won the lottery?"

Not even thinking about it, not like thinking about it thinking about it. Guy probably made half a million bucks in a good year, can't even string together a sentence. "Okay, then," Rollison said. "What happened next?"

Widmer took another sip. Set the bottle down. Waited five seconds and drank the rest. "One day we're talking. Like I said, two guys playing 'what if?' and pretty soon it's like 'what if they were dead?' Then we get to talking about that old Hitchcock movie. *Strangers on a Train*, right? Two guys who don't know each other kill the other guy's wife. No connection. No way for the police to figure it out. It's perfect."

"You ever see the movie?" Rollison knew he couldn't have, if that was how he described it.

"No, but I heard of it. Everyone has."

"So it was Marty who came up with the idea."

"Well, yeah, I guess. I mean we were both talking back and forth. It's hard to remember who said what first."

"But you've never seen the movie, so it's not too likely it was you who brought it up, is it?" Widmer's face clouded. "I'll bet it sounded like a hell of an idea, a little too much to drink, distracted by pussy, playing the big shot."

Widmer fidgeted in the chains. The more Rollison spoke, the more Widmer looked away, tried to move his hands, the chains clanking like the machinery in his head.

"Okay, then. It was Marty's idea for you to go first, wasn't it? Wasn't it?" Widmer nodded without looking at him. "Something urgent came up. It had to happen right away. I bet he had the whole thing set up for you. All you had to do was follow directions.

"The police got onto the Dumpster at Arby's because of an anonymous phone tip. You know that was Marty who called, right? Have you tried to get in touch with him since?" Widmer mumbled something. "Have you?"

"He said not to. Said we couldn't let anything tie us

together until after they were both dead."

"So you killed this woman you never met and just assumed Marty would hold up his end of the deal."

"You weren't there. You didn't see him. Didn't hear him. I knew he'd do it. I think he liked the idea of doing it. Killing someone. He just didn't want to get caught."

"So you figure he's out there now, waiting for a chance to kill your wife."

Widmer got still again. Stared at his hands, spoke so low Rollison practically had to read his lips. "Not now. Not anymore. The day the cops came to arrest me, I saw this guy on TV. The real Marty Cropcho. The guy I'd been talking to was a fake."

"Well, God damn. He *is* trainable." Rollison let Widmer stew for a minute. Spoke when the chain rattling stopped. "Okay, then. I have to find this bogus Marty. We'll work on the assumption he wanted the Cropcho woman dead for some reason. Maybe they had a thing and it went bad, like the cops think happened with you. Maybe someone put him up to it. Could even be the real Marty using him as a blind. No way to tell until I talk to him. The address you have for him is the real Marty's. What about a cell? He'd use a throwaway, unless he's as dumb as you are, but it's all we have. What else can you tell me?"

Widmer described him. Five-ten. Average build, but looked strong. Dark hair with a small bald spot on the crown. About forty. Drank MGD. Narrowed the search down to about ten thousand guys in the Greater Pittsburgh area.

"Would anyone at Tease recognize you and him?"

"Yeah. There's this dancer. Chastity. Five-eight or so.

Black, shoulder length hair and dark brown eyes. About 38-24-34. Twenty-one or twenty-two. She has a mole about an inch above her left nipple and she trims her bush—"

"Okay, that's good enough. I'll find her."

CHAPTER 19

Doc sat back on the couch and listened to his arteries harden. Breaded, deep-fried chicken wings. Breaded, deep-fried onion rings. A salad in case his colon made an emergency roughage call.

"Mom, come in here and watch the game. Pittsburgh's going in to score again."

"I can watch while I clean in here." No mote of dust nor molecule of grease had a moment's rest in Ellen Dougherty's house. A wide gateway connected the kitchen and living room, so she could see while she worked. Doc never sat in her favorite chair, though there was no more chance of her sitting in it to watch the game than there was of Doc lowering his cholesterol without medication.

Tom Dougherty said, "They get six here, the game's over."

"The game's been over since halfway through the second quarter, Dad. Cleveland won't score seventeen points if they play till Thursday."

"I don't know. He still throws stupid interceptions."

"They score here, I doubt he'll throw the ball again. They'll run out the clock."

"That's what I meant. They score here, the game's over."

Six Super Bowls hadn't eased Big Doc's mind about Steeler quarterbacks. Didn't matter who had the job, half of his conversation during a game consisted of yelling either,

"Ellen, come in here and sit down," or, "Get rid of the goddamn ball."

Doc sprawled against one arm of the couch, right foot on the floor. He wasn't lying down as long as both feet weren't on the couch. If the other foot came up he'd be asleep before the Steelers could break the huddle.

He called Jillian Obbink around lunchtime on Saturday to ask if she'd like to have dinner. She teased him about the short notice. Asked how little social life he thought she had. He said it could be another time, no offense meant. He got a good night's sleep on Friday and decided he had more energy that he thought he would, and he'd had a good time with her at Fat Jimmy's. Next week would be okay, too.

Pittsburgh scored on a twenty yard run. Big Doc ran the play back and forth a few times in slow motion on the DVR. "Look at this block. He comes blind side on that linebacker here...*BAM!*" He sat back to watch the televised replays. "That should ice the game."

He picked her up at the house in Fox Chapel. This was the original house, the newlywed doctor starter. The trophy wife *nee* receptionist lived in the big new house. Jillian said she couldn't complain. That was how she'd met him, working together in the hospital. At least he hadn't been married then.

Dinner was at Longhorn in Pittsburgh Mills Mall. There were fancier restaurants downtown. Hell, there were probably fancier restaurants in Fox Chapel. Doc could have found one, or asked Jillian for a recommendation. Closing the Cropcho file deserved a steak, and he ate steak at Longhorn. He was happy for the company, but would have come alone.

A commercial came on. Balloons and confetti and marching bands would greet you at the dealership if you bought a

Toyota before the end of the month, just three days left. Big Doc said, "Hey, Benny, how's your Uncle Stush getting along?"

"He's okay. Closing this case took a load off his mind. That little prick Jack Harriger is still going around behind his back trying to get him fired. Next time I see the mayor I'll tell him what a good job Stush did running that investigation."

"Did he? Just between us."

"He stayed out of the way and let Willie and me handle it. We knew we'd get whatever we wanted, no questions asked. You know I love Stush like he really was my uncle, but he's no investigator. The best thing about him is, he knows it. He finds people he trusts and leaves them alone unless they need help, then he gets it. He's no politician, though, and I'm afraid that'll hurt him some day." That seemed to satisfy Big Doc enough to devote his attention back to the game.

Jillian put on a first class seduction. Made sure he knew both boys would be away. Invited him in for a glass of wine. Music already queued up. A well-chosen level of light. She used the lower voice trick from Friday night, eased him in closer until she didn't say anything one time, waiting for him to kiss her and he did. She returned it, eager but not aggressive. They stayed that way for half an hour on the couch, exploring each other through their clothes until she stood and released a clasp behind her neck. She was naked to the waist before Doc realized she was taking the dress off.

She stepped out of the dress and stood in front of him. Her breasts were full but hadn't depended much on the bra. Her nipples were darker than he expected from her coloring, and hard. Her lips were parted and her eyelids were low. A flush spread across her cheeks and chest.

He shifted on the couch and she straddled his legs to lean into him. Her lips parted and their tongues found each other. Her breasts massaged his chest through his shirt. She slid her hips along his thighs to rub against him and he cradled her head in his hands and kissed her hard. She gave a little yelp and sucked on his lower lip.

"I said, you catch any of that Pitt game last night?"

Doc jerked upright and looked at his father. "Sorry. I zoned out for a minute. No, I was beat. I was going to treat myself to a steak then fall asleep watching the game, but I never got as far as watching the game. I saw in the paper this morning they won."

"It was ugly, though. South Florida must really stink if Pitt could play that bad and still win."

Ellen came in from the kitchen wiping her hands on a dishtowel. "Anyone want something before I sit down?"

Tom and Doc both asked for iced tea. Ellen brought them each a glass and a small cup of jelly beans. "Try these. Giant Eagle had them on sale, three bags for a dollar." Said it *Jian Iggle*. "I think they're pretty good."

Doc felt like one more jelly bean would reverse his belly button to an outie, but he knew to eat them. "These are good. Who makes them?"

"I forget. I got three bags. Take one home with you." Doc still had treats from last week's visit, but he knew better than to beg off.

Jillian fucked with an energy that sometimes passed into desperation. She'd do anything he wanted and hoped he wanted more. Not a submissive begging to be dominated. More like someone who hadn't been fucked in a long time and wanted to be fucked again, and soon. She strained against him, not seeming to enjoy it so much as need it, to lose herself in his desires. It disconcerted him at first, and again later. Not the sharing he was used to in his sporadic love life. More of a strange passive-aggressive encounter, where she insisted to be allowed to be taken.

When they finished the first time she lay with her head on his midsection facing his dormant penis like she was watching for it to revive. The second break she snuggled tight against him, rubbing her body against his so he could rest but not sleep. After the third time they slept.

He left as the sun came up. Kissed her and told her it was early, stay in bed, he had things he had to get done. Went home and made breakfast, read the Sunday paper. Not sure how he felt about what just happened. Wondered how soon he'd do it again.

Doc's right foot came onto the couch when the Steelers went up twenty; he was asleep before they kicked the extra point. The game ended and a smell woke him up. He walked into the kitchen scratching his head. The deep fryer sizzled on the Formica countertop.

Ellen said, "I'm making funnel cakes for a treat."

"Mom, you just cleaned all the grease and mess from the wings and onion rings."

"I forgot I had the batter ready. I was going to surprise you for dessert and put it behind the tea in the ice box. I found it when I got your iced tea."

Doc looked to his father. Big Doc shrugged. *I get this every day.* So Doc got the powdered sugar while his father melted butter and everyone ate funnel cakes.

Doc offered to help clean up. Nothing doing. "I saw you sleeping. Go home and get some rest, unless you want to take a nap on the couch."

"I better go home. I don't want to fall asleep too soon or I'll be up at three in the morning." His mother handed him a plastic bag at the door. "What's this?"

"Your jelly beans. And a loaf of Syrian bread. You need any Eye-talian dressing?"

"That's okay, Mom. I'm good. I go to Giant Eagle myself once in a while, you know."

"Not too often," she said. "I've seen your ice box."

He took the bag. Gave her a kiss. She said, "Had any dates?" like she was trying to sneak it in.

"Nothing lately. Too busy."

CHAPTER 20

The usual Tuesday morning crowd littered Sam Parrotta's barbershop. Sam, his other barber, Dino, and three of a rotating crew of a half dozen retired men discussed the Steelers' dismemberment of Cleveland. Terrorism, Social Security, war, weather. None of those got much air time in Sam's after Cleveland went down.

"I seen Stush Napier on the TV Friday night." Sam worked the clippers around Doc's ear. "What's he doing on TV when it was you and the new guy did all the work?"

"You know how it is." Actually, Sam didn't know. Not like Doc did. Stush wanted Doc or Grabek to get the air time; Doc had to talk him into it. Raise his profile, give him some ammunition if the council came looking for his job. "The cops never go on TV. There's always a spokesman talks to the media. We don't have enough bodies for a PR department, so Stush does it. What's the matter? Doesn't he look official enough for you?"

"He looks like that redneck sheriff Rod Steiger played. You know, in that movie with the colored guy? You know, Potter," one of the retirees said. Doc not sure about his name. Thought of him as Flat Top because of his hair. Today's group included Flannel Shirt and Green Overalls. "Except Stush is fatter."

Doc debated whether to let it drop or stand up for Stush. The question became moot when Harry Waugamann came in. They exchanged hellos and Flat Top had something to say, as usual.

"Day off, Harry? I thought the truck come in on Tuesdays." Harry worked at a local supermarket.

"It does. They cut my hours. I'm down to twenty this week."

"Twenty?" Sam paused cutting Doc's hair to look at Harry. "I thought you were full time."

"You know how many full-time guys they got over there? Twelve. Out of forty. Managers, department heads, and the butchers. Everyone else is part time so they can cut our hours and not pay us benefits."

"You don't get benefits?" Flat Top had interest in this. Former shop steward at a chain store that pulled out ten years ago. "Where's the union?"

"Contract says you got to average thirty hours a week to qualify. That's why I got cut. I'm at thirty-and-a-half and they have to get me under thirty for the quarter. Twenty's as low as they can take me."

"Sons of bitches. Don't you have seniority? Can they give someone else more hours than you?"

"There's exemptions. They can't do it much, and the union'll grieve it, sure. Big deal. Even if we win they only gotta pay me for the time I should've worked. The benefits get figured on the actual hours."

This was why Doc left for the Army, the employment situation unchanged fifteen years later. He knew the feeling, working part-time at the lumber yard and doing demolition and drywall for contractors as they needed it until he got tired of wondering if he'd have to move back home, twenty-three years old. "Hey, Harry. You interested in picking up something else part time? It's seasonal, but I know there's winter jobs coming up for the city. The problem is, they'll need you irregular. How hard would it be to work it around your store schedule?"

"Danny will let me trade if I have to. He's not a bad guy. He didn't want to cut me this week, but he got orders, too. They really hiring?"

"Nothing announced yet, but I'll talk to a guy. These part-time gigs are pretty informal. Not the whole Equal Opportunity process they have to go through for a regular job."

"I'd sure appreciate it, Doc. You think it could lead to something full-time down the road?"

"I can't promise anything, but you never know. You're a good worker, and you're reliable. That has to count for something if a full-time job comes up."

"Unless they need to hire a jig," Flat Top said. "You're screwed then."

"Ignore him," Sam said. "He still thinks everyone lost their jobs at the mill so they could hire blacks. He hasn't noticed the goddamn place is closed for thirty years. No one works there."

Flat Top got red in his face. Green Overalls tapped him on the arm, waved his hand, palm down.

"I'll ask around for you, Harry," Doc said. "I'm going back to the station soon as I'm done here. Public Works is the next door from the parking lot."

Dino finished up with his customer, waved Harry over. Harry looked toward the three geezers. "You guys were here first."

"They don't come in here for haircuts," Sam said. He trimmed along Doc's neck. "They come in here to tell everyone else how things should be. Do we even cut their hair, Dino, or do they go to that joint in the mall? The one with all the chicks who lean over while they give shitty haircuts. The guy getting clipped can look down their shirt and the guy in the next chair can check out their ass."

Flat Top flipped him off. Harry sat in Dino's chair. Doc's cell phone rang. The tone he used for police business. He fished the phone from under the apron. "Dougherty."

Stush Napier said, "We got another body. Eleven hundred block of Fourth Avenue. Barb Smith found him. She's there now with a couple other uniforms."

"Willie around?"

"He's off today. Has that colonoscopy or something, remember?"

"I'm on the way." Doc tore off the apron, pulled the tissue from around his neck. "Sorry, Sam. I gotta go." Across the shop and reaching for his coat before the apron settled on the floor.

"Hey! Whoa! You didn't pay for the haircut," Sam said.

"Here." Doc reached in his back pocket for his wallet. Pulled out a bill. Took one step back and leaned far enough to hand it to Sam. "Thanks."

"This is a ten. You know haircuts are twelve bucks."

Doc didn't stop walking. "I didn't get a whole haircut. You can finish when I come back."

CHAPTER 21

Barb Smith stood on the stoop of the townhouse at 1123 Fourth Avenue with her back to the door, hands under her armpits. Two other uniforms, men, stood smoking ten feet away.

Doc coasted to a stop between the patrol cars. One of his favorite perks, not having to park; wherever he left the car was legal. He waved at the two smokers. They waved back and kept on with their activity. He made note of who they were for mention to Eye Chart Zywiciel. "What you got, Barb?"

"Dead guy in there." She pointed over her shoulder. "Shot at least once in the head that I could see. I didn't touch him to look any closer. Neuschwander's on the way. I guess the ME is, too."

"You all right?" Barb wore her vest, unusual for a Penns River cop. Hugging herself on a warm Indian summer day. She'd worked in Harrisburg for five years before filling a vacancy here six weeks ago. Stush allegedly knew why she transferred.

"Yeah, I'm fine. I've seen stiffs before. This one kind of surprised me, I guess. Last thing I expected to see in there, middle of a nice day."

"What made you look?"

"That car." She gestured to a year-old Cadillac parked in the space marked for 1123. "I thought it looked out of place."

Doc looked from the car to the front door of 1123. "Nice car for a vacant."

"Nice car for this neighborhood, period." The row townhouses on Fourth were built when the low-income apartments that seemed like such a good idea in the Sixties became the inevitable slums of the Seventies. Pride of ownership was supposed to be the answer. Build affordable townhouses convenient to the major employers, working people would buy them, and the problem would be solved. Then the mills and fabricating plant moved out and took the jobs with them. No one who could afford to buy a place wanted to live across the street from the local slum. The developmental tide that was supposed to raise all boats collapsed. Absentee owners bought most of the units to rent. Renters moved from the project across the street and combined three and four households into one. It wasn't like the landlord would be by to complain; hard to exhibit pride of ownership from Pittsburgh, Philadelphia, and Cleveland. The recent credit crisis crushed the leveraged speculators. Now half the row houses were "bank owned," the current euphemism for "foreclosed and vacant." "I made a note and left it be. Wasn't hurting anything, and I thought it might be someone from the bank checking up on the house. I came by again three hours later and the car was still there and I thought maybe something was wrong."

"So you went in."

"Door was closed, but it wasn't locked."

"You mind looking at him again?"

"No. I know what to expect now. Like I said, it kind of surprised me before. I expected someone sick and found brains on the wall."

She pushed the door open with her baton. No furniture in the room. Scattered pieces of paper and dust bunnies scurried across the floor with the breeze. Stairs to the right went up. Straight ahead led past a powder room into a dining area with a ceiling mounted faux glass chandelier. The kitchen beyond that, to the right.

The man on the floor was five-foot-ten, one-seventy or seventy-five. Dark hair thinning on top. Somewhere between thirty-five and fifty. Hard to tell in that light and missing a large chunk of head. Blood and brain made a Jackson Pollock on the nearest wall.

Doc kneeled for a closer look. "Big gun. Forty-four or forty-five, I'd guess. You look for a casing?"

Barb nodded. "There's nothing in this room or the other. I found a few fragments that could be the round, but nothing they'll be able to use."

"So the shooter either policed his brass or used a revolver."

"What do drug crews use for hits around here? I mean, if this town would have a drug hit, this is where it would be."

"Nothing. This is only the third gunshot homicide we've had since I started here six years ago. One was a domestic gone bad and the guy was waiting for us when we got there. The other was a fucked up robbery with six witnesses who were happy to put the shooter away. Couldn't wait to point him out to us. This is the first real whodunit."

Barb shifted her weight foot to foot. Looked at the body

as she spoke. "About this being a whodunit. There's something upstairs you should see."

Doc looked at her, still looking at the corpse. "Show me."

She led him up the stairs. Utility belts made all women look like bowling pins. No way around it. Doc saw Barb come to work in shorts one day and knew to discount the belt handicap. He made a point of looking over her shoulder to the landing above. Very professional.

The stairs turned left at the top. Bathroom straight ahead. Large bedroom to the left, two smaller rooms the other direction. "In here." Barb pushed open the door to the smaller of the rooms on the right.

Open sleeping bags on two inflatable mattresses. Cans of food and two plastic sauce pans. Cheap, unmatched flatware. Plastic drinking cups and pop cans. A power strip had a microwave and two small lamps plugged into it. An orange outdoor extension cord ran out the window.

Doc shook his head. "Someone's living here?"

"It's kids, I think. At least one of them is."

Doc raised his eyebrows in question. Barb opened a closet door and pointed to a child's action figure. "What's that? R2-D2?"

"Jeez, no," she said. "That's EVE. You know, from WALL-E."

"You mean that cartoon movie?"

"You don't have kids, do you? It's not a cartoon. It's a—computer animation, I think they call it."

"So it's an expensive cartoon."

"I guess you could say that. My point is, I think whoever lives here, at least one of them is a kid and they cleared out their personal stuff in a hurry."

"It's possible, but this could've been left from the last resident."

Barb shook her head. "The bank would've cleaned everything out when they tried to sell it. This was brought in since then."

"Jesus." Doc looked once more around the room. Walked to the window and saw where the extension cord connected to an outdoor plug next door. "You talk to where this runs?"

"He said he knew about it, but I don't believe him. He paused when I asked him, like he was deciding what the best answer would be. I don't know if he just doesn't like cops, or if he doesn't mind having squatters next door."

Doc led Barb into the other small bedroom, looking while they talked. "He hear anything last night?"

"Uh-uh. Said he was out watching Monday Night Football at, uh," she checked her notes, "Earl's. Bar across the river on old 28. Got back a little after midnight and the car was already there."

"He knows nobody lives here, right?"

"Sure, but he says people park pretty much where they want with all these units vacant. He didn't think twice about it."

They went into the bathroom. Three toilet paper rolls were stacked beside the toilet. A cake of soap on the sink counter. See-through washcloths and towels hung over the shower rod. Doc turned a handle and clean water poured through the faucet. "Water's still on."

"There's probably a master valve for the whole row. Water bill might be paid out of their homeowner's fees. They can't shut off just one unit without cutting everyone off."

Doc listened, didn't say anything. Passed through the other bathroom door and into the empty master bedroom. Down the stairs to the living room and the body. He stood between it and the door, looked back and forth between them, picturing the victim and shooter when it happened. How they must have come in, who stood where. He spoke without stopping what he was doing. "You check the kitchen?"

"Nothing. I guess with the electric and gas turned off whoever's staying here has no reason to use it."

Doc put his back to the door. Made a gun with the fingers of his right hand. Jerked it back like a recoil. Looked at the body and the spatter behind it. "Anything downstairs?"

"Empty. Cobwebs and some dead roaches."

Doc looked back up the stairs. "I wonder why they live up there. Much easier to avoid being seen in the basement."

"The windows down there don't open, so they can't get the power cord out. And it's cold. Concrete floor. Couldn't be too comfortable for sleeping, even with an air mattress."

She'd done a thorough check of the premises and talked to the neighbor while the other two uniforms spent their time smoking and joking. Something else worth mentioning to Eye Chart.

"Good work," Doc said. A handful of people were on the sidewalk, drawn by the patrol cars and lights. "Make sure those two boobs outside don't let anyone ruin your crime scene. Neuschwander should be here any minute. I'm going next door to talk to the neighbor."

CHAPTER 22

The door to 1125 opened as Doc's foot hit the first step. A black man stood in the doorway, almost six feet tall, back straight as a railroad tie. A manageable amount of extra weight around his middle filled his shirt like a money belt. Kinky gray hair was taking its time about receding. Early sixties, no more than sixty-five. He looked at Doc with a level glare. Not challenging, and not likely to back down.

"You more po-lice?"

"Yes, sir. Detective Dougherty." Doc took both stairs with one step. Showed the man his badge. "Mr. West?"

"That's me. Jeff West. Is there something I can tell you I didn't already tell the young woman was here a few minutes ago?"

"To be honest, sir, probably not. It's routine. She asks some questions, then I ask some. Most of them will be pretty much the same, but each of us has a different perspective. We'll think of different things from the same answer. I know it's tedious for you, but there's no better way to do it. Do you mind if I come in?"

"Do you mind if we stay out here?"

"No, sir. Not at all. We won't get many more days like this. I'd sure rather spend it outside than next door messing with a dead body."

"I expect you would. Can I interest you in some sweet tea?" West held up a tall plastic drinking cup.

"No, thank you, not just now. I appreciate the offer, though." Doc knew the drill. Only a few thousand blacks in Penns River. All but a handful lived within one mile of this spot. Most just wanted to be left alone. West had that vibe. He also had an expectation of respect, and you failed to provide it at your peril. Not the street cred, "treat me like a man, motherfucker," bullshit respect. West would be treated as an equal, or not at all; listened to, not feared. Old school.

This was why Doc worked his way up through patrol when Stush hired him six years ago. His Army experience qualified him to start as a detective in most cities. Stush offered him a chance to run Penn River's small detective force the day he hired on. Doc insisted on riding patrol for four years. Now he knew every neighborhood. Who to talk to. Who to ask about. Most important for today, the culture and politics.

"Mr. West, Officer Smith tells me you were out last evening."

"Monday nights during the season I like to go over to Earl's in Creighton. He sells chicken wings a quarter apiece and Rolling Rock for seventy-five cents a glass."

"A quarter apiece for wings? They any good?"

"I think so. You can get different kinds, but I like them breaded and fried, like they were before everyone started making Buffalo wings. Earl gives the whole wing, too. Not just half and call it a wing. Anyway, I like to get there about quarter after eight, so Earl don't have to fuss to hold my favorite stool for me. Game was over last night, oh, eleven-thirty, little later. I made a stop to the men's room and got back here maybe ten minutes to twelve."

"And that car was here then."

"I parked right next to it."

"See anyone looked out of place?"

"Saw a couple I wished were out of place. Boys from across the street in those apartments, out all night making noise. Wish to hell they was out of place, but they're around most every night."

"Did you see any cars you didn't recognize? Besides this one."

West thought about it. "No, but I'll be honest with you, I wasn't looking. The light here's not the greatest and it was late. All I paid attention to was getting the right key to open the house."

Doc looked away from West, along Fourth Avenue. The smoking uniforms separated a small knot of people to let Rick Neuschwander get through. Another dozen onlookers across the street. Mostly men, with a few women and a couple of kids who probably should have been in school.

"If you don't mind me asking, how long have you lived here, Mr. West?"

West's eyes lifted as though his abacus hung from the portico. "Be twenty-three years in September. Came back and bought this place right after I got out of the service."

"Seen a lot of changes, I guess."

"Not like you mean. More like an erosion. Probably the same number of people not working, but fewer people around. Not like it changed overnight or nothing. I was away for a long time. That's when things really changed. You from around here, Detective?"

"I grew up here, went away for about ten years. Came back about six years ago."

"It would seem like a bigger change to you. You left

pretty much a kid and come back a man. See things you didn't notice when you were younger. Where'd your people live?"

"Up on the Heights."

"Behind the mill or by the dairy farm?"

"Closer to the farm, but not so far up. You know where the old fire hall is, and the Little League fields? Up there."

"Past that big softball complex?"

"About a mile up that hill."

"Saw that fast pitch fella there once. Eddie something. The King and His Court they called themselves."

Doc laughed. "Eddie Feigner. I was there that night. My dad took my brother and me down. I'd almost forgot. We were just kids."

"He put on a helluva show. Pitching from second base and blindfolded and shit."

"Yeah, he was something. Look, Mr. West, I don't want to take up too much of your time." Doc was more worried about his own time, but chatting with the old man might buy him something down the road. "One last thing. Did you hear anything unusual after you got home? These units look pretty well put together, but I'm sure a loud sound would carry through the walls."

"You mean like arguing or a fight?"

"Or a gunshot."

West's lip curled into a joyless smile. "No, I didn't hear any gunshots last night."

"They wouldn't sound like in the movies. Firecrackers, or even a door slamming, maybe."

The smile left West's face as quickly as the accommodation left his eyes. "I'm aware of what gunshots sound like, sir. I have heard all the gunshots I care to hear."

Doc folded his notebook. Put it and his pen into his pocket. "I'm sorry, Mr. West. I didn't mean anything. It's just that a lot of people think they know, but don't."

West's face softened, not his eyes. "I'm sure you didn't. It's a sore spot with me, is all. Have you ever heard of the Lost Battalion? In Vietnam?"

"No, sir. I haven't."

West paused like he wasn't sure whether to tell the story. His voice was soft and flat. "Second Battalion, Twelfth Cavalry. Sent four hundred of us to take out some NVA outside of Hue. No artillery. No helicopters. No armor. I guess they figured we could handle it, there only being about twelve hundred of them.

"We lost half the battalion before we got close enough to do any damage. Then they cut us off. Commander figured we could either surrender, stay put and get killed, or fight our way to a better position and wait for help. So we fought. Held there thirty goddamn hours before they came for us. I did three tours, and it was the biggest cluster fuck I ever seen. Excuse my language. I still have strong feelings about this. Did you know the Army kind of lost the records of that engagement in the official history?"

"No, sir, I didn't, but I have to admit I never heard the story."

"They told us how proud they were of how we held out there. Credit to the unit and all, but they'd rather hide some officers' bad judgment than give us our due." West drank the last of his tea. "I'm sorry, Detective. You didn't do anything to deserve that little speech. It's just that I hear gunshots at night once a week or so, even when there aren't any. I know what they sound like."

"Yes, sir. I suppose you do. You retired from the military?"

"Did twenty-six years and came back here and bought this place." The steel was gone from West's eyes. What remained looked more like fatigue.

"Thank you, Mr. West. I think that's all I need for now. We'll come back if anything else comes up, but it doesn't look like you were home when it happened, unless the autopsy shows the time of death was later than we think it was."

West spoke as Doc's foot hit the sidewalk coming off the stoop. "How long were you in, Detective?"

"It shows?" West nodded. "Nine years, sir. MP."

West inspected him for at least ten seconds before he spoke. "You might only have nine years active duty, son, but you got a lot more than nine years on you."

"What makes you say that?"

"You do. Just looking at you. It hangs off you like a poncho."

CHAPTER 23

Rollison didn't start looking for Chastity in earnest until after the fifth lap dance. Everything since he started his car went on Widmer's tab, might as well have some fun. He never came to places like Tease off-duty anymore. He'd passed the age of self-delusion years ago, never wanted to get so old it wasn't fun to feel a young woman grind on him.

He asked and the waitress told him Chastity started second shift today, be on after seven-thirty. She came onstage as he ordered his third drink. He made his way past three twenty-somethings to the front row. Listened to them hunt for something clever to say she or her partner hadn't heard before. Trumped them all when he slid an expensable fifty into her garter and pointed to his spot against the wall.

She came over when her set ended. Sipped at a Coke, pressed the cold glass between her breasts, let the condensation trickle down.

Rollison nibbled his drink and enjoyed the best thing about a strip joint: no need to pretend you weren't checking out a woman's goods. Losing that layer of bullshit almost made up for the Big Lie, displaying goods and services that weren't for sale. "A friend of mine said I should look you up if I got over this way."

"Really?" She finished her drink. Took her time leaning across him to place it on the shelf built into the wall and give him a look inside the satin top. "Who's that?"

"Tom Widmer. You know him? My height. A little shorter, maybe. Middle thirties."

"Sure. I know him." A few seconds passed and it occurred to her she really did know this one. "Yeah, Tommy. Comes in here with...Marty something. Where's he been? I haven't seen him in a couple weeks."

"He's away for a while." *A long while.* "He says you're worth a trip to the VIP Room. What do you say?"

Chastity took hold of his tie like a leash. "What's your name, sugar?"

"Don." Close enough for a stripper.

"Well, Donnie, I say only you can judge if I'm worth the trip. Let's go."

She led him through the maze to the back. Place about half full. Twenty girls leaned on tables, rested parts of themselves on men's shoulders. Faux intimacy in the name of commerce. Every man here was getting screwed without dropping his pants or getting kissed on the mouth. Rollison appreciated the irony of Widmer paying for action he'd probably never get again.

Double doors separated the VIP Room from the main floor. A guy in a tux shirt and bow tie with arms the size of hams smiled at Chastity and pushed one door open. She paused to get her bearings—even darker here than outside—dragged Rollison to what looked like three pieces of sectional sofa pushed together.

Different music in here. Softer. More sensual. She pushed him onto the couch and positioned his knees apart. Stood between them and moved to the slower sounds, dipping her head to let her hair and satiny top hang low. Slipped the camisole over her head. Ran her hands under her breasts.

Teased the nipples with her thumbs. Slid the palm of her left hand over the breast, lifting it so she could suck one finger. The other hand inside her thong. Stood closer. Watched him watching her. Pulled the thong away from herself to give him a look inside. Eased it over her hips. Stepped out of it. Pulled his knees back together and straddled him, her knees on either side of his hips. Rubbing herself against him. Teasing his face with her breasts.

Rollison let her work. The answers to his questions wouldn't change if he waited five minutes to ask them. He let himself enjoy the show—she *was* good—until she pressed her breasts tight against him and leaned in to bite his ear. He turned his head so his lips were at her ear at the same time.

"I'm looking for Tom's friend, Marty."

She paused, started again with diminished intensity. Her body less languid against his now, not so anyone but him would notice. "Why do you want him?"

"I need to talk to him."

"What about?"

"Tom."

"What about Tom?"

"About Tom is all you need to know."

Right on cue she ground her crotch into his. Turned her whole act up a notch. "I only know him from in here and he hasn't been lately. I don't know what else I can tell you."

"Nothing, if that's all you know. That's okay, if you don't want to talk to me. You'll talk to the police sooner or later."

This pause was longer and the restart less assured. "Why would the police want to talk to me about Marty?"

"You really don't know, do you?"

"Don't know what?"

"About Marty and Tom."

"Just that they've been coming in here once or twice a week for the last year or so." Gearing up again. Laying her weight across Rollison's chest, breasts flattened against him.

"You met Marty first, didn't you? Sure you did. You even know Marty isn't his real name. Don't you?" Rollison raised his arms to hold her still. Tilted his head to look into her eyes. "Don't you?"

Chastity sat up, rested her weight on his thighs. "Who the fuck are you? Or should I just get a bouncer now?"

"Okay, then. Throw me out. I have enough to take to the police now. I was just trying to cut you a break."

"Take what to the police?"

"You expect me to believe you really don't know Tom Widmer's in jail for killing Marty Cropcho's wife? Or that the guy hanging in here with Tom isn't really Marty Cropcho?" Chastity's intake of breath and change in posture told him she didn't really know. "Your buddy Tom and this guy you're calling Marty worked it out, but it was Marty put him up to it. If you were working it with him, that makes you part of the conspiracy."

"I didn't know it was anything like that. Shit!" The bouncer at the double doors looked their way. "Sit back. We have to make this look good or Vic will start asking questions."

Too late. Vic on his way, rolling as he walked the way men his size do, everything about him too big for his arms to swing normally. "Everything okay here, Chaz?"

"Yeah, Vic. Sure." Chastity braced one hand against Rollison's shoulder, turned enough to face Vic. "Donnie here just gave me some bad news about someone I know pretty well. I was a little shocked is all."

Vic gave Rollison the once over. At least thirty years difference in their ages, eighty to a hundred pounds in size. Rollison imagined the calculations running through his head like in *The Terminator* and coming up with "No Threat."

"Okay, Chaz. I'm right over there by the door if you need me."

She thanked him and gave Rollison her undivided attention. He waited until Vic was back where he belonged and said, "Okay, then. Do you know anything interesting now?"

Chastity worked her way into the position they had before. Mouth-to-ear sixty-nine. "I have a name. Just the first, though."

Rollison let her rub against him a few seconds. "What is it?"

"Dave. That's all I have."

"Okay, then. This Dave tells you his real name, but makes you call him Marty when he's here with Tom. Why'd you do it?"

"It wasn't like that. Not right away. I thought his name *was* Marty at first. For like a month, maybe. I'd seen him in here a couple times before, by himself. He told me he had a friend who was going through a tough time and needed some relaxation. Said he'd tip me extra if I'd take care of this other guy the way I'd been doing for him."

"Out of the goodness of his heart, right? Marty just wants Tom to have a good time."

"No. There was more to it than that." Chastity sneaked a peek at Vic. Opened a couple of buttons on Rollison's shirt, slid her hands over his chest. "They were partners in some deal, I don't know what. I think Marty was afraid Tom might pull out, and he wanted them to be like buddies, you know? Keep the deal alive."

"When you say Marty, you mean Dave, right?"

"Yeah. I think of him as Marty. That's how I know him best."

"How did you find out about Dave?"

She spread the shirt apart and rubbed one breast against the hair on Rollison's chest. "He told me if I ever wanted to party for real some time I should look for him at The Foundry. That's a club over by Carson Street. Said to ask for Dave, he was usually there on Fridays in the VIP Lounge."

"You ever go?"

"No, man. I don't fraternize with the customers."

"Club policy, right?"

"Even if it wasn't. I put up with guys dumb enough to blow their money in strip clubs eight hours a day. I don't need to spend my free time with them. I want a guy who knows how to spend money."

"How's that working out for you, looking for him in here?"

Chastity rose up and turned to land hard on Rollison's erection. No hiding that it hurt. "I got to make ends meet till then, right? It's not like I'm out hooking."

"Not with that technique you're not." He squirmed to reposition. "Easy on the dick, honey. It has to last."

"Sorry. You kinda hit a nerve."

"So did you. What do you say we go over to The Foundry this Friday? Look for Dave."

She lifted herself like she might slam down on him again.

He shifted his hips to protect himself. "*This* Friday? Maybe you noticed I'm working nights now? Where I can actually make some money? And you want me to call in the first Friday night I get. They'll bump me back to days. No way."

"It won't be for the whole shift. All I need is for you to point him out. Then you can come back to work."

"Why don't you just go and ask for him yourself?"

"Because he doesn't want to see me. Just hang with him long enough for me to get a look. Then you can come back here. Wear something hot, then bring it to work. Give the guys a different look."

"I don't like it. You said he might've killed someone."

"What I said was he got Tom to kill someone. He's not going to kill someone he wants to fuck. Go on in. Have a good time. Just get him someplace I can see him before you go. Ask him to walk you to your car, maybe. I'll wait outside."

"I still think it's dangerous."

"Fine. Don't do it. Pick him out of a police lineup. That way he'll have a pretty good idea who fingered him. My way, he'll never know."

She let his shoulders support her. Her hips moved against him mindlessly, like jiggling a foot in a waiting room. "You're a fucker, you know that? You should have to pay if this is so important to you. For my time, right? What I don't make here that night."

Rollison needed her enthusiastic cooperation. And it wasn't his money. "That's fair. What do you have in mind?"

"Cindy says she usually makes at least a grand on Friday nights."

"Cindy's a lying twat. *And* she's a regular. No way you

make a thousand dollars your first night. I'll give you five hundred."

Chastity ratcheted up the hip action. Rubbed a hard nipple against his bare chest. "Seven-fifty."

"Six hundred."

"How about six-fifty and a blow job?"

What the hell. It wasn't Rollison's six-fifty. He'd leave the blow job out of his report. No point making Widmer feel worse than he had to.

CHAPTER 24

"Well? How'd it go?"

Eve had enough class to wait for a rehearsal break before she grabbed Doc by the elbow and moved him into a corner. He pretended to resist, waited until he knew they were alone and said, "Uh-uh. You first."

"Me first what?"

"Did you get laid this weekend?"

She looked at him like he'd pulled a live carp out of his mouth. "What the hell kind of a question is that to ask a woman?"

"The same kind of question you were about to ask me about a woman we both know, which is even worse than asking her."

"No, it isn't." The look on Eve's face said she knew it was.

"Did you talk to Jillian?"

"Yeah."

"What did she say?"

"Oh, now you're asking me to betray a confidence."

"No, I'm not. I just wanted to see if you would."

"I don't see why you're so touchy. Since you brought it up, she *volunteered* that you two went out for dinner on Saturday."

"And we did."

"How'd it go?"

"It was nice."

"And..."

"She's smart and funny and great looking."

"And..."

"And what?" Doc took a step back and gave her one of his cop looks.

"And, well, did you, I mean..."

Doc made a show of folding his arms across his chest. His glare held steady. "Did we what? Do you want naked pictures of us, or what?"

"Eww. Not of you. Her—" Eve looked over her shoulder, saw Jillian drinking Diet Coke with two other jurors, "—yeah. Definitely."

"Sorry. Use your imagination. Like I'd have to."

"Doc, that's not a good idea. Nothing you tell me would match what my imagination could come up with." She considered what to say next. "What do you mean, 'like you'd have to?'"

"Why do you assume I saw her naked?"

"Because I know you did."

"She tell you?"

"Not like you mean." Doc opened his hands. *Give.* "It's not like with men. You have to spell everything out. We can talk to each other and just know. It's a woman thing."

"Eve, nothing personal and you know I love you and all, but your track record on 'woman things' is a little light in some regards, if you catch my drift."

Eve's turn to give Doc a stare, fists on her hips. "So you think just because I like to give a little face I don't have woman's intuition? Like I'm not still a member of the club?

That's something men would do to a gay friend. We're not exclusionary like that."

"I'm not saying you're not a member of the club. You know how the Legion works? If you haven't served, you can only be a social member. Or an anti-social member, in your case."

Eve showed her middle finger. "All right. Be that way. At least tell me if you're going to see her again."

"Half of that decision's up to her."

"Jesus, Doc. Are you going to ask her out again? Or is that too personal, too?"

"That's a perfectly reasonable question. The kind of thing two friends can ask each other without fear of talking out of school. I think you're getting the hang of this." He moved toward the stage.

"Wait! Will you?"

"Will I what?"

"Damn it, Dougherty." Eve was torn between laughing and crying. "Will you ask her out again?"

"Who? Jillian?" Then, just before Eve had a chance to scratch his eyes out, "I don't see why not. I had a good time. She seemed to have a good time. Is there something else I should be considering?"

"It wouldn't kill you to show a little gratitude. You wouldn't have said more than hello if I didn't put you together at Fat Jimmy's."

"Don't think I'm not grateful, and don't think I'm dumb enough to make too much of it. It would just encourage your inner yenta for next time."

"What makes you think there'll be a next time? Why do you automatically assume this won't work out?"

Doc's smile was not completely without humor. "You forget. With me, there's always a next time."

CHAPTER 25

Willie Grabek eased himself onto his desk chair like a man who'd had a fiber optic tube shoved up his ass.

"Is it sore?" Doc asked.

"I think it's just psychological. I slept through the whole thing. They could've played Tic-Tac-Toe on my bare ass with Sharpies for all I know."

Rick Neuschwander dropped a handful of folders on Doc's desk. "Here you go. Everything we found yesterday on Fourth Avenue. It's not much."

Doc flipped through the papers. "Two in the head with a nine. I guess this is what the papers would call an execution-style slaying."

"Yeah," Neuschwander said. "Well done, too. First one to the side of the head from a couple of inches away. The body falls and the shooter leans over and puts one in his forehead to be sure."

Grabek stopped leafing through the files. "Son of a bitch."

"What?" Doc said.

"I know this guy. Dave Frantz. We used to talk shit to each other once in a while. Did low level work for the Mannarinos. Not a made guy or anything, he's not Italian, but the Hook would use him for stuff. Frantz always had something going on. Looks like he had some drug action on the side."

"You really think it's a drug hit?" Doc said.

"I don't want to get ahead of myself, but that's sure what it looks like. Connected white guy gets clipped in Tootsie Roll City with a big gun? It's not like Mannarino did him, and I can't think of who else would."

Neuschwander said, "Why wouldn't Mannarino clip him?"

Grabek leaned his chair back into the pontificating position. "Mannarino don't shit where he eats. You think he'd drop a body here? In his home town?"

Doc said, "Maybe Frantz was shitting where Mannarino eats."

"That's a possibility. Like I said, I don't want to get too far in front of this. I just think Mannarino would've made it more public if it was a message killing. Probably want it more public, too. A 'Keep off the Grass' sign is no good if people don't see it."

No one said anything for a minute or two until Neuschwander spoke up. "What about the squatters?"

Grabek looked up from the reports. "What squatters?"

"Looks like someone's been living there," Doc said. "Pirating electricity from the house next door. She thinks it's kids, based on some of the stuff we found."

"You ask the neighbor?"

"Smith did. He said he knew all about it. She didn't believe him." Grabek raised his eyebrows, like that wasn't a complete answer. "She said he paused before he said anything at all, then he was too definite for as short an answer as he gave. She thinks he either knows and doesn't mind, or he just doesn't like talking to cops."

Grabek let the pages he'd been holding relax back into the folder. "Not to sound prejudiced or anything, but if these people spent as much time telling us what they know about crime as they spent bitching about it, it might not be such a shithole down there."

Doc and Neuschwander looked at each other. Neither looked like they wanted to go first. Grabek didn't appear to notice.

"Anybody watching the place?"

"There's a uniform in front."

Grabek said to Neuschwander, "You get everything you need?"

"Yeah. I mean, everything we're worried about being disturbed."

Another pause, then Doc said, "You think they saw anything?"

Grabek answered before Neuschwander could. "They're the only people in the world we can't be sure *didn't* see anything. Be a lot easier to find them if we knew where they were."

"The stuff they left behind isn't the kind of things homeless people walk away from," Doc said.

"Why wouldn't they assume we took it as evidence?" Neuschwander said. "We probably should have, you know."

"Evidence of what?" Grabek said. "It's not like Frantz was smothered with an air mattress."

"What do you want to do?" Doc said.

"Leave the car out front for now. Get the uniform to talk to the natives. They won't tell him dick. Another day or so and we'll make it obvious we're leaving. Then we put a proper stakeout on it. We have any motion-sensitive lights?"

"I can get some," Neuschwander said.

"Send a crew in right before we cut the patrol car loose.

Make a big deal about going in one last time for evidence. Set up a sensor in the room where their shit is. Aim the light so we can see it from the front or the back. Then one guy can watch the place. He calls for backup when the lights go on."

Doc and Neuschwander shrugged. Another Grabek scheme didn't impress them much, the Widmer "interrogation" fresh in their minds. Neuschwander said, "What if they get their stuff and split before then? They could get in the back while we have the car out front."

"Put the car in back, then. Or use two cars. You don't think Napier will approve the overtime? His job's hanging by a thread and we got a goddamn crime wave. Homicides two weeks in a row. It's like Dodge City out there."

Doc's ears showed red. "We can go in and talk to him if you want. He thinks you're a hell of a cop."

"What's this 'we' shit? You're the son he never had. You talk to him. You and Neuschwander can probably use the overtime."

"You're not in?"

"Uh-uh. I signed on eight-to-four. You young guys can sit up all night pissing into Gatorade bottles. Builds character."

Doc thought about pushing it, getting Grabek to pull his weight, decided against it. If Grabek didn't talk to Stush, he had no say in how Doc presented it. Neuschwander probably could use the overtime, three kids now and one ready to drop in the next month.

Stush not in his office. Janine said he was over at Stewart School, "scaring the fifth graders straight."

Doc drove to Fourth Avenue to see if anything was up. Barb Smith had the duty. Doc parked his unmarked car cop style, driver's side window to driver's side window.

"I've seen maybe three people come by here since the kids left for school," she said. "No one looks like they're waiting for me to leave so they can break in. Cars go by every few minutes. I've seen some women waiting for the bus up there on the corner."

"No one just hanging out? Mr. West said there was usually someone around."

"They're not going to hang out with a marked car sitting here. Do we think they're going to walk up to me and say, 'Excuse me, Miss *Po*-lice, we saw everything and we'll tell you if you'll give us back our stuff.' I'm wasting my time here."

"You have a better idea?" He wasn't sure how to take the look she gave him. "I'm not arguing. Just two cops talking, like yesterday. What do you think?"

She didn't answer right away. "They won't come back until we're gone. Let's make them think we are."

Doc suppressed a *déjà vu* comment. "Got to work better than what you're doing now, right?"

"Jeez, Doc, the way these townhouses lay out, I have no idea what's going on in back. People could've moved in and I wouldn't know. Every half hour or so I drive around that way, but you can't see through from Third Avenue and I don't want to go too far up that little alley for fear I can't get out in a hurry if I have to."

Doc lowered his head to look past her to the townhouses. "Yeah, this is kind of a half-assed setup. You see Jeff West today?"

"His car was gone when I got here. He might've had a job."

"Maybe. How's the canvass going? I don't see anyone."

"They're around somewhere. Half dozen guys started on this block, working their way out."

"Any luck?"

Barb shook her head. "There are more people not home today than if the buildings were on fire. The only ones who answer their doors are old folks who want to know why we aren't around more often to bother those boys who make it so decent people can't get no rest here."

Doc chuckled. He'd heard that speech enough to know it by heart. Barb had picked it up right away. It probably didn't change much from city to city. Or race to race, once the old neighborhood goes to hell.

"Okay. I'm going back to the office to talk to Stush about better ways to stake this joint out. I'll tell him what you told me, make sure he knows you're paying attention. Call me if you see anything, or if the canvass picks up something of interest. I'm ten minutes away."

He dropped the car into Drive before she spoke. "Hey, Doc, I was wondering if I could ask you a question? If you're not in too much of a hurry?"

"No. I can talk. What's up?"

She said, "I don't want to keep you," and Doc slid the shift back into Park. Barb spoke as soon as the engine sounds changed.

"It's just, you know I'm still new here, and I'd like to do a good job. This is about the first chance I've had to do anything besides write tickets. So, if you want to, maybe we could get a beer after work. If you have time. You could catch me up on what's what here. In the department, I mean. Ways I can make myself more useful."

She looked along the side of his car until she finished, then up at him only long enough for him to notice her eyes were an unusual shade of blue. Or gray. Somewhere between the two. More blue when a cloud spread a shadow, more gray in direct sunlight. Funny. He thought it should be the other way.

"Sure. You have someplace in mind?"

"I don't really know anyplace yet. You know, quiet enough for us not to have to yell at each other, but not where we're going to bump into a lot of cops and can't talk about some of this."

"You know Fat Jimmy's? Off 356? It's kind of a dive, but it'll be quiet that early and the only time a cop ever goes in there is to break up a Saturday night debate." Doc knew other places. He wanted to see how she'd respond.

"I broke up a Saturday night debate at Fat Jimmy's the week before last. I'll see you there. It'll be fun to see how the other half lives."

CHAPTER 26

Doc ran late from the station. Neuschwander got a report back at 3:30 and Grabek needed time to explain to everyone what it meant to have the firing pin and ejector marks on the casing they found. Not that any of it was worth a shit if they didn't find the gun, which they wouldn't if the shooter was any smarter than Tom Widmer about killing, which he just about had to be.

Barb's car was parked at the corner of Fat Jimmy's. A gray Focus with a Carmax sticker on the trunk. She wasn't in it. Doc wondered if she'd arrested anyone yet.

Jimmy saw him before the door closed. "Jesus Christ, twice this month."

"We been friends a long time, Jimmy. You can call me Doc."

"Be happy I don't call you asshole. You're not trying to make this a cop bar, are you? There aren't enough of you to make up for all the regular business I'd lose."

"A cop bar? Just because I'm here two weeks in a row?"

"It's the company you keep." Jimmy pointed to the corner booth, where Doc had sat with the theater people. "She come in ten minutes ago, scopes the joint out and orders a Corona. I gave her an IC Lite. If she ain't a cop, I'm Batman. A good-looking cop, but still a cop."

Doc looked where Jimmy pointed. Barb Smith sat alone. She wore a pullover sweater and her hair was almost to her shoulders. First time he'd seen it unpinned. He ordered an MGD and went over.

"Sorry I'm late." He pulled out the chair opposite hers and sat. "Grabek had to explain police work to me. I'm a slow learner."

"It's okay. I'm soaking up the atmosphere." She nodded toward the bar. "I take it that's Fat Jimmy?"

"You're wasted on patrol. You ought to be a detective."

"Well, he can barely move around behind the bar, and I heard someone call him Jimmy."

"That's him. He made this place what it is today." Doc swiveled his head to scan the room. "It used to be nice."

Barb laughed and blew a dab of foam onto her nose. "You don't like him?"

"Jimmy's okay. We went to high school together. Under that rough exterior lies an even rougher interior, but if Jimmy tells you something, believe him."

Barb looked from Doc to Jimmy and back. "You went to high school with *him*?"

"He was a couple of years ahead of me."

"He looks ten years older. Did they hold him back in every grade?"

"Hey, Jimmy's led a hard life. Ask his liver."

They drank their beer in silence until Doc broke the ice. "How do you like Penns River so far? You've been here about six weeks now, right? That's long enough to have an opinion."

"I thought I did. The first month about what I expected. Now bodies are starting to pile up. I may have to reconsider."

"How many homicides did you handle in—where was it?—Harrisburg, right?"

"Uh-huh." She nodded as she finished a swallow. "Ten, twelve a year. No more than that. A couple were multiples, but I don't think we had any two weeks in a row the whole time I was there."

"How long was that?"

"Five years. Mostly it was pretty good."

Doc drank half his beer to keep from asking the obvious next question. She'd kept it to herself for six weeks. It would come out when she was ready. "So, setting aside the fact that we're the temporary murder capital of Pennsylvania, what do you think of the place?"

Her smile was uneven, more on the left, where a dimple creased her cheek. "I like it. The people are nice. No one's given me any real trouble, just the usual hassling the police stuff they feel like they have to do sometimes. Chief Napier's been great. He goes out of his way to make sure I'm fitting in all right."

"Stush is a hell of a nice guy. I've known him since before I was born." Barb's eyebrows drew together. "He was a family friend before my parents were even married. I don't think he fixed them up, but I know he was there when they met. I called him Uncle Stush until I went away to college. I came home for Christmas he told me to knock that Uncle shit off."

"I see why you call him Stosh, but everyone else does it, too, don't they?"

"Everyone except that stick up his ass prick Jack Harriger."

"But I thought Stosh meant dumb ass."

"Around here it's pronounced 'Stush,' and it's not always an insult. Pretty much any Polack named Stanley gets called Stush."

Barb looked at him like there was no way he wasn't done speaking. "Napier's not a Polish name."

"It was Napierkowski until they got to Ellis Island." He pronounced it *Napper-kowski*. "His grandmother only spoke English when she went out, insisted we call her Grandma Napierkowski. You see, Stanley is the English version of Stanislaw, and the short form of Stanislaw is Stoshu. It's a term of endearment for the old Polish families, and there's no older Polish family here than Stush's. Just calling someone Stush generically is like calling him a dumb Polack. But if the guy's name is Stan, and he's Polish, it's kind of affectionate for his friends to call him Stush. Does that make sense?"

"I guess. As much as calling someone Doc when his name is Doherty."

Doc raised an index finger. "Ahhhh. But it's not. When spelled with an O, it's pronounced *Dock*-erty. My grandfather said the O spelling with the hard K is Protestant and the A spelling is Catholic. I've never heard that anywhere else, so he might have been full of shit, but we all knew better than to argue with him when he got back from Marriotti's."

"You seem to know a lot about names."

"The way I look at it, a person's name, and what people call him, can tell you a lot if you know the background that goes with it. Take names that end with 'ski.' Most people assume they're Polish, so they must be Catholic. Well, they might be, but if ski is spelled S-K-Y, then they probably came from Russian Jews at some point. Maybe not, and maybe they became Catholic when the family got comfortable in the States, but never assume." He pointed to her empty glass. "What are you drinking?"

"I asked for a Corona, but this isn't one."

"No, it's IC Lite. In this bar a Corona might as well be a Japanese car. How did you like it?"

"It was a surprise when I first tasted it, but it's not bad. I'll take a Miller Genuine if that's what you're having."

"On the way." Doc started to stand.

"No hurry. I'll wait for the server."

"No you won't. Fat Jimmy hasn't had a waitress since before the cleaning crew left."

Barb's eyes widened as she looked around the room. "There's a cleaning crew?"

"That's what I'm saying. I'll be right back."

Doris was behind the bar, the proprietor in back draining Little Jimmy. Not having to listen to Jimmy's wit about incestuous police sex shortened the trip by more than half.

Barb smiled when she tasted hew new beer. "You don't like the Deputy much, do you? I mean, what you called him before."

"I don't remember what I called him before. I call him so many things, it's hard to keep track."

"Something like stick up his ass little prick, I think."

"I must be in a good mood."

"No one likes him much, do they?"

"He likes himself enough for everyone." Doc started to speak and caught himself. "I shouldn't say that. Make up your own mind. Write off what I said so far to a personality conflict between him and me."

"He's a good cop, isn't he?"

Doc took a drink. Swished it around his mouth before he swallowed. *Finally* something handy to buy a few seconds when he needed it.

"He's a promotable cop for a larger department. He does all the things they like to see, everything by the book, and he's very political. The kind of cop who could make rank faster than he could make arrests. There's not much upward mobility here, so he's after Stush's job, and Stush is my boy, so I don't like Jack. That doesn't make me right or him wrong, and that's all I'm going to say about it."

The conversation drifted to how Stush ran the department. What to look for on patrol in certain parts of town. Who to be on the lookout for, who to ask questions of. Where to eat and where to stay away from. Inside baseball for a new cop in a small town. Doc drank another beer. Barb passed.

It was almost 6:30 when he asked if she wanted one more. She shook her head and he pushed his empty aside.

"Don't let me stop you," she said.

Doc pushed out his lower lip. "I'm done. I was just being polite asking you."

"Thanks for all the information. It would've taken me six months to figure all that out on my own. I drove right past Funzie's the other day and never thought to eat there."

"Everyone lies to cops. Cops shouldn't lie to each other. The job's hard enough, even in a town like this."

Barb reached for her purse. "Well, thanks again, and thanks for the beers."

Doc made no effort to get up. "Whoa. I've been answering questions all night. I have a couple for you."

Her face clouded, just for a second. She said, "Go ahead,"

like a dog wagging its tail slowly between its legs.

"I was wondering what they thought about working off the clock in a big city like Harrisburg."

Her body language still showed wary. "Good cops who want results sometimes have to. It's the same everywhere."

"Well," Doc said, "if you're not busy, I thought maybe we'd drive down to Fourth Avenue and see if we could catch us some squatters. You think there's at least one kid involved. Maybe more. Kids are impatient. They're going to want their stuff back sooner instead of later, and they aren't as likely to think we'd keep it."

"They can't come back yet. There's a uniform car parked right in front."

"I make two phone calls and he's gone. The whole neighborhood will know about it, too." The arm holding her purse relaxed as her crooked smile started to grow. "You game?" he said.

"You better let me pee first."

"I wouldn't dream of rushing you. I should go, too. Once the seal's broken, it's every man for himself."

CHAPTER 27

It actually took three calls. One to Dispatch to see who had the duty in front of 1123 Fourth Avenue. One to Mike McKillop sitting in the car to set it up. The third told McKillop to hit the lights and siren and make sure everyone saw him go. Burning rubber and fishtailing onto 12th Street were his idea.

Barb covered the back from the alley. Doc angled in with Jefferson West's Buick between him and 1123. Slid into the passenger seat for a line of sight across the Buick's hood. Sipped a Coke, not worried about any biological impact. The world was his urinal, no one here would pay attention to someone pissing in the street at night. He thought for a second about the logistics a female cop like Barb had to consider until he remembered women can have multiple orgasms. That made it a wash. He didn't listen to the radio or an iPod. He didn't fidget or whistle. He didn't get sleepy. He found a comfortable position braced against the corner of the seat and the passenger door and sat. Thoughts ran through his mind unhindered, never taking residence in his consciousness long enough to distract him. He learned to wait in the Army. Used to be able to sit like this for six hours, sinking into his surroundings so well someone could walk within a few feet and never sense his presence. Nothing out of the ordinary for Special Forces or a SEAL. Plenty good enough for a cop.

His cell phone vibrated at 9:36. He flipped it open without moving his eyes. "Dougherty."

Barb Smith said, "Two of them just went in the window we found in back. They look like kids, one of them pretty little."

"Give them thirty seconds and cover the back. Set your phone to vibrate. I'll ring you right before I go in."

He eased open the door, dome light already disconnected. Placed his right foot flat on the ground and let himself spill out over it. His flashlight was in his left hand by the time he stood erect. He held it along his leg as he walked up to the door of 1123. Took his time, acting to anyone who'd see him like he belonged. Walked up onto a stoop identical to Jefferson West's and listened to muffled noises that sounded like kids trying to be quiet. Hit the re-dial button to signal Barb, kicked in the front door and identified himself to anyone inside. Turned on the flash and took the stairs two at a time, light bouncing off the walls. Turned at the landing for the bedroom where the supplies were found and glimpsed a kid in the hallucinatory shadows, reached and grabbed air when the kid ducked under his grasp. The second was bigger and not as quick. Doc saw motion, wide eyes reflecting light for a second as the kid crossed through the beam. This time he leaned and extended a leg when he reached. Missed again with his arms, but the running kid tripped over the extended leg and fell hard. Doc reached again and caught a handful of shirt, felt it give way as the kid scrambled for the stairs. Let the shirt go and pinned the kid under two hundred pounds before he could go anywhere.

"Lay still. I'm the police. I won't hurt you." The kid was unimpressed. Fifteen or sixteen, from the size of him. Well-conditioned, not real strong. Doc let a little more weight onto him. Put his lips close to an ear. "Calm down before you get hurt accidentally. I just want to talk to you."

The kid jerked his head and caught Doc full in the mouth. He tasted blood and braced a forearm against the back of the kid's neck to push it down, firm but gentle. "Knock it off, goddammit! If I wanted to hurt you I'd of done it already."

The struggle stopped, the kid's body taut with anticipation and adrenaline. Doc said, "I just want to talk. I can help you. If you saw something that night and the killer finds out you were here, he'll come looking, too. He'll hurt you."

The body under Doc tensed once, then relaxed, not all the way. "I'm going to take my arm off your neck. Then I'm going to roll off enough for you to sit up. Don't try to run. I'm not going to let you go that much and you'll just trip. We okay?"

A muffled sound that could have meant anything. The head nodded. Doc raised himself up, rolled to his right to keep the kid between him and wall. Shone the light on his face, then the badge hanging around his neck.

"See? I'm a cop. My name's Detective Dougherty. I just need to ask you a few questions."

The kid stared at the badge, then at the gun on Doc's hip. "You the one they calls Officer Doc?" The voice not yet fully changed, high and reedy with stress.

Doc smiled. His days in patrol earned him some respect from this neighborhood. He used to park the car and walk it at least once a day when he was here, in any weather. Show a police face to talk to, not one to resent as it rolled by. A partner, not the enemy. "Officer Doc coming!" was often followed with greetings and helpful comments on the down low. Those who slunk away bore looking into. They were halfway home if this kid trusted Officer Doc people.

"Yeah, I'm Officer Doc. What's your name?"

"Wilver. Wilver Faison. People calls me Willie."

"You mean Wilver like in Wilver Stargell? The baseball player?"

"You know him?"

"Saw him play when I was a kid, way younger than you. Every time he'd hit a home run, the announcers would holler 'There's chicken on the hill with Will,' because he'd give away free food at this chicken joint he had every time he went deep."

"That's what my Pops say. He call me Chicken Man sometimes. People think it's because I eat so much chicken, but my Pops say it's for that restaurant."

Doc lowered the flashlight until both their faces caught some light. "People used to call Willie 'Pops,' too."

"That's why my Pops likes us to call him that. Willie his favorite player when he a shorty."

"Stargell was a lot of people's favorite player. He could really mash. What's your dad's name?"

"Dennis."

"Doesn't ring a bell. He staying here with you?"

"No. He in Tennessee working for some car company."

"He's not working here?'

"He was working over at a body shop in Tarentum, I forget the name. They let him go last winter."

"So it's your mom staying here with you?"

Wilver lowered his head. Turned it to the side. "She in rehab. Just me and my brother here."

"You don't have any relatives close by?"

"Ain't none who'd take us." Doc waited for a fuller explanation. "My Mom's peoples don't has nothing to do with her. They say she's a ho and she already got everything she getting from them."

"What about your father's people?"

"They don't know nothing about this. They think we in some foster home. That's what my Pops think, too. Far as he know, we living with some family over to Seventh Street."

"Why aren't you? Family Services must've hooked you up when your mom went in."

Wilver gave the noncommittal look kids do when they have the answer and don't think you'll like it. Doc nudged him with his foot. "Come on, Wilver. You're going to tell me sooner or later. Make it sooner and we can round up your brother. What's his name?"

Wilver said, "David" like it crawled out of his mouth before he could stop it.

"How old is David?"

"He ten."

"How old are you?"

"Fitteen."

"Now, about Family Services."

Wilver tried for the sullen teenager voice, couldn't hide the fear. "They put us with these people out Seventh Street, like I said."

When the quiet went on long enough Doc said, "This isn't Seventh Street."

Wilver's thoughts played across his face. "We's there about three weeks. They was nice people and all, didn't hurt us or nothing, but they all the time religious and shit. Told us our moms is going to hell but they could save us with these

Bible doings they had. They had this minister come over couple times and preach at us. He meant well, but, you know, they kept after our moms. Said what she doing was the Devil's work and she be damned and all. I couldn't—*we* couldn't take no more of that. So we left."

"How did you wind up here?"

Wilver rested his back against the wall. Blew air out through puffed cheeks. Fifteen, still a kid at heart, he needed to tell someone. "We live over there, in the Alleghenies." He gestured east, toward the Allegheny Estates project. "You know, when our moms is still here. We saw the peoples live here get—what they call it? When you gets thrown out because you can't pay?"

"Evicted."

"Yeah. They evicted their asses proper. Threw all their shit in the sidewalk. That's where we got the microwave and the air mattresses."

"When did this happen?"

"Couple months ago. We took the stuff home. When they took Moms to rehab and we walked away from those foster people, I knew they'd come looking for us at our regular place. No one lived here. You could tell from the couple boarded up windows. So David and me sneaked back into our place and got some stuff and brought it here."

"Aren't you afraid? This is a pretty tough neighborhood."

"People lives on both sides. Ain't no one using this place for nothing when there's some of them separate houses around just as empty."

Commotion outside. A child's yell and a woman's voice. Wilver got halfway up before Doc reined him in. "That's David! Someone in the house!"

163

"Take it easy." Doc's voice stayed calm. "My partner's down there. She must've caught him trying to get out. Let's go see what they're up to." His hand gripped Wilver's arm before he started down the stairs. "Take your time. They're not going anywhere. I don't want us falling down the stairs."

They found Barb and David in what passed for the back yard: a twenty by thirty foot patch of mostly dying weeds. Doc opened the kitchen door from the inside to get everyone in the house and out of sight. David ran to Wilver, who grew three inches as he held his brother. Doc and Barb let them inventory each other.

"Where'd you find him?" Doc said.

"Coming out the way they got in. It was harder than he expected without his brother to boost him up."

"He give you any trouble?"

"Just what you'd expect. I think he might have wet himself when I grabbed him coming out. Ignore it if he did."

"Or we'll give him a cover story if it's too obvious. You think they're ready for us?"

Barb tilted her head to one side. Turned up a palm. *Who knows?*

Doc stepped forward and turned on the "friendly but serious cop" voice. "Officer Smith, this is Wilver Faison and his brother David. They've been living here for—how long is it, Wilver?"

"Bout three weeks, I guess."

"You were here the night the man got shot, weren't you?" The looks the boys gave each other were all the answer Doc needed. "We could talk right here, but it hardly seems like an appropriate venue. When's the last time you ate?"

"Lunch at school," David said before Wilver could stop him.

"You're still going to school?" Barb said.

"Missed a couple days, but mostly we go," Wilver said.

"Family Services hasn't come looking for you?" Doc said. The boys' expressions said they hadn't thought of that. "Well, a school lunch won't hold you for long. What is it, almost ten? What do you say we all go get something to eat? We can talk there." No objections. "Any preferences?"

"Can we go to Arby's?" David said. Wilver backhanded him across the arm.

Doc put up a hand. "Arby's is fine. We'll take my car. It's out front."

Barb led them out, held the boys on the stoop while Doc shut the door as best he could on the splintered frame. The door closed and stayed shut, but it wouldn't hold up to daylight scrutiny. He'd notify the owner in the morning. Some guy in Aliquippa, Grabek had said.

They were halfway to the car when a light blinded them. "Stop right there! Where you goin' with those boys?"

"Mr. West?" Doc held up his badge. "It's Detective Dougherty. This is Officer Smith. You remember us? From yesterday?"

"I know who you are. Where are you taking those boys?"

The shotgun in West's right hand came into focus as Doc's eyes adjusted. "Arby's, actually. They haven't eaten."

The light didn't waver. "Then where?"

"We hadn't got that far, Mr. West. You want to put that shotgun down? You can come with us if you want."

The light wavered once, then went out. "I'll get my coat."

CHAPTER 28

Wilver ate a small roast beef sandwich and a Dr. Pepper. Jefferson West drank a chocolate milkshake. Barb Smith nibbled fries from Doc's tray. David tried to put cattle on the endangered species list.

Doc wadded up his sandwich wrapping, put it inside the fries' carton and licked Horsey Sauce from his finger. Looked through the window at the Dumpster he dove to find the clothes with Carol Cropcho's blood and tissue on them. Everyone else was finished except David.

"Everyone get enough?" David started to answer. Wilver gave him a look and he reconsidered. "Now gentlemen, you all have some 'splainin' to do." He looked at West. "You first."

West slurped the last dollop through his straw. "I already told you all I know."

"You didn't tell me about the electrical cord running to the back of your house."

"I told her." West nodded toward Barb.

Barb took a breath and Doc said, "She didn't believe you. Did you know about the cord?"

"Does it matter?"

"Yeah, it matters. Sooner or later someone, probably me, is going to have to account for these two. I want to know what happened and I need the straight story. If you have some sort of arrangement, fine. I need to know what it is if I'm going to help them."

"I knew it was back there." Wilver stared at West. David was so shocked he stopped eating. For a moment. "Sure I knew. You boys not as shifty as you think. I'd of taken care of it myself if I didn't see you two coming and going. You weren't doing any harm, and I thought if you needed a place—well, there's hard times and why people do things is none of my business. I would've done something before it got too cold."

"Okay," Doc said. "Nothing we can do about it now, but it's not settled." Then, to the boys, "As for you two, I need to know all about Monday night."

"Which day was Monday?" Wilver said.

"Uh-uh. You're still going to school, so you haven't lost track of the days. Monday was the day a man got shot in your house. I know you remember. What I want to know is what you saw."

"Nothing," Wilver said. "We heard people come in, but we just hid upstairs in the closet so no one would see us if they came up. That's all. We didn't see him get shot and we didn't see who done it. I swear, Officer Doc. We don't know nothing."

"Wilver, maybe I believe you and maybe I don't. We have a problem here way worse than that. Word will get out about you two. Not from me, or from Officer Smith or Mr. West, but someone's going to figure out you're staying there and right after that it'll be common knowledge. Can't be helped. When that happens, whoever killed that man is going to wonder if you were there that night, and he's going to come looking for you, and he's going to find you. When he does, he's not going to care whether you saw him or not."

"Ease up a little, Doc," Barb said, "They're just kids."

"I know that, and I feel bad for them. Really. But they're in it now, and the best way we can help them is to get this guy. Right now they're all we have."

"But you're scaring them."

"They should be scared. *I'm* scared for them. Letting them think it's no big deal doesn't mean it isn't. They're in danger and they have to help us."

"But it's like I told you!" Wilver said. "We didn't see. We was scared and we hid."

Jefferson West cut in. "He's right, boys. You're not safe so long as that man is out there. You got to tell what you know."

"We don't know who it was!"

"Tell me what you do know." Doc kept his voice down. "Easy stuff." He waited for protest. Wilver stared at the tabletop. David kept eating. "How many shots?"

David stopped eating. Looked at his brother. Wilver glanced at him only long enough to send the message. "Can I get some more ketchup?" David asked.

"Go ahead." Doc jerked his head toward the condiments. "Come on, Wilver. How many?"

Wilver's eyes still down, picking at a drop of dried ketchup with a fingernail.

Jefferson West leaned in. "You got to tell him, son. He wants to help you, but he needs you to help him do it."

"Two." He said it so quick and soft Doc missed it.

"How many?"

"Two! I said two! Isn't that what you want me to say?"

Doc stayed calm. "If it was two shots you heard. You're sure?"

What Wilver mumbled could have been, "yeah."

"Were the shots close together or was there some time between them?"

"Not like right away, but pretty quick."

"How quick? Five seconds? Ten?"

"I don't know. Wasn't like I was counting, or nothing."

"Wilver," Barb said. "I'm going to say bang. You say bang again when you would've heard the second shot. Can you do that?'

"I think so."

"Bang!"

Wilver closed his eyes. His lips pursed tighter as time went by, then, "Bang!"

"Seven seconds," Doc said. Nodded. "Sounds about right. One in the back of the head. Step back while the guy falls. Step up to finish him." He smiled at Barb before turning to Wilver again. "Did they say anything? The killer and the dead man, I mean."

"Like I told you, we hid. We didn't go nowhere near to hear what they was saying."

"It's okay. I don't need to know *what* they said. Like tonight, we heard David and Officer Smith all the way outside. Did you hear anything get said? Doesn't matter what."

Wilver watched David come back with his ketchup. Waited for the kid to sit down and start eating. Doc gave him all the time he wanted.

"I heard voices, like you said. Sounded like two people. Could have been three, I don't know."

"Could you tell if they were white or black?"

"Like I could see through the floor, yo? I told you alls I could do was hear a little."

"Come on, Wilver." Doc's voice friendly and patient. "I can guess nine times out of ten if someone's black or white just hearing them talk. Living where you do, I'll bet you're nineteen out of twenty. Take a shot."

"White, I guess."

"Both of them?" A head nod the only response. "Is there anything else you can think of?" David wanted a milkshake. Doc asked if anyone else wanted anything. Gave the kid three dollars and sent him to the counter. "Wilver?"

"No thanks. I'm full."

"I mean is there anything else you can think of?"

"No, man. I told you everything I know." Wilver was going to have to become a better liar if he planned to live on the streets. Nothing to be done about it now. Doc waited for David to come back with his milkshake. He wanted both boys there for the discussion of what to do with them.

Barb and West chatted about how West kept busy in his retirement. Doc and Wilver had their own open channel. Neither used it until David brought his milkshake back and handed Doc his change. "Keep it," Doc said.

David looked to Wilver, who nodded. "Thank you."

Doc tried to include everyone when he spoke. "The question now is, what do we do with these gentlemen tonight?"

"We can't leave them there," Barb said. "It's not safe."

"What do you suggest?"

"Call Family Services. There's nothing else we can do."

"No!" Wilver said. "They just put us back with the people we been with. We don't want to go back there."

"That reminds me," Doc said. "What about those people on Seventh Street? They haven't missed you yet?" Both boys looked down. "Wilver? David? What aren't you telling me?"

"Nothing," Wilver said. "I don't know why they ain't looked for us. Now that you got me thinking about it, I'm a little surprised myself."

"Family Services hasn't missed them yet, either," Barb said, "or they'd have been to the school."

"It sounds like Family Services thinks they're still on Seventh Street. Maybe we should just take them back."

"No!" Wilver said.

"Did you tell them about the car?" David asked him.

"Shut up, David!"

"What car?" All three adults in unison.

"I told you not to say nothing," Wilver said. "Just eat, I said. I'd do the talking."

Doc said, "Okay, then talk. What car?"

Wilver checked every face at the table for a receptive audience. Settled on Jefferson West. "After we heard the shots, the door slammed. I peeked out the window and saw them get into a car."

"Them?" Doc said. "Two people left?"

"Yeah." Wilver's face fell as his stone wall eroded like a sand castle at high tide.

"Both white, right? You knew all along." No answer. "What did they look like?"

"I didn't see no faces. It was dark and I was afraid they'd see me."

"General descriptions are fine. Big? Small? Fat? Anything unusual about their clothes?"

"The man had on like a jacket, you know? Not just a

windbreaker, but with like the same finish. Plastic, like."

The adults exchanged looks. "The man?" Doc said. "Are you saying the other person's a woman?"

"Looked like. Smaller and all. Wore some kind of hat or something on her head so I couldn't see how long her hair or nothing, but it was a woman, mos def."

"What about the car?" Barb said. "Would you recognize it if you saw it again?"

Wilver's face brightened. "That car was phat. A nice ride. One a them German cars. BMW or Mercedes. Not real big, but styled."

"What color?"

"Almost black. It was real dark something. Maybe blue, like the Bears' unis, what they call midnight blue. Or that wine color, kind of purpley red?"

"Burgundy?"

"Yeah. Something like that."

"You guys ever build a car on the internet?" Doc said. "Go to a company web site, pick out the model, change the color, make it however you want it? It's fun. We could take you over to the station and play until we found the one you saw."

Both boys faded into their seats on "station." Jefferson West said, "You can't take these boys in. That'll get word out they're witnesses faster than you were worried about before." He looked both boys over, said, "Come back to my place. I got a DSL line fast as anything they got in a government building. We'll look for the car there." A pause. "An old couch in the cellar folds out. There's a TV down there, and a bathroom. You boys promise to behave, you can stay the night. We'll sort things out after school tomorrow."

"You sure about this, Mr. West?" Doc said.

"I've handled worse than these boys," West said. "We'll be fine."

"All right, then. If we're all done eating," he smiled at David, "let's get back in the car."

"Officer Doc, can I go to the bathroom first?" David said. "I gots to go real bad."

"I guess you do. I'm half surprised you haven't exploded. Wilver, you have to go?" A nod. "You two aren't going to make a break for it, are you?"

"No."

"Uh-uh."

"I could stand a trip myself," West said. "I'll keep an eye on them."

Doc stood and led the way to the short side hallway with the restrooms. Watched everyone else make the trip, Barb to the ladies' room. Saw the doors close, turned toward the window facing the parking lot. Moved to his right. Moved to his left. Stepped back. Closer to the men's room. Closer to the window. Damnedest thing. There was no place in this restaurant where he could see both the door his anonymous caller told him Tom Widmer came through and the Dumpster the clothes were thrown into.

CHAPTER 29

It took half an hour to decide the car was a BMW 528i sedan. The color was trickier. Wilver picked Monaco Blue right away. David wasn't so sure.

"Try that other one again."

"You mean this one here?" Jefferson West moved the mouse over the Deep Sea Blue patch. "On the right?"

"Yeah. That one."

"You know it darker than that," Wilver said. "What you be picking the wrong color about?"

"Show me the darker one again." West changed the car's color back. David took his time studying. "Can I see the other one again?"

Doc stepped up and whispered in West's ear. West nodded. "David, do you think you could settle on one color if I was to let you mess with these cars yourself when we're through?"

"Can I?" Another look to Wilver. He nodded. "Cool. Yeah, I guess it the darker one. What you call it? Monaco Blue."

"I thought it might be," Doc said. "Mr. West, can we talk to you a minute while the boys design their dream car?"

The adults stood at the doorway of the extra bedroom where West kept his computer. "Are you sure you're okay with letting them stay the night?"

West looked past him to the boys. "Look at them. They's

just kids. Nothing wrong with them a little adult supervision won't fix. We need to get in touch with their daddy if momma ain't ready to hold up her end."

"Do you believe what they said?" Barb said. "About the father not knowing, I mean."

Doc shrugged. West said, "I do. I seen things down here the past few years I never seen before. Their daddy going to Tennessee not the strangest story I heard, and I'm sorry to say their momma going away not too unusual, either. Usually it's the other way round, the momma doing right and the daddy falling off, but both parents staying strong don't happen often enough."

"If you're good with it..." Doc let it fade off to invite objection. "I'll come by after school tomorrow and see how it went."

"Not too soon," West said. "I got a plumbing job tomorrow. I doubt I'll get back before four."

"I'll come by when I get off work, then. You mind keeping them on a short leash when you get back?"

"I'll keep an eye on them."

Barb Smith lost her battle to stay out of it. "Why don't we just call Family Services and ask them to swing by the school?"

West said, "No offense, Miss Smith, but is that really gonna solve anything?"

"He has a point, Barb," Doc said. "Aren't you curious why they haven't been missed yet?"

"I know people at Family Services," West said. "Got a niece worked there twenty years now. They're good people and they do good work, but there's more of it than they can keep up with. Maybe we got a chance to do a good thing here."

Barb wrapped her arms around herself. "I don't know. There's a lot of exposure here. If something goes wrong..."

"I'm senior officer," Doc said. "I'll take it."

"That's not what I meant."

"I know it isn't, and I appreciate your concern. Right now we have a choice between calling Family Services and keeping everyone up all night while they go back someplace they don't want to go and we don't know why, or..." he came up for air, "leaving them here for the night and everyone can be asleep in half an hour. They must be exhausted. I never thought to ask where they spent last night, and they've had an action-packed day today. Let's all step back and catch our breath here and see what things look like tomorrow."

The adults turned together. The boys were watching cartoons on YouTube like coming to Jefferson West's home was a weekly occurrence.

"Okay, Mr. West," Doc said. "They're all yours. We'll just say goodnight."

Doc and Barb watched the end of a Family Guy clip over the boys' shoulders. Doc said, "Time to turn in, gentlemen. I don't want to hear you gave Mr. West any trouble. He's sticking his neck out for you."

"We know," Wilver said. "We appreciate it, too. We'll go straight down."

West asked for a minute to find sheets and pillows and went down the stairs. The boys shut off the computer and followed, David still wired. Wilver showed the signs of coming down from two long days of stress. They'd said goodnight, the boys moving through the kitchen toward the basement, when Barb called them back.

"I know it's probably too much to ask, but did either of you see the license plate on the car? Even one number would be a big help."

Doc looked at his shoes and shook his head. The first question he should have asked after they heard about the car.

Wilver and David exchanged their look. Wilver said, "We didn't see no numbers. Didn't see no license plate at all until the car pull away. Then it was too far to see with just that little light on the back."

Doc said, "Did you notice what kind of plate it was? The regular plate, or one of the other ones? You know, the tiger or the otter or the train?"

"Weren't no kind of plate," David said. "Didn't have nothing on it like they usually do."

"Out of state?" Barb said.

"No, not even like that," Wilver said. "It just white. Nothing on it but the letters and numbers. Didn't even look real, like it cardboard or something."

Doc looked at Barb. A smile grew. "Temp plate."

"That means it was sold in the past forty-five days. There can't be too many Monaco Blue 528is sold since then."

Doc showed Wilver and David the good smile. The one he used off-duty. "Boys, you just earned yourself a real dinner. Anyplace in town you want." Talk is cheap. There wasn't a restaurant in Penns River where the four of them couldn't eat for under fifty dollars.

CHAPTER 30

Dan Rollison and everyone else on the block watched Chastity walk across East Carson Street. She couldn't bend over or sit down in the sprayed-on gold dress without risking an exposure charge. The shoes weren't just "fuck me;" they were "fuck me *now*." She wore them as casually as a preppie wore Izod.

She opened the passenger door and slid in. It was artfully done. "You have my money?"

"Right here? There's people all over the street."

"You can't hand me money with people around?"

"There's more to this transaction than money."

She twisted in the seat to stare at him. "You're afraid you won't get your blowjob? Later, after I come out."

"Listen, honey, don't insult my intelligence. I give you six hundred and fifty dollars, I'll never see you again."

"I thought you were a master detective. You know where I work. It's not like I'm going to quit my job and skip to South America on a six hundred and fifty bucks."

True, she wasn't going far on six-fifty. And Rollison did know where she worked. And where she lived. How long she'd been there. What she drove, how she dropped out of Allegheny County Community College. He knew her credit score, which he was sure she didn't. Megan Darcy Callahan wasn't going anywhere with his money. Still, there was principle involved.

"Uh-uh. Cash on delivery."

Chastity shook her head to get the hair out of her right eye. "At least give me something so I can buy a drink or two. I shouldn't have to spot you the money."

"You do this right and guys will line up to buy you drinks."

"Not the first one."

He peeled a fifty off the roll in his pocket, let her see the dozen still there. "Here. Have a ball. Just bring him out where I can see him."

"I was gonna ask you about that. I'm supposed to walk him past your car, and then what? Tell him to get lost? If he's connected like you say, how's that gonna go over? How am I gonna get paid? I didn't miss a night's work to freeze my ass off and maybe get beat up or fucked. Or both."

"What's your idea?"

"You come in after me. I'll show him to you in there, but I leave alone. I'll meet you back here."

"I'm supposed to sit there and watch you?"

"No. I'll call you when I have him picked out. You come in, walk around a little until you see me. I'll make sure you know which one is him. You leave, I'll make an excuse. You pay me and get your hummer before he leaves, then you can follow him nice and relaxed and I'll go to work."

Rollison watched a group of three enter The Foundry. He and his clothes were thirty years too old for this crowd. "I'll stick out in there like a priest in a whorehouse. What's Plan B?"

"That *was* Plan B. You came up with Plan A, and it was shitty. If you don't like my idea, Plan C is on you."

Bitch. He'd forgotten to figure how he could follow this

guy *and* get blown. Marty—David, whatever the hell his name was—couldn't be allowed to make him, and not getting made is a lot easier if you're not seen. Still, he couldn't take the chance the guy would leave the club while Chastity was getting him off or the trip was wasted. No blowjob's worth six-fifty.

"Okay, then. You go in, call me, and point him out. I'll come out, you come out. We'll both wait in the car and watch him until he gets into his. After I get the license number, we'll go someplace quiet and finish our business."

Her forehead furrowed and her lips tightened. Rollison knew she didn't want him to take her someplace dark and quiet any more than she wanted to go home with Marty/David. The night at Tease already a write-off, she wasn't going to walk away from six hundred dollars, either. He watched the calculations play across her face the same as he'd watched them play across faces for thirty years. He knew her answer before she did.

"All right," she said. "We'll do it like that. I'm warning you now. You try anything cute when we park and I'll pepper spray your balls." She snatched the fifty and slid out of the car.

Rollison watched her walk back across Carson Street. Christ, you could see the crack of her ass through that dress. He wondered if she ever sold it. Or even gave it away. Lots of strippers were dykes. Rollison spotted it better in men than in women; he didn't know about Chastity. Wondered what Megan Darcy Callahan looked like in her Catholic high school uniform. Or if they even still wore uniforms at Central Catholic. He knew that about her, too.

He turned the radio on low, listened to a baseball playoff

game on WEAE for background noise. Thought about a couple of other open case files he had working. That got him thinking about detectives on TV and the movies, never working more than one case at a time. What bullshit, all that fighting the system and breaking the rules and coloring outside the lines. The rules were a PI's best friend, if he knew which rules to follow and how to use them.

His favorite rule, what he called Rollison's Rule Number One, was Everyone Wants Money. People who need it sure as hell want it. People who don't need it want more, and they sure as shit don't want to give any up. People with money will pay lawyers and guys like Rollison a million dollars to keep from paying some poor slob half a million for a car accident. So they can say the money was spent, not given away.

Rollison could pay for anything he needed. Private information from the Department of Motor Vehicles? Like calling 411 for him. He knew a guy there with a serious gambling problem. It doesn't take long for a gambling problem to become serious on a DMV salary, so he'd come across any time Rollison waved a picture of Benjamin Franklin at him.

He knew people in half a dozen banks. Banks pay squat until you're way up in the stratosphere. Rollison was amazed more employees didn't peddle information. Brokerage? Guy with a coke habit that didn't recede when his commissions did. Cops? Are you kidding? Rollison was financing more policemen's cars than GMAC. He even got a wire into a confessional once and cashed in for fifty times as much as he paid the priest.

The big three—the real Golden Triangle—were money,

sex, and power. Money trumped; the other two were commodities, purchasable with coin of the realm. Saying money couldn't buy love was laughable. If a woman loved your money enough, she'd love you. Above a certain threshold, women couldn't distinguish a man apart from his money any more than they could think of his arm or foot or pecker not being part of him. Enough money bred enthusiasm and Rollison truly didn't care who or what Megan Darcy Callahan thought of with his dick in her mouth, so long as it was *his* dick in her mouth.

All this thinking made him hard. He adjusted position and almost injured himself when Chastity opened the passenger side and threw herself in.

"What are you doing back here?"

"He's not there."

"Then you wait."

"He's not coming."

Rollison looked at her for the first time since she got back. Pale as ice; her dark hair and eyeliner made her look like one of those *Twilight* vampires all the kids were talking about. "How do you know?"

"Because he's dead!" She turned and he saw how big her eyes were. Chest heaving to strain the dress's fabric. "What did you get me into? What the *fuck* did you get me into?"

"Calm down. How do you know he's dead?"

"How do I know he's dead? How do I know he's dead? Jesus Christ, they fucking told me he's dead! What the fuck did you get me into?"

This hysterical shit had to stop. "Listen to me. If you don't calm down I'm going to have to slap you, and I don't want to do that. Just tell me what happened. Start with the first person you talked to."

"You bastard! He's *dead*! What the fuck did you get me into?"

Rollison slapped her cheek. No arm movement, just snapped his wrist and caught her with his hand. Get her attention. "I didn't get you into anything. You hooked up with this guy and set up his buddy, even after you knew he wasn't who he said he was. Knock off this victim shit and tell me what happened."

She took a minute to collect herself. Didn't touch where he'd hit her. Looked like she might cry, but didn't. "I went in and got a drink and asked about that VIP room or whatever it was where he'd said he'd be. The bartender showed me where. There was a bunch of people in there, and one big guy made you say what you wanted before you could go in. I don't think he worked for the club. I think whoever was in there had him weeding people out. He asked who I was looking for and I told him David and he said 'David who?' and I didn't know, you know, like he didn't tell me his last name. So this guy asks me to describe him and when I do he gets all serious and says I need to talk to a guy and takes me in.

"We get inside and he walks me over to some guy and he leans over and this other guy gets real serious and asks what I want with David. I'm starting to feel uncomfortable, I mean, like, who *is* this guy they're so top secret about him, so I tell him where we met and how he said I should look him up here sometime. This second guy says David's not here and I say I don't mind waiting for him, there were other girls there and it looked like these guys were buying drinks, so I figured what the hell? Anyhow, when I say I'll wait, some other guy laughs real loud, and this second guy, the one that looks like he's in charge, gives him a real dirty look and this other guy shuts up right away."

Chastity talked a mile a minute, stumbling over words, almost forgetting to breathe. Rollison sat back and let her get it all out before she'd have time to come up with something she liked better.

"This guy in charge, he asks me to sit down and says he hopes I wasn't looking forward too much to meeting David because he wasn't coming, not tonight or any other night. I said I didn't get it, and he told me David was dead. Said someone shot him twice in the head up in Penns River. Shot him *in the head! What the fuck did you get me into?*"

Fuck. David Frantz. Rollison knew about the shooting, didn't make any connection to this cluster fuck. Had to be ten thousand Davids in the Greater Pittsburgh area. What were the odds that David from Tease was the same David with two holes in his head twenty miles up the river?

Rollison knew a little about Frantz. Low-level associate of the Mannarino family. Not Italian, so he'd never get made, still wanted to be a player. Usually came up with a decent score once a year or so. Two in the head sounded like a hit, but in Mannarino's home town? And why would Mannarino have anything to do with this Widmer mess? Had to be something else.

Rollison stopped thinking about Frantz long enough to realize Chastity was still in the car, babbling about what the fuck he'd got her into. Crying now, mascara running down her cheeks like she was in some all-girl version of Kiss. He didn't need her anymore.

184

"Here." He pushed the other dozen fifties at her. "Go home. Get drunk. Get a good night's sleep and forget all about this."

"What?" She stared at him like he was speaking Farsi. Not so shaken she couldn't jam the money into her tiny purse. "How can I go home now? Those guys are gangsters, aren't they? They'll come after me, or whoever killed Marty—I mean David—they'll come after me, too. What the fuck did you—"

"You say that one more time and I really will hit you." Gave her a second to let it sink in. "Listen, to them you're just one more twat he wanted to fuck, which is what you are. So go home and forget you ever saw me."

Halfway home he remembered about the blowjob.

CHAPTER 31

Mike Mannarino liked his nickname. The Hook. Sounded big-ass sinister, like he hung guys from meat hooks or some shit. Truth was, he got the name on his high school baseball team, where he threw the best twelve-to-six curve ball anyone there had ever seen. A real yakker. Struck out seventeen in a seven inning game his senior year. Drafted by the Expos, accepted a scholarship at Auburn. He lasted a year before they threw him out for selling steroids way before it was fashionable.

Couple times a week when the weather was good Mike would go out behind his garage where he had a honest-to-Cooperstown mound built and throw a bucket of balls into a net. Couple of times a year he'd work out indoors, get a slow pay tied spread-eagled against a wall, use him for the target. Mike never had a big league fastball, but even upper seventies hurts like hell when you're stripped to your boxers. A good slider sometimes left stitch burns on bare skin. Very effective, and a decent workout.

His job as The Man in Pittsburgh's organized crime structure wasn't always so recreational. Today he had to talk to some spook he wasn't supposed to see ever, find out what the hell his boys were thinking, dropping Dave Frantz like they did. In Mike's home town, no less. Not that Frantz was a made guy, or a good earner; he'd be "Dave Who?" in six months. It was the principle. The Hook didn't care where they sold their drugs or dropped their bodies, so long as it wasn't in Penns River, and so long as the body didn't work for him.

"Donte, please, have a seat. You want something to drink? Stretch, we got any Colt 45 around?"

"I don't think so, Mr. Mannarino. Not a lot of call for it here." "Here" being the Aspinwall Hunters' and Fishermen's Club. Its exclusive clientele included only people who worked for Mike Mannarino. This was where he did business, to keep the taint from his legitimate car dealership in Penns River.

"It's cool, Mr. M." Donte smiled like he meant it. "A little of that Dago Red you drinking be fine."

Mannarino not sure if he'd been insulted, gestured for Stretch to get Donte his drink. "How long we been doing business now, Donte? Three years? Four?"

"Closer to five."

"Five years? No shit? That goes to show, when things go well, time flies."

"Something like that." Stretch put Donte's drink on the bar where he'd have to reach to get it.

"Never a hitch." Mike's tone smooth and measured. "So what I want to know is, why the fuck one of your boys put two in my guy's head."

"I don't know nothing about that, Mr. M."

"You saying this is news to you?"

"No, not like that. Everybody know. I'm just saying I don't know nothing about who did him."

"That's your part of town, Donte. You're supposed to know what goes on down there."

"And I do, if it concern me. I was kind of curious why

your boy be down my way, since we on the subject."

Stretch made a sound, took a step forward. Mike put out a hand. "That's a good question, too. I'd ask him—and he'd tell me—if he was around."

No one spoke until the bulb went on over Donte's head. "Oh, I see. You thinking, since my crew still be around to ax, maybe I should talk to them. See who capped your boy. That be a good idea, if any a my crew had a got-damn thing to do with it. Which they don't, or I'd a known about it already."

"You know your boys that well."

"Fuck yeah."

Stretch said, "Watch your language, spook," and Mike cut him off.

"Take it easy. Donte, forgive what Stretch just said. He lets his glands do his thinking sometimes. He don't mean anything by it." Stretch grunted an apology.

"We cool," Donte said.

"Good. It's five years now we been taking your shipments off the barges here instead of making you do transfers in Pittsburgh where they got real cops. Everything works great. All I ask is two things. You don't sell none of that shit here, where my kids and their friends go to school, and you don't fuck with my people. Did I ever ask for more than that?"

"You mean beside paying you thirty points more than our old connect?"

This jig had a real mouth on him. Mike wondered if it would be more trouble than it was worth to teach him some manners and deal with his replacement. "We deliver a better package. You're still making as much money, right? Even stepping on it more than you used to. And when's the last time you had any issues with the police? Not counting that dipshit selling weight to the undercover cop last year."

"No argument. We doing fine. I'm just saying I know right here," Donte tapped his chest, "my people ain't know nothing about this."

"Okay. You've always known your people before. I'll give you the benefit of the doubt. Here's my problem: I need to know who did this, and my guys can't move around down your part of town without drawing a lot of attention neither one of us needs. I hear there might be a couple of witnesses. Squatters in the vacant where they found him. So I have a job for you. Call it a favor if you want. Find out who did Dave Frantz. If he's one of mine, I want him. If he's one of yours, I want him. He's some dickhead doesn't know anything about anything, I want him. *Capite?*"

"Yo, Mr. M, I *capite* just fine." Donte up and moving for the door, walking that slow-motion pimp slouch they got, take him five minutes to cross the street. Lazy motherfuckers born to sell drugs, only job in the world all you have to do is stand on a street corner and wait for the fiends to come to you. "We on it."

Mike let him get to the door. "Hey, Donte. One more thing. It's on you now. I don't hear back, or I think you're holding out on me, there'll be some logs floating down the river. You feel me, bro?"

Donte turned, just as Mike knew he would. Question their balls or honesty, they had to take it as a mortal insult. Being disrespected. Donte a little smarter than some, still let his crocodile brain run the show.

"Yo, Mr. M, no disrespect or nothing—" *Here it comes* "—but you ain't got but what, three made guys? That's some bold shit to be talking to a crew handle the whole North Side. Just saying, is all."

That was the problem doing business with these coloreds. Too dumb to know when you're trying to do them a favor. Mike could have found out whatever he wanted in a couple of days if he tapped some sources he'd prefer not to just yet. So he gives this one a chance to make some points, earn some real respect, and he talks shit back. "You think three made guys is all I got? Stretch ain't made. You want to fuck with him?" Donte did not seem to be overcome with fear. "You want respect, show some. Carry your weight. There's more to life than standing on the corner waiting for some falling down loser to beg you to sell him drugs. You want to talk shit, we can talk about Wally Ott. You heard of Wally, right? Used to move some weight in Youngstown?" Didn't wait for an answer. Everybody knew about Wally Ott. "Think about Wally and wonder if I'm gonna let some eggplant jack me around."

Donte kept the staredown going. The look in his eyes wasn't at all the same as before.

CHAPTER 32

Rick Neuschwander paused with Doc outside the interrogation room. "Just so I know. Are we going to threaten to violate him if he doesn't help you?" Referring to the man sprawled in a chair inside the room.

"Threaten to violate him? No, Rick, we're *going* to violate him, unless you got some reason not to. Is he a regular snitch for you?"

Neuschwander shook his head. "He comes to me when he's jammed up. How good his information is depends on how bad his problem is. He's on parole for Illegal Entry now, which shouldn't have cost him any time except he was already on probation for Larceny, stealing tires right out of a bay at NTB."

"This guy's a real citizen."

"A real jagov is what he is. Too dumb to even be a decent criminal. I don't know if he's bullshitting me or not. I don't want to waste your time, but if he's telling me straight, you ought to hear him."

Penns River not big enough to have full-time crime scene investigators; Neuschwander handled evidence collection the best he could, which was more than good enough. He'd earned a standing offer to work in Pittsburgh; he didn't want to do crime scenes only. Too dry. He liked working the broader aspects of investigations, putting things together, making arrests. Things CSIs only did on *CSI.*

Neuschwander's problem was he wasn't all that good at it. He lacked imagination and the kinds of interpersonal skills that got suspects to say things they should know better than to say. Things like, "I did it," or, "I'll testify." Grabek and Harriger preferred busting his balls to listening, treated him like a gofer: gather the evidence, bring the reports, stay out of the way. Doc looked past the inability to question suspects and witnesses to Neuschwander's ability to see patterns no one else noticed, spot the one thing that didn't fit. He asked Neuschwander to read files when he was stuck, used him for reality checks, and actually listened to what he had to say. Now when Neuschwander came up with something on his own, Doc got it first.

"Not a problem," Doc said. "Something like this is always worth making time for, even if it turns out to be nothing. You be the good cop. You're the one he knows, you're the one who reached out to try to get him some help. I'm just some hard ass looking to clear a murder who'd just as soon put him in for it as anyone else. That work for you?"

Neuschwander nodded and opened the door. "Detective Dougherty, this is Dwight Wierzbicki. Bick, tell him what you told me."

"And it better be good," Doc said. "I have places to be."

Everything about Wierzbicki said "redneck" clear as a pickup truck with a shotgun rack and Playboy Bunny mud flaps. Stringy hair straggled over a high forehead. Average height, rawboned, angular face. White wife-beater under a cammo field jacket. "You the one working that shooting over by Allegheny Estates?" Doc nodded. "Then you need to hear what I got to say."

"Just so we're all on the same page," Doc said, "tell me

why you're willing to share this valuable information."

"I thought Neuschwander told you that already."

"I need to know first hand how full of shit you are."

Neuschwander cut in. "The Bick has helped me out before, Doc."

"The Bick? Someone with a name like the Bick sounds like he ought to be in a pen. Or the pen. You trying to play some half-assed 'get out of jail' card on me, Dwight?"

Wierzbicki looked to Neuschwander, who said, "Yeah, he's got a little trouble because some stuff stuck to his fingers. It's not serious enough to deserve the time he's looking at if we violate him for a couple of other things, so I thought I'd give him a break." He looked back to Wierzbicki. "*If* he comes through."

"Just so he knows, if he doesn't come through, and I waste my time running down a dead end or harassing some innocent civilian, I'll make a project out of him." Doc sat in one of the chairs, propped his heel against the edge of the table. "Okay, Mr. Career Criminal fuckup, convince me I should talk Detective Neuschwander out of sending you back to jail."

Wierzbicki looked to Neuschwander again. Neuschwander pointed to Doc. Wierzbicki made a show of his disgust. Said, "I was at the bar in the Warszawa Hotel a week or two ago when this chick come in."

"Was it a week?" Doc said. "Or two?"

"I don't know." Wierzbicki caught Doc's look. "Week before last, I guess. Tuesday, Wednesday, Thursday. Somewhere in there." He waited for another interruption. "So I'm sitting there at the end of the bar and this chick comes in."

"What did she look like? This woman."

"Nice looking for an older piece. Had some kind of babushka tied around her hair. One a them trench coat-looking things, but short. Nice rack. Legs up to her ass."

"You said older. How old?"

"I don't know how old she mighta been. Not some young chickie is what I mean."

"Work with me here. Was she fifty? Sixty? Older?"

"Not that old. Thirty-five. Maybe forty. No more than that."

Doc and Neuschwander exchanged looks. Doc said, "How old are you, Dwight?"

"Forty-three. What's the difference?"

Doc waited a beat. "None. I'm just building a picture. Go on."

"Like I been trying to tell you, she comes in and starts looking around. Gets some attention, too, good-looking like she is. The Warszawa don't get too many like that. Not unless they're pros, and the kind of pros the Warszawa gets don't usually look like her."

Doc turned to Neuschwander. "Does he always ramble like this?" Neuschwander nodded. Doc said to Wierzbicki, "Remember what I told you about how busy I am? Get on with it."

"I am getting on with it. I'd a had the fucking story told already if you didn't keep interrupting me." Paused again, looked at Doc like he was waiting for another interruption. Then, "So she scopes the joint out like she's looking for somebody, sees me, and comes right over."

"She goes straight to you? Because bad comb-overs make her wet? What?"

"I'm getting to it. She comes over and asks if the stool

next to me is taken and I'm like, 'fuck, no.' Someone built like her can sit on my face if she wants to. She sits down and orders a white wine. Then, while I'm thinking of a way to move the conversation along, she looks me right in the eye and asks if I paint houses."

"Whoa. You're telling me you're sitting in the Warszawa, which used to be a decent place but now is pretty much a hot sheets and SRO dump, minding your own business, and this classy woman walks up and asks if you'll kill someone for her? Did she bring a clipping from your ad in *Soldier of Fortune*? Twenty percent off with this coupon?"

Wierzbicki spoke to Neuschwander. "Do I have to put up with this? I'm trying to help him and all he does is bust my balls."

Doc said, "Fine. Don't help me, you're so sensitive." He turned to Neuschwander. "Lock him up. I wouldn't fix a parking ticket for this story."

Neuschwander stepped forward, pulled his handcuffs. Wierzbicki, said, "*Hey!*" I'm not done yet! You think I'm so dumb I don't know you need more than that?" Looked from Doc to Neuschwander and back. No one disagreed. "Shit, no. There's more. First thing, I told her right away uh-uh. The only painting I do is with a brush and a ladder. She blushed like I don't know what and this guy comes up, I didn't see him before. He leans in over her shoulder and he's like, 'I can handle that. I do my own carpentry, too.'"

Pause for effect. The cops traded glances. Neuschwander raised an eyebrow. Doc said, "One stop shopping. Kills the guy *and* disposes of the body if she wants." Then to Wierzbicki, "What'd she say?"

"I don't know. He leaned past her before she could say

anything, looks me right in the eye and asks what I'm doing there. I told him drinking a beer and he said drink it someplace else. So I drank it at home."

"Smart man, You recognize this guy if you ever saw him again?"

"I don't know. Maybe. You been down the Warszawa lately? Light's not too good. I didn't get a great look at him."

Neuschwander said, "You just told us he leaned across her right into your face and you didn't get a good look?"

"I didn't *want* a good look, okay? I dropped a buck on the bar and got the fuck out of Dodge."

Doc said, "Dwight's not as dumb as he lets on. You wanted no part of that guy, did you?"

"Fucking A. Not a good idea to get too good a look at someone like that."

"What about the woman?"

"Same deal. The light's bad, like I said."

"The light's not that bad, Dwight. I can understand not getting a good look at the hitter, but her? You wanted a good look at her and you had plenty of time to do it up close. No, you can ID her."

"It ain't that easy. She had on those dark glasses, like I said. Big ones."

"You didn't say anything about dark glasses before."

"Yeah I did." Tried for a softer audience. "Neuschwander? I know I did."

"Uh-uh," Neuschwander said.

"Look at me, Dwight." Doc used his foot to push away from the table and stood. "I outweigh you by fifty pounds, a badge, and a gun. Are you sure I'm the guy you want to fuck with?"

"I'm sure I don't want to fuck with the guy from the Warszawa."

"The woman, then. What you said so far isn't enough for a walk."

Wierzbicki chewed a nail. Ran his hands through his hair front to back. Looked for the same high, corner window Tom Widmer had looked for, the one they all look for, the one that isn't there. "I might. *If* I saw her again. Which ain't likely. We don't run in the same circles."

"I understand that. Detective Neuschwander, will you step into my office, please?" They went to a corner of the room where Wierzbicki could hear them talking, not what they said. Stayed there a few minutes, taking turns looking over at him picking at strings hanging from his jacket cuff.

The cops faced him together. Neuschwander said, "You did good, Bick. Not great. Just good. Here's what we can do. I'll hold this charge for three months. Make restitution and don't let us see you in that time, and I'll throw the paper away. You trip up while you're out on grace and I'll violate you for whatever you do, and this one."

"And Dwight," Doc said, "if you fuck up, I don't care if you have video of someone shooting the pope. You go away."

"Will you for Chrissakes stop calling me Dwight? Neuschwander, you know how much I hate that. Call me the Bick. Or just Bick, you don't want to do that."

"I'm not calling a habitual criminal some cute nickname. What's your middle name?" Wierzbicki lowered his head, muttered something. "What was that?"

"I said I don't like that one, either."

"What is it?"

Wierzbicki said, "David" like he was asking if Doc wanted a blowjob.

It took Doc a few seconds. "Your name is Dwight David Wierzbicki? You're named after Eisenhower?"

"Yeah."

"What's wrong with that? General Eisenhower was a great man."

"Not him. I'm named after the other one. The president. Who's this general? Some Civil War dude?"

Doc and Neuschwander looked at each other like their heads hurt. "Goodnight, Bick," Doc said. "Stay out of trouble."

CHAPTER 33

"You need to talk to Jillian."

Doc set down his side of the jury box façade he'd helped Eve carry backstage. "What's the matter?"

"I'm not sure. She never comes right out and says anything, you know. She hints around and hopes I'll tell you."

"Which you do."

"Right, but she doesn't ask me to, if that's what you're wondering. If we're in it together, I mean."

Doc opened the Coke he'd balanced on the railing. Took a swallow, made a face. Pop machine's refrigeration effective as a government employee on retirement day. "Why would I think you're in it together? Whatever 'it' is."

"That's what I mean." Eve opened her Diet Coke. "There is no 'it.' We have nothing going on. I'm just friends with both of you, is all."

"Eve, we've been friends a long time. We know things about each other no one else knows. In all that time we've never had an awkward moment. We both say what's on our mind. Right?"

"Right."

"So, my old and dear friend, I ask you, with all due respect, what the fuck are you talking about?"

Eve sat one cheek on the rail. "She doesn't know how you feel about her. Wait! It's not like that, one of those woman things where she needs to know your innermost thoughts.

She knows it might sound like that, too. I think that's why she came to me. She's picking up mixed signals and she's kind of bashful about asking you."

"I can think of a lot of ways to describe Jillian. Bashful doesn't come to mind."

"You're right. On the surface." Eve drank some pop. "I don't know how much of this I should tell you."

"Tell me or not, whatever you think is best. I don't want to put you on the spot."

"There! I think that's part of what's bothering her. No. 'Bothering' isn't the right word. 'Confusing' is better."

"Now I'm confused. I'm trying to be a nice guy, not pressing you too hard."

"The nice guy part is okay, but it's putting her off." Doc's puzzlement so obvious Eve didn't wait. "She knows what a nice guy you are. She tells me how well you treat her, how polite you are in your way, and she knows you're careful of her feelings."

"And this confuses her, how?"

"She doesn't know if you treat her like you do because you like her or because you're such a nice guy you treat everyone like that."

"Why is that a problem?"

"Because she needs to know it's for her, that she gets some kind of special treatment."

"Why is she worried about this now? We've only been going out a couple of weeks."

"She says doesn't want to hold back if you're genuinely interested. I think she's afraid she'll get hurt if she's too far out in front of you."

Doc thought of the three nights they'd spent together.

Half afraid to think what she'd be like if she didn't hold back. "Shouldn't she be telling me all this?"

"Yes, she should." Eve finished her drink, tossed the empty toward a trash can. Missed, extending the streak that began with the first rehearsal. "I told her that. I think she's too much like you, though. Won't bring it up until it's too late."

"You think I should bring it up?"

"No! Then she'll know I talked to you about it."

"I thought she wanted you to talk to me about it."

"She did, but she doesn't want you to know she wanted me to. If you talk to her, she'll know I talked to you, which means you know she talked to me, and she doesn't want you to know that."

Doc thought maybe he wasn't missing as much as people said, not having regular relationships. "So what do you want me to do?"

"I don't want you to do anything. I just—I mean you two seem like you'd be good together and God knows you could use a break with a woman, so, I don't know. She used the word 'pursue' when we talked. She might be thinking you're just taking things as they come."

"I am taking things as they come. Like I said, it's been two weeks. I'm not looking for rings just yet."

"Don't be a jerk. I know that. She knows that. She just needs to feel like you want to spend time with her."

"I ask her out, right? I go out of my way to see she enjoys herself. You know me, Eve. I'm not going to kiss ass. I enjoy spending time with her. She seems to enjoy spending time with me. How much time we enjoy spending with each other will evolve. Or it won't. If she wants to be together more, she should say so. Talk to me about it, then we'll both know where we stand. This whole 'pursue' thing bothers me. Makes it sound like she has something I can't live without, and maybe she'll give it to me, if I ask right. No. She can give as much of herself as she wants. Or not. A relationship should be equal partners. Equal partners don't chase each other around. They don't have to."

"You're right. They don't have to. They want to."

Doc banked his empty off the wall into the trash. "But each partner gets to decide when to pursue. If the other pushes him into it, it's not really equal."

"No argument. I just don't know how long she can wait. She has a lot of insecurity, Doc. She needs to know she's wanted."

Doc worked his lower lip between his thumb and forefinger. "I can understand that. She needs to understand everyone has their own timetable. I'm not trying to be passive-aggressive here. I don't know how far I want to take it."

"I'd hate to see the two of you not get together just because your timing's different. Maybe you could bump it up a little. She said she can see you two evolving into fuck buddies. She wants more. If it's not going to be with you…"

"Okay. I get it. Really. Tell you the truth, I'm not sure a fuck buddy deal isn't exactly what I want right now. I don't know Jillian well enough yet to see if I should explore beyond that. I'd rather miss a chance than get myself into something I can't get out of without a lot of hurt feelings."

Eve took her time to say it. "You're not in the army anymore. You know that, right?" Looked at him out of the corner of her eye, not sure how he'd respond.

He'd started nodding before she finished. "I know, I know. You're right."

"You live someplace permanently now. You own the house. You're not going to fall in love and have it fall apart because you have to move and she doesn't want to."

"It's not that."

"Then what is it?"

"I don't know. What's the opposite of that?"

"That you'll fall in love and she'll have to move? I don't think so." She looked at Doc, saw that wasn't it. "You think she'll fall in love, and...what? Who's going to move away?"

"Don't be so literal. What if I'm just worried she wants to go somewhere I don't know if I want to go?"

"Where do you want to go?"

"I don't know."

"Then how do you know where she wants to go isn't where you would want to go if you knew where you wanted to go?"

That took a second to digest. "Let's say she's shown me the brochure and it's a nice place to visit but I don't know that I want to live there. Like one of those Caribbean vacations where the resort is awesome so long as you don't go into town and see how the locals live. Sooner or later you have to go into town."

Now it was Eve's turn to digest a cryptic statement. "How long has it been now, Doc?"

"Since what? I got laid?"

"No. Since you got hurt."

"That's not it. Christ, that was more than five years ago. I'm over it." Eve didn't look convinced. "What?"

"You're going to have to risk something sooner or later."

"This isn't where you give me the 'better to have loved and lost' speech, is it? It's only been nine months or so and you promised you'd only do it once a year. I should be good till December."

"Can't I give it twice this year and skip next year?"

"I let you do it now, pretty soon I'll be hearing the damn thing every week."

"I wouldn't have to give it so often if you'd hold up your end of the deal and get one right."

"Eeeeve." Drew it out to give her a chance to avoid what came next, which she wouldn't want to hear. "I'm done. I just thought you should know."

"And I appreciate it." He opened his arms, waggled his fingers inward. "Give me a hug." They put their arms around each other. Doc kissed the top of her head. "I know you have my best interests at heart. I don't have a better friend than you."

"You hardly have any friends at all."

"I never said I set the bar real high for that 'best friend' shit."

CHAPTER 34

Sunday was Doc's night to stay home and watch a game of whatever was in season. The Pirates never played past September, so most Octobers he'd watch the Steelers with his parents, then come home for a baseball playoff game until it was over or he fell asleep. There was no reason not to go out on Sunday nights, staying in no more than a habit he'd fallen into, but his habits kept him balanced. Eve said boring; Doc called Sunday nights at home his comfort zone.

Tonight the Steelers were the Sunday night game, which threw off his whole day. He almost stayed home, but Steelers games felt funny without listening to his old man yell at the television. His mother offered fish sandwiches to seal the deal, cod fillets from a little joint in Apollo, no place else could touch them.

He was well rested for a change. Came home at eight and slept till noon after a night at Jillian's, during which time she said not a word about anything he and Eve had talked about. Even if the game ran late, his bed was only a five minute drive. He'd tough it out for a couple of fish sandwiches.

"I hope they kick Baltimore's ass for them tonight," Tom said between bites. "Asking the league not to schedule them in Pittsburgh anymore on night games like that."

"Yeah, the Ravens are Super Bowl champions of running their mouth." Doc lifted a handful of curly fries onto his plate, fresh from the deep fryer. Mom always complained

about the things she couldn't cook because of Tom's cholesterol, had the fryer out every time Doc came over. Either she
exaggerated Tom's dietary restrictions, or she didn't care
about Doc's health as much as she said. Or maybe she just
loved him. His aunt's restaurant closed five years ago, the
last place in the valley with anything like these sandwiches.
"Friend of mine from the army lives down that way,
stationed at Fort Meade. He tells me there's a billboard on
the road there with Ed Reed's picture on it. Says, 'Got Health
Insurance?' You know, like those 'Got Milk?' ads? Him and
a couple of buddies got a few dozen beers in them one night
and redid the sign. Now it says, 'Hey, Ed. Got Six Rings?'
Sent me a picture. Painted the Steelers logo up there and
everything. Funnier'n hell."

"Can you e-mail it to me?" Tom still fascinated by any
routine use of a computer that presented a source of enter-
tainment to him. "I called you last night to ask about that
article we talked about. You know, about how they make
that new artificial turf. I want to print up a copy and show it
to some guys at the Legion. They think I'm full of shit. I left
you a message."

"I e-mailed it to you this afternoon. Mom, sit down a
minute. That batch has a while to cook and the fries on your
plate are getting cold." Doc waited for his mother to sit so
she wouldn't miss what he had to say. "I had a date last
night."

"Really?" Ellen held a French fry ready to eat. "How did
you meet her?" Like she hoped it wasn't some dive like Fat
Jimmy's, but she'd get over it if she had to.

"She's acting in the play over at the theater this fall."
Almost said they met at Fat Jimmy's, to see what she'd do.

Thought she might have a stroke and left it out. "Her name is Jillian, she lives in Fox Chapel, she's a nurse with two more or less grown kids. Don't get all excited. We've only been going out a few weeks."

"Two grown kids? How old is she?" Ellen didn't sound happy.

"I don't know. Mid-forties, I'd say. No older than that."

"So she's older than you."

"You're older than Dad." Tom looked over his shoulder like intense concentration could make the game start earlier.

"That's different. We're in our sixties. You're young."

"There was the same difference between you now as then. Unless you're aging faster than he is."

Ellen took her time to chew and swallow. "Well, if you don't think she's too old."

"She seems to be able to keep up with me." If Mom only knew.

"All right. I just wonder why didn't you say anything about her before."

"Because if we only went out once and I said something you'd be disappointed if it didn't go anywhere."

"Do you think it is going somewhere?"

This was the question he'd thought about all day. Maybe it was time to take Eve's advice. Extend himself a little. Bringing it up to his mother obligated him to something more than what he'd done to that point, like telling someone you want to lose twenty pounds is a higher level of commitment than just telling yourself. "Too soon to tell. Let's leave it at I can't say for sure it's not going anywhere." He nodded toward the countertop. "Your fries are burning."

"Shit!" Nothing took precedence with Ellen over making

sure a meal came out right. Tom and Doc would have to talk her out of throwing this batch away if they were overdone. She pulled the basket out of the hot oil and shook it. Complained how dark they were. Doc said he liked them dark. She said she'd make them that way all the time if she knew he liked them better. Doc said he didn't like them darker all the time, but for variety it was nice. Remembered the time she almost tossed six loaves of Syrian bread because they were too thin until he saved them by saying he liked them thin. For the next year he ate Syrian bread he could see through until he told her he'd only said he liked them thin to keep her from throwing that batch away. *All* Syrian bread was good, never throw any away, but, given a choice, thicker was better.

"Nice job," Tom said when he finished. "You're still an amateur, though. I live like this every day."

The fries were saved and Ellen banished the men to the living room to watch the game while she cleaned the kitchen. They played their part in the weekly ritual by offering to help, then took their glasses of iced tea into the living room. All consciences were happy, since Tom could rewind anything she missed on the DVR.

"You owe me," Doc said to Tom when they were situated.

"For what?"

"Now she'll bug me all week about what I'm doing instead of driving you crazy about what I'm not."

"Good point," Tom thought a minute. "Take a six pack from downstairs when you go. That's one I won't need now."

CHAPTER 35

Donte Broadus's patience had worn thin, freezing his ass off waiting for these two shorties to come back to 1123 Fourth Avenue. He wanted to stand and freeze, he could be a hopper down the North Side. Donte had enough of that bullshit. An executive now, he told the hoppers which corners to stand on while he worked directly with the connect. This standing around shit was beneath him, taking orders from that cracker Mike the Hook, what kind of bullshit name was that? Man acted like he was doing Donte a favor, giving him the shit work. Donte stomped his feet, blew on his hands. Mannarino's time was coming. The call had been made.

Donte's indignation got worse every time the wind gusted. He really was freezing his ass off, jeans pulled so low only his boxers covered it. He'd been on the block since noon, walking around to keep warm and not look too obvious. It never occurred to him the boys were in school. He'd made only token appearances since he was fourteen, stopped altogether when he turned sixteen and wasn't legally truant. Almost six o'clock, getting dark, when two boys who fit the description came down Fourth Avenue looking cagey. Donte stepped out when they were in front of 1123. "Yo, shorties, you cribbing in this vacant?"

He knew they were the ones as soon as he said it. The younger one's mouth fell open. He took a step like he'd run, caught himself. The older one stepped between Donte and the other.

"No, man. We living next door." He pointed to 1125. "With our Gramps."

"Bull-*shit*. I seen the old dude live there. He got no young' uns hanging around. I just wants to talk with you about some stuff you might could know about."

The older boy held his position. "We ain't seen nothing. We keeps to ourselves. Ain't no snitches here."

"That's right," the young one said. "Even if we did know about someone get killed here the other night, we ain't say nothing."

"See? That's what I'm saying." Donte angled his stride to stay on the sidewalk ahead of the boys. "You did see something. I ain't here to hurt no one. I just needs to know what you seen."

"David," the older boy said. "Go to the house."

"Which one?" The kid's eyes big as quarters.

"Mr. West. Go. Now."

"Wait right here, little man." The boy took two steps toward the house. "Motherfucker, I said *wait*! I'm talking to you two little bitches and I ain't about to stand here and let you disrespect me by lying in my face. Get in the fucking car so's we can talk."

The older boy stepped up to Donte's chest. "Run, David."

"You stepping to, nigger? You up for this?" Donte threw a looping right that connected above the boy's ear. Pain shot through his hand from the large ring he wore. No problem. It hurt the boy more. "You tell me no when I say come?" Donte slapped the boy backhand twice across the face. "I stand here and beat you like a little bitch. What you gonna do? Cry on me? Have your period? Come on, bitch. Get in the car. And bring that motherfucking shorty with you."

Donte took the older boy by the wrist. Turned to lead him to the car. Teach both these little motherfuckers some manners, showing him up where people could see. Had his free hand on the door handle when he heard someone pump a shotgun.

"You leave those boys be."

Donte looked back and saw the old man from 1125 coming off his stoop. Down the walk right toward him carrying what looked like a twelve gauge. Not for show, either, the geezer looking down the barrel like he knew what to do with it. "I said turn that boy loose."

"Or what, old man?" What kind of fucked up day was this? First that young'un stepped to, now this old bastard throws down on him. People coming out their houses now. Face was at stake. "You'd best step the fuck off right now before you start something I have to finish."

"I don't start nothing I can't finish, boy. The first load is rat shot. For a warning. The rest is buck shot, and I think you know what it'll do. That your car?" He nodded at the car Donte had the door open on, of course it was his car. The old man pulled the trigger. The car rocked against the spray of pellets across the rear quarter panel and trunk. "Now you been warned." The old man locked eyes with Donte, jacked another shell into the chamber.

"Motherfucker! What you do to my ride?" Donte looked to his car. Wilver broke away, ran behind West to stand with David. Donte ran his fingers over the speckled paint. Turned to face West and found himself staring into the muzzle of the shotgun not three feet away. He looked up the barrel to the stock buried in West's shoulder. West's face was impassive, his eyes steady and unblinking. He thumbed back the hammer.

"Get in your car and drive away. Now. And leave these boys alone."

"We not finished, old man. No fucking way. I see you again." Donte held his hands clear of his sides, backed away until he bumped into the car. Kept his hands on it as he shuffled around the trunk to the driver's side, always facing the shottie. "Yeah, I'm watching you, old man. You look like the kind to shoot niggers in the back. You'll see me again and it be the last motherfucking thing you ever see, feel me?"

Donte started the car on his third try. Red-lined the engine once it caught, drove away hollering out the window. "You see me again, nigger! You *know* I'm coming back on this!" A drive-by taunting.

CHAPTER 36

Doc left his supper on the table and was in Jefferson West's kitchen twelve minutes after the call.

"Do you know him, Mr. West?"

"Never seen him before."

"Would you recognize him if you saw him again?"

"You don't forget a face after something like that."

Doc squatted so he was eye-to-eye with David, had to look up at Wilver. "You boys know him?"

"No. I don't think he from here. I ain't seen him round the Alleghenies."

"There's cold drinks in the refrigerator, boys," West said. "Get yourselves each one and go on downstairs, watch some television. I want to talk to Officer—sorry, Detective—Doc."

Wilver got two Dr. Peppers, handed one to David. The boys went through the door to the basement stairs. West held up a finger for Doc to wait until he heard the television come on.

"I'm sorry to bother you like this, Detective."

"I'm glad you called. We have to get them out of here now. No way around it."

"Why?"

The question brought Doc up short. "Why? This is more than we bargained for, and we can't protect you. If I ask for a stakeout now, Family Services has to know. It's better if I just call them up front."

"I can carry this."

"I asked around about you, Mr. West. I believe you can carry it. I need to know why you want to."

"If you asked around about me, then you did the same for these boys. What did you find out?"

Doc glanced toward the basement door. "The mother's two months into a six month hitch for shoplifting. She's been arrested something like thirteen, fifteen times, but this is her first time in. I guess Judge Molchan got tired of her tying up his docket. I made up a reason to see her, asked if she had any kids. You know, worked it into the conversation. She said yeah, but when I asked her if they came to visit, she climbed all over me about did I want them to come see their mama in this shithole? Which I can't blame her for. She's crying about how she loves her babies and she misses her babies until I mentioned she might get to spend more time with them if she didn't get arrested two-three times a year. Probably not the smartest thing to say. You know this isn't the first time they've been in foster care?"

"I figured it wasn't. They know the system too well."

"Mom gave me the full ration, going on about how they were better off in a foster home until she got herself together, which she swore she would this time. Lord knows she's fucked up, but this time is different, she'll get straightened out. She knows there's good people in the system and her babies is safe until she can take proper care of them. Went full martyr on me."

"You've seen it before."

"And done better, but not much."

"So you're not impressed."

"I'm not easily impressed. After that I tried to check into

that foster family over on Seventh Street. That wasn't as easy as it sounds."

"You can't get into their computer, can you?"

"Nope. Juvenile records are confidential. I can go to a social worker for the information, but I'll have to tell her why I want it, and I wasn't ready to do that."

"But you are now."

"I don't have a lot of choices. *We* don't have a lot of choices. We have to assume that banger you ran off was carrying."

"I faced guns before."

"In Vietnam, I know, and you're a capable man. But this isn't Vietnam. You don't have a team with you, and you can't protect yourself using whatever means you see fit. And don't forget the boys. You'd have to protect three people alone. It's too much."

West stroked a hand along his jaw, looked at it like there might be something on it. "Did you check on the father?"

Doc squeezed his eyes shut. Rubbed the bridge of his nose. "He's in jail, too."

"What'd he do?"

"They were right about him, up to a point. He *was* working for Nissan in Smyrna for a while. Went up to Nashville for some fun one Saturday night and found himself a woman. A man has needs, and all that. Anyway, this woman already had a man and there was a disagreement that Mr. Faison—Charles, Chuckie's his name, by the way—anyway, Chuckie Faison ended the dispute with a broken beer bottle."

"Did the man die?"

"Not for lack of effort on Chuckie's part. Cut his face

215

open, sliced his throat. Just missed the carotid artery. Eighty stitches is what I heard. Chuckie claimed self-defense, but the jury didn't buy it."

West asked the question like he didn't want to. "White man?"

"No, but it's funny you asked. It was an Hispanic guy, but a white woman. An equal opportunity cluster fuck."

"So it looks like I'm their best chance."

"Convince me."

West paused, collecting his thoughts. "Would you like a cold drink? Got a couple of Beck's in the refrigerator." Saw surprise flash across Doc's face before he could suppress it. "Didn't take me for a Beck's man, did you?"

"Not a lot of Beck's drinkers around here. Picked it up in the army, didn't you? German tour."

"Heidelberg. Wait here."

West went into the kitchen. Spent longer than he needed to find and open two beers. Carried back two pilsner glasses with half-inch heads on them and a small plate of cheese and crackers.

Doc sipped his beer, wiped foam from his lip. "You put out a nice spread. Ever think of working as a hostess down the Red Raven?"

West chuckled. "I asked, but they don't make them little dresses to fit me. That's Muenster cheese. Something else I picked up in Germany. Get it from the commissary in Oakdale."

"I wondered about the cheese. I picked up a taste for Muenster in Germany myself." Took a bite. "This is good. I buy it around town sometimes, but it's not the same."

"I'll pick you up some next time I'm down there. I go couple times a month, usually."

Doc swallowed, washed it down with more beer. "Very nice, Mr. West. I appreciate it. Now tell me what it is that makes you want to keep these boys."

West took his time placing a slice of cheese onto a cracker. Bit off half. Chewed. Chewed some more. Swallowed when what he had in his mouth was ground so fine it was about to slide down his throat uninvited. Sipped his beer. Looked at the other half cracker like he wanted to eat it, too, before saying anything.

"I was never too good at looking down the road. I got drafted and went in as a grunt instead of reading the writing on the wall and enlisting for a skill that might have kept me out of the jungle. I got my Purple Heart at Hue and figured if the NVA couldn't kill me there they never would, so I stayed in. Already had two boys of my own, got married when I was home convalescent. Wife didn't want me going back, but I re-enlisted anyway. You probably too young to remember, wasn't a lot of job opportunities here just then, what with all the mills starting to close.

"Anyway, keep this story bearable, I never wanted to be away from my boys much, but I never done the right things to stay close. Kept accepting short tours overseas so I could get back sooner, when I could have gone three years and took the family with me. I thought they'd be happier close to home. Never occurred to me until they were about ready to graduate they might learn more about the world if they saw more of it. Turned out they still changed schools every couple of years, but here in the States, so they got the fine education available to black children in places like

Columbus, Georgia and Dothan, Alabama. All that and I still wasn't around much." He ate the rest of his cracker.

"Where are they now?"

"One of 'em living in Maryland, teaching school. Other one's working for the Internal Revenue in Pittsburgh."

"Nothing wrong with that. You must've done something right."

"All I did was pick the right woman to have them with, is all. Adelle raised those boys more or less single-handed. I can't take credit for any of it, which is good 'cause they ain't giving me any. I hear from them three times a year." He ticked the dates off on his fingers. "Christmas, Father's Day, and my birthday. I get cards, sometimes a phone call. Been almost three years since I seen either of them. I never seen my two grandchildren."

Doc ate another cheese cracker so the silence wouldn't seem so long. West said, "Adelle passed two years ago this January. Slid off an icy patch of 28 coming back from visiting the boy in Swissvale. She never could drive for shit in snow. I told her I'd take her. Didn't need to come in, just give her a ride and find someplace to watch a game till she was ready. She didn't want to trouble me." He finished his beer.

"Helping Wilver and David won't bring her back, Mr. West, and it won't change anything with your sons. Family Services will find out sooner or later and there'll be hell to pay."

"What if I gave them straight back to their mother when she gets out? Them people on Seventh Street ain't fussing, so they must still be getting their check. Family Services might be just as happy not to let it get out how they dropped the ball."

Now Doc took his time to finish his beer. "Do you have anyone who can help you day-to-day? You know, stuff like getting them to and from school and keeping an eye open in case a phone call needs made."

"I got a friend I hang with over to Earl's, guy named Sarge. He'll help when I need it. Mrs. Taylor over in the Alleghenies will be happy to help out with some cooking and cleaning for two well-behaved boys. I think we'll be okay if you can give me any help at all with that one came today."

Doc ran through the possibilities in his head. "What the hell. No guts, no glory. Isn't that what they say?" West nodded, didn't speak. "I'll put the word out you had an incident here, but I won't mention the boys. You so much as see him again, call nine-one-one and they'll come right away, and they'll notify me. I'll ask for some extra patrol presence, too. You can call me any time. I mean *any* time."

They stood and shook hands. "How long do you think I'll have to keep my eyes open for him?" West said.

"Not too long, I hope. I have an idea."

CHAPTER 37

The seals were off David Frantz's door; it wasn't a crime scene anymore. Frantz's next of kin could collect his belongings and settle up with the landlord at their convenience. It wasn't like he'd mind if Comcast shut off his cable.

Daniel Rollison let himself in with a set of picks at 10:30 am. No one around, working class building, no shift work anymore. The lock was worn and loose. Set him back until he realized picking it would be easier than expected. Rollison never took a job for granted.

Frantz's place was a one-bedroom flat with a living room, eat-in kitchen, and a bathroom with a shower stall, no tub. No dirty dishes. The expected jug of milk gone over in the refrigerator with a loaf of bread and half empty bucket of KFC. Three cans of Iron City, three six-packs still in the cardboard case on the floor. The living room needed dusting. The carpet color and fabric wouldn't show dirt, so it probably hadn't been vacuumed, either. The clutter of someone living alone. A grease-stained paper towel. Sneakers under the coffee table, one upright, the other on its side, socks stuffed in them. Magazines scattered on flat surfaces. *Guns and Ammo. Antique Trader.* Unmade bed. The *Club International* and bottle of hand lotion on the night stand reminded Rollison Chastity owed him a blow job. The shower walls were clean; a pinkish hue gathered around the floor drain.

Rollison walked through the rooms. Looked at everything. Picked up a few items. He didn't expect to find much. The police had been here, probably more than once. Small town cops or not, they'd take anything they thought might provide insight into how Frantz came to be in the vacant on Fourth Avenue.

But they wouldn't look for anything that associated him with Tom Widmer.

Rollison's second pass was more thorough. He'd searched a thousand dumps like this, knew all the ways to alter drawers and floorboards and drywall to make hiding places. He tapped the walls and felt around the baseboards. Emptied the dresser and desk drawers. Tried to keep things where they'd been so the search wouldn't look obvious in case the police came back. Spent two hours and found dick.

He had his hand on the doorknob to leave when he heard the building's front door open and footsteps come up the stairs. Rollison left his hand on the knob, listening. The steps reached the top of the stairs and stopped. Keys jangled. Something metallic fell into place. Then rustling. Rollison risked a peek outside. A letter carrier dropped mail into the slots for each apartment.

Frantz's mail was definitely worth reading. Rollison had two choices: wait or go now. Going for the mailman was risky. The police might have stopped the mail, or he might know Frantz by sight. Criminals are home during the day more than most, there was a good chance they'd bumped into each other. Worth the chance. Rollison didn't want to have to pick this lock in the open where people might be coming and going from lunch.

He made noise opening the door so the mailman would

hear where he came from. Fast walked to the small lobby area. "Anything for Number Three?"

The mailman finished the slot he was working on, looked over. "You new in Three?"

"My brother's place." If the guy offered his sympathy, at least Rollison would know where he stood. "I'll take his mail if there is any."

The mailman looked at him, pushed his hat up off his forehead. "You got the key, right? I'm supposed to lock it up and let you get it out with a key."

Christ. One conscientious postal employee in the world, and it's this one. "Yeah, it's inside, but I'm standing right here."

"I'm sorry, buddy. I'm supposed to lock it up. They got inspectors going around now, checking up on if we run the route in the right order and handle everything by the numbers. You could be one of them, so far as I know."

"Do I look like a postal inspector?" Rollison spread his arms to show what he was wearing. Long sleeve blue shirt. Dockers. Loafers. Too late it occurred to him he *might* look like a postal inspector. "I'm telling you, I'm not an inspector."

"Maybe not, but who would admit it if they were?" The mailman slammed the door home, hiked the bag over his shoulder. "Nice try, though."

"Thanks a lot, prick," Rollison said under his breath. He waited for the mail truck to pull away and went to work with his picks. Had to stop once when someone came in. Couldn't believe how much trouble the shitty lock gave him. Rollison prided himself on his ability to pick anything—Medeco, Schlage, Abloy, Mul-T-Lock—and this piss ass little mailbox held him up. He had a set of bump keys in the car, hated using them. Smash and grab types needed bump keys. Rollison was a professional, an artist. Sat around watching television in his days with the government, practicing. He got serious about this job after another person came into the building and almost caught him. Went to the car, got the bump keys, and opened the box in fifteen seconds.

Mail had accumulated since Frantz stopped picking it up. Most of the Occupant shit went to a common shelf built into the wall, but anything with a name went into the box. Pledge drive for Channel 13 addressed to a previous occupant. A once in a lifetime chance to buy a house with no closing costs addressed to Neil Shuey or current occupant. A handful of bills. West Penn Power. Columbia Gas. Verizon Mobile.

Bingo.

CHAPTER 38

Bypass Motors specialized in pre-owned cars. Did a thriving business by offering the best deals in town. It was almost like they didn't care if they made a profit. Mike Mannarino learned as a young man a car dealership that handled a high volume of used cars and service could account for a lot of cash it might be inconvenient to report in other ways.

Doc strolled through the lot into the small showroom where Bypass kept a handful of luxury cars out of the weather. Mannarino liked to draw an occasional crowd by bringing in a high end car no one in Penns River could afford, but might see a deal they liked on a Chevy while they were checking out the Bentley. Or the Maybach. Had a Lamborghini in there a couple of years ago. Sat around for a few weeks before it was "sold," probably to another dealer. The high-end cars brought buyers from upscale neighborhoods the other side of Pittsburgh and as far away as Buffalo, Cleveland, and Youngstown. Made everything look shinier for suspicious types in law enforcement.

A salesman intercepted Doc in the showroom. Doc kept walking, said he wanted to see the boss. Salesman cut him off. Mr. Mannarino's with a customer. Doc stepped back, put his arms akimbo so the salesman could see the badge and gun on his belt. Asked if he should announce himself to the other customers. Turned out Mr. Mannarino wasn't as busy as the salesman originally thought.

Mannarino stood when Doc came in, dismissed the salesman. "Detective Dougherty. We don't see you here much."

"You bragging or complaining?"

"Little of both, maybe. We can always use new business..."

"But too much of my kind of business might drive away some of your other customers. I understand. What I'm here for today is sort of unofficial."

"Have a seat. How unofficial?"

Doc sat, crossed his left ankle over his right knee. Watched himself pick a piece of lint from his slacks as he said, "Guy named David Frantz was pulled out of a vacant townhouse on Fourth Avenue a few days ago. I hear he worked for you."

"I knew him. I wouldn't say he worked for me."

"You wouldn't say he worked for you, or he didn't?" Doc flicked the lint onto the carpet and gave Mannarino his attention. "Which?"

Mannarino drummed his fingers on the desk. "How unofficial are we?"

"The Frantz homicide is official as hell. As far as what we're talking about now, I'm not here."

Mannarino drummed some more. "Frantz was freelance. He never worked for me directly."

"But if you told Buddy Elba or Stretch Dolewicz to do something and they needed a body, they might call him in." Mannarino's gesture and expression didn't disagree. "And you'd collect the tax on any jobs he pulled on his own." Mannarino made another noncommittal gesture.

Doc let his gaze drift out the window and across the lot. "We don't get much heavy action here in town. I guess you know we appreciate that."

"*I* appreciate that. My kids live here, go to school here."

"I understand, but you're much more civic minded than most about keeping things that way. How'd this Frantz business get past you?"

"I don't know, but I'd like to. Look, Frantz thought he was big time. He could do good work when he remembered to stay within himself. He had trouble doing that. What I'm saying is, Dave Frantz always had something going. Finding him down in Tootsie Roll City makes me wonder what it was."

"You think Frantz was looking to do some drug business?"

"I hope not, but that's sure how it looks. If he was, good riddance."

"What if he wasn't?"

"It's really none of my business."

"Come on, Mike. Don't go all humble on me. You like to know everything goes on here. Like that smash and grab asshole last year, breaking car windows and taking whatever he could reach. I hear he got warned once, then he got his knees broken. No one minds. Except him, probably. I see him hobbling down the street once in a while, pathetic looking jagoff, and I think how much time I would've had to waste just to get him put on probation. I'm good with it, really, but don't look me in the eye and tell me you'd do that to a petty thief and not take any interest in someone who killed a guy you did business with. It insults my intelligence." Mannarino breathed and Doc raised his hand. "Okay. I'll stipulate you don't know anything about broken knees. Just don't expect me to believe you have no interest in what happened to Frantz."

Mannarino exhaled, sat back in his chair. "Can I talk now?"

Doc gestured as though allowing Mannarino to precede him through a doorway. "I take an interest in what happens here, sure I do. People know that. So when something like this happens, sometimes information gets volunteered. I'm telling you straight when I say so far no one has come to me."

"You send anyone out to look?" No answer. "You're telling me you don't know anything about some hopper roughing up two kids down on Fourth Avenue last night? Tried to get them in his car until an old man faced him down with a shotgun. The hopper said he'd be back."

"This is news to me."

"I'll accept that. Here's some more news. The kids were squatting in that vacant the night Frantz got aced. They didn't see it go down, but they saw two people leave, and they got a look at the car. From everything we know, this has nothing to do with you, or any business of yours. No drug involvement we know of. No gang involvement we know of. No one's making a move on you."

"And you're sure about this."

"Sure enough."

"Why are you telling me?"

"Because I want those kids and the old man left alone. They can't hurt you."

"I told you I didn't know anything about that."

"Maybe you didn't send someone down there to squeeze

227

them. I don't know. Sounds a little heavy-handed for you. But I can't believe it just happened. The hopper asked specifically about that night, and there's no reason someone like that would care about some half-assed wiseguy wannabe getting clipped unless he thought you'd want to know. I'm also having a little trouble believing some ghetto hard case thought he'd dig up some dirt just to kiss your ass. You put out the word, and someone acted on it. Maybe not the way you would've liked, but you might've been vague about methods. You're more of a results-oriented guy."

"You know what, Dougherty? Fuck you. You come into my place, a respectable business, and talk to me like that, like I was gonna have some kids kidnapped, and what? Beat them? Torture them? Make them disappear? Kiss my Italian ass, you arrogant mick. Walking around like your shit don't stink because you're a cop in an asshole town that drops a little farther off the map every year. It don't play here. You want to be a civil servant and make people miserable, see if PennDOT will give you a vest and a flag, direct traffic."

"You want me to take a walk through the Service Department of your respectable business and check the parts receipts? Run a few VINs? Get off your high horse with that 'respectable businessman' bullshit. You're a hood, plain and simple. You get a pass here because you keep the worst of it out of town and you have too much suction for us to do much about it even if we wanted to. Just don't kid yourself into thinking you can bake shit in the oven and everyone thinks it's meatloaf."

Doc stood, leaned over Mannarino's desk. Not quite in his face. "Those kids get a pass. The old man, too. You and they have no common interests. *We* will handle this. I don't care who you play golf with or who you pay. I hear those kids have any more trouble, I'll be back. Unofficial, but not nearly as friendly."

Their eyes met. Mannarino reached a cigarette and lighter without looking away. Lit it, blew smoke out the side of his mouth. "You give me that speech every year, or something close. Probably makes you hard. Now either write me a ticket for smoking at work or get the fuck out."

Doc held the look long enough to pretend it was his idea to leave. He'd said what he came to say, and that was all he could ask for. The price he paid for working in a small town.

CHAPTER 39

Doc walked into the Edgecliff Bar and Grill at 4:15. He liked the Edgecliff, a sleepy little joint with two televisions and the last of the old-fashioned bowling machines, where the players rolled palm-sized balls and the pins folded up above the lane. They sold good bar food, people could bring their kids to the restaurant section without fear of offense. Never empty, rarely crowded, reasonably priced, and within walking distance of Doc's townhouse, so he could get an urge for a bacon burger or a beer and salve his conscience by making exercise part of the transaction.

Barb Smith was already there. They'd started meeting for beers after work about once a week lately. Today made twice this week, and it was Barb's day off, so she made the trip from Washington Township just for this. Doc wondered if that meant she was ready to take their relationship—such as it was—to the next level. He'd managed to keep Jillian from fucking him senseless no more than once a week, and only the night before a day off, so he could rest. Their one mid-week event set everyone at work the next day to discussing what Doc had been drinking and whether he was hungover or still drunk. She offered a blowjob in his car after rehearsal one night. He turned it down with an excuse so feeble not even he remembered it the next day, though it was fresh in her mind that weekend.

The Jillian situation—that was how he thought of it now,

a situation—was supposed to be every single man's dream: a hot woman who'd fuck whenever you wanted, as long as you wanted. In practice it could be unnerving. Jillian screwed with an intensity beyond enthusiasm. Beyond abandon, even. Recklessness came to mind when he thought about it, which he tried not to do too often. He'd slept with women before who said they'd do anything; Jillian's definition exceeded their imaginations. He sensed a neediness in her, like some science fiction movie where the alien life form drew sustenance only though a human dick. He saw a *South Park* episode about a succubus and had a dream just short of a nightmare, Jillian descending on him in his sleep and draining his body so thoroughly all his hair withdrew beneath the skin. That dream had a lot to do with turning down the parking lot hummer.

Barb was ninety degrees different. (He'd told Eve Barb was a hundred and eighty degrees different from Jillian. Eve pointed out *she* was a hundred and eighty degrees different from Jillian and Doc dropped the subject.) Not even he was so dense not to realize Barb was interested in him. It was always she who invited him to Happy Hour. He never refused, but never initiated anything because it didn't feel right, asking her out while he was screwing another woman like a jackhammer. He liked Barb, the kind of liking that could step over the line into something more if both wanted it, or if one wanted it and the other wasn't paying attention. She rode a bike over the Western Pennsylvania hills and played tennis and swam, so she had a compact body and a great ass. Those would be enough to attract any man she was interested in, but she had a greater attraction for Doc, one she probably wasn't aware of. She hung a ponytail through the opening in a baseball cap when she came to work or went out for beers. Something about that told Doc that no matter what else a woman was like—hot, overweight, skinny, blonde, brunette, redhead, airhead, rocket scientist— she was fun. Not just fun, "good, wholesome fun," as Eve teased him about it once. Doc never told anyone else but her, thought it was a stupid thing to attract a man to a woman, but there it was.

He caught her eye and started over when someone called out something close to his name.

"Detective Dockery!"

Doc looked toward the voice and saw Marty Cropcho at the bar. Even from thirty feet in dim light, Doc knew he was drunk and had been for a while. He held up a finger to ask Barb to wait and veered in Cropcho's direction.

"How you doing, Mr. Cropcho? I don't think I've seen you in here before."

"I've been in here every day this week looking for you."

Doc caught Denny Sluciak's eye behind the bar. Denny nodded and said, "Been here since one-thirty or so today."

Doc said, "You could have called or come by the station. I'll make time for you."

"I wanted to catch you away from work. Just you and me. So we can talk. Why I waited for you."

"You off work today, Mr. Cropcho?"

"Haven't been to work. My wife died."

"You haven't been to work at all?"

"My wife died. You don't have to go to work when your wife dies. 'Specially not if you find her dead with her head cracked open like a fucking egg."

Doc looked to Denny. "I can't serve him no more, Doc. He ain't safe to drive."

"It's okay. I got him." Denny moved to the far end of the bar. Doc turned back to Cropcho. "You been drinking like this every day?"

"Why? You gonna buy me another milkshake? What're you doing about the son of a bish killed my wife?"

"We got him locked up, Mr. C. He's not going anywhere."

"Locked up. He's locked up. Why the fuck isn't he dead? Give me a drink. Seagram's and a draft."

"You've had enough for today. Maybe some coffee."

Cropcho turned on his stool and fixed Doc with a look far from mournful. "Oh. You're gonna tell me I can't have a drink, but you let that son of a bish kill my wife. Fuck kind of cop are you?"

It wasn't a scene. Yet. Denny came close enough to talk to Doc. "This is getting into my busy time, Doc. Any way we can get him out of here? I mean, I know he's hurting, I know about his wife, but I got customers."

"You know about my wife?" Cropcho extended his right arm to move Doc back, give him a clear view of Denny. "*You* know about my wife? This cop thinks he knows about my wife. Thinks she was fucking around. Thinks she was fucking the son of a bish that killed her. That's what kind of a cop he is. Blames my poor wife and calls her a slut in the same breath."

Doc stood behind Cropcho, turned him on the stool. Put his lips close to Cropcho's ear. "Come on, Mr. Cropcho. Let's get you home."

"I can't go home."

Doc, softly: "I'll give you a ride."

The manufactured intimacy kept Cropcho's voice down. "I don't need a ride because I can't go home. Not now. I should've been home that night. She'd still be there and I could go home. Now she's not there. What would I go home for? She's not there."

"I understand, but you can't stay here. Is there a friend or a relative you can bunk with tonight? I'll take you."

"She's not home." Barely loud enough for Doc to hear now, standing right next to him. "I go home every night and she's not there. I don't want to go home again. She's not home."

"Please, Mr. Cropcho."

"We go to the movies every Saturday night. I don't think we've missed more than one or two Saturday nights since we started going out. She loves movies. When her father died, we went to the movies after the funeral, that night. Saw *Sideways* because she heard it was funny and wanted to laugh. Cried all the way through it. Saw *Braveheart* the first time we went out. First date was dinner at Arthur's and *Braveheart*." Cropcho turned to face Doc. "If I go home, she won't be there. She was home and I wasn't. Now if I go home she won't be."

"I know, Mr. Cropcho. Where can I take you?"

"Doesn't matter. She's not home. Can I have one more drink, please? I'll be good. I won't yell anymore."

"Can we get some coffee here, Denny?" A cup was there before Cropcho could complain. Doc gave him a light frisk, found his cell phone. Looked through the contacts until he found Mom and Dad. The number was local. Doc called and Marty Cropcho's father came twenty minutes later to collect him. His parents had been looking for him for almost a week. Called his work, drove by the house. Steve Cropcho shook Doc's hand and thanked him for calling and for taking care of his boy. Said his mother would get some food in him and move some things off the bed so he could sleep in the room he grew up in.

Marty Cropcho listened to his father and Doc talk about him like he wasn't there. Didn't say a word until Steve Cropcho took him by the wrist and said it was time to go home.

"Carol's not home, Dad."

"I know, Marty. Let's go and see who else is."

CHAPTER 40

Doc followed the Cropchos outside and helped Steve get his son into the car. It was pushing five o'clock when he carried two beers over to Barb's table.

"That's the husband, isn't? Of the woman who was killed up on Argonne Drive."

"Yeah, that's him. I talked to him when we busted Widmer and he seemed fine. Today he said he hasn't been back to work."

Barb looked toward the door like Cropcho was still standing there. "I can't imagine what it must be like for him. He found her, didn't he?"

"Yeah. Had to be a pisser. Can we talk about something else? I feel bad for the guy, but we've done what we can. The guy that killed her is locked up. We're not grief counselors."

They nursed their beers in silence, Doc irritated that Cropcho had killed his good mood. Watched *Around the Horn* on ESPN with the sound off, the best way to enjoy it.

Barb said, "Anything new on our body?"

Doc finished a swallow of beer. "Nope. No progress, anyway. There was some trouble down there the other night." He told her about Wilver's and David's confrontation, Jefferson West saving them with a shotgun.

"I worry about those two all the time," she said when he finished.

"They'll be all right now. I talked to Mike Mannarino.

He'll put the word out to leave them alone."

"Who's Mike Mannarino?" She fit in so well and so quickly, Doc forgot how new Barb was.

"You want another beer?" Barb nodded and Mike signaled for the waitress. "Mike Mannarino is, we think, the boss of Pittsburgh. There's not much of a family here now, three, maybe four made guys. It's mostly bookmaking, juice loans, and street tax now. You know, taking a piece of all the other crooks' action when they pull a job? Mike likes to act old school, so he's not into drugs officially, but rumor has it he's the connect for the gangs downtown. Claims his grandfather was a big shooter, and a couple of Mannarinos pulled a lot of weight here fifty years ago, but we have no evidence he's more than distantly related."

"Why do you think he'll keep the boys safe?"

"Like I said, Mike thinks he's old school. Acts the whole 'man of respect' routine. Owns a business here in town, makes sure he's seen there working every day. You know Bypass Motors, out on 56?"

"Shit! I almost bought a car there."

"That's Mike. How come you didn't buy it? He usually beats everyone's price."

"He did, but the CarFax information looked sketchy, so I passed."

"Lot of things sketchy about that business." The waitress came with fresh beer. Doc waited until she finished, thanked her. "Anyway, Mike likes to play Godfather. He lives in The River, his kids go to school here, so he makes a big deal about not wanting any crime. Someone steps out of line, he warns them. Once. Next time they get jacked up."

"He kills them?"

"Not anymore, not so far as we know. Time was, back in the fifties, when the real Mannarinos were around, you fucked up here in town and you wound up dead on the front steps of the old Bachelor's Club. Mike's more forgiving. Break your knees, catch you a good beating, maybe use you as a backstop."

"Huh?"

"Mike was a hell of a baseball pitcher in his day. He ties guys down and throws baseballs at them sometimes to show who's boss." Barb stared like she didn't believe him. "Of course, if he was to kill someone, the body wouldn't be left here. That's how we figure he didn't do Frantz."

"I thought this was a nice quiet town."

"It is, thanks to Mike. He likes to know everything that goes on here, so it made sense he'd know who roughed our boys up, or he'd be able to find out. I told him more or less what they saw, and how it all pointed away from him, and I told him I wanted them left alone. He draws a lot of water here in town, but he can't stand too much daylight, so I let him know I was willing to squeeze him on this."

"Why don't we squeeze him anyway? You know, we're the police."

Doc shook his head, swallowed. "Too much pull. Remember, he's a respectable businessman. No one like a councilman or the mayor will socialize with him publicly, but he sponsors ball teams, has billboards at the ice rink and softball fields. He practically owns the high school booster club. A pillar of the community. Don't be surprised if Stush calls me in tomorrow or the next day, wants to know why I was screwing with Mike Mannarino."

"You think that'll be enough? To keep the boys safe, I mean."

"Should be. I mean, they're boys. Boys get into trouble on their own. I don't think they'll have any more trouble over what they saw that night."

"I don't know. Someone out there can go away for life if either of those kids identifies him. The word's out in the neighborhood. I can't believe the killer won't go back looking for them."

"What would you like me to do? Call Family Services?"

"They're a lot better suited to take care of this than Mr. West is."

"Family Services has two choices. They can put them in another foster home, which they won't do because Wilver and David already walked away from one. This time they'll insist on more structure. That means a group home. Is that where you want them? A group home?"

"It's just until their mother gets out."

"Ah, their mother. She'll walk out of enforced rehab, whisk them away like Mary Poppins and everything will be like on the Cosby Show. Damn, Barb, their mother is Choice Three. You depend on her if there's no other option."

"You don't think she'll get them back automatically?"

"I gave up guessing what Family Court will do a long time ago." He finished his beer, pushed the empty glass where the waitress could see it. "Family Services gets a bad rap. People read how these kids that go through the system are screwed up and right away they blame the government. These families were abominations before DFS ever heard of them."

"Didn't you tell me once you couldn't depend on the system to save anyone? You said people had to do it themselves. Who else besides their mother can do that?"

"Jeff West."

"Come on, Doc. He's not going to adopt them."

"He doesn't have to. He sets an example until she gets out. Wilver's on the verge of getting it. He just needs a role model. West can do that. Hell, he's dying for the opportunity. After that, Wilver should be able to tell when his mom's fucking up and either take care of it, or know where to go for help. Like to West. Or me."

The waitress picked up Doc's empty. Looked to Barb, who shook her head, her glass half full. Or half empty.

"Doc?" Caught him watching *Pardon the Interruption* now, Kornheiser and Wilbon holding up sticks with faces on them. A funny bit with sound. "Doc. What if something happens? What if you're wrong?"

Doc gave her his full attention. "I understand you're worried. I don't want to give you the idea I'm not, or that I don't care. It was my call. I'll take the hit if it goes bad."

Barb had the glass almost to her lips, slammed it down harder than she meant to. A few drops sloshed over the side. "No, you won't. They will. Wilver and David. They're who's at risk here."

"West will go to the wall for them. He proved the other night he's up to it."

"Against one guy who wasn't ready for him. What about next time? And what about you if it happens? I'm scared for them, but I'm worried about you and your conscience. You say you're comfortable with your decision, and I'm sure you are. I'm also sure it'll kill you if anything happens to those kids."

She *was* worried. It showed on her face and in her voice.

Hell, it showed in her shoulders, the way she leaned forward when she talked about his conscience. *She* was concerned about *his* conscience. Jillian was concerned about his dick. More than just that, to be fair, but she was concerned about how Doc viewed *her*, and what it meant for *her*. Barb was thinking not just about him, but of him.

Barb said, "Look at that Cropcho guy. He'll never be the same. Never."

"That's different. He found his wife's body. He probably wouldn't have recognized her if anyone else could've been there, the way her face was beat in."

"But he feels responsible, doesn't he? I couldn't hear him, but I bet he does."

"Yeah, he does. He shouldn't, but he does."

"So will you."

She had him. It had been his call, even though West volunteered. Damn right he'd feel responsible. And he'd never be able to undo it.

The waitress brought his fresh beer and he inhaled half of it. Wiped any foam that might be around his lip. Looked toward the television without seeing it.

"We're too far down the road now. We have to play it out. I'll talk to Eye Chart about keeping a car handy. Maybe I'll talk to West. See if he wants me to stay over until this is done."

It felt like putting Band-Aids on a surgical incision. He looked at Barb and knew she felt the same. She didn't say anything, then steered the conversation in a different direction until both their glasses were empty and she said she needed to run an errand before it got late. Doc went home, put three bottles of water and two Hershey bars in an insulated bag. Grabbed a pillow on his way out and parked on Fourth Avenue until false dawn.

CHAPTER 41

It's not like the movies. Private investigators aren't cops. They don't have the authority to break and enter, take people into custody, or shoot them. They do have access to resources beyond anything another private citizen can imagine. For an annual fee and a case number to prove legitimacy, a PI can call up the make, model, and license number of every car registered to addresses on a specific block, and adjacent blocks. The average jerk watching CSI can't imagine why anyone would want this information. The average CSI-watching jerk also doesn't realize most cases are still closed with eyes and ears, feet on the street and asses in car seats. It's good to know which cars belong and which don't on a stakeout. Or a surveillance, to use the politically correct term. Does the car parked on the street in front of the subject's house belong there? Check the list. The car doesn't belong to anyone in the house, but it is registered to the teenage son of the guy three doors down and parking's tight in this neighborhood. Another car across the street doesn't match any addresses. It could be someone parked on the wrong block because parking's tight there, too. Or it could be someone visiting another house, doesn't even know your subject. It's still worth writing down and checking when you get back to the office. A technologically savvy PI can even pop open a laptop in the car and use a wireless card to hit the database without so much as shifting his weight. Get the owner's name, address, phone number, educational, military, and criminal history while he's in there selling insurance or fixing a shower diverter or screwing the lady of the house. This information may not be of any use until the PI sees which house the owner comes out of; then it could be exactly what he's been waiting for.

Phone numbers are pretty much the same. Used to be, anyone could enter a phone number into the Google—remember the dashes—and get a reverse directory search. People caught wise to that and unlisted numbers became more common. Cell and internet phones don't show up. These changes preserve people's privacy and keep the average stalker working at the small appliance repair place from finding out where Fanny Firmtits lives so he can't go over and pay her more attention than she wants after she leaves him her callback number and a smile he mistakes for interest.

PIs have a service for that, too. Pay the fee, login, and reverse directory searches are available for cell, internet, and unlisted numbers. That's how Daniel Rollison spent a rainy Sunday while most of Western Pennsylvania watched the Steelers sneak away with a 17-13 victory over San Diego, reading David Frantz's Verizon bill like it was a Dead Sea Scroll.

He didn't expect much. People who discuss criminal business over cell phones are better known to the general public as convicts. Cells are easy to monitor with the right equipment. The location can be triangulated to within fifty yards or less, depending on tower locations and strength of signal. Doesn't matter if the phone's in use; if it's turned on, it's trackable. Use a GPS phone and someone good enough can tell not just that you're in Fat Jimmy's Lounge, but you're probably taking a leak, because you're in the men's room and only the truly desperate sit on Fat Jimmy's toilet seats.

Rollison didn't need that much technology. He didn't even need the PEN register or DNRs from Frantz's home phone, which was good, because Frantz didn't have one. All he had was the cell, and cell phone companies are considerate enough to provide not just a list of every number called from your phone, but every number that called in to it.

Frantz made a lot of calls. Verizon employees sending their kids to private schools might have to reconsider, having lost him as a customer. Two hundred seventy-two calls out, a hundred ninety-eight in during a thirty-day period. The overwhelming majority of calls were under five minutes; about a quarter were less than one. Not surprising. Don't stay on the phone too long. Call to set up a meeting, or coordinate a call to and from different numbers. A good criminal knew the location of every pay phone within ten miles and cursed every time one was taken out.

Rollison worked with his Oxford cloth sleeves rolled up. A red knit sweater vest kept the chill of the sixty-eight degree house off him. Time was he'd walk around in his underwear in this temperature. His comfort range narrowed as he aged, and sixty-eight wasn't in it anymore. Pete Townshend sang about teenage wasteland on the stereo, turned down low. Rollison wasn't listening; he played the CD for background noise. He'd spent too many nights, cold and otherwise, trying to filter out the sound of his own breathing, listening for anything and everything. Routine settling of the house could wake him from a sound sleep.

He didn't have to do such tedious work himself. He'd

worked for a wife on a child custody case, found enough on her husband to keep him from seeing his kids for the rest of this life and the next. Hubby could only afford to pay enough to suppress the evidence, not destroy it. Rollison reminded him of the outstanding debt when he needed something, teased him with a sample when necessary. Still, there was only so much water in any well, and the kids would soon be of an age where it wouldn't matter anymore. Rollison knew the exact day his hold would end and he'd need someone else. He could pay for it—there was always someone who'd take money—but he'd be screwed if the new contact got cold feet. Always better to have someone to squeeze.

A lot of the calls were to and from Tom Widmer, which saved time. More time was saved by focusing on numbers that appeared after Carol Cropcho died. Whoever Frantz had worked with to set Widmer up would still be in touch.

He found the number that didn't fit on the third day after the murder. A 412 number the search showed as belonging to Thomas Widmer, 2874 Meadow Gold Drive, Penns River PA. It wasn't the house phone; that was 724, like the rest of Penns River. Tom's cell was 412—Pittsburgh—but that number was already accounted for.

Had to be Marian.

CHAPTER 42

Forensics were a bust.

The bullet pulled out of David Frantz's head was too damaged for a ballistics test. The other went through and through far enough to pierce the drywall and smack into a stud dead center. Neuschwander dug it out but couldn't do anything with it.

At least forty-six unique prints from no fewer than eleven people were recovered from the death room alone. Fourteen belonged to either Wilver or David Faison. Most—maybe all—of the rest could belong to the former residents. Or to a realtor. A possible buyer. Workman. The computer couldn't match them to any known record. Didn't mean the killers didn't leave prints, but they'd have to be caught to be matched.

Doc and Grabek sat in their office eating the doughnuts Stush brought in once a week, said it was his way of keeping tradition alive. Each of them had one of David Frantz's phone bills. His address book and e-mail directories were dead ends. Prints in his apartment belonged to him and possibly two other people, one of whom was probably a woman. The woman's prints didn't match any found at the crime scene.

Frantz had no landline; did all his talking on a cell. The one they needed was the most recent. As usual, the phone company took its sweet time processing the court order and the Penns River postmaster insisted on a federal warrant to hand over the mail.

"We should just take the mail out of the box," Grabek said. "We have the key."

"Uh-uh," Doc said. "I do not need Harriger crawling up my asshole again. He wants to go by the numbers, we go by the numbers." Grabek had made the mistake of floating his idea of simply taking the mail while the warrant was pending past the Deputy Chief while memories of the Widmer interrogation were still fresh. Much as it pained him to admit it, Doc saw Harriger's point: anything they learned as a result of reading the bill would be tainted if a judge ruled the seizure out of order. They'd get it soon enough. What bothered him was Harriger's attitude when he gave Grabek the word. He seemed less interested in protecting subsequent prosecutions than in letting the investigation linger, and the only reason to drag out the investigation was to make Stush look bad.

Neuschwander came in and Doc said, "The warrant doesn't really matter. This is Neuschwander's fault. Gil Grissom on *CSI* would've had these phone records waiting here by the time I got back from the crime scene."

"Grissom doesn't need phone records," Neuschwander said. "He can tell from the fingerprints on the phone what the last number dialed was."

"Yeah, and get DNA from the spit on the mouthpiece. How come you're not that good?"

"You're just jealous because you think Grissom gets to bone Willows and you don't."

Doc set down the bill he was reading. "Really? You think Grissom was doing Willows? I thought they had this professsional and platonic thing going."

"You assume because you never get laid that no one else does," Grabek said. "There's no way Grissom and Willows don't get together for an occasional grind."

"That makes no sense," Doc said. "Why would he ever leave the show?"

Grabek looked at Neuschwander over his reading glasses. "Tell him."

Neuschwander sat on the edge of Doc's desk, dangled one leg. "It's a television show, Doc. Gil Grissom didn't really quit, William Peterson did. He's not on the show anymore, so Grissom can't be, either. And, before you ask, let's not even discuss if Peterson and that Marg Helgenwhatever had anything going. Even if they did, that's real life. They could still get together if he worked there or not."

"Wait a minute," Doc said. "Your name is Neuschwander and you can't pronounce Helgenberger?"

"I don't need to be able to pronounce it. I'm not hot for her. Let it go. She's too old for you, anyway. She must be, like fifty. What are you? Thirty-three? Thirty-four?"

"I'm thirty-seven, and it doesn't matter. I thought she was hot on *China Beach*."

"She was a lot younger then."

"So was I."

Neuschwander did a quick calculation. "You in high school then?"

"Yeah. So?"

"She played a hooker on *China Beach*. All teenage boys think hookers are hot, because they just figured out the only thing you need to get some is cash. You're still getting over your adolescent infatuation with the idea that sex can be available at any time and projecting onto her."

"And you're full of shit. What did you come in here for, anyway?"

"I wondered when one of you ace detectives would ask about that. Your report's done."

"Which one? We only have about a dozen pending."

"Dark blue Beemers sold in the past two months." Neuschwander held up an envelope.

Doc looked toward Grabek, who didn't look up. "Anything interesting?"

"How would I know? I'm just the jagoff gathers the evidence. I have no idea how things fit together. That's your job."

"Give me the goddamn envelope," Doc said. Neuschwander smirked, held it out so he'd would have to reach.

Doc scanned down the list. Stopped when he got to a line highlighted in yellow. "I thought you said you didn't look at this."

"Not in detail like you would. I just kind of skipped down to see if anything jumped out at me. Did I do good?" God, he was frustrating when he got like this.

"I don't want to jump to any conclusions. Hey, Willie." Grabek typed something into his computer, read the screen. A tight smile creased his face, not far enough to show teeth. He rocked back in his chair, clasped his hands on top of his head. His reading glasses fell onto his chest, hanging by the chain. "Does it interest you that Marian Widmer bought a car matching the description of the one Wilver Faison saw the night David Frantz was shot?"

"Depends," Grabek said. "Does it interest you that Frantz made and received calls to a number on Tom Widmer's account that wasn't Widmer's phone?"

"Marian's?"

"Unless you can think of someone else who'd have a phone on Widmer's account."

"His kids?" Neuschwander said.

"Why would Frantz call Widmer's kids?" Doc said.

"That wasn't the question. You asked who else might have a phone on Widmer's account."

Doc and Grabek exchanged glances, shifted their chairs to face each other, excluding Neuschwander. Doc said, "What would David Frantz and Marian Widmer have to talk about? She didn't call him on the day he got clipped, did she? That would be too much to ask."

"We don't have that bill yet."

They sat. Doc started thinking out loud. "Okay, what *do* we know? A car with T plates was seen driving away from the vacant on Fourth. It just happens to match the descripttion of Marian Widmer's new car, which also has T plates. A woman was seen getting into it."

"With a man," Neuschwander said.

"With a man we know not to be David Frantz because he's in the living room dead by this time." A pause. Neuschwander nodded. Grabek sat stone-faced. He never thought out loud, acted like he knew everything all along and had been waiting for everyone else to catch up. "Leads me to believe she was there when he got aced."

Grabek deigned to join the conversation. "Prove it."

"I don't have to yet. I'm just thinking. Now I'm going to think about why Marian Widmer and David Frantz talk on the phone. How often?"

"Three-four times a week, sometimes more than once a day," Grabek said.

"For how long?"

"Now that I know the number, I been looking back through. It's at least six months."

"What the hell would Marian Widmer and David Frantz have to talk about that often for six months?"

"Fucking, probably," Neuschwander said. "I've seen her. She's hot. If Frantz was alive I'd shake his hand."

"I can see why he'd fuck her. Why would she fuck him? He's a low-life. She wouldn't run in his circles."

"Does the autopsy say anything about the size of his johnson?"

"Forget about his johnson." Grabek sat up, acted like he was finally interested. "This isn't the only case we have where Marian Widmer figures in. Her husband's locked up next door for killing Carol Cropcho. We've been assuming he killed her over an affair gone bad. What if his wife knew about it?"

Silence while Doc and Neuschwander tried to get their heads around it.

Neuschwander said, "I don't see the connection. If Widmer's wife knew and felt like doing something about it, she'd of killed one of them. We know Widmer killed the Cropcho woman, so where's the connection?"

"We know Widmer killed her based on the evidence we have now, right?" Grabek said.

"Right."

"We can't let that give us tunnel vision. We had two murders within a couple of weeks in a town that averages maybe a homicide and a half a year. One person has connections to both. That's a hell of a coincidence."

Neuschwander took his time forming the words. "But we don't know for sure that's her at the Frantz hit."

"Don't worry so much about what we can prove. We're not that far yet. Look." Grabek stood, walked to a dry erase board on the room's longest wall. Erased the lunch orders from a previous day and drew a circle. "You've seen Venn diagrams, right? Okay, this circle is everything we know about the Cropcho killing. That's a dead bang case. We're not worried about it."

He drew another circle. Smaller, overlapping a tiny part of the original. "Marian Widmer's married to Carol Cropcho's killer. We don't know if she had anything to do with it. Hell, we have no reason to think she has anything to do with it. But there's a relationship there."

Doc stared at the board deep in thought. Neuschwander said, "You could draw that circle for everyone Widmer knows. Friends, family, people he works with. Anyone."

"Okay, I will." Grabek drew similar circles around the perimeter of the original. All overlapped it by the same amount as Marian's circle. None of the new circles overlapped with each other. "Now, some of these would overlap each other if we were doing this right. His family's circles would, his co-workers' would, some of his friends'.

"*But.*" Grabek drew another large circle slightly overlapping both Marian's and the original. "None have them have any known connection to this other homicide. She does, even if it's only coincidental."

Neuschwander pointed to the diagram. "What's the connection between the Cropcho and Frantz homicides?"

Doc said, "Proximity," and walked to the board. "Time

and place both. This is a small town. Not a lot of murders. Now we have two within a couple of weeks only a few miles apart. They're connected by time and place."

Neuschwander's hand wavered, like he was looking for something specific to point to. "It's thin."

"What do we have on Frantz?" Grabek said. "Shit. You know it and I know it."

Doc softened his voice. "Noosh, you're stuck on the hard evidence, and we're not getting anywhere with it. Willie's saying there might be something we don't have, but it's not a great leap of logic to suppose it's there. Remember that article you showed me about dark matter? How they can't see it, can't measure it, can't prove it's there, but evidence from how planets and stars and light moves says there must be something else we can't see?"

"Dark matter?" Grabek said.

"Okay. Yeah." Neuschwander's eyes roamed across the diagram. "I think I see what you're getting at. Even if you're wrong, it's not like working on this will keep us from following up any hot leads."

Doc turned to Grabek. "What next?"

"Let's go talk to her."

"Just like that." The Widmer interrogation sprang to mind. "We don't have enough to pin her down to anything. We might just spook her."

"Her husband is charged with killing someone, and the best reason we can come up with is he was cheating on her. I think we've waited way too long to have this chat. Once we get there—well, conversations drift. Who knows what we'll talk about?"

Doc checked Neuschwander, who looked like he'd had his picture taken and still saw spots. Turned back to Grabek. "What the hell. I'll drive."

CHAPTER 43

The Widmer woman was hot, no question. A different kind of hot than Chastity, who was slutty hot and twenty years younger, still learning how to leverage the effect she had on men. Marian Widmer appealed to a more refined taste. A twenty-year-old kid wouldn't see past the stray line or sag. She was vintage for a man with an appreciation of experience and class, even if it was all external.

Rollison followed Marian through the house to the living room. She gave him the full treatment, or as much as she could wearing jeans and a sweatshirt. The jeans were cut for someone much younger, though women her age still tried unsuccessfully to wear them. Marian Widmer got away with it better than most. Getting away with it wasn't the same as belonging in them.

He hadn't tried anything cute to get in. Identified himself as a private investigator, said he was looking into the David Frantz homicide, waited for her to tell him she never heard of Frantz. She handled it better than expected. Frantz? Wasn't he on the news? The man killed in the Allegheny Estates a while ago? She didn't know him, though. Never met him. Then Rollison asked why she'd been talking with him on the phone for over a year—once he found the connection he decided to squeeze his contact at the phone company after all. Her face didn't fall, her smile hardly changed. Her eyes got hard as a hammer and she invited him in to watch her ass as she led the way to the living room.

She offered him a glass of wine and he accepted. Then she excused herself to go to the bathroom, came back wearing a blouse fitted like a man's shirt, three buttons undone. Sat barefoot on the couch, one leg tucked under her. Took a sip of wine. "What makes you say I talked to this Frantz person for over a year?"

Rollison said, "Honesty" just to see what she'd do and got no reaction. "I read his phone bill. Your number comes up a lot."

"And you came by his phone bill...?"

"I took it out of his mailbox a week after he died."

She looked at him over the wine glass through hooded eyes. He'd seen it before, deciding whether to play him soft or hard. "What is it about our phone chats that interests you?" she said.

"You're talking about phone chats you denied having a minute ago."

"I never said we didn't talk on the phone."

Rollison took a sip, held eye contact. "You never heard of him until you saw him on the news, dead, but you talked to him on the phone. You know it's only a matter of time before the police come. They're not going to buy that story, either."

"Let them come. What I can tell them is embarrassing, mildly, but not criminal."

"What would that be?"

"Why do you care, Mr. Rollison? I see no reason to tell you anything."

"Okay, then, think of me as a friend of the family, someone to try your story out on. Get an opinion how it might play with the police."

Marian turned the eyes up a notch, leaned forward to place her wine glass on the coffee table. "It's the kind of thing I wouldn't want to get out ordinarily, but, I don't suppose people would judge me too harshly now that they know about my husband. Are you familiar with phone dating?"

"You mean phone sex?"

"That's usually what it evolves into. I met David Frantz on a web site that caters to Pittsburgh area people who are looking for a little excitement but don't want to run the risk, or carry the guilt, of actually cheating. We had phone sex. Quite good phone sex. We never actually met, not face-to-face. So I wasn't lying when I said I never met him."

"What's the name of the site?"

"Discretion. It's actually www dot discretion something dot com. I don't remember exactly."

Rollison swirled the last swallow of wine around the bottom of his glass, then downed it. He liked to play a scene as much as the next guy. "That's very good, Mrs. Widmer. I'm sure the site checks out. I'm also sure when the police take a look you'll have a profile there. You're too smart and careful not to have taken care of it. There's still a hole in your story."

"What's that?"

"The police don't know David Frantz was passing himself off as Marty Cropcho to your husband. Only I know that."

She didn't handle that news nearly as well. The wine sloshed around the glass as she raised it. Redness on her cheeks and the hollows of her throat. Her voice lost some of its resonance. "And how do you know that?"

Rollison made her wait. "He told me. He doesn't know it was Frantz, of course. He just knows he was set up. He told me where to look and I figured out Frantz was the one."

"You sound very sure."

"If I wasn't before, I am now. Your poker face needs work."

That brought a different shade of red to her cheeks. "What do you want?"

"What are you offering?"

"I can't fuck you right now. The kids will be home from school soon."

The suggestion of a smile creased his face. He exhaled once through his nose, sharply. An unfunny laugh. "I had something more tangible in mind, Mrs. Widmer. That was an opportunity to name an amount, not embarrass yourself."

Her face had used its allotment of heat. Now it came through her eyes with a concentration that might have unsettled him twenty years ago. "You sound like you have everything figured out. What do you suggest?"

"How much do you think you're taking him for?" Marian's eyes got big and she drew back. "Have you spoken to a lawyer yet? I didn't think so. You couldn't afford to appear to be ahead of the game. Have you ever studied law?"

Her glare told him she considered it a rhetorical question, even if he didn't. "Me, either. I spend enough time around lawyers that I pick up what I need. If he's convicted of first degree murder, the jury has to decide between the death penalty and life without parole. There are aggravating circumstances and mitigating circumstances they have to consider, but they have to vote one way or the other: life or death. If he goes down for first degree, you can divorce him and probably get everything."

"You said 'if.' After what he did, what else could they convict him of?"

"Juries are unpredictable. Even if they think he's guilty, they might not want to have to decide whether he lives or dies. Then they'll take the easy way out and convict him of second degree. Let the judge sentence him. Thirty to life, or something like that. Could be out in ten."

"How could any rational person not call what he did first degree murder? It wasn't like he just happened to be there and something came up and things got out of hand. He went there to kill her. Everyone says so. What's the term? Premeditated?"

"No question, but think about this: what if the jury had reason to believe he was duped into killing her? He testifies about how he was up against it and not thinking straight and they can't help but see he's not too bright. He's greedy and venal and no one wants him anywhere near their daughter, but he's never done anything remotely like this before." He held up one hand. "Don't say it. The beating stories won't hold up. His lawyer will prove Frantz wasn't who your husband thought he was, and he knew him long before your husband met him. I don't know if a grand jury would indict you on that, and I don't see any way it establishes the kind of reasonable doubt your husband needs to get off. It could be enough for a jury to cut him a break. Or for a prosecutor to cut a deal if he thought you could be brought into it. *If* anyone had evidence he'd been played. Right now I'm the only one who has it. If only I have all the dots, no one else can connect them, and that's worth something."

Rollison watched the color drain from Marian's face like snow melting in a microwave. "Relax. I don't want it all. You'll still do well if he gets death or mandatory life. I'll settle for half of what you get above and beyond fifty percent. So long as the number has at least six figures."

"Or what?"

"I take the dots to the police. It'll be tricky, working for his lawyer and all. Privileged information. I'll find a way."

"You won't give it to the fat bastard Flaherty?"

"Why waste it? It won't do him any good. There's no question your husband's going down, it's only a matter of for how long. This information incriminates you. Accessory, murder for hire. Maybe accessory to murder for hire. The DA will think of something."

Marian finished her wine. Recovering already. "Do you have any idea how much you're talking about?"

"Do you?"

A beat. "Not precisely."

"Okay, then. You're not going to cheat me."

"You trust me?"

"Absolutely. You can't afford to let me feel slighted and go to the police anyway. It might cost my license, maybe even an extortion charge I can probably beat. You'll go away forever."

"You're a disgusting man."

"I may be, but I didn't trick anyone into killing an innocent woman just so I could take his money. How did you pick her, anyway?"

"Get out."

"I understand. You need some time to think about this."

"Get out!"

"Don't take too long. Two or three days, no more. The clock's running now."

She threw her wine glass at him. It missed, shattered against the wall. *"Get the fuck out of my house!"*

Rollison set down his glass. Turned and took his time moving for the door. Marian Widmer stood to hurry him along. He stopped at the threshold into the kitchen so suddenly she bumped into him.

He pointed to the broken glass near the corner. "You should take care of that. You don't want the kids to get cut up."

He felt her quivering behind him, her body tight as a bow string. He led her through the kitchen and stepped onto the front porch. She stayed in the doorway.

"I understand getting the money will take time, but I want an answer in three days, before things move too far along with the police. We can work out a payment plan." He looked her up and down. The tops of her breasts were dappled with color and her chest swelled with suppressed rage. "If you're still interested in giving some away, I'd call it interest."

Marian brought her right hand up from her hip and stepped into the slap. Rollison half expected it, still rocked his head back. He reached into his shirt pocket and took a card. Tucked it into the breast pocket of her shirt.

"I'll give you credit. You've got more balls than the one they have locked up."

CHAPTER 44

Grabek touched Doc on the arm before he could turn into the Widmer driveway, pointed to the Lincoln Town Car. "She has company," he said. "We don't want to disturb her."

Doc drove past, parked fifty yards up the street, rolled down the windows halfway and killed the engine. Semi-rural area, no sidewalks, four or five houses per mile of road. Anyone who didn't look too closely might think the car was empty, assume someone was hunting rabbits in the wooded area behind. Hunting illegal in the city limits but there were unofficial areas where it was tolerated if only shotguns were used.

They sat for twenty minutes. Sun halfway to the horizon, air getting cooler as a breeze picked up from the woods. "Put my window up a little, would you?" Grabek said. "Draft is going down my collar." Doc keyed the ignition without starting the car, put up the passenger window.

Each sat in his own way. Grabek looked half asleep nestled in against his door. Doc rested one elbow on the center storage console, tapped the steering wheel with an index finger. Both sat up with movements smooth as wax being extruded into a mold when the Widmers' storm door opened.

A man about Grabek's age came out, stopped on the porch and turned around. Marian Widmer stayed in the doorway. "You recognize this guy?" Doc said.

"Uh-uh. She's pissed about something, though. Look at her."

The man said something and Marian slapped him. Hard. The detectives exchanged sidelong glances. "You think we've come at a bad time?" Doc said.

"Maybe we should make sure everything's okay."

The man offered something to Marian. She shook her head and he slid it into her shirt's breast pocket. Walked to the Town Car and started it.

Doc tapped the glove box door. "Field glasses inside." Grabek opened the compartment, handed him small pair of binoculars. "Pennsylvania plate KSD-1147." Grabek made a note.

Marian Widmer slammed the door at least as hard as she'd slapped whoever it was. Doc pulled into the Widmer driveway less than a minute after the Town Car drove off. "You lead. She already knows you from court. I'll lay back in case it's to our benefit to have one less familiar face."

Grabek nodded and went first up the stairs to the porch. Rang once with no answer. He'd raised his hand to ring again when the door flew open.

"What the *fuck* do you want now?" Her right hand was cocked at the wrist.

"Mrs. Widmer? Marian Widmer?" Grabek held up his badge. "I'm Detective Grabek. This is Detective Dougherty, Penns River police. May we come in? It won't take long."

"Police?" She looked at her hand as though surprised at where it was, relaxed after a few seconds. "I'm sorry. You're with the police? What's this about?"

"About your husband, ma'am. We have some questions

we'd like to ask, clear up a few things. Do you mind?"

The tension left her so fast Doc thought she might fall. "No. No, of course not. Please come in." She stepped aside and offered seats at the breakfast nook table.

The signs of a recent flush lingered on her face and neck. The mannish shirt had no bra under it. "I'm sorry, but the kids will be home from school soon, so I don't have a lot of time. I'll be happy to help if I can."

"Is everything all right?" Grabek said. "You seemed a little, uh, agitated when you answered the door."

"I'm sorry about that. Some salesmen can't take no for an answer."

"None of our business, ma'am. You know to give us a call if he hassles you. A man's got to earn a living, but there's a line. I also appreciate the situation you're in. A woman in your position doesn't need any extra harassment."

"In my position?"

"Where your husband's put you. I guess you're getting a lot of attention you could live without."

"Only for the first few days. A handful of cars drove by and slowed down. I imagined the people inside, pointing to the killer's house."

"Was the press bad?"

She shook her head. "I referred them to my attorney and he asked them to respect my privacy."

"Did they?"

She smiled tightly. "We were—what's the term?—'overtaken by other events.' There is always someone willing to talk to a reporter, even if they don't know what they're talking about. I'm just happy to be left alone."

"Has someone been spreading bad information?"

"You know, rumors. I'm a news junkie. Cable news is always on, and I get half a dozen internet feeds. I never thought I'd be nostalgic for the days when all we had was the newspaper and a half-hour of TV news for information. At least they verified their stories then."

Doc looked around the breakfast nook and what he could see of the kitchen. Whatever he could to keep from looking down Marian Widmer's shirt, which she gave him every opportunity to do. Acting like he was only riding shotgun for Grabek, nothing important to be gained here, can we just get on with it and get to Happy Hour?

"Before I ask you anything, Mrs. Widmer," Grabek said, "I have to tell you you're under no obligation to talk to us. A wife can't be forced to give evidence against her husband. You can put us out now, or ask us to leave whenever you want."

"I understand. Ask what you want and I'll answer, within limits. Before we start, can I get either of you something to drink? Coffee? Iced tea? I'd offer you a beer, but you're on duty." Doc suppressed a snicker. Why did everyone who'd ever seen a cop show on TV feel obligated to say that? Like she was reminding them in case they were thinking of breaking out the Jack Black and asking if maybe did she have any heroin around?

"Iced tea would be great. Thank you," Grabek said. "Doc?"

"Anything cold and wet. Iced tea is fine, thanks."

The cupboard she opened required her to reach overhead for the glasses, in case they'd missed her ass on the way in. She was a good looking woman, but Jesus Christ. Show some decorum.

She brought back three glasses with lemon wedges and tea spoons, pulled the sugar bowl where all three could reach. "Here you are, Detectives. It's unsweetened."

"Thanks," Grabek said.

"Just how I like it," Doc said. "Not *too* sweet." Grabek kicked his ankle under the table.

Everyone took a minute to get their tea how they wanted it before Grabek spoke. "Mrs. Widmer, we're looking into the possibility that your husband was having an affair with Carol Cropcho. I'm not going to lie to you, we have him dead to rights, but juries like to know why people get killed. Frankly, sitting here with you, I'm not too sure about the idea of an affair, but we're checking everything. Did your husband ever give you cause to suspect he was unfaithful?" He made no effort to hide his interest in what was inside her shirt.

Marian sipped her tea. Took some time to steel herself for the answer forming in Doc's head, wondering if he could guess it word for word. "My husband...is an indulgent man. In himself, I mean. He indulges himself whenever he can, and, I suspect, however he can. He drinks, he gambles, and he comes home late smelling of cheap perfume. Have I ever caught him in the act? No. Have I ever intercepted a call or message from a...paramour? No. Do I have any doubt he's indulged himself in any willing vagina that came along?" She gave Grabek a look, shared a little of it with Doc. "No."

"I see. Do you have the names of any female acquaintances he might've had more than a friendly interest in? We're not looking to get anyone in trouble, but showing a pattern is often helpful in supporting a case."

"There's a woman he works with—worked with. Jane

Weigert, I think her name is. They were very familiar with each other at last year's Christmas party."

"How do you mean, familiar?"

Marian reached across to touch the inside of Grabek's left forearm. They both looked at her hand. "That's a gesture of familiarity, wouldn't you say? Some might say intimacy. That's how she touched him when they were chatting. It was practically erotic, the way she did it."

She cut in as Grabek started to speak. "There's also a woman named Molly Garrett I've wondered about. He goes through assistants on about an annual basis. Check their personnel records. There should be plenty to work with."

"Yes, ma'am," Grabek said. "I need to ask about the beatings you mentioned in court."

"Do we have to talk about that?"

"You don't *have* to talk about anything. You're the wife. I'm only asking because of the level of violence shown in Carol Cropcho's murder. What you described in court—and I apologize for saying this, I'm sure it was terrifying for you—that was pretty pedestrian domestic abuse. What happened to her isn't the kind of thing we'd expect based on what you described."

She took her time, looked down at the table when she spoke. "Thomas has always had a temper. Not violent...I don't know what to call it. Mean spirited? He says cruel things and makes what I guess most people would call aggressive gestures, but never so you'd worry about him doing anything."

"I'm not sure what you mean."

"He'll smack a fist into his palm or hit a door jamb. Throw something across a room, but never anything breakable and never toward anyone. Out of frustration, I suppose. I never worried about any of us getting hurt. Mostly it just makes him look like an impotent ass."

Grabek's pen paused above his notepad. "So you've seen nothing to make you believe he could beat someone the way Carol Cropcho was beaten."

"Well, not before. Recently, since the economy changed, he's—he's been drinking more. Moody. He's always been a mean drunk, mean the way I said before. It's just lately he started getting physical and hitting me. He was methodical about it at first, getting the phone book because he knew what he wanted to do. But there have been a couple of times..." She drank some tea, swallowed it hard. Looked into the glass as she spoke. "He's pulled back before he took it to another level. You know, cocked his fist but didn't actually hit me with it. It was very frightening."

"I'm sure it was," Grabek said.

Now Doc *was* getting impatient. Tom Widmer's temper was their cover story, not the issue. They were here to ask about her and David Frantz, not waste time with irrelevant questions so Grabek could look down her shirt. "Willie," he said, tapping his watch. "We have an appointment at four."

Grabek turned toward him sharply, then let his face soften. "Damn, that's right. I forgot all about it. Doesn't matter. We're about done here. Thanks for your time, Mrs. Widmer. I know this is hard for you."

"I don't know how to feel," she said. "I mean, he's my husband, and I'm loyal to him, but what he *did*. I'm afraid to have him here, and there's no way to know what he might do if he got out, now that I've told everyone what he's like. I don't want to be the one who puts him in prison for the rest of his life, but it looks like that's a foregone conclusion?"

Grabek flipped his notebook shut, slid it into his pocket. "Don't worry about that. He's going away no matter what you tell us. We're just here crossing Ts and dotting Is for the file so no one can say we missed anything. I don't think I've ever seen a case go from whodunit to dead bang so fast."

They all stood. Grabek nodded for Doc to lead the way. The two of them were on the porch, the storm door swinging shut, when Grabek pulled a Columbo and caught it before it closed.

"One last thing, Mrs. Widmer, if you don't mind. You just bought a Monaco Blue BMW 528i, didn't you? My brother-in-law's a big shot doctor down at UPMC looking into one. How do you like yours?"

She couldn't help herself. Her eyes shot over the cops' shoulders. Crown Vic the only car in the driveway and the garage door was closed. "It's-it's fine. I mean, I'd never driven a German car before, so it feels a little stiff sometimes, but it steers well and it's very quiet."

"I guess you haven't had it long enough to know how reliable it might be. Couple months is all, right?"

Doc watched her face darken, wondered how long Grabek would run with it. "Uh, no, that's right. It still has that new smell. No problems with it yet. Knock wood."

"Just thought I'd ask. I know they're good cars and all, but those German rides cost when something does go wrong. It's not like he can't afford it, but I still want to see him get a good deal. Never know when I might need open heart surgery. Wouldn't want him wondering why I didn't warn him when he's got me cut open in front of him." No one laughed but him. "Thanks for your time. I don't think we'll have to bother you again."

Neither cop spoke until Doc had the car out of the driveway. "I'm sorry if I hurried you back there, making up that meeting," he said.

"It was perfect. Put her off her guard. For a young guy, you got potential, Dougherty."

"Did you see the broken glass in the living room? In the doorway? Looked like plain glass and something else glazed, like a vase or something."

"Yeah, I saw it, and she made sure we didn't go in there. I'd love to know what went on with her and the guy she slapped."

"I'll check him out when we get back. Did you get what you wanted when you asked about the car?"

Grabek cracked his window, leaned back. "Oh yeah. She was there, she knows we know, and she knows we took the trouble to look it up. I wonder what size bricks she's shitting right now out of that ass she worked so hard to show us."

"What's next?"

"We shook her tree. Now we sit on her and try to get taps on her phones."

"Do we have enough for the warrants?"

Grabek made a face. "Depends on the judge. Might be worth shopping around, see who's on duty when we submit."

"Andy Molchan's the only game in town for criminal warrants. He has a backup magistrate when he's away, but it's not often."

"I was afraid you'd say something like that. I keep forgetting this isn't Allegheny County. Okay, fine. I'll work

on the warrants and see what I can find out about her
mysterious visitor. You watch her. See where she goes and
who she sees."

"Alone?"

"Ask Stush to get Neuschwander to help you. It'll give
him a chance to pretend he's a real cop."

CHAPTER 45

Jesus fucking *Christ!* The only way this day could be worse would be for the doctor to call with a positive pap smear.

Marian Widmer wanted to break something, but the kids would be home any minute and she couldn't let them see her in mid-tirade. Clean up the current mess and try to figure out what the *fuck* to do now.

She got a broom and dustpan from the kitchen closet. What was she thinking when she drove Frantz to Fourth Avenue in her own car? The killer she hired—Stark—told her it was a bad idea. Use Frantz's car, he told her. How was she to know Frantz had taken his piece of shit in for service? She didn't want to wait, not once she was committed, so she used her own car. Who was going to notice on Fourth Avenue, for Christ's sake, nothing but dopers and coloreds down there.

Did the police know about her and Frantz setting up Tom? They couldn't, or they would have asked her about it more directly. They know about the car, though. Someone must have seen it. She knew better than to say she loaned it out. She should've called it in as stolen as soon as she got home. Or had Stark drop her somewhere, claim it was stolen from there.

Too late now. There must be some good reason for her to have driven past there that night, though she couldn't think of one now. The police were fishing today, would have asked harder questions if they had any real evidence, so she had time. She hoped.

The private cop was the problem. He knew about her and Frantz, and had to assume she had a hand in the murder. How much time had she spent under that sweaty pig, faking orgasms, feigning ecstasy by raking her nails down his back, knowing it got him off, hoping he'd hurt in the morning. How she almost gagged when he put his dick in her mouth, shutting her eyes and thinking of what she would do with the money to keep from yakking, only to maybe ruin everything with her own impatience.

She put away the broom and dustpan. Poured herself a glass of wine. Her hands shook, not enough spilled any. Went into the living room, sat in the wing chair she liked to read in. She should have known when everything came together so easily. She knew Tom fooled around, had been since the first time she got pregnant. She could divorce him, but she'd only get half, and she deserved more. All those years as arm candy to make his co-workers jealous, when she could have had a career of her own, used her degree from Carlow for more than a memento on the bedroom wall. She carried and raised his children, and he had the nerve to screw around on *her*? He'd never been as successful as he'd told her he was to get her to marry him. A blind stockbroker throwing darts at a list of company names would've made money during the credit bubble. Then the bubble burst and Tom's whole Master of the Universe routine stank like the bullshit it had always been.

Pure dumb luck, meeting Frantz. A friend put them together, said her husband knew someone who got great deals on furs. She saw right through it, played along until she discovered what else he might be good for. A couple of bottles of wine into an evening he suggested killing Tom, which was about what she'd expected him to do, all the smarter he was. Too obvious, she told him, they'll look at me right away. She wanted no part of an insurance company, looking for excuses not to pay legitimate claims. She and Tom had plenty of money she could legitimately control, if she got to it before Tom pissed it all away. How could she get it, and rid of Tom? Prison, Frantz said. Frame him, get him sent away for something bad enough, and you might get it all. Marian wanted to be sure she'd get it all, and Frantz laughed at her. Tom would have to kill someone to be sure.

Marian sipped her wine and smiled. Carol Cropcho was perfect. Marian had spent weeks—no, *months*—teaching her the cunnilingus technique Tom had never bothered to learn, and the slut dumped her for someone younger. Goddamn feminism. Now even women wanted someone younger and prettier, never mind what you'd done for them. Marian had never thought of killing Carol before—never thought of killing *anyone* before—but if someone had to die, Carol was as good as anybody. Damned thoughtful of her to return the expensive tennis bracelet when they broke up.

The trick was to get Tom to kill her. One night Marian saw *Strangers on a Train* on Turner Classic, wondered how such an idea might work in her favor. She had to admit, Frantz really came through for her. He wanted half of the extra half—same as Rollison asked for—and was a good enough con man to trick a dumbass like Tom.

All the complicated pieces—finding Frantz, talking Tom into killing Carol, getting him arrested—fell together easier than she'd imagined possible. It was the easy part, killing

Frantz, causing all the problems. No question he had to go; he was a thief, after all, and no thief walks away from a guaranteed source of income. He'd be back for more, again and again. Finding Stark was as easy as an Internet search and a meeting at the Warszawa bar. And $20,000. Which hurt, but Marian considered it an investment. It was supposed to look like a drug deal gone bad, sever all relationship between them; who would look? Now Rollison knew, and he'd tell the police if she didn't pay. He'd come back again and again, too.

If Rollison found it, the police would make the connection sooner or later; not even Penns River cops were that dumb. Maybe the Discretion story would work. She needed time to think. She'd been careless once, not thinking of the phone records pointing back to her, and she couldn't afford to make the same mistake twice.

Marian needed to buy time, and she had a pretty good idea how much it would cost.

CHAPTER 46

Seventy-three miles per hour not bad for a forty-three-year-old man who hadn't pitched competitively since freshman year of college. Mike Mannarino didn't have the twelve-to-six yakker that fell off the table tonight, but the deuce he did have showed good movement and he threw it for strikes. Live hitters might hammer it, but that was the fun of garage throwing sessions: Mike could imagine all the foul balls and pop-ups he wanted.

He knew the pitches were strikes because he consistently hit Donte Broadus between the nipples and the kneecaps. Donte so skinny, Mike figured he threw more strikes than he gave himself credit for, counting only the hits, not balls that crossed the plate and failed to make contact. Stretch had Donte tied to a backboard sixty feet, six inches from the pitcher's rubber Mike kept in his back garage. Two balls left from the bucket of fifty. Mike let Donte know what was coming by flipping his glove over for a curve and just nodding before a fastball. Not that Donte could do much to cover up, spread-eagled against the backboard.

Mike enjoyed reminding Donte never to let business trace back to him. It wasn't all Donte's fault that arrogant asshole Dougherty guessed Mike was indirectly behind what happened on Fourth Avenue. Dougherty had the smarts to put that together on his own. Probably would have left well enough alone if Donte hadn't overreached. That forced

277

Dougherty to do something about it, and Mike was the logical person to see.

What bothered Mike was how Dougherty went about it. Time was, no cop would walk into the office of a man like Mike Mannarino and *tell* him anything, unless his ambition in life was to work mall security. Even cops who weren't on the pad had better manners than that. Those days were gone. Mike was entering his prime while his business lost ground in a changing industry.

Fifty, sixty years ago, men like Mike Mannarino ran Penns River. Virtually appointed the mayor, city council, and the police force. Always in the background. Those assholes in New York wanted to make headlines, let them. Pittsburgh made money, and Penns River was their Cicero.

Then the blacks got into selling drugs and the Soviet Union broke up and Communist China turned capitalist and now the Italian gangs had competition like they hadn't seen since they ran off the Irish and Jews. Except now the spooks and Russians and Chinks were hungrier, more ruthless, and full of don't give a shit. Russian boss wanted a guy dead, his boy would do it in front of fifty cops. Jail meant nothing to them, like taking a cruise compared to what they were used to.

He flipped his glove hand and caught Donte with a beautiful curve along the left floating ribs, one of the better hooks he'd broken off all night. Donte made a halfhearted grunt, having given up yells and screams twenty pitches ago. The stupid fuck deserved this. Mike should give that old coon a medal for keeping Donte from getting carried away. What had he planned to do if they did say what they'd seen? Take them home? No, he'd probably kill them and bring down shit all out of proportion to the trouble they could have caused, since none of Mike's crew was involved in the first place.

Life is what it is; Mike was no whiner. He'd cut his deals and do what he had to do to keep up in an evolving world. He'd tried being a nice guy; it worked better with some than others. Most of the town appreciated it. A few like Dougherty were hardasses, knew the benefits and still ignored them, like there was honor in being poor when you didn't have to be. Some—Donte came to mind—were too fucking stupid to get it. So, a lesson.

He gave a nod and drilled Donte with a heater midway between the navel and balls. Stretch read the numbers off the radar gun. "Sixty-eight." Mike windmilled his arm and rubbed his shoulder. Used to be able to hit eighty-five, even after a workout like this. Well, eighty. Still, not bad after the equivalent of three or four innings.

Mike put his glove on the workbench, walked off the mound. Donte's head hung down, though he hadn't been hit any higher than the shoulder. Mike got up close and gave him a once-over.

"You don't look too bad. Maybe you're dark enough the bruises don't show. Now pay attention." He squeezed Donte's cheeks between a thumb and forefinger, held up his head to make eye contact. "There was a time they'd of found your black ass dead tomorrow morning. I give you a job, I don't just want it done. I want it done right. Nothing rolls back on me. Ever. Now Stretch is gonna cut you loose so you can pick up all these balls and put them in the bucket. Then he'll give you a ride back to that shithole you live in. What happened here tonight will never happen again."

WORST ENEMIES

Mike left Stretch to cut Donte loose. No need to ask if he got the message. No one misunderstood Mike Mannarino more than twice, and Donte had just used his free one.

CHAPTER 47

Doc did interval training to and from work. Barely two miles door-to-door, old breaks in his feet wouldn't let him run all the way anymore. He'd run a minute, walk a minute; it was better than not running at all.

He came home, showered, and made himself a hard-core Burgh meal: chipped ham sandwich on his mother's home-made Syrian bread, with lettuce, American cheese, tomato, and Vidalia onion. Wise potato chips and a glass of lemon Blennd and he probably would have read the evening edition of the Pittsburgh *Press* if the paper hadn't gone under twenty years ago.

He'd drunk half the glass of Blennd and taken one bite of the sandwich when his cell went off. Jefferson West.

"Detective Dougherty, I'm sorry to bother you at home like this, but Family Services is here. They're taking the boys."

Doc warned West not to do anything rash and made it to Fourth Avenue in under ten minutes, aided by Eye Chart Zywiciel giving him a pass for going seventy-five on Leechburg Road.

The front of 1125 looked like a crime scene. Two county-owned sedans, two sheriff's deputies vehicles, lights turning. Half the neighborhood gathered around. Doc pulled in blocking the sedans, never stopped walking as he flashed his badge at the deputy working the crowd.

West opened the door before he could knock. "They're in the living room. I held them off the best I could."

Wilver and David Faison sat on West's couch. David was crying. Wilver did his best to look defiant and unafraid, didn't quite pull off either.

Doc said, "Who's supposed to be in charge here?"

A middle-aged woman with light brown hair stepped forward. "I'm in charge. I assume you're Detective Dougherty." Five-foot-one, no more than a hundred and ten pounds. Her voice told everyone she didn't give a shit that Doc was a cop, a foot taller, and a hundred pounds heavier. This was her party.

"These boys are my witnesses. What's going on here?"

"If they're witnesses, we should have been informed," the woman said. "All I know right now is they're runaways and truants."

"You boys miss any school?" Doc said.

"No, Detective Doc," Wilver said. "We go every day." David wiped snot from his nose with the back of his hand and nodded.

Doc turned back to the woman. "They're not truants."

"Acting clever isn't going to help these young men."

"Do you have a name, lady?"

She produced a card. "Kathleen Whitmore. I'm in charge of foster care for Neshannock County. These young men were removed from a foster home. I'm here to see that they get put where they belong."

"No one removed them from anywhere, Ms. Whitmore. They walked away on their own. Where you should be is over on Seventh Street asking the alleged foster parents why they didn't report that but keep on cashing your checks."

"An investigator is there now. The situation is under control."

Doc looked toward the boys. Another social worker asked if they were hungry. "Mr. West fed us," Wilver said.

"Pork chops and corn and beans," David said. "It was good."

Doc stayed looking at the boys when he spoke to Whitmore. "Where are you taking them?"

"We have a place."

"At the county group home?"

Whitmore softened her tone. "No. We have a family. That's why we're here so late. We had to get their approval to bring the boys over." She put her hand on Doc's elbow. "Come with me into the other room. Please."

Doc nodded for West to watch the boys and followed her into the kitchen. "We could've come for them three days ago," Whitmore said. "We waited so they wouldn't have to spend time in the county facility while we found someone. We've kept an eye on them since then. We saw you come and go. I understand what you're doing here. I don't approve of it, but I'm not unsympathetic. Your heart's in the right place, and they seem to be well cared for."

"Then leave them here."

"I can't. No. Wait. That's not fair. I won't." She laid three fingers on his hand. "It's not just the regulations. My conscience won't allow it. We have a good organization in Neshannock County. We really do. It works well and everyone looks out for everyone else. I defy you to name a story from here like in some of the bigger counties, of kids getting lost or abused. It doesn't happen here, and it doesn't happen because we have good policies and everyone does their jobs. I know what went on here a couple of weeks ago. About Mr. West and his shotgun."

"And they're fine. How could putting them in a different home ensure the same level of protection if someone came looking for them again?"

"Well, first of all, they wouldn't be next door to the first place he'd look." She let that sink in. "Like I said, we have tested policies to protect everyone, and they work. Do you realize what could have happened if things had turned out differently that night? What if someone had been shot? Anyone? The repercussions to you and Mr. West, even though you both have the best intentions?"

"So your regs will let everyone cover their asses."

Whitmore paused to show Doc she was working to maintain her patience. Didn't make a big deal of it, just enough to let him know there wasn't an unlimited supply. "We can make this come out right. No one wants to take action against you or Mr. West. I already told him I'll start the process myself to get him certified if he's willing. He'll never lack for children who need him."

"What if it's not just children for him, but *these* children? There's a bond there. We talked about it some. There's something about these two that resonates with him, and they're picking up on it. Jeff West is the closest thing they've had to a caring adult in their lives for a long time, and he's *good* at it. How is this other home going to do any better?"

Whitmore started to speak, changed her mind. "The infrastructure is in place for better supervision. This is a family who's accustomed to our practices and policies."

"Like those good folks on Seventh Street?"

Whitmore rubbed her chin. "I have to give you that one. We dropped the ball there."

"Can you guarantee it won't get dropped again? Not you personally, but your wonderful, foolproof system?"

"It's not foolproof. We both know that. But, yes, I can guarantee it won't get dropped again." She held up a hand to cut him off. "Be*cause* of what happened on Seventh Street. Do you think we're—*I'm*—going to write that off and just hope for the best? This time will be different because it *has* to be. We owe those boys, and I always pay my debts."

She meant it, too, and Doc knew it. He hadn't lost this argument yet, but he would, sure as winter was coming. He cupped a hand on the back of his neck, stared into the nearest corner. "Jesus Christ."

Whitmore stepped closer, spoke so no one else could hear. "I'll talk to Mr. West to see if he's interested in becoming a foster parent. For Wilver and David, I mean. There are ways we can expedite it. If he's willing, and I can get it approved, we'll bring them back."

Doc turned his head enough to see her without looking at her. "I thought that was *your* gig. Can't you just approve him now? Let them stay?"

"It has to be done right, and not just to cover ourselves. A home can't be certified on my say-so alone. If you think about it you'll see it has to be that way. My opinion carries some weight, but we still have to do a background investigation. What he's done for them so far will count a lot.

"I don't like doing it like this." She waited for Doc to make eye contact. "Taking them out, then maybe bringing them back. It's hard on the children, and hard on both sets of foster parents. I'm willing to consider this a special case, but I'll need your help."

"My help? I'm the one fucked it up."

"You got a little ahead of yourself is all. I need you to tell them what's going to happen. They trust you. I need you to trust me."

The whole thing reminded him of a death notification, looking for an easy way to tell something there's no easy way to tell. Except with death notifications he spoke to adults who understood the fragility of life. These boys would see it as another bond broken, two fewer people they could trust. For a second he thought of their mother. Almost asked Whitmore how she entered into it, remembered Mom's name hadn't come up, so maybe she didn't enter into it at all. "All right. I'll tell them. Well, we'll tell them together, but I'll do the talking. I won't mention the chance of them coming back, though. I won't get their hopes up so they'll feel like I lied to them if it doesn't work out."

"I don't want you to. I'll ride with them and stay a while this evening. The other family is waiting with some pie and ice cream, and I'll stay for that, too, to be sure they're as comfortable as we can make them. I'll need one more favor from you."

"What is it?"

"Will you talk to Mr. West about my offer? Give him a night to sleep on it, and I'll come back tomorrow. I think you might be onto something; he and the boys do seem to have a bond. It would be a shame to waste it."

"Okay, I'll talk to him. And thanks for your cooperation."

"I'm glad you see we're not as heartless as we're made out to be."

Doc almost said something. Instead he brushed past her toward the living room. Get it over with. He was almost to the doorway when it occurred to him. "Just one more question, if you don't mind. The boys haven't missed school, and the current alleged foster parents sure didn't call you. How did you find out?"

Whitmore thought no more than a second. "Referrals are strictly confidential, but since this was an institutional call, I don't suppose it will hurt anything. I'm surprised you don't know already. The Penns River police department called us."

CHAPTER 48

Doc found Barb Smith working a traffic stop on the bypass. Pulled in behind and put the magnetic battery-powered light on his roof.

He leaned down to speak through her window. "How far'd you get with this one?"

"I just called in for warrants. What's up?"

"He have any?"

"No."

"You write him yet?"

"No. What's wrong?"

"That his license?"

He took it from her clipboard before she could answer. Walked to the pick-up she'd pulled over, an old Dodge with the gate broken off. Rapped on the dented door with his knuckles. The driver's head came slowly through the open window.

"Here's your license. If I ever see you speeding I'll write you up for every violation I can find on this piece of shit. Now get the fuck out of here before I change my mind and take you in for being a redneck in a triple-digit IQ zone."

The Dodge driver didn't need to be told twice. The truck was already moving by the time Barb got close enough to speak to Doc.

"What was that all about? What the hell's wrong with you?" Doc didn't consciously do anything. Over six feet tall and more than two hundred pounds, all he had to do was fix Barb with what Stush once called The Look and she took an involuntary step back. "Doc?"

He didn't have to raise his voice to show the anger. "You called Family Services."

"No, Doc, wait—"

"You called Family Services and they just took those kids away. Who the *fuck* do you think you are? I'm not saying I was right or you were wrong about not wanting to leave them there, but goddamn it, you come to *me*, not behind my back like that."

"I didn't call them! I swear to God, Doc, I didn't!"

"Bullshit. The woman from DFS just told me they got the call from Penns River Police. I told Zywiciel they were with family when I asked him to have patrol keep an eye on them. Only you knew the whole deal."

She made a short gasp, one hand to her mouth. "Oh, Doc. Oh my God. I'm so sorry. I didn't know, honest to God I didn't."

"What? You just now remembered you called them?"

"No, I didn't call them. I—I just—my conscience was bothering me. I was worried about them, about keeping them off the books like that. They're just kids and couldn't really help with the decision or know what they were up against. I didn't know who to talk to, and I wasn't sure how things worked around here. I needed someone I could trust, and I don't know that many people that well."

"Who'd you tell?"

"I needed someone who'd been around, and had some authority. Someone who'd know better than how to handle something like this."

"You talked to Sherry Gibson, the juvenile officer? I've known her for twenty years. I can't believe she wouldn't come to me."

"No, it wasn't Sherry. I should have gone to her but she was off that week and I couldn't wait any longer—"

"Who did you tell?"

"Doc, I really wanted to help and he seemed most likely to—"

"*Who, goddamn it!!??*"

"The Deputy. Jack Harriger."

Doc stood for a second with his mouth open, stupefied. Felt the shoulder of the road slipping away under him, then his rage overtook the shock.

"Jesus *fucking* Christ! Forty-one cops in this town and you go to *him*? Not Stush. He only got you the job and looks out for you. Not Sherry, whose job it is to worry about this kind of stuff. Not even Janine Schoepf, who sits on her ass in the office all day but hears every little thing that happens because she's universally trusted. No. You go to the one guy guaranteed to screw whoever he gets the opportunity to do. You have got to be the stupidest bitch ever wore a uniform."

Doc didn't melt down much anymore; the Army taught him how not to. The fire still burned, banked through conscious effort. Or like now, sparking at the edge of combustion. Barb stepped back again. Her hand twitched toward the mace on her hip.

"Doc, I'm sorry. I really am." She kept her voice level, working him like a domestic disturbance on the brink. "You're right. I should have gone to the Chief. Or anyone else. I really didn't think the deputy would do anything like this. He said he'd take care of it, and I should sit on it until he decided what to do. I thought he'd go to the chief. Or maybe he'd call someone he knew over there, you know, off the record. I never thought he'd do this and not tell you. I'd never go behind your back to hurt you. You know I wouldn't."

Doc looked past her shoulder to the ice rink across the bypass. The eruption past, his hands shaking with excess adrenaline. Lips pulled tight, not trusting himself to speak.

"You have to understand why I did it," Barb said. "Why I had to talk to someone else. You have a way of making every decision seem like it was the only logical choice. I don't mean you argue or get defensive about it, but you have this confidence in what you do. That it'll turn out. I don't."

"It wasn't your decision to make." Still looking past her shoulder.

"I know. You made it, and I knew you'd stand by it. I needed someone who'd look at it from my point of view to tell me not to worry about it. Or to tell me I was right and to do something about it. Because there's more to it for me. I— it's because of something before."

She turned away from him, looking across the bypass at three o'clock to his twelve. Neither said a word. Doc immobile, Barb digging at the gravel with her toe.

"Do you know why I left Harrisburg?" she said.

"I know it's a big goddamn secret."

Barb stayed facing ninety degrees away from Doc. "I was working a beat in Allison Hill. The neighborhood's on the edge. You know, used to be nice, going to hell, but parts are coming back again. We knew about this drug house with little kids living in it. We tried everything, but never got what we needed for a bust. We thought about getting the kids out, but then we'd have to show evidence we didn't want made known.

"One night we get a nine-one-one call. I'm first on the scene, went in with the EMTs. It's a little girl, six months old, and she's not breathing. Nobody knows anything, they thought she was asleep, now she's not breathing. EMTs started working on her, carried her down to the ambulance to take her to the hospital. One of them started giving her CPR and his partner told me 'We can't pronounce them, but this one's gone already.'"

Barb's voice was flat and distant. "I got a call to go back up and start questioning people. Detectives were on the way. This might be the excuse we needed to shut them down. So I went up."

Took her the better part of a minute to continue. Doc kept staring toward the rink.

"The detectives separated people into different rooms to talk to them alone. A lot of 'What goes on here?' and 'Who the fuck are you?' kind of stuff. I kept inventory. No one out and no one in. Who'd been questioned. Stuff like that.

"The preliminary ME's report came in about the time we were looking for excuses to stay. Baby died of a heroin overdose. The mother went crazy when we told her. She wound up in the hospital herself. All we could figure was the mother's sister, the baby's aunt, was a heavy user. They kept some lactose around to cut the heroin, and Auntie must have been high and the baby was hungry and she mixed the wrong stuff into the formula." Crying now, obvious from her voice, though no tears or sobs. "I don't know. All we had were guesses."

Doc raised his eyes over the top of the ice rink, above the

lights into the darkness of the hill behind.

"We never proved a thing. There was no evidence against anyone specific. Just traces of drugs in the apartment. Of course, they didn't call us until they'd cleaned house. Their lawyer made it sound like no one in the house was at fault, maybe Gerber keeps heroin around the factory and some fell in.

"We could've got her out weeks before, but we were more worried about making the case. We figured the kids would be all right until we were ready, then everything could go down at once. So she's dead. They left her to die so they could move their stash out before they called for help. And they got away with it."

She looked Doc's way, tried to make eye contact. He stared at the ground, hand on his hips. Neither had moved since she started her story.

"I had to drive past there all the time. I couldn't take it. They transferred me, got me counseling, finally put me on a desk. Every time Allison Hill came up I thought about that little girl. Tamika Stewart. That's why I had to leave. My chief knew Stush from conferences, and told him I was a good cop. He thought a small town might be good for me. So Stush brought me here."

She turned to look directly at Doc. "I should've gone to Stush. Or waited for Sherry to come back from vacation. I'm so sorry I picked the wrong person, but I'd do it again. Ask someone, I mean. Just not him."

She waited for Doc to speak. After thirty seconds he raised his eyes to the level of the ice rink again. Didn't turn.

"Don't ever go behind my back again. Ever."

CHAPTER 49

Tailing Marian Widmer with Neuschwander not as much fun as usual today. Not Neuschwander's fault; Doc's mood had not improved since the Family Services-Barb Smith confrontations. Wilver called on the way to school; all seemed well. Jeff West said he wasn't sure about interrupting his retirement to raise children, since he hadn't been that good at it the first time, but he'd give the approval process a try for Wilver and David.

Doc didn't know if he was madder at Barb, or at himself for showing his ass like he did. No anger for Harriger. Getting mad at him for something like this same as being upset with a stone for sinking in water. He'd been pissy all day, not like himself, which made it worse, wondering why it still bothered him. Maybe he'd been too hard on Barb. She'd tried to do right by the boys, not hurt him. He felt no hurry to clear the air, even though he knew the longer he waited the harder it would be until the prospect looked so daunting he wouldn't do it at all and a friendship could be lost. Wouldn't be the first time.

A steady drizzle came in through the half-open car window while they waited for Marian to do something worth following her for. A cold front moved through overnight and the windows kept steaming up, so he let the rain drip in and savored the discomfort as his due.

Marian came out at 11:00, drove the Beemer down one

hill and up the next to Hillcrest Shopping Center. Every third storefront had signs in the window. For Lease. Under New Management. Everything Must Go. Marian spent twenty minutes in the bank while Doc and Neuschwander sat in the car.

"She's been in there quite a while," Neuschwander said.

"They're busy. I'd send you in, but we can't risk her leaving while we're separated. I might have to leave you behind to keep her from making us."

"Shouldn't we have two cars for this?"

"Absolutely."

Two minutes passed. Neuschwander said, "How come, you think?"

"How come what?"

"We don't have two cars."

"One's all they gave us."

"I could use my personal vehicle if you think it would help. I just hate to leave Judy without, you know, in case she needs it." The Neuschwander family condensed from two sedans to one minivan when they learned they'd need room for another car seat.

"Never use your own vehicle. I used mine once and got it totaled. Insurance wouldn't pay and I had to kiss ass for the city to make it right."

That satisfied Neuschwander for the time being. He contented himself—such as it was—by jiggling his legs, first one, then the other, then alternately. As methodical as he could be when he worked, he hated to wait. Slid his watchband on and off his wrist. "How long now?" Not looking at the watch in his hand, like Doc was the official timekeeper.

"Twenty-three minutes. She's talking to a manager."

Neuschwander kept playing with his watch. Open it, slide it up his arm. Slide it back into place. Wait five seconds. Repeat. "You find anything out about that guy come to see her the other day when you were there? The one she slapped?"

"He's a PI from Pittsburgh, Something Rollison. Daniel, I think. Supposed to be hot stuff, some kind of retired spook. Willie knew of him from working downtown. He's there now, buying some guy lunch who might be able to fill him in."

Neuschwander was quiet for a minute, watching people come and go at Merchant's Tire, still screwing with his watchband. "Shouldn't someone follow Rollison, too?"

Doc shifted his eyes, calculated whether the band would go around Neushwander's neck. "Probably. Thing is, we don't have the manpower to follow both, and he probably has other things going on, so a lot of the time spent on him would be wasted. Plus, he knows what he's doing and would be hell to follow. Not to mention she's the one we know for sure has a connection to both murders. So we follow her."

"I'm not complaining. It's just I don't like the idea of following her somewhere far if Judy needs me for something."

This was when Doc would usually tease Neuschwander. Call him pussy whipped or ask if maybe they should bring Judy with them tomorrow. Bring the kids, too, use the minivan. He'd say it so Neuschwander knew he was kidding, run him around for a few minutes until they were both laughing, pass the time and keep Rick from worrying so much and becoming a pain in the ass.

Not today, Doc still on the rag from the fight with Barb.

The ongoing Jillian situation didn't help. She called every day, sometimes twice, asking when he was coming over, could they go out after rehearsal, how come it was always her who called. He would call her, he said, but she always did it before he had a chance. Reminded him of an old country song: How can I miss you if you won't go away?

"Here she comes." Neuschwander sat up, fastened his watch. Doc started the car as Marian unlocked the Beemer. They followed her out of the parking lot, left onto Wildlife Lodge Road, across the bypass past the VFW. She turned left onto Milligantown Road and Doc said, "She's going to Penn State."

"That's on 780."

"She can cut over on Slusser or Hartge."

She didn't cut over on either. Drove east to Manchester Hill like she was taking the air and doubled back toward town on 780.

"Now she's going to Penn State," Neuschwander said.

"Helluva roundabout way to do it."

Following her through a wooded area had its pitfalls. The lack of traffic made it hard to blend in, but few reasons to turn off meant people didn't think twice about seeing the same car in their mirrors for several miles. Of course, they'd lose her if a slower car got between them. Doc held back a hundred yards. Near enough close the gap if she turned, keep anyone from cutting him off.

He dropped back another hundred yards as she approached Penn State, then had to catch up when she went past it. She did turn onto Hartge this time, over to Milligantown Road. Turned left. Back the way she'd come.

"What the hell?" Doc said, not in the mood.

"Maybe she wants to see how a BMW handles potholes."

Marian took the left turn lane at the light for the bypass. Doc let a car pulling out of the VFW lot get between him and Marian. The woman in the middle car concentrated more on her phone than the light and almost fanned on the green altogether. Doc caught the last nanosecond of yellow, would have passed on the right but she drifted over, still working the phone. Marian three hundred yards ahead now. She'd be gone if she made the light at Craigdell Road and Doc missed it.

She didn't. Doc stayed back, kept the driver with the phone between them. The light turned green. Marian went and the middle car stayed put again, driver's head down. Too much traffic in the left lane to pull out. Doc did a slow burn, tapped the horn. The woman flipped him off.

"Go around on the right," Neuschwander said.

"Fuck this. Keep an eye on Marian."

Doc was out of the car before Neuschwander could answer, trotting up the bypass between lanes of traffic. Slapped the window of the car in front and pressed his badge against the glass.

The woman finished her text message and opened the window. "What is it?"

Doc reached in, took the phone from her hand, threw it as far as he could into the field across the road, near to where he'd stood with Barb the night before. The woman stared at him, open mouthed.

"Be grateful I didn't shove that phone up your ass," Doc said. "Now get off the road and stop interfering with police business before I take you in."

The woman still too shocked to speak. Doc trotted back to his car, ran the red swerving around her on the right.

"Which way?" he said to Neuschwander.

"Take the right. Toward the bridge."

Good driving and luck caught them up at the light next to the City-County complex. Doc stayed a lane to Marian's left and two cars behind. She drove across the river and through Tarentum onto 28 south.

Doc and Neuschwander turned to each other and said in unison, "The Mills."

Pittsburgh Mills was an schizophrenic mall halfway between Tarentum and Harwick, full of national big box stores and businesses that sold things people didn't need. Steelers and Penguins gear, indoor remote control car track, and stores where everything cost less than five dollars shared space with Macy's and Victoria's Secret. A banner hung above the entrance to Dick's Sporting Goods: Welcome to Pittsburgh Mills. Official Mall of the Pittsburgh Penguins. No ice rink within ten miles.

Marian parked near the theaters and went in. Neuschwander parked two aisles over and looked at Doc. He nodded and they trotted after her. Spread out across the Food Court while she walked straight through the center, across the concourse and into the Caress Day Spa. "Grand Opening," the sign read. "Specials for Every Budget."

They lingered near a kiosk that sold cell phone accessories. Marian went to the desk, gave her name and took a seat. Ten minutes later a buff, blond man of dubious sexuality shook her hand and led her into the back of the suite.

Doc and Neuschwander moved to the store across the

concourse to window shop where they could keep an eye on Caress's entrance.

"See if I'm making a mistake here," Doc said. Neuschwander lived for this kind of thing. Harriger dismissed him; Grabek mocked him openly. Doc asked him for reality checks, bounced ideas off him, wanted his opinion. Actually paid attention when he spoke, so Doc got his complete attention. "Don't look at me, Noosh. Anyone sees us, we want to look like two guys bullshitting."

"Sorry." Neuschwander turned away.

"We're bullshitting, Rick, not ignoring each other. Come on, man. Work with me."

Doc waited for Neuschwander to strike an acceptable pose. "Okay. We have witnesses who can place her car at the murder scene. A woman was seen there, too, but we didn't get a description. Seems reasonable to assume it was her, but we can't prove it."

"Right."

"Meanwhile, your buddy Wierzbicki meets a woman in the Warszawa he swears was looking for a hitter."

"Right again."

"How nice would it be if Wierzbicki could identify Marian Widmer as the woman at the Warszawa?"

"Very."

Doc motioned for Neuschwander to follow him several feet along the window. Stopped in front of a display of watches. "Do you have anything decent on Wierzbicki you'd be willing to trade away? I don't want to cost you a pinch, but it could come in handy."

"Nothing right now, but I will. It's always only a matter of time with him."

"You have his number?"

"Yeah."

"I don't see any way she's in there less than an hour. Tell him get his ass down here and maybe we can do him a favor someday."

CHAPTER 50

Dwight Wierzbicki sucked down the last of a Mountain Dew Code Red and shook his head in admiration at two sweet young things walking past the food court. He'd made it in twenty-five minutes. Doc told Neuschwander to look for crimes with the Bick's MO. His haste implied a guilty conscience.

"You know what's fun?" Wierzbicki said.

They'd been there over an hour. Doc bought their lunches and Neuschwander took his to the car in case Marian got out unnoticed. Wierzbicki only stopped running his mouth to swallow. Doc wanted to know what he thought was fun about as much as he wanted to see Grabek's colonoscopy photos.

Wierzbicki took the silence for assent. "You get a young girl like those two, and she don't know something's dirty? She'll do it. She don't want to look like she's not cool, or inexperienced or something, so she'll let you."

Christ. *And* they were going to give him a pass on something they didn't even know about yet. No crime to be an asshole, or half the people Doc knew would be inside. Something should still be done about evolutionary cul-de-sacs like Dwight Wierzbicki.

Doc tried to think of a way to guide the conversation away from topics that might end with him strangling his potential witness. Marian Widmer saved him the trouble, walking out of Caress and down the concourse to their right.

"There," Doc said. "Blue blouse, navy pea coat. That the woman asked you about painting houses?"

Wierzbicki craned his neck, squinted. "The hair's wrong."

"Maybe she got it cut."

Wierzbicki gave another long look. "Could be. Hell, man, it was dark and she was wearing that babushka thing. I didn't get a real good look at her."

"Make up your mind before she's gone. It's not like we can chase after her."

"I don't know. Maybe if I heard her voice. I talked to her more than I got a good look at her."

"You asking for a formal introduction?" Doc made a quick calculation. "Stay close and keep your mouth shut. I don't want her to recognize you."

They followed her through the mall, gradually closing the distance. She turned into Charlotte Russe and Doc pulled Wierzbicki into the store across the way. Marian came out empty-handed ten minutes later.

Doc tugged Wierzbicki's sleeve. "Come on." Took an oblique course toward Marian. Halfway to her he turned to intercept.

"Mrs. Widmer!"

She turned, startled. Her face fell for a second, the recovery too quick for anyone but a pro to spot.

"Detective Dougherty? Penns River police? We spoke at your house a few days ago. With my partner."

"Yes, Detective Dougherty. I'm sorry. I didn't expect to see you."

"Same here. This is my cousin, from Butler. We get

303

together here for lunch once in a while." Careful to block Marian's view of Wierzbicki.

"Yes. How do you do?" She extended a tentative hand. Wierzbicki reached around to take it and Doc stepped hard on his foot.

"Sorry," Doc said. "We don't let him out often. He's kind of hideous, actually. It's nice to see you off the clock. I felt bad, having to question you the other day. It's not like you did anything wrong, but you're having to suffer for it."

"I understand. You were just doing your job."

"I appreciate you saying so, but sometimes it's a crap job just the same." Doc made eye contact and she held it. "I— uh—you know, it's not the optimal way to meet someone."

Marian's voice teased more than it scolded. "Is that what we were doing? Meeting? I thought I was being questioned."

"Yeah, well, that was the official reason for the visit. I wouldn't have been there otherwise, not working a case and all." Her pea coat was unbuttoned. He let his vision drop to her breasts, made sure she saw it. Looked back up after she'd had the chance. "I'd seen you before. At court that day. The arraignment."

"And I made a good impression?"

She turned enough to give a line of sight inside the blouse should he choose to peek again. Wierzbicki tried. Doc moved in front, like dancing with someone to whom his back was turned. Took another quick look, knowing she'd see. "Let's say it was worth remembering."

"I'm flattered."

"Don't be. Flattery implies dishonesty, buttering someone up."

"And you're not buttering me up?" She ran her tongue

over her lips. Hot or not, she was subtle as a neon sign on a church.

Doc maneuvered in front of Wierzbicki again. "No need to. Not while you're even peripherally involved in an investigation I'm working. I'm a good cop."

"Are you good at anything else?"

He let that one sit a few seconds. Wierzbicki poked him in the back. Dumb bastard still didn't get it. "It's not good form for someone to talk about how good he is at something. It's better for others to make up their own minds."

Marian smiled. A lesser man would have thought it was real. "Well, you know where I live."

"Yes, I do, and I'm not likely to forget." He half turned into Wierzbicki to start him moving. "Time to go. We both have to get back to work. I hope to see you again."

"Me, too." Marian walked away—back the direction she'd come, away from the Food Court and her car—turned after about ten steps. Gave a fingers-only wave. Doc nodded back. She kept walking.

Doc pushed Wierzbicki back toward the Food Court. "Is that her?"

"Fuck, man, you coulda give me a better look than that. She's fine."

"You had a look. You said you needed to hear her." Walking faster, wanting to get out before she circled back to her car.

"Yeah, but still. A boy can dream, can't he?"

"Is it her?"

Wierzbicki looked back over his shoulder. "Lots of differences. You know, the light's different, the noise is different—"

"*Is it her?*"

Wierzbicki paused, weighed the criminal ethos of not ratting against what he had to gain. "Yeah. That's her."

"You'll swear to it? In court?"

Another pause. Then, "Yeah. Yeah, I'll testify."

Doc got him outside, looked for Marian. "Make yourself scarce. I did you a favor in there. If she is the one had Frantz clipped, and sees you eyeballing her with a cop, you're next."

Wierzbicki's face showed this was a revelation. "That's a shame, man. A fucking shame. I'll bet she was some piece of ass in her day."

Doc shook his head. "In her day? Grow up. Remember when you asked if I knew what was fun? You know what's *really* fun, Bick? Kick ass fun? When you have an older woman, an experienced woman, and she knows something's dirty, and she does it anyway because she *likes* it."

This was no less shocking to Wierzbicki than the thought Marian might have him killed. Doc felt good for an instant, shutting him up, then thought of Jillian, his mentor in such matters. That didn't feel nearly as good.

CHAPTER 51

"Come home with me tonight, Benny."

Jillian sat a row behind Doc watching the rehearsal, her lips so close he felt her breath on the tiny hairs of his ear. He didn't like being called Benny. People who knew him since he used to shit his diapers could call him Benny. His parents. Stush. Not in the mood to like much at all tonight. Got there late—which he hated—should have skipped it altogether. In the last twenty-four hours he'd endured the Family Services-Barb Smith fiasco and spent over an hour with Dwight Wierzbicki, who could inspire the Dalai Lama to steal a knife to stab him with.

Now Jillian. He'd tried to cut back on their time together, at least do something besides eat and fuck. He knew a guy could get him into Pens games if he didn't abuse the privilege. Pitt tickets were easy to get. A movie, for Chrissakes. Something normal couples did.

He'd mentioned it to Eve. Of course she gave him hell. "Normal couples fuck, Doc."

"They do other things, too."

"You've never been in a strictly sexual relationship before?"

No, he hadn't. Always thought it would be fun. Now he was in one, he supposed, and the sex was incredible. It was erotic, exotic, hot, sweaty, noisy, painful, sensual, breathtaking, mind-numbing, intoxicating, dirty, and illegal in several

Southern states. What it wasn't, was fun.

"Not tonight, Jillian. Okay?"

"What's wrong, Benny?. You have a headache?"

"No, but I've been working twelve-hour shifts and I have to get up by a quarter to six tomorrow morning for another one."

"I'll have you up all night, if you want."

"I don't want." More edge in his voice than he intended. The recognition flickered across his consciousness and was dismissed. "Not tonight. I have too much going on right now. I need a good night's sleep. Even if I just come over and sleep, I'll have to get up that much earlier in the morning. Not tonight."

She sat back in her chair. He couldn't see her without turning, and he wasn't turning. She never pouted. He expected her back with Plan B within two minutes. He was too generous by thirty seconds.

"I called you last night."

"Last night? What time?"

"About eleven-thirty."

"Christ, Jillian, I wasn't coming out at eleven-thirty."

"I just wanted you to talk dirty to me." Lowered her voice to a more conspiratorial tone. "Sometimes my toys just can't do it for me. I think you spoiled me."

Talked for ten seconds, got "me" in three times. "Sorry. I didn't hear it. I was out cold by ten-thirty."

"Are you sure you didn't hear? I'll bet you would've answered if they were calling about another dead body."

"That's a different ring. I'm used to waking for that."

"And not for me? I think my feelings might be hurt."

"Not tonight, Jillian. Please."

"I mean, as intimately as we know each other," her voice got throaty on "intimately," "I'd think you'd wake up for me. Part of you wakes up for me like Pavlov's doggie."

"I said not tonight." It came out louder than he intended. Heads turned, though the actors on stage didn't miss a beat. He stood. "Come on. We'll talk in the lobby."

She followed him out, rubbed against him as she passed the door he held for her. Waited for the door to close, took his hand. "Let's go into the little boys' room. I'll suck your cock for you."

"*No!*" Doc took her hand from his wrist, placed both his hands on her wrists to move her an arm's length away. "No. How many times do I have to tell you? Not tonight. I want to go home and get some sleep. That's all."

Her look was thoughtful more than hurt or confused. "This isn't fair, Benny. I'm doing all the work. You pick and choose how much you want to be involved. A girl likes to be pursued once in a while."

"How can I pursue you? You're on me like stink on shit, every day." Knew he'd made a mistake before he finished the sentence. "You said it yourself. It's nice to be pursued once in a while. Everyone likes it. But there's being pursued and there's being chased, and being chased all the time gets old. You like to be pursued sometimes. Great. I like to set limits once in a while. Give me a chance."

"You'd like to set limits?" Her face reddened as her blood came up. "What do you think you do every time I call or ask you to go out or come over and you say no? Are you 'setting limits?' Or are you just a tease?"

He couldn't help snickering. "A tease?"

"I was trying to be nice." Her voice rose to match her

blood. "What I wanted to say was, are you just a manipulative bastard? You want what you want, and fuck what I want."

"Far as I can tell, all you want is to fuck." Not in the mood to be harassed, Doc sure as hell wasn't in the mood to argue. "The whole point of contention seems to be you're not getting enough."

"You never complain about that when we're doing it."

"That's not the kind of thing that comes to mind in the middle of incredible sex like we have. Don't misunderstand me: sex with you is like nothing I'd even imagined. There's more to life than sex, is all."

"You want more? Have you ever tried to do anything else with me?"

"You mean aside from the movies and other events I've suggested?"

"Oh, so you want more than dinner and a fuck? You want dinner and a movie and a fuck. Or dinner and a ball game and a fuck. Thank God there's no NASCAR track close by."

"Tell me what you want. It sounds like what you're after is for me to invite you for a fuck instead of you doing it every night."

"I don't do it *every* night, and yes. That would be a nice start."

"As you've no doubt noticed, I don't necessarily want to fuck every night."

"We could do other things."

"Such as?"

"Talk. Real couples talk."

"What would you like to talk about?"

"Right now we're already in the middle of something."

"I mean in these regular couple talks you'd like to have."
Her color showed again. "How we spend our days. You
never tell me what you do all day at work."

"Okay. Today I spent twelve hours in a car with a guy
nervous because his wife's about to have a baby, watching a
woman we think might be a killer just in case she does
something incriminating." Doc's blood coming up to match
Jillian's, and he was good with it. "For lunch I hung with a
low-life criminal whose idea of a good time is tricking young
girls into nasty sex acts. There wasn't one goddamned thing I
liked about my day while I was doing it. Why the hell would
I want to go over it again?"

"You could ask about my day."

"Fine. How was your day?"

Took her a little time to collect her memories. "It was
okay. You know, days are never the same at the hospital, but
the work doesn't vary all that much. I'm working in Quality
Control now, not actually doing nursing. I check all the
charts and records to make sure everything gets done prop-
erly and we've performed our due diligence." She paused to
look directly at him. "You don't care about any of this."

"It's not that I don't care. I'm sure it's interesting to you.
I'm sure some of it's fascinating. It just doesn't mean anything to me. Half of what you'd tell me, I'd say, 'Why don't
you do it like this?' just like you'd do about my job."

"No I wouldn't. I'd listen to what you had to say. I don't
always have to look at every conversation as a problem to be
solved."

"Not every conversation. Just the ones where someone
tells me something's wrong. If it's wrong, I want to fix it."

"That's a stupid guy thing."

"And I'm a guy. It doesn't mean I can't or won't listen. I lack the patience to listen to the same sad stories every day. Sooner or later I'm going to make a suggestion."

"You can't just listen, give the other person a chance to share some of their stress."

"Sharing stress that way just means pushing it off onto me, and I have plenty already."

"That's selfish. I was right before. You want what you want when you want it and to hell with everyone else."

"Which is different from you how?"

She glared at him and Doc saw the full potential for that whole "woman scorned" thing. "We are nothing alike. I give myself to you in ways you've never known, and this is the thanks I get. All you do is take and take and take and take."

"It's enough to make a reasonable man wonder why you put up with me."

He didn't expect the slap. She snapped his head to the side, Doc too surprised to slip it. "Fuck you, Benny Dougherty, and your idea of how to treat people. The least I should've been able to expect was a little consideration for my feelings. I should've known you'd treat me like this after you talked me into letting you fuck me in the ass. I hope you and your right hand are very happy together." She bumped open the panic bar to the outside door with her hip and left. The director should have given her a bigger part than jury member. She definitely knew how to make an exit.

Doc didn't realize the rehearsal break had begun until he turned to go back inside and saw twenty people trying to look like they hadn't been there. Eve walked up, put a hand on his shoulder, gestured with her head toward the door

Jillian had just used. "Think you used enough dynamite there, Butch?"

"How long have you been standing there?"

"Since about the time there wasn't one goddamned thing good about your day and why would you want to go over it again."

"That long, huh?" Eve nodded. "Thanks for coming over and defusing the situation."

"Defusing it? I was thinking of selling tickets. You really didn't know we were there?"

"Uh-uh. I guess I was in the moment, like you're always telling me to be. Not overthinking things."

"You definitely didn't overthink anything I saw." She passed her glare over the remnants of the cast and crew who hadn't left the lobby yet and they melted away like frost off a windshield. Doc wished he could disperse a crowd like that. "You're better off, you know."

"Better off than what?"

"Better off without her, I mean."

"Whoa whoa whoa, wait a minute." Doc held both hands at chest level, palms outward. "You've been telling me for weeks—*weeks*—that Jillian was exactly what I needed. How I should make a few allowances, not worry so much, everything would be fine. Now you tell me I'm better off without her. What happened?"

"You saw her just now, right?"

"Me and half the cast and crew."

"Psycho bitch, right?"

"If you want to be technical about it, yeah."

"So why would I want my best friend to hook up with some psycho bitch?"

"And it occurred to you just this minute she was that way?"

"Uhhhh, maybe not exactly just now, but, you know, I thought it might be fun. You'd get your ashes hauled and not have to worry about a lot of complications." Doc tilted his head and glared at her. "Okay, it got a little more complicated than I expected."

The director called everyone back for rehearsal. Doc put a hand on Eve's arm before she could leave. "Am I really your best friend, Evie?"

She blushed. "Yeah. I guess you are."

Doc pulled her close into a hug. "Then I have nothing to complain about. Why would I need Jillian when I'm your best friend? I mean, how many psycho bitches can one man handle?"

He was amazed someone Eve's size could kick so hard.

CHAPTER 52

The first voice Doc heard coming into the station the next morning was Stush's. "That you, Benny? You got a minute?"

Quarter to seven, Doc there early for the surveillance car, then pick up Rick Neuschwander. Stush never came in before eight.

"Want some coffee?" Stush said when Doc sat. Doc held up the twenty-ounce from Mr. Donut. "Probably already have a doughnut, too."

"Half dozen for Neuschwander and me. Figured you'd want us to, early morning surveillance and all. Tradition."

"Goddamn right. Look, I don't want to hold you up. I know Neuschwander will have a fit if you're late, but I need to talk to you about something."

"Shoot."

"We got a call yesterday. This woman says a Penns River policeman stole her cell phone and threw it away, right there on the bypass by the Ice House. Said he threatened her, too. Something about shoving the phone up her ass, except she was way too dignified to say 'ass.' Said something like, 'He said he'd stick it where, you know, people aren't supposed to stick things.'"

"Uh, Stush—"

Stush put up a hand. "So I ask her if she got the unit number off the car and she said it was unmarked. I asked her how she knew it was a Penns River cop, and she gave me the

315

whole, 'We were in Penns River, where else could it be from?' So I explained to her how cops from other jurisdictions use the bypass all the time. That's why it's called the bypass, because it lets them go around town instead of through it."

He sipped his coffee, pulled it away with a "too hot" face. "So she gives me hell about how I'm trying to push it off, how this cop—big guy, dark hair, wore a jacket kind of like the one you've got on there—ran back to the car and swerved around her. Took off like a bat out of hell, though you know that's not exactly what she said, either.

"Well, I told her we only had three unmarked cars. One's in the shop. Willie Grabek had one, but he was in Pittsburgh most of the day. The only other car was the one you and Neuschwander signed out, and you were on a surveillance nowhere near the bypass, not as far as I knew. So that's what I'm checking. You followed Marian Widmer out to Pittsburgh Mills, right?"

Doc felt the near miss rush past his ear and relaxed. "Yeah."

"Well, hell, the direct route from her house to Pittsburgh Mills don't go anywhere near the bypass. I told her I was sorry and we'd look into it and asked if she needed any help finding the phone. Thought I'd send Eye Chart out to walk around with her calling it, hope the battery didn't run down."

Stush sipped his coffee again, found it more to his liking. "I didn't want her to go away mad, but I know none of our cops would do something like that. Sorry if I interrupted you there before. Was there something you wanted to say?"

"Uh, no, not really. Did Grabek get anything good on this

PI we saw with Marian Widmer? What's his name, Rollison?"

"Willie was gracious enough to share some of what he got with me before he went home yesterday. Go on and have a seat. Neuschwander will get over it. It's just some extra time with his wife and kids. Doman had the overnight, and he's probably asleep, anyway, so you're not keeping him from anything."

Stush waited for Doc to settle. "This Rollison guy. I guess he's been a pain in the balls downtown for a while now, so they checked him out. Informally. He has suction somewhere up the line, so they didn't get much. He used to be some sort of spook, but no one's saying what agency or what kind of work he did, so it's safe to say he didn't ride a desk. He has contacts everywhere and isn't bashful about leaning on people to get what he wants. Warrants and court orders aren't a big deal to him. He knows how to get information off the record we have to wait for a judge to sign for." Another sip. "You get anything good yesterday?"

"One of Neuschwander's sources identified Marian Widmer as the woman who mistook him for a hitter a few weeks ago. Asked him if he painted houses."

Stush whistled. "Only makes sense it's her."

"Should be enough for a phone tap."

"I'll put Grabek on it when he comes in."

They sat for a minute, Doc waiting for Stush to either say something or let him go. Stush sipped his coffee like it needed to be drunk slowly but right now so he could savor the taste before it went away. "This Rollison. Pittsburgh looked at him pretty hard from what Grabek told me. No one would help them. Couldn't even find out which letters of the alphabet he worked for."

"So he was covert. You think he was black ops?"

"I wouldn't normally. It's the easy way out. But we have this Widmer broad looking for a killer, witnessed at the scene, and connected to this Rollison. True, it's after the fact, but we don't know what they talked about. So I have to wonder if the mysterious Mr. Rollison was a wet boy."

Doc knew a little about such things. "Covert, even black ops, doesn't mean he killed people."

"Doesn't mean he didn't, either. Someone killed Frantz, though, and it looks like she was in on it. Now she's tied to Rollison. I want you to find out how."

"What would you like me to do?"

Stush finished his coffee. "Even I know he can't be squeezed. So go after her. Shake the tree if you think it's the right thing to do. She's an amateur, maybe she'll panic. I'll leave how you do it up to you, you're better than me at these things. But find out."

CHAPTER 53

Doc had the car door open—*thisclose* to getting on with the day—when his name was called. He recognized the voice before he turned to look.

"I need a word, Detective."

Jack Harriger.

Doc rested his elbow on the car's roof. "Can it wait, Deputy? I'm already late to pick up Neuschwander."

"You're off to a leisurely start. Five more minutes won't hurt."

"I've been here since quarter of seven. My day only appears leisurely because I spent the last twenty minutes with Stush."

Harriger's approach lost momentum. "The chief's here already?"

Doc sipped his coffee. "He wanted to talk to me, too. I'm in demand today."

"Was it about the Family Services fiasco you got us in the middle of?"

Damn, he should have said something to Stush. "No. This was some mistaken identity thing. I don't know that he's aware of that Family Services business. Did you say anything to him about it?"

"What I say or hear from the chief is none of your business, Detective. I'll write it up for him when I know all the facts. What I want from you is a full report, including what the hell you were thinking, removing two juveniles from DFS custody and hiding them with a civilian."

"First off, I didn't remove them from anything. They were roaming the streets when I rounded them up. DFS didn't know any more about their whereabouts than you did."

"That still wasn't your call to make."

"I was the only one there and I had to make a decision right away. I'll admit, putting them next door might not have been the best place, but I was pressed for time and didn't have a lot of options."

"You don't need options in a situation like that. The book says call Family Services."

"DFS would've either sent them back to the family that never reported them missing, or hauled them off to the county home. Neither option seemed attractive."

"You want to make those kinds of decisions, Dougherty, be a social worker. You're a cop. You do police work."

"I was doing police work. Everything we know about this case—everything—we got from those two kids. They go to County, they get the 'stop snitching' drill twenty-four hours a day. We send them back to Seventh Street and I lose the connection we were building. The older kid knew about me; that's the only reason he talked to us at all. We treated them right, fed them, took care of them, and they trusted us. We send them back into the system and they got no reason to talk to anyone."

"Are you finished?" Harriger drew himself up in full bantam rooster mode. Doc gave a modified version of The Look: no physical manifestations, but anyone paying attention would know to tread lightly. He knew Harriger was about to do the one thing that made his hundred other petty sins unforgiveable.

"What's wrong with you, Detective Dougherty, is that you've been allowed to get away with acting like your shit doesn't stink for too long. You're the spoiled kid of this department, and Chief Napier enables you. You do what you want, when you want, in the manner in which you feel like doing it. That is not good police work. That is television bullshit. No good department can function if one of its members thinks he's too good for the rest of us. You put those juveniles at risk, and left the department open to one hell of a lawsuit if something had happened to them."

Doc had several pet dislikes. Cramps in his feet that sometimes curled his toes over each other. Restaurants where the Vegetable of the Day was broccoli, no substitutions. The Designated Hitter. None came close to getting berated for something he'd already decided was a mistake, especially when he'd have to defend his position.

He did leave Wilver and David too close to the crime scene. He should have called Stush, worked it out with DFS, found them some way to be safe and still get to school. He knew all that and let Jefferson West keep them because he trusted West to do the right thing more than he trusted any component of the system. Kathleen Whitmore was right: Neshannock County DFS had an excellent reputation, well earned. Still, Wilver and David had fallen through the cracks once. Fall through again and they might be lost forever.

And...he wanted to put that case down. Barb Smith's comment hurt more than he'd let on. The boys *were* the case. Phone records linking Marian Widmer to David Frantz were nice, a circumstantial finger to tie a bow around for a jury.

The boys could place her car at the scene; with Wierzbicki's help, they'd place *her* there. He didn't know that at the time. All he knew was they could lead him to the car, and that a woman was there. But they were all he had, and that made him do something he would counsel against in more reasoned circumstances.

So now Harriger had carte blanche to bust his balls, and he couldn't argue with him, and he sure as hell couldn't agree with him. Coming clean and taking your medicine not an option with Jack Harriger; you'd never hear the end of it. Ten years down the road there would be a discussion and Harriger would say, "You were sure about those kids on Fourth Avenue, too." Doc took the only option left, impaled Harriger with the Modified Look that showed disgust short of insolence, and let him talk.

Harriger had continued his harangue while Doc thought. He set up a pause for breathing with, "Well? Don't you have anything to say?"

"Do you want an argument off the record, or do you want a report? I don't see any reason to do both."

Harriger needed a few seconds to shift gears. "Listen, all right, you're right. I want a report, and I want it today."

"Come on, Deputy. You know Stush won't let Neuschwander surveil Marian Widmer alone so I can do paperwork. Grabek should be able to get the warrants for her phones today. Then we won't have to stay on her so hard. I'll get to it then."

Harriger tried to maintain control of the conversation by sounding like he was giving orders. "All right, but the first day you're off surveillance, I want it."

"Fair enough." They stood without speaking. Doc sipped his coffee. "Is there anything else?"

"Yeah, look here, Dougherty, you're a good cop, a hell of a cop. Practically a natural. You just need some experience." Harriger two years older than Doc, talking to a man who worked as an Army investigator for three years and done a tour in Iraq while The Deputy chased speeders and poachers in Emporium, population 2,500. "I never understood why you came back here. You're cut out for bigger things. I could put a word in for you with the state police. I have friends there.

Only because you're not there anymore, Doc thought. "I was born here, Deputy. I went to school here. I probably know one in ten people in Penns River by name, and half the rest by sight. I like it here."

"You change your mind, let me know. Like I said, I got friends all over the state." *Except here.* "Be happy to put a good word in for you. Hate to see you get too old to make a career move before you figured out you should have."

"Thanks. I'll keep it in mind. I really need to pick up Neuschwander now. Doman's been out there alone since seven last night."

"Right, sorry. Don't let me keep you. Just remember what I said. About your career."

Sure, Doc thought. *I'll remember you want me to go away.*

CHAPTER 54

Stark left the stolen car in the Elks' parking lot, carried the .30-06 in its case across the road and up the hill. He'd marked the place on Milligantown Road where the spring came aboveground, where she'd park the car. Worked his way across the hill to a spot with a clear line of sight. The walking harder than he'd expected. Unseasonably cold the past week, leaves turning and falling earlier than usual, getting slippery as the rain made them wet.

Stark not his real name, of course; just the name he gave her. Took it from a series of books by Richard Stark, the main character a serious badass much the way Stark thought of himself. He liked borrowing a name other than his own from a writer using one other than *his* own, knowing the author wasn't Richard Stark at all, but Donald Westlake.

He shouldn't have taken her second call. She'd almost fucked up the hit in the vacant building with her lack of subtlety. He told her he preferred to take care of it himself, but she insisted. Made up some half-assed story about not letting Frantz suspect anything when the last thing anyone suspects is two behind the ear getting out of his car in front of his apartment, which is how Stark would have done it. No, she wanted to be there. He saw how hot it made her, practically smell it on her, surprised she didn't come when he pulled the trigger. Maybe she did. Stark not watching her just then, other things on his mind.

Twenty large for that job, and another twenty for this one. Ten already in the box behind the downstairs bathroom sink at his mother's house. She owed him ten more on completion, and he wondered as he lowered himself in a prone position if it was worth collecting. She insisted on getting cute this time, too, *lure* the target into the middle of the boonies. Just point the unlucky bastard out and let Stark do his business. He'd be dead within a week.

An hour and a half to wait. Stark here early so no one would happen onto him crossing the road. Plenty of leaves and deadfall for concealment and to gather into a firing support. Lots of time to think if the last ten grand was worth the risk. She thought of this like a reality TV show, Marian Widmer and her hit man, and there was no question she'd give him up if they squeezed her. The extra ten grand would be nice, but he already had thirty, and shooting her instead of the assigned target would get Stark free and clear, though it offended him to leave money on the table.

It wasn't like he did this full-time. Worked out of Youngstown, Crime City, mostly sharking, doing muscle as needed, the occasional shakedown. One or two hits a year like bonuses. He was good, he was reliable, people on the in knew who to call. Her being a third generation referral—she talked to a guy who knew a guy who knew Stark—didn't disqualify her. He'd worked for less money and worse references.

He spent an hour deciding whether to kill the man and take her ten grand, or to kill her and walk away clean. Went back and forth with himself until his indecision irritated him and he pushed it out of his mind. Make it a game time decision. See who presented the best shot.

CHAPTER 55

"Where the fuck is she going this time?"

Neuschwander driving in a steady rain, Doc slumped in his seat, thoroughly sick of following Marian Widmer while she acted like a housewife. The tap on her home phone would go up later that afternoon, but the cell people were dragging their heels, as usual. So Marian stayed under surveillance twenty-four-by-seven until they could account for her actions remotely at least some of the time.

The turn that set Doc off was a left onto Seventh Street Road. She'd followed the bypass again, bore left across town, left again opposite the high school. Not much out this way except Penn State, where they thought she'd been going the other day. Neuschwander kept a safe distance. Never impatient, steady as a metronome. Doc preferred to drive, but he liked Neuschwander relaxed and quiet in the driver's seat more than driving him crazy with his fidgeting as a passenger.

Marian turned left on Hartge. "She's going to Milligantown Road again," Doc said. "What the hell is so fascinating out here?"

"Maybe she likes to watch the leaves change color."

Neuschwander could be right; prime season for it. Something still felt off. Why come all the way to the other side of town, missing most of the foliage, just to drive home through it, when she could have turned half a dozen places and seen trees everywhere?

"Awfully dreary for sight-seeing, even if she is the nature loving type, which I don't think she is. Give her some room, Noosh. She might be looking for a tail."

Marian drove northeast, back toward the bypass. Parked in a small turnout where a spring opened out of the hill to run through a pair of pipes. Doc stopped here a couple of times a month, fill up an empty Gatorade bottle and taste real water for a change.

Neuschwander looked over, worried. Doc nodded. "There's no place to pull over where we won't stick out. Drive past and we'll think of something." Lowered his head, blocked his face with his hand as they drove by. Looked over his shoulder as the car went around a bend to make sure they were out of sight. "Haul ass and turn around in the Vets. We might be able to pick a spot in the Elks' lot where we can see her."

"She'll recognize us when we go by the second time."

"We don't have a lot of choices. We stay at the Vets, she could bail out on Puckety Church or make a huey and go back Milligantown. We'd miss her either way. If you can find a spot between here and there we can hide and not be seen if she drives by, take it. Otherwise, we have to go to the Elks."

Marian was raising the hood when they came back. "Pass her while her back's turned," Doc said and Neuschwander pulled it off. Went by a hundred yards or so, turned into the parking lot for the Elks. Couple of cars there already. Someone cleaning up, or left behind from last night, owners who'd needed rides home.

The lot itself twenty feet below the level of the road, down a steep driveway. Neuschwander turned around, pulled up far enough to keep the car on the driveway and still have a line of sight to Marian's BMW.

"Can you see her?" he said.

"Sort of." Doc twisted in his seat. "I can see the trunk. Tree's in my way to see the front. How about you?"

Neuschwander leaned out his window and got a face full of rain. "I can see the whole car like this. Sort of make her out inside." Sat down to look through the windshield. "Here I can make out the car's there if I keep the wipers on. I'd know if she left, but I can't tell what she's doing now."

Doc tried two more angles. Got out to look over the roof. Not much better. Leaned back into the car. "Something stinks. I can't believe she pulled over and popped the hood in this weather just because the Check Engine light came on." He reached into the glove box for the field glasses. "Call Grabek. Tell him get his ass to the Vets parking lot and keep his eyes open. I'll walk the hill on the other side of the road. Call me if you see anything, but don't wait for me. Stay with her and get Grabek to help you. I'll find a way back."

He eased the door shut. Walked another fifty yards away from Marian to where she couldn't see and crossed the road. The rain steady, more than a drizzle, less than a shower. A passing car's tires hissed on the wet pavement. Doc jumped across a berm onto the hill, grabbed a sapling for balance. The rain falling on wet leaves muffled external sound; he heard his breathing inside his head. He pulled on the sapling, started up the hill.

It was steep going and the leaves were slippery. He slid a couple of times, caught himself on tree branches. Worked his way to a promising spot and looked around. Turned and saw straight into the windshield of Neuschwander's car; couldn't see Marian's. Went down and to the right fifty yards hoping for a usable notch in the hillside. Stopped to try the glasses again. No joy. He scanned across the hill, looking for a break in the trees where he could see but not be obvious. Stopped when something in a small clearing forty yards to his ten o'clock caught his eye. Took another look to be sure.

A man lay on the ground. He wore a dark brown jacket, blue jeans, and Timberland boots. He had a baseball cap on backward. Tufts of brown hair crawled out either side. Leaves covered the backs of his knees. He pointed a rifle with a scope through a gap in the trees toward Marian Widmer's car.

Doc had trained on slow, silent movement in the Army. Not as good at as he used to be. No matter. Rain falling through and on wet leaves would cover any sound he was likely to make. He slipped his gun from the hip holster. Advanced one foot at a time, stealing looks at the man with the rifle while paying attention to where his foot would come down next. Picked his way through twigs, careful not to break any. Invested nine minutes covering twenty yards—half the distance—when the man stirred and Doc froze.

The man shifted, brought the rifle up, took the covers off the scope. Doc followed his line of sight and saw a dark Lincoln Town Car that looked familiar pull in next to Marian's. A man got out. He looked familiar, too. Hard to say without the binoculars and he couldn't risk using them.

Marian got out of her car. The rifle scope shifted as she and the other man moved. Doc started again, less carefully, counting on the rain and the rifleman's concentration to cover what extra noise he might make. Fifteen yards. Ten. At twenty feet the man locked the rifle into his shoulder and Doc knew he was close as he'd get.

He spoke with the voice the military taught him. Not shouting, not even loud. Projected with a tone that discouraged disagreement. "Penns River police. Lay the weapon down and extend your hands away from your body, palms up. Now."

The rifle relaxed from the shoulder. The man's body twisted no more than a couple of inches. His left hand moved, not the right.

Doc used the same voice. "Don't. I'll put one up your ass and one through your heart before you can reach anything useful."

The man's head dipped an inch, then he shifted position to lay flat. Extended his arms. Doc moved quickly, placed a foot in the small of the man's back. Drew his handcuffs. Said, "Left hand," and the man turned enough to present it. Same for the right.

"Can I get up?" the man said. "Fucking wet down here."

"In a minute." Doc took the rifle by the end of the barrel, slid it away. Took out his cell, dialed Neuschwander. "Call Grabek. Arrest everyone at the spring and wait for me. I'm bringing one more."

"What's the charge?"

"Let's just get them to the station. Stush has a whole book of charges we can pick through."

CHAPTER 56

"I was hunting."

"Hunting what?" Doc said. "Deer season isn't for six weeks yet."

"Rabbits."

"You hunt rabbits with a rifle."

"More of a challenge."

Doc flipped through a sheaf of papers. Driver's license and a fingerprint check showed his guest was Frank Orszulak, 1665 Benning Street, Youngstown, Ohio. Eight months in Mahoning County jail for assault. Five other assault charges, all dropped. Arrested for assault with intent to inflict grave bodily injury for beating an alleged debtor with a baseball bat. The charging document even specified it was a Louisville Slugger Model C-271. Charge dismissed when the witness and victim both recanted. One conviction for usury; sentence suspended. Questioned and released in connection with four homicides in Youngstown and Cleveland.

"You know it's illegal to discharge a firearm within the Penns River city limits."

"I guess you stopped me just in time. Thanks."

One of the cars in the Elks parking lot had been stolen that morning from a supermarket in Vandergrift. Cute, stealing a car the wrong side of the logical escape route.

"That's a stolen car in the parking lot."

"I don't know nothing about that."

"Where's your car?"

"Little town out the road there. Vandergrift."

"Why's it there?"

"I didn't want to drive it here and leave it somewhere it might not be safe."

"So you walked here from Vandergrift." About nine miles.

"I got a ride."

"From who?"

"Some guy. I was hitching."

"You get his name?'

"Uh-uh."

"What'd he look like?"

"You know. White guy, forty-fifty. Hair getting gray, pretty good belly on him. Wore a flannel shirt and a Steelers hat." Thirty percent of the population.

"Okay, Frank—you mind if I call you Frank?"

"Not at all."

"Okay, Frank, let me get this straight. You drove from Youngstown to Vandergrift yesterday. Hitched a ride back to Penns River, which you drove through on the way to Vandergrift, so you could hunt rabbits with a rifle, but without a license. That about right?"

"Yeah. You got me on that hunting license thing."

"We're awful fussy about that."

"My bad luck."

Doc scanned the paperwork one last time, trying to conjure an open warrant for anything—jaywalking, incorrect postage—that would justify an overnight stay. Nothing.

"Wait here, Frank." No comment. Orszulak probably knew more about waiting in police stations than Doc.

Grabek stood in the hall chatting with Stush. "Is Neuschwander still around?" Doc asked.

"He just went home for dinner," Stush said. "He's not going to like coming back in."

"I don't care if he comes in or not. I need him to get a hold of Dwight Wierzbicki, tell him to get his ass down here to eyeball a suspect." He nodded toward the room holding Frank Orszulak.

Stush looked at Doc, then the door. "I'm on it."

"You talk to her?" Doc asked Grabek when Stush was gone.

"She lawyered up. Been in there about twenty minutes with some guy from downtown."

"She say anything at all?"

Grabek shook his head. "Walked in like she'd been shopping on the Strip all day, sat her tight ass down and asked for a lawyer. I didn't even get a chance to introduce Stush or turn on the tape."

Doc had gone to the men's room and come back with Cokes for him and Grabek by the time her lawyer came out. Late thirties, dark hair, thousand dollar suit. "You can talk to her now," he said, "but she's not saying anything."

They followed the lawyer into the room where Marian waited. Grabek made the introductions, turned on the tape, and repeated the cast for the record.

Q (Det. Grabek): Interview with Marian Widmer. Penns River police represented by Detective William Grabek and Detective Benjamin Dougherty. Mrs. Widmer is represented by her counsel, Dennis Lattimore. Mr. Lattimore, is there anything you'd like on the record before we begin?

A (Mr. Lattimore): Only that my client wishes to

cooperate to the extent her rights are not waived, and that I will be the sole judge if any question is appropriate or answerable.

Q: Very well. Mrs. Widmer, where were you on the night of this past October 7 and 8?

A (Mr. Lattimore): That's a pretty broad time frame, Detective. Can you narrow it down a little? Say, between this time and that time?

Q: Very well. Mrs. Widmer, let's say between the hours of eight PM on the seventh and three AM on the eighth.

A (Mrs. Widmer): I was at home, alone.

Q: Where were your children?

A: I had made plans to go out, so they were at my mother's house. I took them over right after school, but I started to feel ill a few hours later and decided to stay home. I didn't want to disturb them, so I called my mother and told her I'd be home, but the kids could stay.

Q: Are you aware your car was witnessed at the scene of a homicide that evening?

A (Mr. Lattimore): Do you have a positive identification?

Q: We have the make and model. The car had a temporary plate. We narrowed the list of all similar vehicles with new temp plates in this area. Mrs. Widmer's was a match.

A: But you don't have a positive match on the license plate?

Q: We contacted the other possibilities and eliminated them.

A: Eliminated them how?

Q: Either the cars don't match, or the owners have established alibis.

A: So you're eliminating other matches, but you don't have positive ID on her car?

Q: That's correct, Counselor. I think you'll find that's more than adequate.

A: In conjunction with other factors, sometimes. Are you saying her car killed someone? Is she to be responsible for that?

Q: I'm just wondering how her car came to be at this location at that time and she not know anything about it. She doesn't know anything about it, does she?

A: Ask her.

Q: Mrs. Widmer, do you know how your car could have come to be on Fourth Avenue that night?

A (Mrs. Widmer): No, I don't.

Q: Were you on Fourth Avenue that night?

A: Earlier, perhaps. Coming back from my mother's—she lives in Springdale—I crossed the Ninth Street Bridge. Sometimes I come home along Fourth Avenue, then up Drey Street.

Q: Did you that night?

A: That was weeks ago, Detective. I wasn't paying that much attention. I didn't think I'd need to know.

Q: Assuming you had gone home that way, about what time would it have been?

A (Mr. Lattimore): We're not assuming anything. You can prove an assertion, or you can't.

Q: Her car was seen there, with a woman meeting her general description.

A: A car much like hers was seen there. Do you have a witness who can positively identify her?

Q: We haven't put her in a line-up yet.

A: Do you plan to?

Q: It hasn't been decided.

So it went for two hours. All Grabek was able to establish through a hundred and twenty minutes of Marian's obfuscations and Lattimore's objections was that she knew Daniel Rollison because he was working on her husband's defense team. She pulled over near the spring on Milligantown Road because her Check Engine light came on and she was afraid to drive a brand new car any farther. (Doc smiled to himself at that.) She called Mr. Rollison to help her because he knew about cars and had said to call if she needed anything. No, she didn't know why the light didn't come on again when Grabek started the car. Yes, she had slapped Mr. Rollison at her home several days earlier. That was because he'd made an improper advance to her—exactly those words, "improper advance." Doc felt like he was in a Forties movie, though Marian Widmer was hotter than Barbara Stanwyck. She'd called Mr. Rollison for help, even after that episode, because he'd apologized to her over the phone and she wanted to give him a chance to make amends.

Marian asked for a bathroom break. Doc, Grabek, and Lattimore walked her to the ladies room. Doc waited outside while Grabek used the men's, then they switched, both while Marian took her turn. Lattimore didn't need to go, confirming Doc's suspicion that defense lawyers don't have bodily functions.

Back in the interview room, Grabek ramped up the questioning.

"How did you meet Carol Cropcho?"

Doubt flickered behind her eyes so quickly only a pro would catch it. "You mean the woman my husband killed—

is accused of killing? I didn't know her."

"You're sure?"

"I know who I know and who I don't."

"Is there a purpose to this line of questioning, Detective?" Lattimore said.

"We're not in court, Counselor. I ask what I want. She answers what she wants. Or what you tell her she wants. Can I go on?"

"Within limits. If I think you're just fishing, we're leaving. And I'm close."

Grabek gave him and Marian time to add comments, then went on.

Q: So you're sure you didn't know Carol Cropcho?

A (Mrs. Widmer): I never heard of her before I saw her name in the paper. When she was killed.

Q: Then I wonder if you can explain this. (Hands papers to Mrs. Widmer.) These are cell phone records, yours and Carol Cropcho's. You used to call each other regularly until it stopped about nine months ago.

A: What do you want to know?

Q: Why you kept calling someone you didn't know.

A: I told you. I didn't know her.

Q: Then why does her number show up on your cell phone bills?

A: I don't know. All I can think of...I believe you said yourself Tom was having an affair with her. He must have called her from my phone.

Q: Why would he do that?

A (Mr. Lattimore): You're asking her to read his mind?

Q: She's the one who brought the idea up. I only wondered why she thought of it.

A: You can ask about facts. Her opinions are her business.

Q: Then I guess you won't like it if I ask her why Mrs. Cropcho called her husband back on Mrs. Widmer's number. Seems indiscrete to me.

A: That's all. Mrs. Widmer, we're leaving.

Q: We're not finished here, Counselor.

A: Yes we are. Unless you have a charge.

Q: I'll charge her when I'm good and ready.

A: Then you'd better get good and ready in the next thirty seconds or we're gone.

Q: (Detective Dougherty): Hang on, hang on. Let's all take a deep breath. We've been here a long time. Mr. Lattimore, Mrs. Widmer, do you mind if I ask a couple of quick questions, then maybe we can wrap this up?

A: (Mrs. Widmer): I suppose that would be all right, if my attorney agrees.

A: (Mr. Lattimore): Very quick questions, Detective. Five minutes.

Q: That'll be fine. I appreciate the courtesy. Mrs. Widmer, have you ever been to the bar in the Warszawa Hotel?

That shook her more than the Carol Cropcho question. She recovered quickly—had to hand it to her, she was good—not quick enough to get past Doc. Grabek made no sign, Doc sure he couldn't have missed it.

He let Marian's silence linger until anyone who might view the tape would have to be aware of it. "Mrs. Widmer? Have you ever been there? The Warszawa?"

"Is that over on Sixteenth Street?"

"Seventeenth, actually, but close enough. Have you ever been there?"

Marian's voice was strong, but not as solid as before.

"I've lived here all my life. I'm sure I've been there once or twice."

"Can you remember a specific time?"

Lattimore spoke up. "I get the feeling you have a specific time in mind, Detective. Why don't you just ask her so we can get on with it?"

"I'm thinking in the past month or six weeks. Not so long ago your client would have a hard time remembering."

"What's your reason for asking?" Lattimore said.

"I'm trying to clear something up. I have this guy. He says he's a witness. I don't know. Mostly he's a jagoff, pardon my language. He says he saw Mrs. Widmer there, at the Warszawa, one night in that time frame. I didn't think much of it at first, the Warszawa not the kind of place a woman like Mrs. Widmer's likely to spend much time."

"Are you saying you're asking as part of another investigation?"

"I'm not saying anything. I just asked the question."

"How would this witness recognize Mrs. Widmer?"

Doc took his time. Made eye contact with Marian Widmer and held it while he spoke. "He didn't know her then. They've since been introduced. This guy, he's sitting in the Warszawa having a beer and what he described as a hot-looking woman walks in and sits next to him. He figures what the hell, starts his spiel." Still in the stare-down with Marian. "Imagine his surprise when she asks him if he paints houses."

"Paints houses?" Marian said it like Doc had been speaking Greek.

"Means 'do you kill people?' It's what gets said when someone's meeting a hit man."

Lattimore got to his feet. "That's all. Let's go."

Doc raised a hand to wait. He and Marian were still locked onto each other. "So while he's wondering whether to shit or wind his watch, a hard case sits on the other side of her, says he does some painting, and his own carpentry, which is a way of saying he'll dispose of the body. Oh, and by the way, our witness is told to get lost, which he does."

Marian said, "And can this witness identify the other man?" and Lattimore got pale as frostbite.

Doc said, "Hasn't tried yet. He's on his way in."

"And if he does?" Sherbet wouldn't melt in her mouth.

"Then he does."

One corner of Doc's mouth curled up. Marian returned it. They sat like that, almost smiling at each other, no one speaking, until Lattimore couldn't stand it anymore and took her home.

CHAPTER 57

Doc stepped into the hall and almost ran Stush over.

"Your witness is here. Wierz-the hell the rest of it is. At your desk."

"Think Orszulak will go for a line-up?"

"He'll need a lawyer."

"Maybe he'll waive. He thinks he's smart. We'll get him a PD if he insists."

"So go ahead and ask him. Let me know. We'll need some guys."

"I can get us guys. Stand by."

Doc knocked once on the door, stepped into the room with Orszulak.

"You got to be the politest cop I ever seen. Knocking before you come in like that."

"I didn't want to catch you jerking it and embarrass us both. Here's the deal. I could write you a ticket, maybe two. Then you'd have to come back to contest them and that would be a pain for everyone."

"Who says I'll contest? I'll just pay. You caught me fair and square."

"Even so, I'm willing to let the tickets slide if you'll do a little thing for me. Won't take but a few minutes."

"What?"

"I need you to stand in a line-up."

"What, as one of the—what do you call them—distracters? No. I got a long drive ahead of me."

"You're not getting it. I want you for guest of honor. There's a guy needs to take a look at you."

"For what? Hunting?"

"In a way, but not like what the tickets will say. Tell you what. I'll even give you a ride back to your car in Vandergrift if you stay for it."

"Fuck you. I'll call a cab." Orszulak made to get up.

"Uh-uh. You're staying, either way. I was just trying to be a nice guy about it."

"Fuck you again. You can't make me stay. I got rights."

"You have the right to a lawyer. You want one?"

"Fuck yeah."

"Wait here."

Doc stepped out, told Stush Orszulak asked for a lawyer, could he set it up.

"Where are you going?"

"Edgecliff Bar." Stush gave him a look. "I'm gonna fix us up a line-up."

The Edgecliff Bar busy with regulars taking advantage of Happy Hour's seventy-five-cent drafts. Doc stepped to the bar, held up three twenties.

"Who wants to make twenty bucks for an hour's worth of standing around?"

A few looked confused. Most of the regulars knew Doc and what he wanted. He had half a dozen volunteers, picked the three best and loaded them in his car.

He saw Grabek coming out of the men's after he dropped his line-up off to wait. "Did the PD come yet for Orszulak?"

"On the way. He wanted someone in Ohio, said it was his regular guy. I don't feel like waiting here for some Cleveland asshole to crank up his Model A and drive all the way to civilization. Told him our witness was here now. He could take the PD for the time being or I could charge him and make him spend a night or two. He asked what the charge would be and I said wait, went out and got the penal code, brought it in and dropped it on the table. 'Take your pick,' I says. 'Gotta be something in there likes you.' He took the PD. It's almost like he thinks we're a bunch of rubes here. You get someone for the line-up?"

"Picked up three at Edgecliff. We can use them and see who else is here looks even a little like Orszulak."

"I got a better idea." They went into the detectives' office. Doc drew himself a cup of water from the cooler. Grabek assumed his usual feet-on-desk position. "Let's put Rollison in."

"Rollison doesn't look all that much like Orszulak."

"He's a middle-aged white guy. We all look pretty much the same. I got to thinking while you were gone, if Rollison was a wet boy, those skills transfer to civilian life. Maybe he's the guy Wierzbicki saw."

Doc took a sip while he considered the possibility. Stush stuck his head in before he could make up his mind. "PD's here for Orszulak. They're talking now. You get enough guys for the line-up?"

Doc said, "I got three. We were talking about whether Rollison might make a good fifth."

"Then we'd have to lawyer him up, too. He's not going anywhere. Cut him loose and find someone from next door to sit in. That one janitor looks close enough the lawyer won't object. We can always bring Rollison back if what's-his-name can't ID this one."

Grabek left to release Rollison. Doc went next door to the
county side of the complex to borrow George Squitieri for an
hour. Gathered the Squirt and his three Edgecliff Bar volunteers together with Orszulak. Told them the drill, left a uniform to watch them.

Penns River didn't have what a larger city would call a
lineup room. The interview room Orszulak had been in had
lines drawn on the wall opposite a two-way mirror that had
Doc, Stush, Grabek, Wierzbicki, and Orszulak's public defender on the other side.

The PD was named Sylvia Coates. Short, around thirty,
gave the impression she was building her resume for heaven
now before the opportunity to make serious, conscienceless
money came along. She had teeth like an English rodent,
wore her hair in a bob that needed attention, and acted like
she'd been disturbed from something far more entertaining.

"This is very irregular," she said in a voice coated with
nicotine. "Mr. Orszulak has a personal attorney in Ohio.
Has he been contacted?"

Grabek gestured toward the mirror. "His decision. He
didn't want to spend the night. So here you are."

"Spending my night. Thanks." A job like his, Doc usually
sympathized with someone called out to work on their
personal time. He made an exception for Sylvia. "Let's get on
with it. What's your witness's name?"

"Uh-uh," Grabek said. "You'll get that later. Orszulak
has a record of violent crime, and we're looking at him as a
murder suspect. There's no way you, or he, gets this name
until we have to give it at discovery."

"Oh, good," Coates said. "A cop who knows the law.
Almost worth coming in for. All right. Bring them out."

Grabek pressed a button in the wall. Five men filed in, Orszulak fourth. The drill never changes. "Number One, step forward. Turn to the left. Turn to the right. Step back. Number Two..."

Doc saw Wierzbicki tense when Orszulak entered behind George Squitieri the county janitor. Watched his eyes move down and around, only sneaking looks at Orszulak while everyone else stepped forward, turned left, turned right, and stepped back. Looked away for Orszulak's turn, then back to roaming when the last man stepped forward.

"Take your time," Doc said. "Let us know if you want to see anyone again. We can ask them to speak if that'll help."

Wierzbicki stared at Orszulak, his skin the color of newsprint. His jaw moved and he swallowed.

"He's not here. I never saw any of these guys before."

CHAPTER 58

Donte had never been to Baltimore. Most of what he knew he learned from watching the Steelers play the Ravens on TV, pictures of the water and the old boat in the harbor. Looked nice. Now he was hanging with his cousin, a West Side boy, driving through a hood made Homewood look like Strip in Las Vegas. Not that Donte had been to Vegas, either, but he'd seen those Ocean movies so he had an idea.

The cousin's name was Walter; everyone called him Tookie. "Over there where they did my boy Nardine. Shot his ass up then run him over with the car when he fell in the street all bloody and shit. This here," he pointed to a viaduct passing overhead, "this where they made that homeless city in *The Wire.*"

Donte knew *The Wire.* Fancied himself as Stringer Bell, he got some money and schooling. "You think we could go down by Hamsterdam, where they let the slingers set up legal and shit?"

"Naw, man, they bulldozed that shit for real. I don't even know could I find the motherfucker now, way they changed it."

Tookie pulled up in front of a half dozen row houses on Fayette west of Amity. Knocked on the third door from the left and said a few words. Made Donte show himself. Someone snickered and the chain came off the door and they were inside.

The interior was a hopper's dream. Sixty-inch TV, X-Box, PS2, Wii. Game cartridges everywhere. Guy with arms like Donte's thighs handed them each a Rolling Rock and pointed up the stairs. Tookie turned left at the landing and knocked twice, quiet. Someone said, "Yeah," and they went in.

The room was fixed up like an office. Desk with a leather chair, three other chairs in front of it. Safe in the corner was closed, not locked. Man behind the desk wore an open silk shirt over a wife-beater, baggy shorts past his knees even with his feet on the desk. Wore what looked like brand new Reebok ZigTechs.

"Have a seat, please. You understand, I don't usually see people I don't know, but since you and Tookie family and Tookie's my boy, I make an exception. He tells me you a player in Pittsburgh and might has a proposition for me. I'm always ready to hear a proposition, 'specially if it make me money."

"That's why I'm here, Mister—uh—Mister..."

"No disrespect, you understand, but you don't need to know my name just yet. Tookie my boy, but I don't know shit about you. You don't have a name, be harder for you to lead Five-O back to me just in case you got ideas along those lines. Not saying you do, I respect you and all, but a man in my position gots to be careful, you feel me?"

"I understand completely. Man like you's got to be careful. I only axed because I don't know what to call you, you know, like while we talking."

The man's voice dropped twenty degrees in temperature. "You don't need to call me a got-damn thing. Just tell me what the fuck you want."

Donte forced himself not to acknowledge the sweat on his

forehead. Pittsburgh was a major league sports city, but he was definitely Triple-A in the life. This man here had it going on, where Donte wanted to be if he could get out from under that ofay Mannarino.

"Tookie maybe told you I run a crew on the North Side of Pittsburgh. I got a connect for some quality goods, and I'm doing a little wholesaling with the crews on the Hill, Homewood, a little action in Wilkensburg. I'm doing all right, coming along, but this guy delivers my package keeping me down. Treat me like his house nigger, got me running errands and shit."

"Mike the Hook, right?"

Donte thinking this nigger's for real, doing his research, knowing shit before Donte even had a chance to tell him. Might as well cut to the chase. "Right, the Hook. Thing is, he don't do shit for me except take his points. He hand me the package and take a cut big as mine just for moving it one hand to the other. I don't see no what you call value add there. So, what I'm thinking is, why fool with him when I can go with someone show me some respect? Man I could learn from. And right away I think you might be that man, what I hear from Tookie."

The man sat behind the desk, cracking his knuckles one at a time while Donte talked. Made a steeple of his fingers, tapped the tips against each other irregularly. Donte out of his league, knew this was a test, could he keep his mouth shut until he heard what the man had to say, not try to oversell the proposition.

"How much the Hook charge for a key?" Donte told him. "Oooo-weee, boy, don't your ass hurt, the way he fucking you so regular?" He laughed, Tookie smiled; Donte missed the joke. "Look, I tell you straight up. I can sell to you for a price halfway between what I pay and what you pay and still make a nice profit. Everybody happy."

"Except the Hook," Tookie said.

"Fuck the Hook," Donte said.

"I'm sure you'd like to fuck the Hook, motherfucker not ever giving you the courtesy of a reach around." The man quit playing with his fingers, looked more or less at Donte for the first time. "See, what you bring me here is a good proposition. I appreciates that. I could make a lot of money working with you, and you'd do fine yourself. There is a problem, though. Big problem."

Donte couldn't resist. "How big?"

"Motherfucking deal breaker big. See, I get my package same place Mike the Hook. My boys even runs into his time to time. It's all good, just business, right? Now, if I start to move an extra twenty, twenty-five percent, my connect gonna want to know what I'm doing with it, dig? He know my business didn't just go up that much overnight, so I must be wholesaling."

Donte barely kept his mouth from falling open. Here he was, talking about buying his whole supply, and this man telling him it's just a small percentage of what he moves regular.

The man not done talking yet. "The problem is, when my connect see this big increase in my package, he also see Mike the Hook dropping off the same amount."

"Why would he give a fuck? He making the same money."

"He might not give a fuck. But he might, too. Him and Mike the Hook goes way back, and these Dagos some clannish motherfuckers. He might not like the idea of taking bread off his boy's table, give it to some niggers wearing rags on they heads. Maybe he get the ass and I lose my whole package. Or at least lose my preferred pricing, which I worked so hard to achieve.

"I axed around about you. I know you got some skills. I'd like to help you. But you gots to understand, I got me a business to run. People depends on me. You stay tight with my boy Tookie there. I see an opportunity for us to do business, I'll reach out. You see an opportunity, I want to hear about it first. Spend some time, us building a relationship and shit, everything be cool. Then, when the time right, opportunity present itself, we ready. You feel me on this?"

"Absolutely. I understand completely." Understand completely this man was a punk ass playing Original Gangster. Fine. Donte knew how to be patient. His time would come. So would Mike the Hook's. Motherfuckers line up to do business with Donte then.

CHAPTER 59

Sally Gwynn draped her suit jacket on a hanger, hooked it to the coat tree in her office. Popped open the can of beer Doc handed her and gestured for Grabek to close her office door.

"No drinking in the county building." She took a sip, waited for it to trickle down her throat. "Since it is my sworn duty to enforce that law, I insist on closing the door when drinking with two cops who just talked me into indicting a case I can't win."

"Come on, Sally," Doc said. "We still have time to work it, and you have that hot shit investigator. How hard can it be?"

"My hot shit investigator," Sally said, taking another sip and propping both shoeless feet on her desk, "is the best I've ever seen at making sure everything we have goes to court in perfect condition. Most anal retentive, OCD little bugger you ever want to see. He verifies everything you give us so well most defense counsels that work here regularly don't even make us submit most of them as evidence; they stipulate. He'll take those phone records you got and probably be able to tell if the call was made by pressing one number at a time, or speed dial, or voice dial. I don't know how he does it."

She leaned back in the chair to stretch and Doc was mesmerized by the pulse in her throat. That didn't make him special, and Sally knew it. This was her move. It guaranteed the attention of almost all men, and women of certain tastes.

"But ask Darrell to find one original fact on his own and he'll look at you like a dog you asked to turn a doorknob. He's a sweet man and a hard worker but I don't think he's had an original thought since—well, ever."

"How long till the trial?" Grabek missed Marian's arraignment for a doctor's appointment, playing catch-up.

"Early January. Gives us about seven weeks," Sally said.

"Plenty of time, assuming no one else gets killed," Doc said. "And I think we have all the parties who've been running around killing people pretty well under wraps."

Sally crushed her empty and threw it in the trash. Not a small woman, she'd played field hockey at Penn State and once subdued a rowdy defendant before the bailiff had a chance to even look like he was protecting her. Gestured to Doc for another can. "Okay. Let's talk about how you boys are going to spend your holidays, assuming no one else gets killed."

"Marian outsmarted herself trying to tell us Tom used her phone to call Carol Cropcho *and* had Carol call him back on it. No one's ever going to believe that. Had to be Marian and Carol who were having the affair, and they had to have gone places besides each other's houses. That means someone saw them together. We get photos and shoe leather and find a few of them. Then let her deny she knew Carol."

"That's nice, but it's gravy," Sally said. "It's not worth the trouble to tie her to the Cropcho killing. Not with Frantz dead."

"Sure it is. She admits she knew Frantz. Sure as hell no one will believe that phone sex story. Frantz is the link between her and the Cropcho murder. Wierzbicki can place her at the Warszawa looking for a hitter."

"But he can't identify the hitter."

"It was him." Doc finished his beer, tossed the can in a wastebasket across the room. "Orszulak, I mean. Our boy about shit when he come in the door. Couldn't look away until it was Orszulak's turn, then he couldn't look at him. He's afraid, is all. We just have to work on him, convince him it's in his interest to speak up, and that we can protect him."

"Or make him more afraid of us than he is of Orszulak," Grabek said.

No one spoke while Sally thought. Her gig now. Her decisions would make or break the case in court. She stared at a point near the ceiling, midway between Doc and Grabek, eyes half closed. She looked almost sleepy.

"You want me to argue in court that Marian Widmer, working in conjunction with David Frantz, persuaded her husband to kill Carol Cropcho. What's the motive?"

"We're not sure," Grabek said. "Revenge, maybe. Could be the Cropcho broad dumped her and Marian wanted even."

Sally kept her gaze on the ceiling. "Juries don't do could be."

"That's why we have to find someone who saw them togethef."

"And that alone will establish vengeance as a motive? You take this woman scorned shit pretty seriously, don't you?"

Grabek not used to hearing his judgment questioned. "We can prove she lied about knowing her. Why bother? Had to be something serious enough that perjury is a shorter fall."

"Forget about Marian and the Cropcho case. We have her

husband for it, and we don't need to muddy the water."
Sally's voice showed her mind was made up. "Let's work on
the Frantz hit. We have actual evidence there."

Grabek wasn't ready to give up. "The Cropcho thing is
the motive for the Frantz hit. He's the weak link, the only
thing that could trip her up. One leads directly to the other."

"You're asking the jury to make too many leaps. Stick
with Frantz."

"I am. Frantz won't go down without the Cropcho
connection."

Sally moved her head to face Grabek. Opened her eyes.
"We're not charging Marian Widmer with Cropcho. We're
working her and Frantz. Period. How are we going to do it?"

Doc sensed Grabek getting the red ass and stepped up. "It
works either way. Leaving Cropcho out of it creates a
minefield for the defense, a lot of things he has to avoid or it
opens the door for us to hammer him on her credibility.

"Here's what we have for sure. Marian knew Frantz. We
have the cell phone records. It's just a matter of time before
we put the two of them together just like Willie wants to do
with Marian and Carol Cropcho. We have a witness who can
identify Marian as the woman asked him if he paints houses,
then sees her meet someone who says he does. We can place
Marian's car at the scene, with a woman who looks not
unlike Marian, along with an unidentified man."

"It would really help if your witness could ID Orszulak as
the house painter."

"Yeah, well, we'll work on it. Rick Neuschwander has
some outstandings he's willing to forgive. We have to make
sure our witness understands the best way to stay safe is to
put Orszulak away forever, but if he doesn't talk, Orszulak

will be running around loose, knowing Wierzbicki's the one guy can put him in the jackpot."

Grabek interrupted his sulk to say, "So can the Widmer broad."

"Not if she beats the case," Sally said. "If we don't put her down, Orszulak never has to worry about her. Double jeopardy."

"And she's more likely to go down if Wierzbicki identifies Orszulak," Doc said.

"Those two kids can't positively ID either the Widmer woman or Orszulak from that night?" Sally said.

"Not for sure. I wouldn't want to put them through it." The new foster home working out better than Seventh Street. Jefferson West still not cleared to take them back, and every snag of red tape only delayed the next. "They're just kids, Sally."

"They may be all we have. The hit was a professional job, so we won't get the gun and motive's not an issue. We need to put Marian Widmer together with the shooter, and put them both at the scene. That's your task. Put them there together. Marian's the amateur. Get enough around her and squeeze. Convince her there's no reason to take the whole fall when he's the one who did the actual shooting."

"Far as we know," Grabek said.

Sally and Doc both froze and looked at him. "Huh?"

"As far as we know, he's the one did the actual shooting. I wouldn't put it past her."

They sat, finishing the beers already in hand. Sally looked at Doc, then Grabek. They both sighed and stood.

"Looks like evenings at the Warszawa," Doc said. "Someone else besides Wierzbicki had to see them that night, and they had to meet somewhere before they went over to do Frantz. We find even one other guy, maybe the Bick grows a conscience."

CHAPTER 60

Daniel Rollison reached into an old-fashioned brief case at his feet and withdrew a two-inch sheaf of papers.

"Here you are, counselor. Everything I have on the Widmer case."

Aiden Flaherty laid the stack on his desk without looking. "A synopsis, please, but take your time. You've never offered to tell me anything worth hearing about this case before. I want to savor the experience. It *is* worth hearing, isn't it?"

"You'll like it." Rollison laid it all out. Marty Cropcho was really a nickel-and-dime criminal named David Frantz. Frantz and Marian Widmer exchanged phone calls for an extended period of time. Frantz is dead. He didn't say how he came to have any of this knowledge. Rollison still worked on a need-to-know basis, and Flaherty only needed to know what, not how.

The lawyer rubbed his forehead. "Very impressive. What does it prove?"

"Enough for a plea deal, maybe."

"Because..." Flaherty hated criminal law, all the rules of evidence. Reasonable doubt, probable cause, exclusionary rule. He liked contract enforcement, writing weasel words into documents to interpret as he saw fit when the time was right to convince a jury his client was the offended party.

"Because you don't have anything else. He killed her. You know that, right?"

Flaherty made four-fifty an hour and didn't care for Rollison's tone. "That was never really in doubt."

"He broke into the house to kill her and make it look like a robbery. That's premeditation, first degree, probably natural life. Best he can hope for is the jury might feel sorry for him and go for Murder Two, which is what? Thirty to life? What you have here gives the DA a sexy prosecution she didn't know she had. A wife setting up her husband to kill another woman. That has to be worth at least an appearance on *Dateline* or *48 Hours*."

"Do you really think this Gwynn woman is going to make me a deal for *that*? To accuse Marian of conning her husband into killing someone she didn't even know? Just because you have some phone calls between her and the man her husband thought was the victim's husband? No actual conversation, mind you. Just records of the calls."

"You don't think a jury will think that smells?"

"Of course it smells. It still doesn't prove anything we can use. Showing she conned him—if she did, which I still doubt—leaves us with the inconvenient fact that Tom Widmer killed Carol Cropcho. You're expecting me to plead he's so stupid she could talk him into doing it through someone else and he was powerless to stop it. That's not helping."

Rollison waited for Flaherty to come up for air. Guy was missing the whole point. Rollison didn't care about Tom Widmer any more than he cared about who'd win the next election in Kuala Lumpur. He owed Marian Widmer now and Flaherty was his best chance to clear the debt.

"The relationship between Marian and Frantz is important because Frantz was her intermediary. It was Frantz who talked Tom into killing Carol Cropcho."

"Refresh my memory. Which one is Frantz?"

Idiot. "Frantz is who your client thinks is Marty Cropcho. His drinking buddy. Tom thought Frantz would kill Marian for him, except Frantz was sleeping with Marian all along, probably more than Tom was. You got all that?"

"Better than you do, I suspect. What should I ask Ms. Gwynn to charge her with? Since we're bringing this to her on a silver platter, she's going to feel entitled to know the charge."

Talking to this lawyer was like teaching a fish to count on its fingers. "They might like to charge her with hiring someone to kill Frantz so she couldn't be connected to the Cropcho business. What you have here gives them motive. It's the kind of case that makes a prosecutor's career. You're probably still looking at second degree, but they can ask for leniency. Give him fifteen to thirty, your client gets out in ten or twelve."

"Our client."

"Pardon?"

"He's *our* client. Yours and mine. You're in too much of a hurry to wash your hands of him."

Rollison willing to drink bleach to wash away the memory of Tom and Marian Widmer by now. "Right. Our client. Sorry." He stood, snapped shut the brief. Patted the pile of papers on Flaherty's desk. "Everything you need is here. I'll send a bill."

Flaherty let Rollison see him choke back a laugh. "We won't get ten cents on the dollar for this case. Not once the wife gets through with the property and bank accounts."

"All the more reason for you to put her in on it. Remember one thing." He gestured at the papers. "The techniques I used to get all that? They'll work on you, too."

CHAPTER 61

Jefferson West already in his favorite seat at Earl's when Doc walked in the Monday before Thanksgiving. Half a dozen middle-aged and up black men sat at the bar. Another half dozen were sprinkled among four white guys watching the six-foot television against the opposite wall. West spoke to the man next to him, who moved over one seat. Doc thanked the man and the bartender asked for his order with a look. Doc pointed to West's glass, held up two fingers, then pointed to the almost empty glass of the man who'd made room. He turned so he could talk to West and watch New England whip Washington's ass at the same time.

"Haven't heard from you in a while, Mr. West." Doc nodded to the bartender for his beer, accepted thanks from the man next to him. "Wondered how things were going."

"You know how it is, Detective. Long as they go, I'm not complaining. Thank you for the refill." He tipped his glass toward Doc

They watched the game in silence for a few minutes, sipping. New England kicked a field goal and Doc said, "See the boys any?"

"New family brings them around once a week. I been over there a couple times. They seem happy."

Neither spoke during a Bud Light commercial. Doc said, "Not to pry, but I was wondering if you kept after that foster parent thing we talked about."

"You didn't check with Family Services yourself?"

"No, sir. This is personal business. I figured you'd tell me if there was anything you wanted me to know."

"But you come over here just to ask me tonight."

"I'm a cop. It's not my nature to let things go." The bartender came close and Doc ordered a dozen wings. "I really don't want to put you on the spot. If you changed your mind, I trust your judgment. I was curious, just thought maybe I could help if anything had stalled."

West slid a sidelong glance Doc's way. "They approved me last week. You sure you didn't know about that?"

"Nope. Like I said, anything I heard, I wanted to hear from you." Cops are good liars when they want to be.

"You been by to see them?"

"Couple times, as part of the investigation. Kathleen Whitmore asked me not to make any social calls until things shake themselves out. She doesn't mind if I'm friendly when I'm there, only that I don't make special trips just to visit."

"What do you think of where they are?"

"It's nice. Yard in back. Family takes good care of them. Damn nice of the wife to get them to their regular school every day."

"I thought so, too."

They watched Washington drive to midfield before punting. The wings came. Doc pushed the plastic basket where West could reach it.

West broke a wing in two, gnawed on the drumstick. "Those boys seem happy to you?"

Doc swallowed what he had in his mouth, licked the grease from his fingers. "You were right. These are good wings. Quarter apiece, huh?" Not as good as Ellen's, but still worth leaving the house for. "Yeah, they did. They were throwing a football around the back yard last time I was there, with the father. I enjoyed watching them."

"You don't think they're better off with a real family? Not just some old man keeping an eye on them until their parents get out of jail?"

"Families grow into what they are, for better or worse. I have a couple of gay friends adopted a baby a few years ago. There are a lot of people who wouldn't call that a real family. I see them once a month or so and I don't know two better parents, and haven't seen a happier little kid. Okay, so it's not normal. Anything say normal has to be better?"

West chewed a wing, watched the game with exaggerated interest. Doc gave him time.

"Do you know how old I am?"

"Sixty-six."

"Not for three weeks. Don't rush me." West swallowed the wing, washed it down. "How long is it before you figure those boys won't be able to depend on me anymore?"

"From what I've seen, about twenty years. What's your point?"

"I don't want them to come to depend on me, then not be there for them."

"Wilver's almost fifteen. Couple more years and he'll need you as an advisor more than anything else. David's got longer, but not that long. Look, I understand if you don't think you're up to it. Maybe there's an issue I don't know about, and I'm not asking. If you truly think they're better off where they are, I'll say fine, you see them more than I do. I get the feeling there's something else. That's none of my business, either, and we won't talk about it if you don't want to. One thing I will argue about is whether you're qualified to take proper care of those boys. That's been well—"

"What about when the mother comes back?"

"Ah." Doc had wondered how West would take it when the time came for the boys to go. He hadn't considered the old man would think of it so soon. "I guess that'll have to be worked out when the time comes."

"You met her. How do you think it'll go?"

"Not well." Now Doc chewed a wing and washed it down to buy time. "You know how these people are, Mr. West. She's all about her babies when it's to her advantage to act the concerned mother. She gets out, she'll want them back, then she'll do what she'll always done. Knows judges and social workers will go easy on her for the sake of the boys, trying to keep the family together, when that's the last god-damn thing they should be worried about. Let someone worry about the boys for their sake for a change. Fuck the mother. She's had her chances."

"Leaving your opinion out, the first half of what you said's all I care about. She'll get them, and things will go back the way they were before."

"Which means Wilver and David will need someone they can depend on more than ever."

"You think that should be me?"

"I don't think an institution can do it, no matter how good a reputation DFS has, or what Kathleen Whitmore says. Too many competing needs."

"What are you saying? That I should try to keep them?"

Doc thought before he spoke. "No. She'll contest it, and that wouldn't be good for anyone. What I'm suggesting is to strengthen the bond you have with them. Where they're at now is good, the family cares for them, but they know the boys will be leaving and they'll get another kid or two to watch over. Build up your connection with them and they'll always know they have someone to talk to if things get rough with mom again. I'm not walking away, but we both know I can't be the primary caregiver."

West signaled for two more beers, pushed a five across the bar. "So you want me to get closer to them before I give them up."

"They're only going up the block, Mr. West. It's not like she's moving to California."

West nodded to acknowledge the fresh beer and collected his change. "Mother will still have the say in how much I see them."

"Let me handle her. Mothers like that talk a good game about doing right by her kids, but she'll take the easy way, so long as it's offered right. A cop with contacts in Family Services can make things unpleasant for her if he wants to."

The conversation lapsed while New England moved eighty yards in the last two minutes of the half to go up 24-3. West said, "I guess I need to make up my mind and let people know. You have any more advice for me?"

"Me?" Doc drained his beer, put the coaster on top of the glass. "I'm just a neutral observer who thinks they're happy where they are but could maybe use some longer-term stability down the road. There's not a lot of people who can do that for them, but I think you knew that before I came in here. Now, if you'll excuse me, I have an early morning. Good wings. Thanks for the tip."

CHAPTER 62

"That's our boy Orszulak, isn't it?" Grabek said.

Doc nodded. "Uh-huh. He looked better with eyes."

Doc's Tuesday started even earlier than expected. Quarter to five in the morning, cold and dark as Stalin's conscience on Third Avenue. Frank Orszulak lay along the stairs leading down to the Bachelors Club like dirty laundry. Ice crystals coated his skin.

"What do you think the odds are the autopsy finds baseball-sized bruises on him?" Doc said.

"They won't find dick. Mannarino's smarter than that."

"You think it's him? Not the Widmer woman, cleaning up?"

Grabek shook his head. The scent of a heavy drinker seeped from his pores. "You hire a hitter, strictly business, it goes down like Frantz did. Two in the head and walk away. This, marking up the face like this, this is disrespect. Mannarino owns this joint, doesn't he?"

"I think so."

"Two for the price of one. This is his way of telling people from out of town they can't shit in his back yard. He's also telling us he doesn't care if we know. I'm impressed. I didn't think he had this kind of old school shit in him."

They stood there a couple of minutes, breathing clouds over Orszulak's corpse. Waiting for the Medical Examiner to come. Neuschwander got there first. "Is that who I think it is?" Doc flashed him a look that told all he needed to know. "ME here yet?"

"Yeah," Grabek said. "We made him wait. We weren't done freezing our balls off yet."

Neuschwander walked past, kneeled to start setting up his lights and kit.

Doc said, "That's our case laying there."

"How you figure?"

"It breaks the chain. There's no one left for us to threaten her with, say he might roll over on you, maybe you should go first."

"It doesn't matter." Grabek hawked up a wad, turned his head to spit it away from the body. "We still have all the connections. Her to Frantz. The car. The boys. What's his face—Wierzbicki—is more likely to testify now that he knows Orszulak won't come for him. We're okay, and this one's out of the game. Mannarino did us a favor. Now there's nothing to muddy the water about Marian."

Headlights flashed across them, went out. A car door slammed. The medical examiner walked over. "You guys got a regular crime wave here," he said. "Maybe next time you can find a body when someone else is on call, middle of the goddamn night. Neuschwander here?"

Grabek pointed to him, not twenty feet away. "Good," the ME said. "The Gil Grissom of Penns River. A good man. This shouldn't take long."

"Not for you," Grabek said under his breath. "We'll be here half the fucking day."

The detectives stood, not speaking, listened to Neuschwander and the ME trade pleasantries. Poke around, show things to each other, compare thoughts. The ME stood, pulled latex gloves from his hands as he walked toward them. Looked for a place to throw the gloves, put them in his coat pocket.

"Cause of death is a gunshot wound to the back of the head, right about here." He tapped his head an inch above the right mastoid bone. "Small caliber weapon, probably a .22. I'd be surprised if it was more than a .25, since there's no exit wound. I'll know for sure when we cut him open. It's still in there."

"What about his eyes?" Doc said.

"Post mortem. The shot to the back of the head put him away. The eyes are just decoration." Grabek grunted. *What I told you.*

"Thanks." They waited until the ME's car started. Doc said, "What do you think? What now?"

"Same as we been. I told you nothing's changed. Lean on Wierzbicki. He saw them together."

"So what? We have nothing, not a goddamn thing, to tie Orszulak to any of it. This means we have nothing solid to try to push Marian Widmer into a deal. What are we gonna do? Ask her to put Orszulak in, now that he's dead?"

"What? Is he gonna argue?"

"She knows there's no risk that he'll either come after her or roll over first. This woman's a lot of things, Willie, but she's not stupid."

Grabek spat again. "Uh-uh. She's good for it, Doc, and she's going down." His voice had the tone of a zealot unwilling to tarnish his argument with facts.

CHAPTER 63

Pool night at the Legion. Skip Jacobs shot the Eight too hard, as usual. Ball rattled in the jaws of the pocket and died on the lip. Doc raised an eyebrow, made sure Skip saw him. Made the Thirteen in the side and let the cue ball run to the far rail. Put on a show of lining up the Eight. Walked around the table. Leaned over to make sure a piece of lint or pill of fabric didn't deflect it in the half inch it had to travel.

"Just shoot the fucking ball, Hemorrhoid." Skip stepped over like he might push it into the pocket.

"Uh-uh-uh. Don't make me draw my weapon, Skippy. I've still haven't taken half as long as you did with that bunny I left you last week." Doc chalked his cue. Took his stance, cheek almost resting on the shaft. Three warm-up strokes, then he rolled the ball only hard enough to kiss the Eight into the pocket and touch one rail.

"It's like sex, Skip," Dewey Augustine said. "Finesse and tenderness goes a lot farther than just blasting away with brute force. You should try it at home sometime."

"What do you know about how I do it at home?"

"Me and Lorraine have to talk about something to pass the time when we're done." Lorraine being Skip's wife.

"She wants you so goddamn bad, she can have you. Who wants a beer?"

Skip's usual MO after a waxing. Keep playing, trying to salvage one game out of a night of beatings, then give up and pay for a round like a magnanimous loser who could've played one more and beat you but took pity.

The Doughertys sat next to each other facing the big TV in the corner. Olympic hockey.

"Surprised you came out tonight. Big hockey game on," Big Doc said.

"Slovakia will kill Germany in this one. The game to see's Czech Republic and Sweden. I'll be home in time."

Chick the bartender set a beer in front of each. "From Skippy." He nodded to the other end of the bar. The two Docs raised their glasses in Skip's direction. He missed it, already arguing with Augie and Jack Bubus.

Big Doc sucked foam off his beer. Wiped the back of his hand across his lip. "Is that woman lives on the hill going to get away with it?" Marian Widmer lived no more than a mile from Big Doc's house as the crow flew.

"Already has."

"Did she do it?"

"Yep. Damned if I can prove it, though. I told them that, Willie and Sally, after the hitter from Youngstown went down. I think Sally agreed with me for a while."

"What happened?"

Doc took a swallow, set down the glass. "We probably pushed Sally too hard to charge in the first place. We told her we'd find a stronger link, and she agreed she had enough to indict. Then the hit man got killed and the other lawyer insisted on a speedy trial. Sally probably could've dropped the charges without prejudice and tried again later, but by that time she was invested and wanted the Widmer woman as bad as we did. I'll tell you something. We had enough evidence for a trial. No one could look at everything we had and come to any other conclusion. I know she was involved. Did we prove it? Enough to send her away for life? You ever see her?"

"No."

"She's hot, Dad. She has those high cheekbones and tight jaw, looks like she could've been a model twenty years ago. Good coloring and a fantastic body and she knows how to use it all. Wore suits to the trial that showed nothing and everything at the same time. A friend of mine—you remember Eve, the lesbian—came to court one day and said she got wet the second Marian walked into the room. The women on the jury thought she was getting the shaft and the men all fantasized about a gratitude screw. The closest thing we had to an eyeball witness—guy she spoke to about a hit in the Warszawa, before she realized she had the wrong guy—he waffled on the stand. We had a circumstantial, borderline case; she had a good lawyer and all the intangibles. We never had a chance."

They watched luge for five minutes. Neither spoke except for the occasional "crazy bastard" from Big Doc. Doc finished his beer, swept his money off the bar. His father said, "One more?"

"I don't think so. I want to get something to eat before the Sweden game comes on."

"Stay for one more and I'll pay for a poor boy from Edgecliff."

Doc re-settled. "I'll get the sandwich. What's up?"

Big Doc waited for Chick to bring fresh beers and leave them alone. "I only ask for your mother. You know that."

"It didn't work out, Dad." No formal announcement had been made about Jillian's ex-ness. "Things fell apart when I was so busy last fall and I guess I forgot to say anything. I haven't seen her in months. She quit the theater group and everything."

"Jesus Christ. What did you do?"

"It's what I didn't do. I didn't pursue her enough. Her word. It's a shame. She was smart, she was funny, and she was good-looking, but she was insecure to the point of being psychotic. She had bunny boiler potential."

"What's a bunny boiler?"

"You saw that movie with Glenn Close, right? *Fatal Attraction*? Where she boils Michael Douglas's kid's pet rabbit because she's not just going to be *ignored*."

"I never got that movie. Glenn Close is a nice looking woman and all, but he had Anne Archer at home. Why trade down?"

There was no good answer to that. They drank beer and watched some of the two-man—"Greek luge", Big Doc called it—until Doc finished and pushed his glass across the bar with a coaster covering it.

Big Doc tapped him on the arm. "One more thing."

Doc laughed. "What the hell, Dad? You trying to get me to talk the Playhouse people into doing a Columbo so you can be him? Is anything wrong?"

"No, no, nothing wrong. You know I hate to ask, but I have to report back when I get home."

"It's been three months since this went down. I've seen Mom maybe twenty times, talked to her on the phone at least that much. Why doesn't she just ask me herself?"

"Says she doesn't want to be a neb shit."

The comment hung in the air three seconds before they both laughed. "Okay. What does she want to know?"

Big Doc put a coaster on his glass and pushed it away. "There was this woman cop you mentioned a few times. Your mother thought—I don't know what she thought. She says you talked about her like there might be something going on."

"She's a cop, Dad. She's nice and all, but she's a cop. Not a good idea to mess around at work."

"That's what I told her. Tried to, anyway." He looked at his watch. "You coming over on Sunday?"

"Sure. What time?"

"Your mother's making a roast for five-thirty. Is that good?"

"You want me to come early and we can see about that tree fell over out back by the creek?"

"No. I went down there today. It's still too wet to move around much and it's supposed to rain or snow tomorrow. It's not like someone's going to sneak back there and cheat me out of a chance to drag the bastard out of that hollow. The more I look at it, the more I think I'll just pay Jimmy Novotny to cut it up and haul it away."

They walked together to cars parked next to each other.

CHAPTER 64

Marian Widmer felt the first drops of rain and abandoned her gardening project. Middle of April, none but the most adventurous flowers dared show themselves. Her garden the only thing Marian had a sense of do-it-yourself pride about. She paid for everything else: car washes, lawn mowing and landscaping, housecleaning, and any home improvement more complicated than changing a light bulb. The flowers around the house and flanking the walk were hers.

She wore an Allegheny College sweatshirt and sweatpants big enough for herself and a pre-teen child. Hair gathered in the back with a clip. She put her gardening gloves and implements back in the garage and had undone the clip when the doorbell rang.

It was the big cop. Dougherty. The one who thought he was clever, setting her up in Pittsburgh Mills so some low-life could get a look at her. She opened the door only far enough for introductory conversation, not any kind of invitation.

"Hello, Mrs. Widmer. Sorry to bother you at home. I wonder if I could come in for a few minutes. Out of the rain."

No rain on the porch. She let him in, anyway. Said, "Am I under arrest again?" as she stepped aside.

"No, nothing like that. I guess I'm here to tell you I'm *not* going to arrest you."

It seemed as if he should say more. Marian gestured to a

seat at the kitchen table. Started to sit herself, felt the baggy sweatshirt rub against the chair. Stood up, said, "Will you excuse me for a second, Detective?"

"No need, Mrs. Widmer. I've seen the show before. It's impressive, but that's not why I'm here, either."

Temper rose in Marian's cheeks and midsection. She showed some of it in a glare before she remembered to keep cool. They'd tried everything to trip her up before, this one and his partner and the prosecutor who thought she was hot. Marian was still free to work in her garden whenever she wanted. Weather permitting.

"Why are you here, Detective?"

"I hate to be presumptuous, ma'am, but I've been running around all day. You wouldn't have something cold to drink, would you? I'm parched."

Marian wondered how long it would take to chill some Liquid Plumr. "The kids always have pop in the fridge. Will that be all right?"

"What do you have?" Making her get up and check.

"Pepsi and orange, looks like. There's some lemonade in here, too. Or ice tea. Whatever they put in the pitcher."

"Some orange pop would be great. A little ice, if it's no trouble."

She got ice from the door dispenser, handed him the bottle and the glass. He poured, let the fizz settle. Poured again. Like he'd come just for a cold drink.

"Have you ever met Marty Cropcho? The real one, I mean. Not David Frantz pretending to be him."

"Why are you asking?"

"I'm a cop; it's what I do. I'm not asking if you knew him well. Did you ever run into him when you and Carol were out? Get introduced as a friend. Anything like that."

"How would I know him? I told you before—I testified under oath—that I never met Carol Cropcho, let alone her husband. It was my husband—ex-husband—who knew her."

"Speaking of your almost ex, how are the settlement negotiations going? I'll bet you never heard the term 'equitable distribution' before all this happened."

If a gun had been handy, Marian would have shot him and taken her chances. "Equitable Distribution" was how the Commonwealth of Pennsylvania sorted out property in a divorce if the parties can't reach an agreement. None of this fifty-fifty shit; each spouse owns one hundred percent of everything they've accumulated since the wedding. The judge can divide it up however he thinks is fair. Fault in causing the end of the marriage didn't come into consideration. Tom had earned all the money; he now had zero earning potential. Marian could work, but she had the kids and was entitled to support. The judge wasn't likely to leave Tom penniless before knowing of a conviction or sentencing, in case he needed the money when—if—he got out. It was a cluster fuck of cosmic proportion and Marian would be lucky to collect ten cents on the dollar by the time the lawyers got through with it.

"The lawyers are discussing it. I don't care about the money. I just want him out of my life. Out of my children's lives. Finish your drink and get out if that's all you came to talk about."

Dougherty sipped his pop while she talked. Took a second to dry his lips. "Sorry, it just popped into my mind when you mentioned your husband. I came to talk about Marty Cropcho. I've gotten to know him a little since his wife died. Hell of a nice man. He's still shaken up over it after—what is it?—six months now."

"I'm very sorry for him. If you want to make someone feel guilty, you should talk to my ex-husband."

"Marty had to take leave of absence from his job to keep from getting fired. Missed a lot of work, and he was in no condition to work when he did show up. He drank a lot for a while, but that's much better now. He works some handyman jobs, manual labor to keep busy and make a few bucks. Too hard for him to sit still at a desk all day. Has to be doing something physical all the time, so long as it requires at least a little thought."

He sipped his drink again, like he was waiting for her to move the conversation along. She was already tired of him and let the quiet grow.

"There's only so much tinkering and heavy lifting a man can do. Everyone else goes home at night and there's Marty with no place to go. Doesn't want to sell the house because it reminds him of her, but he probably should sell it. Because it reminds him of her."

Another swallow. "So what Marty does, now that it's spring more or less, is clean the house. Organize things, gather up Carol's stuff so if he ever does decide to do anything with it, it's ready. A couple of weeks ago he's cleaning out the bedroom and he finds something stuffed away under a false bottom in Carol's lingerie drawer."

"What did he find?" Marian's voice had less resonance than she'd expected. Or hoped.

Dougherty took a small book from his inside breast pocket. The book didn't close all the way, held open by a sprung lock. Dougherty laid it on the table out of Marian's easy reach.

"He looked everywhere for the key. Tore the house apart. Finally decided he wasn't sure he wanted to know what was in there and brought it to me. I got it open right away." He fingered the lock's broken clasp.

"Carol Cropcho was quite a romantic. Even a quick reading of this shows she was crazy about you. For a while. Makes me wonder why she called it off. She did, didn't she? I haven't read all the way to the end—I think it's cheating to skip ahead—but the phone calls stopped months before she was killed, so she must've ditched you. It just took you a while to get even."

Marian didn't trust herself to speak. Dougherty tapped the book with a finger.

"Some of this is pretty steamy. I don't know what Carol was like in person, but she didn't have many inhibitions as a writer. Very graphic. They could make a movie about the time you taught her how to get sixty-nine exactly the way you liked it. January 19, I think it was. Up at Seven Springs. And that business with the strap-on? At your house? I had to go home after I read that."

Marian felt the floor fall away from her. Like she was slipping into a hole, the tile sagging only beneath her chair while everything around her stayed where it was.

"What are you going to do?" Her voice sounded like an old woman on her deathbed. "Are you going to arrest me?"

Dougherty let her wait while he finished his drink. "I already told you I'm not here to arrest you."

The first prickles of fear scurried along Marian's scalp. "What do you want?"

"To make sure you know that I know. About you and Carol. You and Frantz. I know for a certainty you and Carol Cropcho had an affair. She broke it off around the same time you met David Frantz. You were having marital troubles of your own, and were afraid your husband would leave you with half of a portfolio that shrank every day. Killing him would make you the obvious suspect and tie up the money forever. So you got Frantz to pull this half-assed 'Strangers on a Train' con. Promise he'd kill you if Tom killed Carol. Tom was pretty forthcoming about how that played out once we showed him everything else we had that linked you and Frantz.

"Then you had Frank Orszulak clip Frantz. Your mistake, hitting on the wrong guy at the Warszawa. Bad luck the guy you hit on always needs a favor from the police. Such is life."

"I'm innocent. We proved I didn't kill Frantz."

"No. We didn't prove you did. There's a difference."

Random thoughts ran unimpeded through Marian's mind. *Why is he here? Don't say anything. What does he want? Who did he tell? Don't say anything. What comes next? What do I do? Don't say anything. Don't say anything. DON'T SAY ANYTHING!*

She couldn't bear the silence.

"I suppose you're going to ask the District Attorney for an indictment."

"Been there already. She passed." Marian thought he must be screwing with her. "Don't worry. I'm not messing with you. DA told me she only lets any defendant make her look foolish once. You had yours."

Now Marian really was afraid. *Why is he here?* Dougherty was a big man, well put together. Rollison tried to blackmail her; she doubted Dougherty cared much about money. What was left? Better to get it in the open now so she could evaluate her options.

"What do you want?"

"Like I said, I want you to know that I know." He tipped his glass, cracked and chewed an ice cube. "And—I want you to know I'm not going anywhere. I'll be on this job at least twenty more years, and there's no statute of limitations on murder. Every so often I'll pull into some nice, romantic place and show pictures of you and Carol around. David Frantz, too. I'll check all of Frantz's known associates. These guys talk, and there's no way Frantz tapped a hot number like you and didn't tell anyone. Couple of drinks in him, hard to guess what else he might've said."

He stood. Pushed back the chair. Marian stayed seated. "They say every good cop has a case that stays with him. One he couldn't close that he thinks about even after he's retired. A mission. Maybe this is mine. I have a better deal than those other guys, because I know who did it, and now you do too. Every time I show your picture in a bar, or open the case file instead of reading a book or watching a ball game, I'll know you're looking over your shoulder. And you should be, because I *will* show those pictures and read those files."

Dougherty walked to the door. Paused with his hand on the knob, turned back to face Marian. "That's good pop. I don't think I've ever had Fanta before. I'll have to get some. Keep it in the refrigerator where I'll see it every day. So I don't forget."

ACKNOWLEDGEMENTS

No author writes in a vacuum. We draw upon all experiences, memories, and interactions with others when creating our fictional worlds. In my case a few individuals and groups stand out:

The Writers of Chantilly, where continuous support in semi-monthly meetings gave me the confidence to show my writing to people I didn't know and whose support in my too infrequent appearances is unflagging.

John McNally and George Washington University's Jenny McKean Moore Writers Workshop of the spring of 2002, where I learned the craft of both genre and "serious" fiction were the same.

The handful of stalwarts from John's workshop who continued on in monthly meetings, for their support and for finding ways to improve everything.

The Beloved Spouse, for being a dedicated and insightful first and last listener, attributes that are the least of what she gives to me every day.

Charlie Stella, for his comments, improvements, encouragement, and friendship.

My parents, to whom much of this entirely fictional work will seem vaguely familiar.

Eric Campbell, Lance Wright, and everyone at Down & Out Books for bringing the Penns Series together and giving it a home; and to Eric Beetner for his patience and creativity with the covers.

Those with knowledge of the Pittsburgh area may recognize the three small cities that inspired Penns River. Much of the area's prosperity left with the closing of the steel and aluminum mills. Subsequent improvements in Greater Pittsburgh's economy never seem to move northeast, yet the towns survive. They are proof that Nietzsche was right: what does not kill you makes you stronger.

Dana King owns two nominations for the Private Eye Writers of America Shamus Award, for *A Small Sacrifice* (2013) and again two years later for *The Man in the Window*. His novel *Grind Joint* was noted by Woody Haut in the *L.A. Review of Books* as one of the fifteen best noir reads of 2013. A short story, "Green Gables," appeared in the anthology *Blood, Guts, and Whiskey*, edited by Todd Robinson. Other short fiction has appeared in *Thuglit*, *Spinetingler*, *New Mystery Reader*, *A Twist of Noir*, *Mysterical-E*, and *Powder Burn Flash*.

Dana's lives in Maryland with The Beloved Spouse. His blog, One Bite at a Time, resides at danaking.blogspot.com.

OTHER TITLES FROM DOWN AND OUT BOOKS

See www.DownAndOutBooks.com for complete list

By J.L. Abramo
Catching Water in a Net
Clutching at Straws
Counting to Infinity
Gravesend
Chasing Charlie Chan
Circling the Runway
Brooklyn Justice

By Trey R. Barker
2,000 Miles to Open Road
Road Gig: A Novella
Exit Blood
Death is Not Forever
No Harder Prison

By Richard Barre
The Innocents
Bearing Secrets
Christmas Stories
The Ghosts of Morning
Blackheart Highway
Burning Moon
Echo Bay
Lost

By Eric Beetner (editor)
Unloaded

By Eric Beetner and
JB Kohl
Over Their Heads

By Eric Beetner and
Frank Scalise
The Backlist
The Shortlist

By G.J. Brown
Falling

By Rob Brunet
Stinking Rich

By Mark Coggins
No Hard Feelings

By Tom Crowley
Vipers Tail
Murder in the Slaughterhouse

By Frank De Blase
Pine Box for a Pin-Up
Busted Valentines
and Other Dark Delights
A Cougar's Kiss

By Les Edgerton
The Genuine, Imitation,
Plastic Kidnapping

By Jack Getze
Big Numbers
Big Money
Big Mojo
Big Shoes

By Richard Godwin
Wrong Crowd
Buffalo and Sour Mash
Crystal on Electric Acetate (*)

By William Hastings (editor)
Stray Dogs: Writing
from the Other America

(*)—Coming Soon

OTHER TITLES FROM DOWN AND OUT BOOKS

See www.DownAndOutBooks.com for complete list

By Jeffery Hess
Beachhead

By Matt Hilton
No Going Back
Rules of Honor
The Lawless Kind
The Devil's Anvil
No Safe Place (*)

By Jerry Kennealy
Screen Test
Polo's Long Shot (*)

By Ross Klavan, Tim O'Mara
and Charles Salzberg
Triple Shot

By S.W. Lauden
Crosswise

By Paul D. Marks and
Andrew McAleer (editor)
Coast to Coast vol. 1
Coast to Coast vol. 2 (*)

By Terrence McCauley
The Devil Dogs of Belleau Wood

By Bill Moody
Czechmate
The Man in Red Square
Solo Hand
The Death of a Tenor Man
The Sound of the Trumpet
Bird Lives!

By Gary Phillips
The Perpetrators
Scoundrels (Editor)
Treacherous
3 the Hard Way

By Tom Pitts
Hustle

By Robert J. Randisi
Upon My Soul
Souls of the Dead
Envy the Dead (*)

By Ryan Sayles
The Subtle Art of Brutality
Warpath

By John Shepphird
The Shill
Kill the Shill
Beware the Shill

By Ian Thurman
Grand Trunk and Shearer

James R. Tuck (editor)
Mama Tried vol. 1
Mama Tried vol. 2 (*)

By Lono Waiwaiole
Wiley's Lament
Wiley's Shuffle
Wiley's Refrain
Dark Paradise
Leon's Legacy (*)

(*)—Coming Soon

Made in the USA
Monee, IL
15 June 2023

35926805R00236